I0594983

This is a work of fiction. All the characters and events portrayed in this book are fictitious or used fictitiously.

DEN OF THIEVES

ISBN: **979-8-9920397-2-6**

Portions of this book appeared in Analog Science Fiction:

Den of Foxes, *Analog*, December, 1990
Den of Sorrow, *Analog*, March 1991
Den of Wolves, *Analog*, July 1991

Cover Design by Jay O'Connell

Bigwaves Publishing

ASGARD

Second planet of Mu Cassiopeiae, a G5 star in the Perseus Sector, 7.7 parsecs from Sol.

Radius: 4812 km
Day: 30 hr 13 min 12 sec
Year: 215.636 standard days
    171.253 Asgard days
Axial Tilt: 18 degrees
Surface Gravity: 0.91 G
Atmosphere: 28 percent O_2
    70 percent N_2
    2 percent other
Mean Pressure: 1110 millibars at sea level
Distance from Primary: 0.73 A.U.

Planetological Description: An Earth-type planet with 30 percent land, 70 percent ocean, currently in advanced stages of continental glaciation with ice cover extending as far south as the 40th parallel.

History: Scout team landed in Year 32 of New Era. Breakthrough colony followed in Year 87.

– The Scout Service Handbook of the Stars and Planets

DEN OF THIEVES

Daniel Hatch

The Slow Space Series Book 1

Guy Stanger downed the last of his hot fuzzasaur soup and stacked his plastic bowl with the others. He refilled his cup with black coffee and watched while the other nine scouts finished their supper. He could tell they were hungry – there was no shouting, no joking, just the energetic slurping of soup.

"Billy, you help Tad wash up," he said when they had all finished. "Walt, you help Joan with the horses."

"Yes, sir, Mr. Scoutmaster," Walt said with mock submission, then he turned to the others and said: "One of these days I'm going to be bigger than my big brother – and when I am, he better watch out."

"Yeah," said Billy and Tad. "Us too."

Guy ignored his brothers and handed out tasks to the remaining scouts. "I'm going to make sure the security fence is secure," he said. "It's getting warm enough for maxidons to be up, and we don't want to lose the horses."

The scouts got busy while Guy went off to inspect the fence and its automated lasergun defenses. It took him fifteen minutes to make a circuit of the 300-meter perimeter and check each of the fence posts.

He paused for a moment on the back side of the cabin to look at the sun as it dropped behind Thor Mountain. A thin cap of clouds hugged the ice at Thor's two-kilometer-high peak, catching the colors of the sunset. He turned around to see Loki, close behind him with half the altitude, where the glaciers caught the ruddy light and danced across the snowy ridges that embraced the ice.

Guy drew in a deep breath of crisp, clean air. Winter was only a few days gone and already he could smell the sweet south wind.

A big snow could still blow up the coast or a heavy chill could roll in from the Deep Freeze to the north, but spring was finally here.

And this spring, this special spring, was the one the scouts had been waiting to arrive for nearly a century. In just two weeks, it would be Colony Day.

But for Guy, Colony Day carried a disappointing irony.

All his life, he and the others his age had been told how lucky it was to be born when they were – for they would all be young adults when the breakthrough colony finally arrived at Asgard. Guy's birthday, however, came in November, half a year from now. He was still short of 35 Asgard years, equivalent to 21 standard years – the age of majority. And until that day, when he could cut his hair like an adult and take his place as a full member of den Iroquois, he would remain something less, something in between, emotionally an adult, but legally, a child.

Lyle Sanderson, the scoutmaster at the Main Post, had tried to brighten Guy's mood as the big day approached, but there wasn't much he could do.

Sanderson had given him this patrol to lead up to Glacier Valley, but three of the scouts were his brothers. And the spring inspection patrols never needed an adult along.

The one thing he wanted most – to lead a regular patrol as a full scout on Colony Day – he could not have. This assignment was a poor substitute.

He returned to the campfire and sent the scouts into the cabin to make up their bedrolls. He had them fill the fireplace, but did not light the fire yet. The night was too gentle and inviting for a troop of kids who'd just spent six weeks cooped up in winter quarters.

While they were inside finishing up, Guy watched Loki turn gold, red, then stark white as the sun edged out of sight. Darkness followed quickly as the scouts came dashing out of the cabin to take their seats around the fire circle.

When they were all in place, the ceremony began.

Guy let Walt take the lead. His younger brother was only 25, but already taking charge. While Guy had to think things out before making a decision, Walt just did things. He was a natural leader, popular, athletic, independent, and Guy envied that. He seemed to fit with the other people effortlessly, while Guy struggled between being acceptable to them and accepting them. There had been more than a few times while they were growing up that Walt's easy self-assurance had clashed with Guy's insistence on being in charge.

"The Great Spirit is with us," Walt said.

"And we are with the Great Spirit," they replied with one voice.

"Long ago, the Great Spirit walked upon the Earth and made it great and bountiful," Walt said. "Clear waters sprang from the ground where he walked. Fruit grew where he paused. Forests arose where he slept."

"Great was the Great Spirit."

"He walked with the other spirits of the world."

"The Spirit of the Wind," said Joan.

"The Spirit of the Sea," answered another.

"The Spirit of the River."

"The Spirit of the Forest."

"The Spirit of the Ice."

And on around the circle it went until Billy's turn came up. "The Spirit of the ... uh. It ..."

A chorus of giggles echoed across the fire circle. "The Spirit of the Forest," he said finally.

"We already said that one," Tad said in disgust.

"Billy gets the first story," Walt announced. "Go ahead, Billy. Make it a good one."

"Do a Wind Spirit," said one of the girls.

"How about a River Spirit story?" asked another.

"Shh – this is my story and I'm going to pick the spirit. I'm doing a Ice Spirit."

A few critical remarks were made, but the children settled down quickly.

***

"Back on Earth, the Ice Spirit lived at the North Pole. Every winter, he would ride south and cover the world with ice and snow. In the spring, he would ride back to the north, with snow gliders and hangplaners following behind him. He also left icebergs in the ocean. They were the tears he cried because he was sad to leave the south.

"But one day, man came. Man burned the oil and the coal and the forests and filled the air with carbon oxide."

"DI-oxide," the others corrected in a harsh whisper.

"Carbon DI-oxide. That made the world warmer and warmer every year. And the Ice Spirit got real sad. In the winter, he didn't travel as far. And in the spring, he cried harder and harder, filling the sea with bergs. He cried so much that the oceans got higher and waves flooded the cities. But still man burned the carbon dioxide."

"He didn't burn it – he made it by burning trees," said Tad. Billy looked down at his brother and glared, then continued.

"The Ice Spirit was so sad that he finally decided to go away. That was when the Great Spirit told him about the other spirits, who were also sad. They wanted to go away too.

"So the Great Spirit told them about this other planet they could go to, and he took them away in a giant spaceship. And they traveled for 25 years until they got to Moo Cap – I mean, Cassiopeia – where they found a planet named Asgard.

"And all the spirits went down and landed on the planet and decided live there. The Ice Spirit was so happy on the new planet that he decided not to live all the way up at the North Pole. Instead he lived in Skandia. And instead of going south every 12 months, he decided to go every six months. And that's why we have the glaciers on Loki and the Deep Freeze and everything."

He looked around nervously and added: "And that's the end of the story."

Walt started the applause, and the scouts responded by overdoing it, whistling and cheering and stamping their feet. The Osborne twins even stood up and started clapping each other on the back.

Guy smiled, recalling the earliest days of his childhood when Grampa Bob told him his first Great Spirit story. Grampa Bob had started the storytelling tradition more than 90 years ago when the first scouts came to Asgard. When he was still a youngster, Guy had believed the stories and thought the white-haired old scout was the wisest man in the world. His awe was a little more restrained now, but not his respect.

The stories were always fun – but just a little bit more. They made the scouts feel like they had an important job to do on their new world, like it was up to them to protect it.

That meant even more to Guy this spring.

"Boy, was I nervous," Billy told Guy when he was finished.

"You did really good, though," Guy said, mussing Billy's hair. "Yeah, but now I have to go pee real bad."

Guy laughed as his brother ran off stiff-legged towards the latrine.

***

Next up was one of Walt's monster stories. Walt had a talent for horror. His method was simple and direct. First, he got everyone scared. That wasn't hard to do – he just stuck very closely to the truth.

"Once upon a time there six – " He looked around the circle, counting off on his fingers. "I mean nine scouts out on patrol. They were the only scouts on the whole planet. There was no one around them for thousands of klicks but the wind, the mountains, the sky, the river and the ice. And It."

The giggling subsided, and the youngest of the scouts fixed their attention on Walt.

"For two days, the scouts rode across the empty planet. Alone, defenseless, just the scouts and their horses. No one saw them come or go because there was no one there to see them. Nothing but emptiness as far as they could see. Nothing but It."

The Osborne twins stopped poking each other, and the girls stopped making faces at them.

"At night they camped out and they built a fire. And when it got dark, the fire was the only light for thousands of miles around. There was nothing beyond the flames but darkness. Only It."

By now, even Guy was starting to feel a little nervous. As the leader of the patrol, he was acutely aware of how helpless and alone the scouts were.

"It was three meters tall. It's tail was three meters long. It's mouth was a meter wide and full of sharp teeth. It had bad breath. And it liked the taste of scouts."

The children sat riveted and motionless, their eyes staring wide. The monster Walt described was not what gripped their imaginations. They were all thinking about the great emptiness of Asgard that stretched out in every direction around them. Their parents were all a day's ride away, and the darkness truly held carnivorous monsters – though none so large as the one Walt was describing.

"The scouts saw It's great wide eyes glowing from the fire light. Outside the camp. Beyond the fence."

The youngsters suddenly began craning their necks and looking around behind them at the darkness beyond the camp.

"It was there in the morning when they woke up. Waiting. The first scout went out to face It. It snapped off the scout's head and ate him in three bites."

He growled and swung around suddenly to poke his face at Joan, baring his teeth and eliciting a yelp.

"When It was done, It looked for more scouts. But they went running off in every direction. It looked around, smelled the ground and went chasing after two of them – the biggest scout and the littlest one. When they saw It coming, the littlest scout reached into his pack, pulled out a pair of running shoes and started to put them on.

"The biggest scout said to his brother – I mean, to his friend, 'That won't do any good, you'll never outrun that monster.'

" 'I know that, but I don't have to outrun him,' the little scout said, trying his laces and jumping to his feet. 'I only have to outrun you.'"

At just that moment, something came crashing through the

bushes to Guy's rear.

Little Peggy Mojidor creamed. The Osborne twins leapt to their feet. and Walt turned to face the intruder. The scouts hadn't even had time to laugh at Walt's punchline.

Guy rose as a small figure burst into the yard.

"Tad! Walt! Guy! Everybody – you've got to come see this. Right now!"

It was Billy.

Guy sighed in relief as his skin crawled with goose bumps. He had half-expected to see a maxidon come out of the dark and had not expected his little brother at all.

"What is it?" he said, catching Billy's hand and trying to calm him down. "Lights. UFO's. Up there near the tree line on Loki."

"Oh Billy, you don't know what you're talking about," said Walt. But Guy wasn't so quick to dismiss him.

"Where were you when you saw them?" he asked. "What did they look like?"

"I was coming back from the latrine. They were colored lights – red and green and white – and they were moving. Right across the face of the mountain. I kept walking around the edge of the perimeter so I could keep sight of them. That's how I got over by the bushes there."

"Moving fast or slow?" Walt asked, following Guy's less skeptical lead. "Slow. Come quick, you still might be able to see them."

He lead the way back through the bushes to the edge of the perimeter fence. They walked off to the south a few dozen meters in quick step, but i: didn't help. There were no lights to be seen.

"Show me where you were when you first spotted them," Guy said.

They returned to the cabin and the latrine and Billy showed them the precise spot where he was standing. "Up about as high as that pine tree over there, but about way off to the left."

The sky above them blazed with light. The Milky Way crossed it in broad band from east to west with the thicket of dust and star clouds that marked the galactic core centered halfway up from the southern horizon. Sol lurked in there somewhere, Guy thought as he scanned the heavens, and off to one side Eta Cassiopeiae burned brightly, an intruder in Centaurus.

But there were no moving lights to be seen anywhere.

"Wouldn't that put them up over the horizon?" Walt said as he measured the angle with his arms.

Guy crouched down to try and simulate the viewpoint of his shorter sibling. It was hard to tell if the lights could have been in the sky or passing in front of the mountain.

"Because if they were over the horizon, that means they could have been stars, planets or who knows what," Walt continued.

"Are you sure you saw something?" Guy asked.

"Positively. I swear by the Great Spirit."

Guy just shook his head.

"What do you think it was, Guy?" Walt asked him.

"I don't know. They say stars can look like they're moving when they're near the horizon. But he says they flew in front of the mountain. That would mean scoutships or miniplanes. And I don't know how that could be. They wouldn't take the minis out after dark unless it was an emergency. And if there was an emergency, someone would have called us."

"Well, I know it was something," Billy said, as they walked back to the campfire. He stuck his hands in his pockets and kicked a stone into the tall grass.

"Maybe it was just Loki up to his old tricks," Guy suggested.

Billy looked up at his big brother and sighed. "Cheesh, Guy, even I don't believe that."

The patrol was up bright and early the next morning – extra early. Just before sunrise, the perimeter alarms went off.

The noise of the alarms startled the horses and now they were going wild.

The camp was wrapped in a thick fog that glowed with dawnlight, but which limited vision to a few meters. Guy was on his feet, but had nowhere to go. The fence alarms whooped away off to the north and the horses were rearing to the west.

"Walt, grab two scouts and take care of the horses," he said.

He pulled on his boots and slid the rifle from its case beside his pack. He made sure it was loaded, then tucked the butt tight against his shoulder and clutched the grip tightly just like a range exercise. With the barrel pointing straight up, he switched off the safety. Then he went outside.

He walked slowly towards the source of the noise. What if the fence posts had failed? Would the lasers work in this kind of fog? Could he be walking straight into a maxidon or something worse? Maybe even a Ward's dragon, drawn down from the forest by the early spring thaw?

Guy peered into the fog, searching for the intruder.

He dropped the barrel down to eye level and sighted over the end of it. That didn't seem satisfactory, though, because the weapon and his arm blocked his view of the ground – and some of the local carnivores were small enough to come in low. He relaxed his grip on the rifle and held it at hip level and looked all around him as the fog closed in behind him and he lost sight of the cabin.

But before he got to the perimeter, the alarms stopped.

He found the fence posts that had sounded the alarm, lights flashing atop the laserguns, but there was nothing there. He walked the gap between the two posts and, despite the fog, made a close inspection of the ground – no tracks, no signs.

By the time he got back to the camp, Walt and the others had calmed the horses down. Since everyone was already up, Guy had them start breakfast and get ready to break camp.

"Must have been a maxidon," Walt said later. "The horses wouldn't get worked up over a grazer."

"I don't know – maxis are allergic to horseflesh," Guy said.

"Only if they smell it first. He must have stumbled on the camp before the air began to stir."

But later, when the sun had burned off the fog, Guy and Walt checked the ground beyond the perimeter. In a sandy patch they found the five-toed prints of a ripper, smaller than a maxidon, but just as nasty. Guy tightened his grip on the rifle as he briefly pictured one of the toothy fuzzasaurs watching them from the brush – a ripper was similar in design to the monster in Walt's story the night before, only a quarter of the size. How far away could it be now?

"You better watch your horror stories," Guy said. "One of these nights, one of them is going to come true."

***

They mounted up as the sun peeked over the shoulder of Loki.

The horses and riders filed along the trail at a leisurely pace, the scouts all bundled against the cool air and trailing thin streams of fog from their breath. The sun took an hour to dissipate the morning chill.

Ordinarily, the patrol up to the Valley post waited until the second week of spring, but this year they were sending the inspection teams out early. With Colony Day coming, there would be a million things to be done at the last minute.

The trail ran about 30 kilometers from the Main Post to the Glacier River and another 35 kilometers up the river to the valley itself. The river itself cut through the broad grassy savanna that ran the length of South Valley, broken only by a few clumps of woods and the thin fringe of trees along the riverbanks.

A few klicks upstream, they came across a crowd of grazers – bluenecks. The scouts heard the whistling and hooting of the fuzzasaurs before they saw them.

Then they turned a bend in the trail and came upon the entire crowd all at once. The bluenecks were crossing the river at a shallow point. The fuzzy lizards stood about a meter tall and wore dusty coats of tan fur with blue ruffs at the base of their long necks.

Guy watched as the lizards worked their way across the waterway. They were bipedal creatures, with an architecture that resembled a bird, despite their mammalian overcoats. Long hind legs were equipped with powerful thighs while weaker forelimbs appeared to be designed for grasping. Their mouths were wide and round and filled with flat teeth.

They jammed together at the river bank before pressing into the water, leading Guy to wonder if the bluenecks were going to make it or be washed under. The first of them splashed across, though, straining to keep its head above water. The rest followed and soon there were a couple dozen fuzzasaur heads leaving thick wakes behind them as they struggled across the river.

The scouts stopped to watch the spectacle. A few minutes later, Guy laughed at the sight of the awkward grazers scrambling up the bank on the far side. When they were all up on the grass, the leaders took off at a trot towards the east. The rest of the crowd followed, and they disappeared into the distance.

For Guy, the ride was like a trip through his boyhood.

He had made this journey to Glacier Valley many times. When he was younger, he had filled the hours by imagining himself as one of the heron in the books he devoured by the disk back home. And as he passed each familiar landmark, he recalled vividly the memories of those earlier patrols.

Here was the waterfall where Daniel Boone had explored the early Appalachians. This was the clearing where Col. George Custer had been attacked by a war party of wild Amerinds – though the duckasaurs who had stood in their place were always a poor substitute. And over there was the great boulder where Arthur drew the sword Excalibur and became king.

He was almost embarrassed by it all now. If his brothers knew what was going through his mind, they would surely laugh at him. But Guy had grown up with a thirst for the life of the imagination, surrounded by books and stories – fantasies and histories, atlases of old Earth and the stars.

And at the same time, he had a serious side. He looked across the Asgardian environment with a studied eye. As they passed through the riverside meadows, he cataloged the flora and the fauna as he had been taught from his earliest days.

He saw brassweed and thistlefoot, blossoming in the new warmth of spring, while fuzzwort and beastthorn sprouted along the river. The smell of the meadowweeds was enough to bring back the memory of summer days spent with a tablet and a meterstick, taking inventory of a meadow just like this one.

Snowflowers like the baby's nest and rose petals still bloomed in the shadows of the boulders around chunks of persistent ice. And a sweetheart vine that had wrapped itself around the trunk of a fern tree seemed to be pushing out tender green buds.

The list went on – each item a precious gift, the reward for hours of hard work learning their names and characteristics. Being a scout meant more than just running around in the woods alone pretending to be a great hero.

It meant learning the language of the world that had been entrusted to his care while it awaited the colonists who would one day call it home.

***

At 1300, after crossing Hart's Bridge in a thunderous, clop-clop-clopping procession, he stopped the patrol for lunch. High noon wasn't for two hours and by then he hoped to be at the Valley Post. But it wouldn't be fair to make everyone wait that long for lunch. And the horses were getting restless about their own feeding schedule.

The ground had grown steep and broken by rocks. The path lead ever higher, with glacial boulders and gravel washes spilling onto the grasslands. From the meadow where they ate their lunch they could see the treeline where the upland forest began. The valley wasn't far beyond that.

Just before the treeline, they reached a kilometer-wide ledge that extended along the front of the trees for several klicks. Stretching away to the east was a long course of flat ground covered with gravel – the landing strip.

The runway was only a few years old, one of the last of the big construction projects the scouts had prepared for Colony Day. It, and six more like it, had lain dormant since completion, covered with snow in the cold months, sprouting grasses, snowflowers and meadowweeds during the warm ones. In the next few weeks, though, it would see plenty of use as the colonists arrived.

Guy and Walt made the inspection together, riding the five-kilometer length of the strip, taking careful notes on the condition of the runway.

The weeds were not bad – the winter had seen to that. But the drainage from melting snow had caused some serious problems. There were nearly a dozen washed out spots that would require filling before the landing strip would be safe to use. Guy made a record of their location and dimensions for the patrol's inspection report.

At one point they even found a boulder beginning to break the surface where the rainwater had forced it up.

"It's awfully quiet down here," Walt said when they reached the far end of the strip. The wind had fallen away, the other scouts were far out of earshot and there was nothing to be heard but the occasional whistle of a wilbur gliding overhead. Above them, the white peak of Loki caught the sunlight and shined with pristine majesty. To the west, a thin gray haze hung over the valley, with Thor rising out of it more than a hundred klicks distant. The sky was turning yellow beyond the big mountain's shoulders, a portent of an overnight snowstorm.

"Wait a few weeks and that'll all change," Guy said.

"I don't know about you, Guy, but I'm getting knots in my stomach just thinking about it – Colony Day, I mean."

"I feel the same way," the older Stanger said. "I'm not sure how I'm going to like having thousands of new neighbors stomping all over my favorite scenery. In some ways, I can hardly wait – but in others, I wish it would just never happen. Like Grampa Bob."

"He doesn't want the colonists to come, does he?"

"I don't think so. Maybe he did once, but that was a long time ago. Nowadays he mostly complains about the whole idea."

"You know what I'm looking forward to most?" Walt asked.

"What's that?"

"The girls. I just can't get excited about the Majidor girls and Joan is nothing special. There's something funny about the idea of getting romantic with kids you grew up with. I want to meet someone new."

Guy smiled. "I didn't think of that myself," he said. "But you're right about the Majidor girls. And the Gilmartins and the Sweeneys and all the rest of them that keep hanging around the house to talk to you. Maybe it's about time you gave them a rest and started a whole new crowd coming around."

"Ah Guy, you're just jealous."

"Of you and Deena Majidor?"

"Well at least she still comes by the house – not like Jeannie Gilmartin and you."

Guy blushed. Last year, he and Jeannie had carried on quite an active sex life for a few months. The relationship was purely physical, just two kids exploring biology together, and after a while they grew tired of it. Or one another.

But he had never told his brother about it. Secrets were a precious thing in a community as small as the Main Post.

Walt realized he had struck a tender spot, though. "Admit it, you like her. Especially those big teeth that stick out so far in front."

"Why you – " Guy scowled at Walt, but his brother was already spurring his horse on, racing down the strip, leaving Guy to chase after his dust.

***

The entrance to Glacier Valley was not immediately visible from the trail. All that the patrol could see at first was the spray from Valley Falls, then the cataract itself, plunging 20 meters down along a 100-meter front. The roar of falling water filled the air, and the mist gave the native evergreens sparkling coats that dazzled the eyes where the sun caught them.

They rode on past the falls and around a broad stand of terrestrial fir trees planted by previous scout patrols, then they circled a deep kettlehole, a hollow left when the retreating glacier left a chunk of ice behind. On the far side was a gravelly wash that ran uphill for a half a klick.

The scouts knew what was at the top. They broke ranks and spurred their horses into a gallop to get over the crest. Guy was the only one to keep his mount under rein as the rest of them rushed past, and they were already halfway to the post when he reached the top of the rise.

The valley that stretched out before him was about four klicks wide here at the mouth, with sharp stony walls rising from the floor. A long, narrow lake ran back for a few klicks, waves lapping its shore just a short distance down a grassy hill from where Guy sat. Along its banks and along the base of the cliffs grew stand after stand of majestic greenwoods – the Asgardian equivalent of the sequoia. Chloroplasts in the bark gave the 100-meter-tall trees their name. Clutching at their feet were forests of pine and fir trees, planted by the scouts to provide building lumber for the colonists who would one day make their homes here.

At the far end of the valley, more than a dozen kilometers away, the glacier rose from another small lake ringed with more greenwoods. It looked like a great white tongue extending down from Loki's snowy peak.

Valley Post consisted of 45 log cabins and wooden frame buildings shielded behind a windbreak of greenwoods and Douglas fir on the shore of the lake. The main lodge sprawled across a low hillside, with porches, chimneys and rooftops spreading towards a large beachfront. More than a dozen dormitory buildings ran along a path that struck deep into the woods and a few utility buildings clustered in the lee of the main settlement. And, of course, there was a large horsebarn just off the main trail.

The first lodge had been built almost 90 years ago by the earliest scouts, and successive generations had added on to it. But about 20 years ago, the post had been idled as the scouts who lived there migrated out of the Prime Site for unexplored lands to the west. The property was used in the summer, and kept up by the scouts who from the Main Post, but its main function was as reserve housing for the colonists.

The rest of the patrol had dismounted and tied up their horses by the time Guy rode into the post. They were fooling around, the Osborne twins chasing each other behind the barn and his two youngest brothers laughing at the sport of it.

"Come on, patrol," he yelled as led his horse to the rail and tied up the reins. "Let's get organized. Do this right, or you won't be sleeping in real beds tonight."

"Real beds? Did you bring mattresses?" Walt asked.

Guy frowned – the post's bunks were not yet equipped with those niceties and they all knew it. "At least it's better than sleeping on the ground. And if we don't get busy, that's where we'll be tonight."

They moaned and complained until Guy added: "And it looks like snow before morning."

Guy opened the barn, and the scouts brought in their horses, removed their saddles and gear and broke open a few bales of green savanna grass hay. Then, with their most important responsibility out of the way, they moved on up to the main lodge.

The logs and rails for the building had been rough-cut and there was never time to do much finishing work, but there was still a certain style and flair to the old place. The sound of the scouts clomping across the wooden porch sent a pair of orvilles flapping away from their rooftop perch.

But when they reached the main doors, they all stopped at once.

The doors were open.

The two-meter beam that normally barred the entrance was lying on the floor in front of them. The doors themselves were undamaged, but swung freely.

The inner doors beyond them were closed, but the inner doors were mounted on springs – they formed a baffle to keep out cold drafts – while the outer doors were supposed to be shut tight and secured.

Two months earlier, Guy had closed those doors himself and then helped John Squire, the patrol leader on the fall inspection, lift the beam into place. Since then, no one had returned. No one that the scouts knew about, at least.

Guy felt his blood run hot and cold. He looked back as Joan gasped. Walt's face twisted in surprise and the younger scouts stared with eyes wide and mouths open.

3

No one was more afraid of what lay beyond the doors than he. And it occurred to him that he had carelessly left his rifle back in the horsebarn.

But as patrol leader, it was up to him to go first. So he imagined for a moment that there was a perfectly rational explanation for the open doors – one that involved an empty room on the far side. Then he tried to picture how he would act if that explanation were true.

Forthright. And unafraid. As if it were the simplest thing in the world.

"This is certainly odd," he said, trying to talk himself into believing the perfectly rational explanation. There was also the thought in the back of his head that anyone on the other side of the doors might be warned by the sound of his voice so they would have ample time to leave.

Then he found himself stepping up to the door and pushing it open.

The old spring overhead squeaked loudly, almost as loudly as the hinges. He walked boldly into the foyer of the lodge, looked around quickly and, with a sigh, realized it was empty.

That seemed to be enough to restore his nerves and his good sense. He stepped quickly to the doorway into the dining hall, then back across the foyer to the library. Both were empty.

"Walt, you take Billy and the Osbornes with you, the rest come with me," he said. "You go through the west wing, we'll go upstairs and on through the east. Meet back here in five minutes."

They raced through the building, up the stairs and down, opening doors, checking bathrooms and closets and making as much noise as possible to scare away the intruders – if there were any. They found nothing, then turned back. Walt and his party spilled into the dining hall just as they did.

"Nothing," he called out.

"Look around," Guy said. "Has anything been touched?"

"Check the fireplace," said Billy. "Is it still warm?"

Guy and Walt were there at the same instant. The hearth was still as clean swept and spotless as it had been when the scouts cleaned it in November.

"What about the kitchen?"

They all ran in together, shaking the walls as they went. The stone counters were empty and spotless. Guy checked the wicker trash basket in the corner – nothing. Walt wiped his fingers across the stove while the rest of them checked the larder.

"What is going on here?" Walt demanded in a shout that rattled the windows.

"Calm down," Guy ordered, glaring at his brother. If ever he needed to establish that he was the patrol leader, regardless of his age, it was now. "There's got to be a reasonable explanation for this – and we won't figure it out by losing control. Let's all go into the library, get a fire going and work it out. And let's try to walk through the halls instead of run. We're scouts, not duckasaurs."

A sour groan from the youngsters helped break the tension as they filed out of the kitchen. Walt just snarled and glared at Guy as he walked past. That was just what he needed – a rebellious and uncontrollable Walt.

There wasn't much to the library but a few tables, a couple of readers and a hard disk full of books. They sat down around one of the long tables, Guy at the head.

"Whoever left the doors open obviously didn't stay long or disturb anything," he said once they were all settled. "Did anyone notice anything out of place in the barn?"

There was no response. "I didn't think so. Now let's approach this rationally. Who could have opened the door? Not a fuzzasaur – they haven't got the brains to come in from the cold, let alone unbar the door. No one but a scout. Right?"

A few heads nodded in agreement.

"So who did it? Anyone from the Main Post? Not me. Not Walt. Or Billy or Tad. We were home all winter. Did any of you sneak up here? Do you know anyone who disappeared for a few days during a thaw? No, I didn't think so. So that leaves us with three choices – North Valley, Highland Post or one of the outland posts."

"Do you think someone from North Valley came through Vogelberg's Pass and opened the doors?" asked Tad.

"That's one possibility."

"That's a stupid possibility," said Walt. "Why would they leave the door open? Where did they go? They didn't show up at the Main Post. Guy, none of this makes any sense."

"Maybe they never got as far as Main Post," Guy said, sensing the weakness of his own proposition, but determined to rationalize the mystery by any means he could. "Maybe it was a mini-pilot who had to put his plane down and who's trying to find the Main Post."

"Then we would have run into him on the trail," Walt said. "You're just guessing. You don't know if anyone from North Valley came through here. You don't know anything. And you're just as scared as the rest of us, no matter how calm you try to act."

Guy held his temper and his tongue until his brother ran out of steam.

"I guess you're right, Walt. I don't know for sure who was here. But I'm sure they're gone. And I'm sure they didn't leave us a clue as to who they were."

"You're not sure they won't be back, are you?"

"No, I'm not. Maybe we'd be better off if they do come back. Then we won't have to wonder anymore. In the meantime, we have work to do. And we're wasting time sitting around here making ourselves nervous. There's no place else to go, so we might as well get over the willies right now and get to work. Walt, we'll sort this out later."

"But – "

"No buts," Guy insisted. "Later. First, I want you to take the girls and Billy on an inspection tour of the post. Check for snow-damage, ice invasions, byte colonies and glider nests. You know what to do, Walt. I'll join up with you in a while. I'll take the twins and we'll start hauling up the stuff from the pack horses. I figure on dinner in about an hour, and then we've got a few more hours of sunlight after that to finish up. This place has got to be tight before the snow starts to fall tonight."

Walt's hard eyes only seemed to soften a bit, until Guy shot a pleading wordless expression at him, then the younger Stanger seemed to melt.

The change was almost instantaneous. "All right, ladies, you heard Mr. Scoutmaster. Let's go."

"Don't call me a lady," Billy snapped back.

***

Guy tried for nearly an hour to raise the duty scoutship before its orbit brought it into acquisition. Then the receiver crackled and the scoutship's AI came on the line.

"Please stand by. Your call is in the queue."

Then there was some more crackling and then a human voice.

"Main Post, Lyle Sanderson here."

"Hi, Mr. Sanderson. This is Guy Stanger with the patrol up in Glacier Valley."

"Hey, Guy, how are you kids doing up there?"

"We've got a problem," he said, and he told them about the open door and their fruitless search.

"Beats me, Scout," Sanderson said. "I'll have to pass it along to the North Valley posts, but I don't know who could have done it. I'd like to find out, too. It seems pretty irresponsible to me."

"Things are pretty tight up here otherwise," Guy reported, giving a quick rundown on the landing strip and the post. "Must have been a mild winter."

"I'm glad it was mild somewhere. Keep your eyes open and record anything you find that doesn't look right and maybe we'll figure this out before you get back," Sanderson said before signing off.

Guy packed up the phone and set it in the dining hall where it could be heard easily if someone called back. Then he took out his rifle and checked the load. He set it in the rack beside the main entrance. That was Scout Law – weapons in the rack when scouts are indoors.

The scouts carried out their duties in an eery silence, unbroken by the normal joking and playing. Guy also felt an uneasiness borne out of too much of the unexpected. Add to that the general tension that had been building all winter long as Colony Day approached and you had real trouble. Like Walt getting all worked up.

Guy tried to relieve some of the tension by making dinner something special.

He dug some eggs out of their cool-pack, break-proof cartons and some vegetables, onions, and mushrooms and some pots and pans in the kitchen cupboards and a few logs in the hearth. A half an hour later, he was turning out omelets to order and nine hungry, nervous scouts regained some semblance of order.

Even Walt tried to settle things from their earlier spat.

"I've been thinking about it all afternoon," he said. "I don't know about you, but I'd rather die than go off and leave the door to the lodge unbarred. So would any scout. And if I came in here at night, for sure I'd start a fire. Look at you – you cooked omelets, for goodness' sake. And I'd leave a note on the chalkboard saying who you were and why you came here."

"So it doesn't add up. It doesn't make sense. What's your point?"

"My point is that it couldn't have been a scout who opened the doors," he said. "It had to be someone else."

"Who else could it be, Walt? There's no one else on Asgard but scouts. If a scout didn't stop here, who did?"

"A Native?" asked one of the Osbornes

"An Alien Ancient?" asked Tad.

"I didn't say that," Walt said.

"You're right, you didn't. That's because there ain't no such things. That's just stuff you tell around the campfire. This is real."

"Well damn it, Guy, I don't know!"

"Neither do I, Walt. But that's no reason to argue about it. All right, you've convinced me that whoever it was did a lot of unscoutlike things.

But that only makes it harder to figure out."

"So what do we do?"

"We wait until we have more information instead of pounding our heads into a brick wall over the little we do have."

That seemed to settle it for the moment. At least Walt seemed to give up the fight.

"All right, all right," he said. "Just remember to be careful. Don't expect Grampa Bob to come through that door during the night. And please don't leave the rifle where someone who does come through the door can reach it ... "

Guy sighed. "Walt, you know the Scout Law."

"I don't give a damn about the Scout Law. It's not safe. Not now, anyway."

He struggled with the idea for a moment, balancing his brother's fears with his own sense of duty. He wanted to tell Walt he was being irrational, but he didn't want to start another argument. And it seemed like such a small thing to do. He retrieved the weapon from the rack, brought it into the dining hall and set it on the table.

"I'll keep it with me all night, if it makes you feel better."

"Thanks, big brother," Walt said. "I don't know what I'd do without you." He wasn't the least bit convincing.

***

Aftersupper duties kept everyone busy until almost dark. Guy assigned them sleeping quarters – three to a room, his own bunk alone in a room next to the door nearest the main entrance.

When the light finally faded from the skies, the scouts returned to the lodge and boiled up a soup kit for supper. When the kitchen was cleaned up, they laid in a fire in the dining hall and camped out in front of it to tell stories. But there weren't any stories to tell – nothing they made up could be as scary or mysterious as what had really happened.

And on top of that, they were all exhausted. They'd already put in more than 18 hours today and with all the excitement, they were ready to drop.

Guy fixed some coffee for himself just to keep his eyes open long enough to get them all settled in. When he went back into the dining hall, he noticed that Billy was gone.

That little monster. When he got his hands on his little brother, he'd teach him to run off. Where could he be?

"Did anyone see Billy?"

"He went out onto the porch," Tad said.

Some of his anger ebbed at that. But still, what was he doing outside? He found Billy at the far end of the porch, looking up the valley at Loki. A moist wind was picking up out of the south and the trees were beginning to shake and rustle in its grip. The sky was black with a thick coat of clouds that a short time earlier had blotted out the sunset.

"It's going to get cold up here pretty soon, you know," he said softly. "I know. I just thought I'd take a look again tonight. Just to see if they came back."

"Makes sense," Guy said. "But I'm not sure it's a high-probability event."

"We can watch for a little while, can't we?"

"I guess it won't hurt. Might improve our chances if we gave it more of an interval."

They stood there in the dark, listening to the waterfall in the distance and the wind nearby. The horses whinnied in the barn. A few sparks danced overhead from the chimney.

Billy had picked the right spot. During the day, this end of the porch provided a view of the top of Loki and the glacier, framed by the great boles of the greenwoods. Now there was nothing but the imagination to posit the mountain's great bulk.

The wind was beginning to turn from southwest to northeast now, with a confusing effect on the trees. It reached around the corner of the lodge and tugged at the two brothers, but Billy stood his ground a little longer.

And a little longer.

Until Guy was past the end of his patience and ready to call it a night. Then they saw it.

A set of lights – red, green and bluish-white. Aircraft warning lights. And they were certainly there. It wasn't stars – not through this cloud cover. And it wasn't ghosts. Ghosts didn't carry standard red and green running lights.

Guy wasn't surprised that his brother hadn't recognized the lights. Scoutships never flew at night and, since a night accident when he was younger than Billy, neither had the scouts' few remaining miniplanes. But Guy remembered the sight of running lights at night.

They watched it for a minute as it crossed from east to west, and then a second set of lights appeared behind it.

"Where did that come from?" Guy said.

"From the middle of the valley," Billy said. "Look – I've got it triangulated." He pointed to a row of sticks resting on the railing.

"This stick is the western ridge line and this one is the east. The first middle one is the glacier and the second is the peak. They didn't fly in from outside the valley. They were here all along and they just took off."

The two aircraft climbed to the west. It took them almost long enough to convince Guy that they weren't going to clear the valley walls, but they did: Then they vanished from view.

"It was real, Guy. You saw it. They were real and we know where they came from."

"That's right, Billy. We certainly do. But what we've got to find out now is who they were and what they were doing."

***

There were three inches of snow on the ground when the scouts got up the next morning.

They'd been up the night before for another hour after Guy and Billy saw the aircraft, but they still had logged eleven hours of sleep, and were ready to take on the world – even covered with wet frosting. Sunrise was still an hour away when they began shuffling around the lodge, washing and grumbling and stirring.

By dawn, Guy had three horses saddled and ready to go. He decided to take along Walt, because he wanted him to see everything first hand, and Billy, because he had a right to find out the source of the strange lights.

They rode for two hours until they reached a meadow at mid-valley where they found the evidence they were searching for.

Strewn around the ground were wrappings and cans, binding straps, plastic insulation and wire. A half-eaten piece of fruit, a paper bag and some bones covered with red sauce marked a second find some meters away.

But the big prize was the large stack of equipment that had been staked into the ground. There were seven of the black boxes, each with its own little instrument panel, some with vents and fans, others with wires and antennas. Each had a little identifying tag with an incomprehensible technical name and a system number beside it. A serial number was embossed in the corner of each plate.

"What is it?" Billy asked.

"A weather station. And some other sensors," Guy said. "It's the kind of stuff we use for remote monitoring. But we don't need remote monitoring up here in the valley. Where did they get this stuff? Is someone moving our monitor stations around?"

"What for?" asked Walt.

"This is more than we can figure out," Guy said. "I'm calling the Main Post."

It was half an hour before he could raise the duty ship. An hour after that a mini appeared out of the west and circled for a landing. Guy was relieved to see Mr. Sanderson step out after it came to a stop.

The next few days were not a lot of fun for Guy. He wanted to rush back to the Main Post and help solve the mystery of the intruders. But Mr. Sanderson had given him no such orders, leaving him to complete his job as leader of the inspection patrol.

There was plenty to do. They had to check the interior of each dormitory for byte and chitinoid infestation, examine all the roads and major pathways for drainage damage, test the water lines in all the buildings and inspect the tent flats.

He spent the hours of daylight after dinner compiling the reports of the inspection parties and logging them in his tablet. The winter had been easy on the post. In the eight weeks since they had left the place, all the buildings had remained secure and the most damage they'd found was a nest of bytes that had fouled a closet in one of the dorms.

With all that had to be done before the colony arrived, even the minor damage would not get attention. That would be left to the new tenants. But there was a lot of satisfaction in knowing that the scouts were turning over a post in as near perfect condition as possible.

When darkness finally came, Guy put away the reports, packed his tablet and fixed himself a duckasaur sandwich for supper. The fireside story session was more lively that night – now that everyone could put a label, however uninformative, on the intruders. But Guy couldn't help noting that there was a nervous edge to the laughter.

The next morning, they cleaned up, closed up and locked up, replacing the bar across the entrance to the lodge carefully. Then they mounted up and were on their way home.

The ride was long, but tempered by the rapidly proliferating signs of spring. In the two days since they had passed up the trail, a whole world had begun to blossom.

The plains were beginning to take on a golden glow as the savanna grass returned to life. Vines were budding out and some had even begun to flower – the sweethearts and fleur-de-lis especially. Mossback and thistlefoot had painted the meadows orange and blue. And silverbacks and redcrests had crossed over the South River in substantial numbers, judging from the size of the crowds Guy saw grazing on the newly awakened savanna

The scouts reached the riverside camp by lunchtime and struck out west along the overland road. They had dinner in their saddles as the afternoon sun beat down on them and forced the jackets off their backs. A warm rain rolled in out of the south as they rode the last leg of the journey home and they passed through the Main Post Gate as darkness fell.

***

Henry Schmidt came for Guy while he was still in the barn taking care of the horses.

"What I can't understand is why they want one of you kids to come to this meeting," Schmidt said. "But Smiling Lyle said to come get you. He's up in the lodge now, so you let Walt tend to that and come with us."

Schmidt was Sanderson's assistant, and Guy didn't like him. He was a young man, only in his 40s, but he was always trying to make Guy feel unwanted. Schmidt was more interested in ceremony and custom than he was in work or knowledge. His wife was unattractive and whined a lot and Schmidt spent a lot of his time in the lodge instead of at his cabin.

Guy didn't know what to say to him – partly out of surprise and partly out of fatigue after spending most of the day in the saddle. He wanted to say something sharp and cutting, but he was so angry at the easy way Schmidt put him down that he couldn't think straight. He decided any remark he might make at the moment would only get him in trouble. Schmidt was a large man with 20 centimeters and 20 kilos on Guy – although some of that mass was confined to his waist.

Guy followed along through the dark drizzle as Schmidt splashed across the post towards the lodge. The air was sharp with the smell of woodsmoke and cookfires, and the lighted cabins among the trees signaled the reassuring presence of other scouts.

They clomped into the foyer and stripped off their wet rain ponchos. Then Schmidt led the way into the library.

More than two dozen scouts formed a semicircle around a man seated in one of the few upholstered chairs in the place.

The man was a stranger to him.

While the young scout didn't know all of the more than 4,000 adults on Asgard, he had seen most of them. This man's face wasn't even familiar. Then Guy realized his hair was grown long over his ears like a boy's. Like his own, he realized with a lump in his throat. And his clothes looked different – made of some odd material that didn't resemble fuzzy leather at all.

"Excuse me," Sanderson said, interrupting the gathering. "I'd like to introduce our visitor to one of our younger leaders. Mr. LeClerc, this is Guy Stanger. Guy, this is Pierre LeClerc."

He stepped forward and shook hands with the odd scout.

"I'm afraid your friends gave Guy and his patrol quite a scare this week," Sanderson said. "Mr. LeClerc is from Tikarahisat – at Eta Cass."

Guy felt his jaw drop, but hoped no one would notice his loss of muscle control. Probably not. They were probably paying more attention to the distracted mumbling he was producing in response to Schmidt's introduction.

"A pleasure to meet you, my friend," LeClerc said. "I was just saying that den Iroquois has really lived up to its reputation for hospitality with tonight's supper. And as a representative of den Algonkian, I'd like to extend my thanks. I also want to apologize if we had you worried with our little expedition, Mr. Stanger. We meant no harm."

"Eta Cass?" The words were all Guy could muster. He looked around the room for help.

"Mr. LeClerc is part of an expedition from Eta Cass," Mr. Sanderson said. "They've been in system for a few weeks now. That equipment you found in Glacier Valley was theirs."

"And it was our two minis that you saw while you were up there," LeClerc added.

"But why? What are you doing here?"

"That's just what I was about to explain," LeClerc said. "Have a seat and I will tell you all."

***

There were about a hundred men, women and children in the party from Eta Cass, he said. They were colonists, mostly. LeClerc was one of the few scouts who had come along. Tik was an older settlement, closer to Sol. When LeClerc and the others left, the breakthrough colony had been there 14 years.

They had crossed the six years between Eta and Mu Cass in a borrowed scoutship – a risky enterprise for all involved. And once here, they decided to take a look around before disturbing the local scouts. It was not what LeClerc had suggested, but colonists tended to do things their own way, no matter what anyone said.

Why were they here? Why did they come all that distance?

To offer their help to the new colonists at Asgard, of course.

"The Good Lord, He has smiled on Tik," he said. "We got the best of everything – land, sky and air. And we learned how to do things right, us. Now we come to offer what we know to help the new colony do it right the first time around. Me, I came because I like adventure."

He tilted his head in jaunty manner.

"But really, you must listen to what we have to say. Our leader, Peter Kolberg, he'll explain it all to everyone. But the Kolbergs, him and his brothers, they have a good idea. We can give you what we know – technology, management methods, organizational ideas – all that we have learned in 14 years of making a colony. Give you all a head start on the world you want to build here."

"And what are you asking for in return?" Lyle Sanderson asked softly.

"The Kolbergs say all they are after is some back country real estate. Just among us scouts, I think they want to be big shots and run a big show. But they do a lot of good things, too. Me, like I said, I want some adventure.

"They sent me down here to talk to you scouts after you started calling on the radio. They finally listened to what I said. You can't ignore the scouts, I told them. You need their help. So here I am. Maybe, when we're done, I can get some back country land, too. But more likely I'll be moving on to the next world before she gets all filled up with colonists."

LeClerc talked for a long time without revealing much about the Kolbergs or their specific plans or anything else that would have been useful. But he was a colorful character and he knew how to captivate an audience.

Guy was amazed at the sight of a man from another world. In a way, it made a life of waiting for Colony Day become an imminent reality instead of a distant faith. And the idea that he had crossed six years of interstellar space – solar years, at that – sent a chill up Guy's back.

But somehow, it didn't mesh. If LeClerc and his friends were interested in back country real estate, why were they poking around up in Glacier Valley?

LeClerc was good with his rambling manner. He deflected serious questions and evaded any attempt to elaborate. "Wait for the Kolbergs," he said. "They told me not to give away the show before it goes on."

But Guy didn't trust the man.

***

Neither, it seemed, did Lyle Sanderson.

After an hour or so, LeClerc begged off on the questioning. He asked for some coffee and a little breathing room and the scouts obliged by heading off on their separate ways. Sanderson caught Guy on his way out the door.

"You probably haven't had supper yet, Guy," he said. "Why don't you join me in the kitchen and we'll see what we can scare up?"

The invitation caught Guy by surprise. Sanderson had never expressed much interest in his nutrition in the past. What was going on?

"I was on the phone to Grampa Bob this afternoon, and he said to tell you hello," the scoutmaster said as he handed Guy a wooden bowl and pointed him towards the soup. "He also told me I should keep an eye on you because you're a smart kid."

"I was always told not to believe everything Grampa Bob said," Guy replied. He filled the bowl with thick fuzzasaur soup and found a chunk of fresh-baked bread in the breadbox.

"So what do you think of Mr. LeClerc?"

"I don't like him much, sir," Guy said. "He talks too much. Grampa Bob would probably tell you the same thing."

"He did, pretty much. Tell me what you saw up at the post. What kind of people are we dealing with?"

"They're sloppy, careless and irresponsible. That's pretty obvious, isn't it. They left the door open to the lodge. They were lucky we came along as soon as we did or the place would have been full of chites, rippers and bytes. And they left trash all over the place. Packages and food garbage. Things that any scout old enough to walk would have picked up and carried away. Is that because they're colonists?"

Sanderson shook his head. "I don't know, Guy. Those are some of the things that worry me, too. But I think you and Grampa Bob and I are in the minority. Henry Schmidt is all excited about it. He thinks it's a great idea. Treats LeClerc like a long-lost cousin. A few of the others have some doubts, but they aren't talking about it. But they don't have the problem I have."

"What's that?" Guy asked.

"LeClerc has asked us for a favor. He and his friends want the database for North and South Valleys – the township grid, resource surveys, the works."

"Well, that's supposed to be public information. I mean, that's what we're here for, is to collect that data for everyone to use. I guess we have to give that to them whether we like them personally or not."

"No, Guy, when I said the works, I meant they want the township assignments that we've drafted for the breakthrough colony. They want to see our proposal for how the colony is going to be laid out – which dens go where. That's not public information – that's the political sense of the scouts of den Iroquois. It's our hope for this world, our request to the new colony as the caretakers of Asgard."

"That's different," Guy said. "I guess we don't want to hand that over to these outsider before we've even approached the colonists."

"I get nervous just thinking about showing it to the colonists. They're the ones who are going to have to approve it."

"What are you going to give LeClerc then?" Guy asked.

"As little as I possibly can – and then I'm going to check the family strongbox to make sure it's still there."

"DRIVE ACTIVATION COMPLETE." Emily Baxter stared at the words on the big screen at the far end of the gymnasium. Barely seconds ago, it had read, "PREPARE FOR DRIVE ACTIVATION." Now it was over.

And in the interval a third of a lifetime had passed.

Her mother turned and hugged her and her twelve-year-old brother.

"Aw mom," Joey complained as he squirmed loose. She ignored him, turned to her stepfather and kissed him. Emily was a little disturbed to see the tears in her mother's eyes, even more so to see them in Ray's.

All around the chamber, the scene was being repeated hundreds of times. There were smiles and shouts and sobbing and tears.

But Emily wasn't sure why. She wondered if there was something she was missing – some essential part of the jump across the stars that she still hadn't experienced. What did they feel that she didn't?

A rising crescendo of sound filled the great cylindrical chamber.

The announcement on the screen was replaced by an image of Captain Gallo, her dark curls framing a humorless face. She was looking off-screen, at another part of the control deck, while someone's voice counted off numbers: " ... 17 ... 18 ... 19 ... that's all, sir."

Then Captain Gallo turned and faced the colonists gathered in the gym. The size of the face on the screen made the compartment shrink in Emily's eyes.

"It's my sad duty to report to you that only nineteen of our ships have completed the journey from Sol," she said. "Our friends and comrades on the *Hollister* have been lost. A moment of silence in their memory is now in order ... thank you."

The image dissolved into a blank screen. Then another announcement appeared: "STAND BY TO SECURE FROM SOLITON DRIVE QUARTERS"

The moment of silence continued long after the Captain disappeared from the screen.

Then the significance of the report sunk in.

Until that moment, the risks that the Asgard Breakthrough Colony faced in their interstellar flight had all seemed academic to her. She was never very good with math anyway, and percentage of failure rates involved one set of fractions too many. Of course it was dangerous. Everyone knew that. But she didn't have any way of weighing what that meant to her personally.

She hadn't realized how the survivors would feel.

There had been 5,000 people on the *Hollister*. Three dens. Mothers, fathers, children, babies. Livestock and equipment. Plans and hopes. And now they were all gone.

Emily thought about all the hard work involved in preparing for the passage to the new world – she had been at it since her last year of high school, three years now, survival training, camping and hiking, planetary and plant science, first aid, navigation and meteorology, and a whole catalog of other subjects. Like her, those colonists had given up their homes and possessions on a crowded Earth, suffered through the same training, and now it was all a waste. They would never see the world they had sacrificed everything for. And the rest of the colony would never know what happened to them.

Out of that dark ignorance, all kinds of things appeared in Emily's imagination, fueled by what little she could remember of the list of fates that could befall the unfortunate.

The soliton drive could have been caught in an uncertainty loop and sent the *Hollister* on an endless journey at the speed of light. Or the ship could have hit a comet or a brown dwarf or a cosmic string or some other hazard in midflight and dispersed the soliton field, leaving the ship stranded in interstellar space. Or it could have hit one of those things and been destroyed, both events that could now be a dozen years in the past.

Now she realized why her mother and the other parents were so relieved to make it through the drive activation intact. Now she understood why the entire membership of all three dens had to be together in the gym when the colony made the jump.

They wanted to be together with their loved ones. In case the jump across space was the end, and not the beginning, of their lives.

Emily couldn't help but think of what it must have felt like for the families on board the *Hollister*. Did they wait for the announcement to appear on the lightboard and then step into oblivion without warning? Did they find themselves in the middle of nowhere, condemned to a slow, cold, breathless death? Did they cry out? Did they feel pain?

She was swept by a wave of embarrassment. How selfish she had been that first moment when everyone was so relieved and she was so unconcerned. And now the first blush of relief had been destroyed by the knowledge that they had lost 5,000 of their comrades. For Emily it was a lost feeling that she could never regain.

Why did life have to be so unkind? Why did the joy of a safe arrival have to be stained with the sorrow of such a great loss?

Now that the reality of the event had caught up with her, she felt a sudden hunger for human contact. She looked for her mother, even though that was not a normal impulse for her. Suzanne Baxter stood next to Ray, Emily's stepfather, who had his arms wrapped tightly around her.

Emily hesitated. She and her mother had never been close or affectionate towards one another – a situation that only worsened when her father left. And now she was reluctant to get too close to her mother and her new stepfather. But the strain was too much, and she pressed forward awkwardly and huddled against her mother.

Joey was there, too.

"A 62 percent chance of losing one," said her precocious brother. "A 38 percent chance of losing two and a 12 percent of losing three. Looks like we were well within the curve. Welcome to Asgard, Em."

***

Suzanne Baxter barely had time to get her family back to their cubicle before a call came for her. The leaders of the other two dens aboard the *Hamilton* wanted a meeting on the control deck.

She kissed Ray on the cheek and told Emily to keep an eye on her brother before dodging out the door into the crowded passageway.

Her nerves were wired up as tight as she could stand them. A week of freefall aboard the *Hamilton* while they finished loading and a day of spin gravity had stressed her to the limit. The activation of the soliton drive had almost made her ill. What kind of a mother would do that to her children? Turn the key on that machine and send them across 25 years of empty space – or worse? What kind of a mother was she to let them do it?

If only Lee Baxter hadn't joined the scouts. If it had just been the divorce, she could have lived with it – even if it meant being both a mother and a father to the children, even if it meant putting even more distance between her and her daughter. But she was not about to let him outdo her, becoming a distant hero to Joseph and Emily while she had to stay behind and do the dirty work of raising them. So she switched from pre-med studies to wildlife biologist and signed the kids up with her for a colonial den. She'd been just as surprised as anyone when they were selected for the Asgard breakthrough colony.

She was even more surprised when the faculty and staff and families of Middlesex University chose her as leader of the newly formed den Middlesex. Although she had expressed an interest in the position, she never dreamed that she would win the election – and the responsibilities that went with the office.

Harry Bayard and Brad Karlsen were talking with Captain Gallo when she reached the control deck.

Harry was a small, heavyset man with white hair and a red face. His hands were scarred from years of working the frozen Alaskan earth. He headed up den Matanuska, one of the toughest agricultural dens in the colony.

Brad was leader of den Bunyan, a woodsman two meters tall with shoulders a meter wide. His long red beard had fluffed up in zero-G, and his oversized frame seemed to bump into everything.

"The *Hollister* was carrying a service den and two agricultural dens – Calumet, Boone and Kenosha," Gallo said.

"Mary Covetti, Brian Ash and Eric Heidegger," Suzanne said, listing the names of the den leaders.

"And a few thousand more," added Harry. "May they rest in peace."

"And the other 95,000 of us?" Suzanne asked.

"Are doing as well as can be expected," Gallo said. "Most of them – most of us – are still suffering from soliton shock. Relief and guilt in generous doses. It's probably just as well that we'll be spending the next few days working off our proper motion before we can make orbit. Gives everyone time to recover."

"Which brings us to the subject of this meeting," Harry said. "We've already received a message from the scouts, and I don't think you're going to like it."

"What did they say?"

"They invited us to postpone our landing schedule while we listen to a sales pitch for an alternate plan."

"The scouts have an alternate plan?" she asked.

"No. Someone else does."

"There isn't anyone else, Harry. Just them and us."

"There is now," said Brad.

They told her what the scouts had passed on about Peter Kolberg and his offer. "They want to make a full presentation to all the colonists once we make orbit. And they'd like us to put the landing schedule on hold while we discuss it."

"And would they like anything else while they're at it? Our virgin daughters, our cattle and our grain?"

"We don't know, Sue," Harry said. "We won't be able to get a two-way going with the scouts until tomorrow. We've got to synchronize our clocks and get on their time. It's the middle of the night at the main scout post right now."

"They must think we're crazy," Suzanne said. "I don't want to spend a single minute more in these egg crates than I have to. The sooner I'm on solid ground, the better. They've got three days to give us their pitch. After that, the Doctrine says we're supposed to start landing. I move we follow the Doctrine. Let the Kolbergs go back to Eta Cass if they want to direct traffic."

"It's not so simple," Harry said.

"Why not?"

"Some of the dens like the idea."

***

Guy finished his morning session in his family's vegetable patch, weeding the rows and following the instructions on the tablet for planting the collection of seedlings the nursery had given them. This year, they were trying a mix of gene-tailored cherimoya, arracacha and yams and some force-bred native vegetables like beastfruit and duckroot. If they followed the pattern of past seasons, only about half of them would be successful, but it would be up to him to dutifully record which were which in the fall.

He set down his trowel and wiped the sweat from his forehead just in time to see the miniplane circle overhead. His neck ached as he looked up to follow its track. It buzzed by only a few meters off the ground then came down on the landing field with a bounce and a bump.

When he saw who had arrived, Guy broke into a trot and ran to meet him. It was Grampa Bob.

He was a portly man with a white mustache, white eyebrows and an old fashioned ranger-style hat. At 140, he was the oldest scout on Asgard – one of the few surviving members of the first generation. He had waited 93 short Asgard years for this moment – for the colony to arrive. And now he was mad.

"What do they mean they want to put off Colony Day?" he roared as he greeted Guy and Lyle Sanderson, who appeared at the last minute from his office.

"That's what they told the colonists," Sanderson said.

Guy was stunned. This was the first he'd heard of it. When he awoke, his brothers were already running around the house shouting that the breakthrough colony had arrived. And his mother and father told him in hushed and serious voices about the loss of the *Hollister* and the 5,000 colonists aboard.

"What a terrible price to have to pay," said his mother.

But no one had told him that the Kolbergs' wanted to postpone the landings.

"When did they say that?" Guy asked.

"Last night, when the colony ships arrived," Sanderson said. No wonder Grampa Bob had flown in from the Highland Post.

Guy's feet and legs felt suddenly liquid and insubstantial. Or maybe it was the ground that he was standing on. Nothing seemed to be happening the way it was supposed to.

"They're supposed to make orbit Sunday," the scoutmaster continued. "Colony Day is Wednesday. The landings start Monday with the pathfinder groups, then the first wave of dens. It'll take a week to get them all down. And the rest of the summer to land the cargo."

"Not if they don't get started," Grampa Bob said. "What in the name of the Great Spirit are these interlopers after?"

"I'm not sure what they want," Sanderson said. "But I know what they've got – and that's our proposal for the township assignments."

"Oh damn, you can't be serious. How'd they get that?"

"Henry Schmidt. He claims he did it by mistake while he was uploading the database. His story is that he miskeyed the command to edit that file out of the transmission."

"You don't sound like you believe him."

"Well, there's not much I can do but call him a liar, is there?"

"Guy, don't look so astounded," Grampa Bob said, shifting his gaze up at the young scout. "Scouts can be selfish just like anyone else. Henry always seemed a little uncomfortable out in the wilds. Maybe he wants to make friends with the colonists."

Guy realized that his mouth had been hanging open in surprise. He never had liked Henry Schmidt, but he always thought it was just a matter of his personal taste. He realized now that there was more to it than that – it was also a matter of character. Schmidt was not trustworthy. And Guy didn't like the idea that there were scouts that he couldn't trust.

"And has anyone told us what the Kolbergs want?" Grampa Bob said.

"Not yet. LeClerc is useless and the rest of the crowd has stayed holed up in their scoutship – wherever that is. We haven't seen it in orbit.

They must have landed somewhere nearby, but no one's spotted them yet."

"It doesn't matter. I know what they're after."

"What's that?" Guy asked.

"Power. Pure and simple. Power over other people's lives."

6

One by one, at various intervals over the day, the nineteen ships of the Asgard breakthrough colony fell into orbit about the icy world that revolved around Mu Cassiopeiae.

Each ship contained three dens – sixty in all when they set out, now only fifty-seven.

Half of them were agricultural dens – Lincoln, Imperial, Banf, Windhoek, Jasper and more, gathered from the United States, Canada, Australia, southern Africa and Europe. Some of them brought livestock – horses, dairy herds and sheep – and others carried seedstock – corn, soybeans, potatos, yams, beets, coffee, quinoa, arracacha, pepinos and naranjilla. Each den included 400 families and each family was equipped with a truck, a tractor and part-share in a harvester. In addition to their 46,000 colonists, the farming dens brought to Asgard 700 horses, 2,100 dairy cattle and 2,100 sheep. And 14,000 tons of feed grain.

Only the two ships carrying the transportation dens – Pullman and McDonnell – were larger than the ag-ships. In addition to their members, each of them carried 100 light trucks, 150 heavy trucks, 50 buses, 50 boat engines, 20 airplanes and 10 heavy tow trucks. That added up to more than 7,000 tons of equipment in each ship. It would take the colony's landers 140 trips to set the entire load down on the surface.

Six dens of service workers had accompanied the colony from Sol – there were five now. They carried no cargo but themselves and offered no equipment but their own labor. They came from urban centers where life was raw and useful skills were few. Dens Franklin, Munchen, Midland, Gotham and Angeles, tucked away in the big ships where space was at a premium.

Five educational dens came equipped with the makings of 500 classrooms each. The university den – Middlesex – brought along a library. Each of the four health dens – Schweitzer, Salk, Reed and Nightingale – was a fully equipped mobile hospital with a staff that included 20 obstetricians, 20 pediatricians, nine internists, four surgeons, three psychologists, two orthopedists, a diagnostic radiologist and a dermatologist.

Two special services dens – Harley and Levesque – provided an eclectic mix of hairdressers, police, morticians, comedians, television producers and cameramen, nine reporters, three editors and a dozen printing presses. Five specialist dens formed the industrial sector of the colony: Gompers, the apparel den; Larington, food processing, or as it was more commonly known, the cannery den; Carnegie, the specialty manufacturing den; Yorkshire, the machinist den; and Bunyan, the lumber den. Two construction dens provided carpenters and tools to build the new colony.

And to keep everything running smoothly – and to insure that the colonists did not entirely escape the world of red tape and paperwork – the colony also included three professional-management dens – Putnam, Hancock and Elliott – that included bankers, bureaucrats, planners, lawyers and judges.

While the executive dens were equipped to carry out the functions of government – both political and commercial – they were not political centers in their own right. Policy direction would have to come from the colonists themselves, in whatever form they eventually decided. That fact was amply demonstrated any time the dens were asked to give a straight answer about anything – and could not.

And therein lay the problem facing the colony as the last of their ships locked itself safely within Asgard's gravity well.

They had not yet decided how to organize themselves as a political body, make decisions as a single entity and take action to implement them. At the moment, they were only 57 separate dens spread around 19 ships in 19 different orbits.

It was enough to make Suzanne Baxter scream.

***

Emily had put it succinctly.

"You mean no one is in charge?" she'd asked innocently.

"That's exactly the problem," Suzanne told her daughter. "The den is a great piece of social organization. The Colonial Corps did a great job of creating and training them and getting them here. But they didn't give us a method for acting as a group. No government, no constitution, no social contract. Nothing. Just the Doctrine – which is nothing more than a landing and unloading schedule."

"But why not? Mother, that doesn't sound like a very smart thing to do."

"That's because adults don't always do the smart thing, Emily," she'd told her.

Now, tethered to a table on the control deck, watching a half dozen Corps officers try to get all nineteen colony ships linked together on the same communications channel, she was struck by that more than ever. The 57 dens couldn't even speak to each other, let alone decide their future together.

"If they just put us down on the ground and let us do what we've been trained for, we'd solve all these problems," Brad Karlsen said. "That was the idea in the first place, wasn't it?"

"That's what I thought," Harry Bayard added.

Suzanne shook her head. "I don't think they even figured it out in that much detail. Have you read the plain language translation of the den's contract with the Corps? 'The Corps will put you on a ship and send it in the direction of Mu Cassiopeiae.' End of document. As far as we're concerned, the Corps is history. That was 25 years ago – not last week."

"So what did they expect us to do?" the Alaskan farmer asked.

"Land – and then work it out from there," said Karlsen.

"I'm with you," said Suzanne.

She was still on edge and tired out from trying to adapt to the Asgard 30-hour clock. She couldn't believe she had once looked forward to the prospect of having an extra six hours in the day. The longer days were matched with endless nights that seemed filled with the distant, muffled and inescapable sound of crying babies, and dreams that seemed obsessed with guilt for having lived while the 5,000 colonists of the *Hollister* perished.

On top of that, the changes from the thrust-gravity to spin gravity had thrown everyone out of phase, only adding to the stress.

And now the colonists from Eta Cass wanted them to wait, hold off on the landings and consider their proposal. Why wait? What did they want? And did they realize what they were doing to the poor people in the colony ships?

Probably not. That must have been fourteen years back in their pasts. After all, who could be so callow as to subject 25,000 families to this kind of suffering?

"Greetings to the Asgard breakthrough colony!" a voice

announced from a monitor overhead. "This is Peter Kolberg of the Tikarahisat Colony at Eta Cassiopeiae. An important message will follow shortly at 2500 hours Asgard Base Time. Please stay tuned to this channel ... Greetings to the Asgard breakthrough colony. This is ..."

An officer turned off the message that issued suddenly from a speaker in one corner. "That's just a few minutes from now," she said.

A two-meter-wide monitor at one end of the control deck suddenly came to life, the image of the Asgard colony logo, a spaceship in front of a snow-capped mountain. Surrounding it were twelve smaller images of den leaders and Corps officers.

Then the image of the logo was replaced by the face of the commodore of the colony fleet.

"Colonists, this is Commandant Marlow. As you all know by now, the colony has been preceded to Asgard by an expedition from Eta Cass. They have asked for a chance to address you and make a request. Their transmission will begin in a few minutes. When they are finished, we'll open up the common channel to questions and responses – just key in a query on B channel, and we'll make a speaker's list. Ladies and gentlemen, this is Peter Kolberg."

The image of the commandant was replaced with that of a middle-aged man with thick eyebrows and wavy blond hair. His face was creased and dark. He wore a white shirt, open at the collar to reveal a hairy chest. He smiled, but Suzanne found no humor or warmth in it. To her, it looked like the predatory grin of a fox.

***

"The colony on Tik welcomes its brothers and sisters to the stars," he began. Suzanne detected a slightly European accent, hard edges on the consonants and a rumble in the R's.

"We share your sadness at the loss of your comrades. And we celebrate your arrival at a new world. We also want to extend the hand of friendship and cooperation between Asgard and Tikarahisat. And to make that friendship formal, a group of us have traveled from Eta Cass to Asgard to help you as you break the ground of a new colony.

"My name is Peter Kolberg. My family and our friends came to Tik fourteen years ago – twenty now that we are here at Asgard. In that time, we built a strong and stable colony. But we made mistakes. We wasted time. We lost money, work and lives. We are so small out here, there is so little room for error, that each of those mistakes cost us dearly. We want to save you that cost and help you reinvest it in building your world.

"Which brings me to the subject I call upon you to consider tonight.

"The Kolbergs want to offer you all the assistance we can. We have formed a management consultant team to help you organize your colony. We have brought some of our technology – we have extensive experience with gene-adapting terrestrial plants to alien ecologies. We have brought our technical libraries. And we have brought ourselves. We wish to offer you a contract with us that will make Asgard grow and thrive and flourish.

"In return, we ask only for a stake in your world – a few tiny pieces of land here and there. Let us build and grow with you. We are natural trading partners, you and we. Sol is 25 years away from here, we are only six. Beyond us are a dozen worlds ready to be settled in the next few centuries. Asgard and Tik will be the gateways to those new worlds. We have a long future together.

"And to prove our worth and demonstrate our value, we would like to begin our mission by helping you to establish your colony on Asgard. The scout den below has already provided you with their recommendations for township assignments and den organization.

We are sure they have been careful and exacting in their suggestions. But we would like a chance to show you what we can do. Maybe our experience on Tik can bring a new perspective to the scouts' plans.

"Give us a few days to study their recommendations and let us come up with our own. The delay cannot hurt you, and it could give you all a chance at a world much richer and stronger than you would believe.

"According to the colony Doctrine, you are scheduled to begin landing the dens on Wednesday. Give us until the end of the week. By Friday, we can present an alternative to the plan. Then you can vote on which of the two you wish to use. In fact, you may choose our plan, use it freely, and then tell us to go back to Tik, if that's what you want. We offer it to you without charge, without obligation.

"The choice is yours."

***

Suzanne could not quite bring herself to believe him.

Part of it was the man's appearance. He did not look sincere or paternal or solicitous. He looked uncomfortable. Peter Kolberg was not a charismatic politician or a wise leader.

What was he back at Eta Cass? He struck Suzanne as a cool, calculating, passionless man, despite the emotional appeal of his words. Someone else had written those words, she realized. He may have rehearsed them, but they were not his own. What was he hiding?

The rest of her distrust came from the odd convenience of the Kolbergs' offer and the colony's current chaos. There were people out there on the colony ships who would soon be begging for someone to tell them what to do, she realized sadly. Some were already at that point.

Maybe she'd been wrong about the kind of people who had

preceded them to Asgard. Maybe they remembered the fearful days at the birth of their colony all too well.

An image of the Kolbergs and their followers clicked into place in Suzanne's mind.

If they wanted to weaken the resolve of the colonists, this would be the perfect way to do it. First of all, make them wait. Look at what it accomplished. It would make them question, then abandon the Doctrine. Without its natural authority, the dens would need a new mission and a new organization to rally around. And if they stayed sealed up in their ships for a few more days, they would be ready to do almost anything.

The Kolbergs had to know what was going on. They had to know what impact their maneuverings would have. She just couldn't figure out why they would allow it.

What were they after?

The answer had to be in the landing plan – and the township assignments. "Captain Gallo, have we received the final recommendations from the scouts on landing assignments?" she asked.

Gallo turned, a quizzical frown on her face. "I'm not sure – I'll have to check."

Suzanne turned her attention briefly to the screen on the wall. The leader of one of the educational dens was on.

"It's not fair," she said. "How are we going to decide this issue? How will we vote? These are important questions that should have been decided before we left. The Colonial Corps was responsible for that, and they didn't follow through. I want to know what we're supposed to do now."

She went on like that for several minutes, until Suzanne let her eyes glaze over. Then she sneered at the screen and cursed the woman speaking. Commandant Marlow was doing a lousy job of chairing the meeting. Instead of managing the speakers' list and cutting off the mindless chatter of leaders like Loparo, he was letting them go on far too long.

"At this rate, it'll be hours before everyone's had a chance to make their speech," she said.

Gallo returned and smiled. "The scouts' landing recommendations were transmitted to the commodore's ship earlier today, but they haven't been forwarded to the rest of the fleet," she said.

"Why not?"

Gallo just smiled helplessly.

Suzanne held back her anger. There was so much of it growing inside that she didn't dare let even the smallest bit of it out, for fear the rest would follow. "Do you think you could open a line to the scout post down there so we can get some firsthand information instead of waiting for someone to do it for us?"

"I'll see what I can do," Gallo said. She didn't seem pleased with the request, but there wasn't much she could do. The Corps was only responsible for the ships and their crew – not the colonists. And Gallo and her fellow officers were bound by duty to obey the orders of the colonists, not the other way around.

Suzanne turned her attention back to the screen where the schoolteacher had been replaced by a suntanned, blond-haired farmer with a foreign name she couldn't quite remember.

"These are wise men," he said. "They can help us. We need their expertise. There's no reason why we have to follow the scout plan. Maybe the Kolbergs can come up with something better. I think we should follow them."

She stuck out her tongue at the man, but no one on the control deck noticed.

Guy Stanger sat in the administration office of the lodge, watching the colonists debate their future over a repeater from the library. He wasn't sure if he understood all that he saw and heard, but the parts that he did made his stomach churn.

This wasn't what he had expected.

They weren't organized. They didn't know what to do. And they sounded like his brothers arguing over who was going to get the last piece of spineyball pie while their father ate it all himself.

Guy had never pictured the colonists as regiments of efficient, dedicated and selfless men and women in sharp blue uniforms – at least not after Grampa Bob got a hold of him. But he had never expected this kind of embarrassing confusion either.

In the past hour, he had watched a parade of foreign faces with strange accents whine and whimper and boast and argue. It was like a scout council, only more formal. But the clash of personalities was still the same. Only ... only scouts had more self-respect. And honesty. Judging from what he heard, some of the colonists seemed to be lying.

"We need these people. They have the expertise," said the man on the screen – a bald fellow with a sharp nose and sour face. Guy had never seen anyone who looked so sad and angry at the world. Who was he? The leader of a service den? Or was he in machinery?

Out in the lodge, the library and lounge were both packed with scouts watching the show. They'd brought the large repeater screens out just for tonight. The duty scoutship had taken up a synchronous orbit to relay the communications down to all the scout posts on this side of Asgard.

Guy stood phone watch in the administration office, while Mr. Sanderson sat with Grampa Bob and the senior members of the post.

It seemed like a pretty easy job until the satellite phone began to chime.

His heart seemed to flutter and for a moment, he almost forgot what to do. But his training got the better of him and he put on the headset and said: "Main Post, Scout den Iroquois, Scout Guy Stanger speaking."

For more than a year, Mr. Sanderson had made the young men in Guy's class practice the correct protocol for answering communications from the colony ships. They had to give a good impression, and it helped to show that the scouts hadn't gone to seed over the past 93 years, he said. And who knows, he'd added, it could always be a colonist on the line.

Guy had never expected to be the one who answered the call.

"Scout Post, this is Captain Gallo of the Colony Ship *Hamilton*. Stand by for Suzanne Baxter of den Middlesex. You will have six minutes before loss of signal as we cross the horizon."

His heart jumped up into his throat. What did they want? Where was Mr. Sanderson?

"Hello, Baxter here. Is this the Main Post?"

"Scout Guy Stanger speaking, Scout den Iroquois, Main Post." Damn, he'd said it all backwards.

"Well, Scout Stanger, what's the weather like down there?"

Guy was speechless – but only for a moment. "It's, uh, been a nice day, ma'am. Warm and sunny. But it's starting to get foggy now."

"The fog's getting pretty thick up here, too, if you know what I mean," she said. "Listen to me, Scout Stanger. I need a favor. We're stuck up here without a lot of information and no one seems to care how long we stay ignorant."

"I'll do what I can. Would you like to speak to the scoutmaster, Mr. Sanderson? I can get him for you in a minute."

"No – there isn't time. I need to have you do something for me. Are you familiar with the landing assignment plan that you scouts uploaded to the commodore's ship? I need to know if you can send a copy to us as well."

"You don't have the landing plan yet?" Guy stammered in disbelief. "But why not? I mean, the Kolbergs have had it for more than a week now. I would have thought you colonists would have already studied it."

"I'm afraid we're having a little trouble getting organized up here just now. But we'll be down there just as soon as we sort things out. You said the Kolbergs have had this information for a week?"

He told her about Henry Schmidt's indiscretion.

"Then you must send it to me right away," Suzanne Baxter said. "Can you do that? Is there enough time?"

"If I hurry, there is. If not, you'll be back in 90 minutes, won't you?"

"I don't know. Maybe 90 minutes will be too long. Hurry, please."

Guy went to the screen of the computer at Mr. Sanderson's desk and scrolled through the menu to the proper file. He knew which one it was – he had called it up many times before, playing the colony game, making up the landing assignments himself, then adding the immigrant dens that would follow each year.

He dragged the file over to the uplink menu and readied the computer for the command to transmit the file to the colony ship.

"Are you ready to link up?"

"Stand by," the woman said.

"What's going on here?" asked the man in the doorway behind Guy. The young scout turned and saw Henry Schmidt – nearly two meters tall, 90 kilos of well trained beef. He swallowed hard.

"Nothing, Mr. Schmidt," he said.

"Stand by," said the tiny voice in his ear.

"It doesn't look like nothing," Schmidt said. He smiled, but there was a glare in his eyes that made Guy shake inside. "Who are you talking to, Guy?"

"Ready," the tiny voice said. Guy pushed the key to execute the command.

Schmidt saw the bar on the computer screen turn red to indicate that it was uploading the file. It only took a few seconds for the light of recognition to appear in his eyes. He went for the keyboard. Guy realized what he was after and blocked his way.

Then the older scout grabbed Guy by the arms, squeezed them tightly against his ribs and picked him up off the floor, moved him to one side and set him down in a chair. He turned to the computer, but it was too late. "File received," said the colonist on the phone.

"Scout Post out," Guy said. He took the headphone off and set it on the desk. Then he walked up to Schmidt and stared him in the face.

"Mr. Schmidt, don't you ever touch me like that again," he said.

"If you have any questions for me, you can ask Mr. Sanderson."

Schmidt stared at him with eyes that radiated self-righteous hatred, but he didn't move a muscle. He was back under control now.

"Don't get in our way, Stanger," he said. "This is a lot bigger than you are."

***

Gallo found Suzanne a terminal she could use to look through the file. She called it up, then keyed it to life.

The image began with the globe of Asgard. A long collection of tectonic plates formed the main continental mass, with a scattering of large islands floating about in the ocean half of the planet. Land masses encircled a polar sea. There was the problem with the planet. Long ago, the cold, wet polar air had deposited snow on the continent to the south. The snow became ice, the ice piled high and, after a few dozen millennia, the ice cap extended itself more than halfway to the equator.

The ice had pulled back just a little in recent centuries, but it still lingered in the highlands of the continental interior and along the high coastal mountains north of the Prime Site – the target for the breakthrough colony.

Near the center of the continental mass, just east of a place called Skandia Bay, the shoreline turned south and ran that way well past the equator. The Prime Site sat on the coast at 25 degrees north latitude – far enough south to avoid the worst of the Deep Freeze's influence on the climate, but not so far that the 30-hour days made outdoor life impossible during midday.

A young mountain chain descended along the coast from the north. Near its southern end, two peaks – Thor and Loki – divided the land into the North and South River Valleys. The Prime Site was

150 kilometers from north to south and ran 300 kilometers west from the ocean, cut by the two valleys.

The scout surveyors had divided the site up into more than 100 rectangular townships each of which contained at least 225 square kilometers of arable farmland. It was just enough space to give an agricultural den 400 hectares for every family. Some of the townships contained substantial land up above the treeline – those would have to wait for the gradual clearing of the wood by the lumber and construction dens – and others were bound by the rugged ridges of Loki and Thor, but there was plenty of good land for everyone down there.

Suzanne was amazed by the maps and orbital photos that the file presented as it laid out the townships in quick-step on the screen before her. She wished she had a holo-tank to watch this in. Watching the file reach its climax with the display of the den assignments took her breath away.

The Doctrine and the Plan – the two were always meant to go together. The Doctrine was the unloading and landing timetable – a trolley schedule. But the Plan was a world ...

The scouts had picked the Prime Site, explored it, studied it and lived in it for half a century. They had surveyed each township, tallied its strengths and weaknesses, noted the fertility of the soil, the way the rivers flooded in the spring and how the snow piled up in the winter. And they had planted dreams, nurtured and fed them and then put them into the Plan.

The farming dens appeared first. They were easy – two dens for every three townships to provide room for growth. They spread up and down the two valleys, more in the south where there was more open land. The farmers provided the base for the community. Each agricultural den would have to provide food for a counterpart den in the non-farm economy. Every family had to grow enough for two. The planners hoped it was a modest goal.

Then the service dens went onto the map, distributed evenly among the farms, followed by the educational dens.

But the suspense built for the specialist dens – construction, transportation, health and management. What did the scouts have in mind? Where would they put them?

Decentralization was the theme of this drama. The plan was simple – spread the specialists around just like the farmers. Every non-farm den was paired off in a township with an agricultural den. Suzanne found den Middlesex on the map, tucked into the highlands near the base of Loki Mountain, on a glacier-fed lake in a valley somewhere, with den Matanuska nearby to feed them.

The strengths of such a system were immediately evident. Transporting food would not be a problem with that organization. There would be no hinterland where services were few and unreliable. Instead, they would be accessible to all on a more democratic basis.

Then she sighed. This was not going to work.

The scout vision was beautiful in its simplicity and its dedication to the values that made scouts special and unique. But it was not what the colonists needed and she knew it. The Kolbergs knew it, too.

The radical decentralization of the dens would be just too much for them to take. They needed something to hold them together, strengthen them and forge them into a unit. This plan would only disperse their energies. There were ways the scout plan could be modified to accomplish that, she was sure. But who would modify it and to what end? That was the crucial question before the colonists.

What were the Kolbergs going to come up with?

They'd had a week already. If they were supposed to be such experts, why hadn't they already come up with a plan of their own?

Or had they?

A week on Asgard. That was ten days old-fashioned time, wasn't it? No – less than nine, she realized after doing the math. It was still too much time. They should have been able to do better than that.

That meant only one thing – the Kolbergs were lying. They wanted the colonists to delay their landings, certainly, but not to give them more time. It was only to strengthen their hand among frightened and crowded colonists. What kind of thoughtless creatures were they?

Suzanne made up her mind without forming an answer to that question.

If the Kolbergs didn't want the colonists to start the landings on time, then she was going to do everything in her power to get them going.

***

After two hours of speech-making by the long-winded den leaders, Suzanne was fighting to stay awake. She was afraid to ask for another bulb of that vile liquid the Corps officers passed off as coffee, but there didn't seem to be much choice.

Another short, dark farmer was speaking in favor of the Kolberg offer. "We need their expertise," he said.

"Maybe I'm getting punchy, but these fellows are all beginning to sound the same to me," said Harry Bayard.

"I noticed the same thing," Suzanne said. "It's as if they're all giving the same speech. The same words, over and over again."

She realized with a start just what she was saying. It was as if they'd been coached.

"Are you thinking what I'm thinking?" Bayard asked her suddenly.

"They had three days to get them ready," she said. "And I wouldn't put anything past the Kolbergs."

"What do you suppose they've been telling the other dens?"

"And why didn't they contact us?" she asked.

"That's easy," said Brad Karlsen. "Our reputations precede us. They would have started with their natural allies and worked their way out – if they were smart. That's not a logic-tree that leads to us."

"How many more speakers are there on the list?" Suzanne asked.

"Only three – woops, correct that. It's back up to ten in the last few minutes," a Corps officer reported. "That's odd. No one signed up for nearly an hour, and now, all of a sudden, there's a half dozen."

"Oh no!" Bayard cried in lament.

"What's going on?" Suzanne wondered aloud. She looked at the speakers list and saw that the new sign-ups were topped by the leader of Elliott, the management den. The rest, who had followed quickly, included the other two management dens, the machinery den and one of the special services dens.

Something was afoot. She knew the leaders of those dens fairly well – they were a good bunch, sharp and honest.

She called to the communications officer: "Put my name up there, too." Bayard and Karlsen looked at her in surprise. "For Pete's sake, Suzie, haven't you had enough?" Bayard asked.

"It's just getting started," she said.

***

John Porter, the leader of den Elliott, started things rolling by proposing a few simple organizational actions – setting up a chairman to run the rest of the meeting, creating a committee to study their options, another one to draw up some rules for voting.

The other dens moved to back him up. Annie Kovalev, a design artist who spoke for den Harley, ended it up by calling for a vote. With nothing else as an alternative, the proposals drew immediate and total support.

In less than thirty minutes, they had a rudimentary form of government in place and adjourned the whole thing until the morning.

"Why didn't they do that two hours ago?" asked Bayard.

"Why didn't you suggest it two hours ago?" Karlsen shot back.

"Because everyone would have spent the time talking anyway," Suzanne said. "And I think they must have thought of it only after everything began. That parliamentary maneuvering wasn't spontaneous. I think they worked it out on another channel while the rest of them talked their brains out."

"Well, it looks like we may get some action now," Bayard said.

Suzanne shook her head skeptically. "Committees don't do anything, Harry. People do. Everyone seems to be overlooking one thing in all this – what about the Doctrine?"

Bayard and Karlsen looked at her blankly.

"According to the book, we're supposed to start the preliminary landings tomorrow – or has everyone forgotten that schedule?

"So far, no one has said if we're going to follow the Doctrine or not. They didn't appoint a committee to study that question – because no one had the nerve to bring it up. But that's what we really have to decide. I don't know about you two, but I'm going to take my tablet to bed with me tonight and go through the Doctrine line by line. Tomorrow should be a very interesting day."

"The way I see it, you've got two problems with the landing plan," Annie Kovalev said. "You've got to figure out what mix of dens you want. And then you've got to assign specific townships to each den. But that gets a little complicated now that the Kolbergs are in the picture. From what we've been told, they're promising their friends the choice townships and threatening to leave their enemies with the bogs and granite."

"Well you can do the assigning tomorrow," replied Suzanne. "Today, you've got to start working over the scouts' plan. The way they've set it up, we get locked into the chaos we went through last night. Complete decentralization means no concentrations of power and no leadership. Have you seen what their plan looks like?"

Annie frowned, wrinkling the gray circles under her eyes. Suzanne felt guilty about calling so early. It was 0700, still a half-hour before sunrise, Asgard Base Time. But there was too much to do and too little time – even with bonus hours.

"Yes. I was lucky enough to catch it when it first came in. That's why it was never sent to the other ships. If everyone sees it as a choice between the two, the Kolbergs will win, sight unseen."

"Can't you fix it up?" Suzanne asked. "It only needs a few changes. Dispersal makes sense to an extent, but this is too much."

"I suppose we can do our best, Suzie. But if you're so excited about it, maybe you should join the committee and work on it yourself."

"Afraid not," she said. "Today, I have other plans."

***

An early morning fog had given way to a clear sky. Guy had a good view of both Thor and Loki as he walked across the post from his family's cabin. His clothes were still wet with the dew accumulated since sunrise while he took a turn at planting duties, but he didn't have time to change. He wanted to get to the lodge before 0900 to watch the colonists resume their multichannel council.

As he climbed the steps to the building, Guy spotted Henry Schmidt, sitting on a fence next to the horse barn, talking to one of the Gilmartin brothers. Guy tried to pretend he didn't notice the man. He'd told Mr. Sanderson about the incident in the office, and the scoutmaster said he'd take care of it. But that didn't satisfy Guy. He wanted to find some way to settle the score that wouldn't get him killed.

The lodge was crowded and noisy, and the smell of hot grease wafted from the dining hall where they were serving a late breakfast. It was enough to start Guy's mouth working, so he took a detour through the steam line and loaded up a plate with scrambled eggs and fried duckasaur cutlet.

The meeting had already begun when he got to the library. He hadn't even found a seat with a view of the screen when he heard the voice of the woman who was speaking. He recognized that voice. It was the colonist who had called him the night before.

She had a round face with thick blond hair cut in curls that framed her eyes. She must have been over 50, but Guy wasn't a good enough judge of age to say more than that. He was disappointed. For a while, he had pictured the mysterious caller as someone younger, more interesting. This woman was probably somebody's mother. At the bottom of the screen it said: "Suzanne Baxter den Middlesex."

He grabbed the cutlet in one hand and bit off a chunk as he dropped into a seat on the couch next to Jeanie Gilmartin's father.

" – and the question before us is not what to do about the Kolbergs' offer," Suzanne said. "It is whether or not we are going to ignore the Doctrine and start making things up as we go along. No one has yet suggested that the Doctrine is no longer in effect. I have not heard anyone make a motion to abandon the Doctrine as our basis for common action.

"Please correct me if I am wrong, but we are still, theoretically, supposed to complete a number of important tasks today – at least according to my copy of the Doctrine. I looked at it last night and found that by sunset tonight – that's 2230 for those of you still trying to adjust – we are supposed to complete our review of the recommended landing plan presented by the scouts and decide on any changes we want to make.

"And we are also supposed to have six pathfinder groups on the ground, preparing for the full landings scheduled to begin on Wednesday. Has anyone started making preparations for those landings? Since I am assigned to a pathfinder group, I intend to see what can be done to get my party ready for landing.

"And until the Doctrine is revoked as the legal authority for our actions, I suggest that the other dens involved in today's missions make ready as well."

Her image dissolved into the colony logo. Guy looked down at his plate and realized he hadn't eaten anything after the first bite.

"Did she say she wants to start the landings?" Mr. Gilmartin asked.

"I think that's what I heard," Guy said. "The question is, can she do it?"

Grampa Bob, seated in a chair in front of them, turned and said: "The question is, can anyone stop her?"

***

The *Hamilton* had two landers. Suzanne hovered outside the No. 3 lock of the starboard aerospacecraft, Emily beside her. Another 240 colonists floated in the wide passenger assembly compartment, linked by orange safety lines, ready to board the lander.

Suzanne looked at them, but did not see. Her mind was still replaying the brief conversation she'd had with Peter Kolberg before leaving the control deck. Her hands still trembled with anger, and she was sure that if there were gravity in here her knees would be shaking.

Damn that arrogant son of a bitch!

The lock opened before her in a hiss of escaping compressed air.

"You go ahead in, kid," she told her daughter. "I'll catch up to you later." She kissed her on the forehead as the crew of the lander began reeling in the safety line, pulling the colonists one-by-one through the hatch.

Suzanne had her fingers crossed as they slowly filled the lander. The den leaders were still debating the pathfinder landings, and it was possible that at any minute, they would decide to stop her from going.

The uproar had been tremendous, but unfocused. The Kolberg supporters had accused her of trying to sabotage the colony. They said the "unilateral" action threatened the colony's unity and said the pathfinder landings were unnecessary until the landing plan could be decided on.

But no one wanted to be the first to suggest abandoning the Doctrine. Until they did, the schedule had to be followed and the landings had to go forward as planned. She was sure the vote wouldn't come up – not today. She had taken the Kolbergs by surprise. They weren't ready for her yet.

Everyone knew the Doctrine would win on the first vote. The colonists had been training for years to follow the prescribed schedule when they arrived at their new world. To overturn it would require planning and coordination. Tomorrow they might be able to do it, but not today. At least she hoped they wouldn't do it today.

Then Kolberg had called the *Hamilton*.

His image had appeared like an evil ghost on the screen of the control deck. His hair was slicked back from his low forehead, his eyes were red and he needed a shave. And he wasn't nearly as cordial as he had been the previous night.

"What are you trying to do to me?" he asked in a soft monotone. "Are you trying to interfere with my plans or are you just terribly ignorant?"

She'd mustered her best professional face and cooed at him sweetly, "Why Mr. Kolberg, I haven't got the slightest idea what you're talking about."

"Mrs. Baxter, I didn't come six years across space to have an ignorant woman waste my time. You are getting dangerously close to standing in my way. That is something you should avoid. If you are doing it because you are stubborn and foolish, you need to be warned. If you are doing it because you oppose me, then make no mistake – I will not be stopped."

His voice had never wavered in tone or volume. He sounded as cold and sterile as the continental ice sheets on the planet below. And the chill penetrated down to the center of Suzanne's soul.

"There is a great deal more at stake than you can imagine. If you value your life and the lives of those you love, you will stay out of my way."

As an undergrad, she had once had a fancy for clinical psychology. She'd taken the courses in abnormal psych and knew what kinds of pathologies the human soul was subject to. Kolberg was one of the most frightening – intellect without affect, thought without emotion, relentlessly self-interested and ruthlessly amoral. He was the product of social forces that denied life, rejected feeling and destroyed spirit – the failed product of humanity's advanced technetronic culture. Suzanne knew that intellectually. But when she looked into his eyes, all she saw was an endless hunger for power.

And it scared her.

She realized with a start that the last colonist was aboard and it was her turn to go through the hatch. Just before she did, however, she saw Captain Gallo step into the assembly chamber. Her heart went into her throat.

Then Gallo stuck her thumb into the air and smiled.

They waved to one another, and Suzanne stepped through the lock and into the lander.

***

Guy was playing chess with Grampa Bob in the main hall of the lodge when the first sonic boom hit. It echoed off the hillsides and shook the windows and resonated in his chest. They went outside to watch and by the time they reached the door, two more had thundered through with a cannonade of echoes.

"Sounds like the Fourth of July," said Grampa Bob.

"The fourth what?"

"Never mind," Bob said. "How many of them were there supposed to be?"

"All six," Guy said. "One each for North Post, the Highland strip, Lake Geneva, Glacier Valley, North Lake and Upper Post. They voted to follow the Doctrine half an hour after the last one broke orbit."

Grampa Bob snorted in disgust. "It's always the same – no one gets any guts until after the boat leaves the dock."

The sun was high in the sky and a hot, muggy wind was pouring up out of the southeast, pressing down on the fast-growing savanna grass to make waves. The midday haze gave the sky a brassy look, while over the mountains, an inversion layer caught the moisture and shaped it into lens-shaped clouds that molded themselves to the icy peaks of Loki and Thor.

"Is there any chance that we'll see them?" the old scout asked.

"The lander for Glacier Valley may come close enough," Guy said. "That's only 100 klicks away. How big is a lander, anyway?"

"Bigger than a scoutship by half."

The deep blue dome of the sky began to show the streaks of condensation trails as the landers hit the lower reaches of the atmosphere. Guy counted two to the north and another to the southwest. "Here they come," he said.

Another boom shook the trees and the windows of the lodge. A fourth trail appeared to the northwest while the first three began to curl as the landers began their terminal area descent.

Almost fifteen minutes elapsed from the time of the first boom to the time of the last one. Three of the landers had dropped from sight and their contrails were dispersing on the upper winds. The fourth and fifth had disappeared to the west, presumably to land at Highland and Upper posts. The sixth and final lander was leaving a short and indistinct contrail, but after a while, Guy realized with surprise that he could make out the shape of the craft itself, a tiny gray triangle at the head of the white cloud.

It was getting larger and larger, but didn't seem to be moving across the sky until it came around to the north. By the time it veered off to the east, Guy could make out the details of the delta-wing lander with the upturned wing tips. He could see the rudder markings, tail flaps, engines and wing numbers. By now, it had killed off all of its orbital velocity and was making its final approach on its own engines.

The big plane lumbered along through the haze, then tipped its wings tentatively before banking around to the right. The lander was both ungainly and graceful – at least it was being gracefully flown. He wondered for a moment at the piloting skill that kept that huge craft and its 100 tons of cargo from plummeting into Asgard.

He watched it descend as it circled around the to the northeast, in the direction of Loki and Glacier Valley. But when the lander continued to circle around to the south, he became puzzled.

"That's odd," he said. "If they were going to land at the valley, they would have kept on going to the east. But they look like they're curving around and coming back this way."

Indeed, the lander was steadying up on a direct bearing towards them out of the southeast.

"I think they're going to land here," Grampa Bob said.

"But they're not supposed to. Something's gone wrong."

The awkwardly huge shape of the lander plodded along at its own persistent but pedestrian pace, growing to menacing proportions as it dropped closer and closer to the ground. Guy felt his heart beginning to pound at the sheer size of it. A scoutship could get into orbit too, but it was a sleek and well-cut vessel. The lander looked like a dormitory with wings.

The dinner bell rang out up at the lodge just as the craft passed directly over their heads. Guy craned his neck and twisted his head as it went by, watching the doors in its belly open up and the landing gear emerge.

"They may not be invited, but I think they've arrived just in time to eat," said Grampa Bob. But Guy didn't have time to answer – he was already on his way to the barn. The landing field was four kilometers away and while he was excited enough to run the distance, it made more sense to grab a horse.

The ride down in the cockpit of the lander was an experience unequaled in Suzanne Baxter's life.

She watched out the windows, gripping the arms of her seat with white knuckles as they plunged into the atmosphere and the leading edges of the wings began to glow cherry pink.

The nose dropped somewhere just west of Thor Mountain as they streaked along at Mach 3, giving her a magnificent view of its icy peaks, gray rock ridges and the glaciers that flowed into the valleys. Off to the north, she could see the endless bands of white – ice, snow and clouds – that wrapped the top quarter of Asgard.

Then they plummeted down into the South River Valley, the ground rushing up at them. The snowy slopes of Loki Mountain loomed ahead of them and Suzanne was sure they were going to smash into it if they didn't slow down.

Then she heard the co-pilot curse.

"Damn it, we just lost our beacon," he said.

"What? How come? Our equipment or theirs?" the pilot asked. "Never mind, where's the alternate?"

"Main Post. Coming up on it now. Beacon activated and operational. We're going to have to make a tight turn to get back to it."

Suzanne's stomach, barely used to having returned to gravity, twisted as the plane tipped to the right.

Were they going to crash or not? The earth seemed to tilt sharply, giving her a view of a river flowing down a steep slope. The ground kept coming closer and closer, while remaining at its unnatural tilt for what seemed like an eternity.

"Air speed 500," she heard the co-pilot report as they finally leveled off and steadied up on a heading.

"Gear down," the pilot replied.

And in a few minutes, they were taxiing down the gravel landing strip, rolling past an endless grassy savanna dotted with crowds of grazing fuzzasaurs.

When they had stopped and the crew and passengers were straining with their newfound weight, Suzanne leaned forward to talk to the pilot.

"What happened up there?"

"The beacon for our primary landing strip went out just before we started our final approach. I don't think the glitch was ours because we picked up the secondary beacon without any trouble. Something must have quit on the other end."

"You mean there was something wrong with the beacon."

"Yes."

Or someone had simply shut it off.

"Were we in any danger?"

"Not really. I'm sorry if that radical turn gave you trouble. We'll try to give you better service on your next flight."

"The turn was no worse than the rest of the ride," Suzanne said. "And I think next time I'll take another airline."

Maybe it had just been an innocent accident, but she didn't think so. There were too many interests to be served if she were delayed or distracted. And Peter Kolberg himself had warned her. There was something more going on, and while it frightened her, it did more to make her angry. She wasn't about to let him get away with this.

She pulled herself to her feet and headed back into the passenger compartment where her daughter and fellow colonists were moaning in exaggerated pain.

"Come on, gang," she called to them, her voice quickly swallowed up in the tight quarters. "How can you expect to carry your packs if you can't even carry your backs?"

She was met with a chorus of groans.

"Don't give me that. You all had gym time scheduled for the past three weeks, so there's no excuse for lost muscle tone. Besides, we've only had a few hours of freefall the whole trip."

"It's not the gravity that bothers us, Mom," Emily piped up. "It was the ride down."

That met with another chorus of groans, fewer and not as loud.

The lander crew finished the post-flight checks, then opened the main locks and lowered the ramps to the ground. Suzanne and Brad Karlsen were the first ones out, but the rest of the colonists followed quickly.

***

Emily Baxter watched the sky deepen to dark red as the setting sun painted the top of Loki Mountain a succession of gold, rust and amber. In the center of the yard, youngsters tended several large carcasses on spits, turning them slowly over open fires.

The idea that the scouts were going to eat the animals was both revolting and fascinating to her. Like most residents of Earth, she was a vegetarian, by necessity, not choice. Meat eating seemed so barbaric and primitive, but the scouts seemed like nice, civilized people in so many other ways.

From the moment they stepped out of the lander, the colonists had been swept away by a wave of hospitable, smiling faces and ready hands. The scouts hadn't been expecting colonists to land at this strip, they told her, so there were a few delays. But within a few minutes, the scouts had put up tent canopies to shield them from the sun and a short time after that, trucks were unloaded from the lander to carry them into town.

The scouts were strange to look at, she thought. It wasn't just their leather clothes and the odd way the adult men cut their hair – shaved bare for two inches above the ears. There were also strong signs of family resemblance among many of them, and only a few families at that. Emily noticed a strain of red hair and freckles that cropped up everywhere she went. And there was a shock of black, curly hair that seemed to have made its way around.

The ride to the post in the back of a truck had been like a trip through a game park, only without fences to keep the animals in. She was thrilled when they had to wait while a herd of animals – or a crowd of silverbacks, as the scouts said – crossed the road

There were at least thirty of the things, a little more than a meter tall with gray fur marked by two silver stripes along their backs. They ran with a birdlike, hesitant pace, stopping to dig at the ground every few steps.

The strange creatures were a surprising thrill – tangible evidence that this was indeed another planet. But what surprised her most about the new world was the sand and the gravel and the pine trees at the scout post and the flying creatures in the sky and the bugs that rose in waves from the savanna grass as the trucks roared by. The thousands of ordinary things that worlds had in common that she had never expected. The way the ground crunched against the feet, or the way the sun felt warm on her back.

Only she kept being jarred by the recognition that instead of green, the leaves on the trees were yellow, gold and, in the case of a limbless native evergreen that reminded her of the palmettos at the space center in Florida, a deep red that seemed to radiate with energy.

And the chitinoids that filled the insect niche on Asgard had acquired the ability to grow bright pigments in their exoskeleton. Emily noticed a small bug with a black body a centimeter long and triangular wings of silver, red and gold that looked like they had been painted by hand.

Now, here at the Main Post, the familiar world of human structures again clashed with the sensations of a new world – this time the collision of cultures as the scouts and the colonists celebrated the safe arrival and landing. The roast in the middle of the square was only one example.

She noticed a handful of the oldest scouts and overheard them talking about the streets and sights and cities of Earth. And she noticed the youngsters following her, giggling and hiding when she looked at them, but racing ahead of one another as she walked around.

She stopped for a while at the barn and watched the animals eating in their stalls. The dimly lit stable was rich with the scents of hay and horses. A young scout – he looked like a young teenager to Emily – appeared.

"Hi, my name's Walt, what's yours?" he asked with an engaging smile.

"Emily." She looked him over carefully. He must have been five years younger than she was and a good ten centimeters shorter.

"Did you ever ride a horse, Emily?"

He smiled a lot and seemed to stand awfully close to her, but she didn't know if he was being overly familiar or if all the scouts were like that. "Yes, once. On a ranch in Wyoming."

"Want to try it again?"

"Not right now."

"Oh come on," said Walt. "It would be fun."

He took her hand and tugged. She walked stiffly through the barn, her arm outstretched as he pulled hard to hurry her on.

"I don't think so. I'm not really dressed for it, and I'm still not used to the gravity. I'm afraid a few weeks in space can leave you feeling pretty weak."

When they reached the far end of the barn, just before the door, Walt suddenly stopped and reversed direction. He took her by surprise, sweeping her arm behind his back and putting his free arm around her. He raised himself up on his toes to put his face level with hers.

Then he kissed her.

A half dozen little scouts who had been lurking in the stable yard burst into giggling fits. Emily felt her face burn with embarrassment, then she broke her hand free from Walt's grasp, pulled his arm out from behind her and slapped the back of his wrist hard.

"Look, little boy, I don't know how they do it on your planet, but where I come from, that kind of thing is not allowed."

He looked up at her with bright eyes that seemed to darken suddenly. Then he backed away, a worried look on his face.

"I – I'm sorry," he said.

"Can I help you?" Another scout appeared at the far end of the barn. "Walt, is that you? What are you up to?" he asked. Then, when he came within easy sight, he hesitated. "Uh-oh, excuse me."

"Hi, Guy," Walt said.

"Is this child related to you?" Emily asked in a chilly voice.

"He's just my brother," the newcomer said. She looked at him closer as he came under the light of a glowb hanging from the rafters. She recognized him as the young scout who had come riding up to the lander shortly after she reached the ground. She remembered his big shoulders and ready grin.

"That's too bad," she said.

"I'll make him apologize, if you'd like."

"You and a maxidon," Walt shot back.

"That won't be necessary," she said, trying to decide if the older scout would be any better a prospect than his younger brother. She decided to seize the opportunity. "But you could escort me back to the party, if you don't mind. All kinds of things can happen to a girl alone in this place."

***

For a few minutes, Guy Stanger had been walking among the stars.

In all those times with Jeanie Gilmartin, he'd never felt anything like this. This woman was different.

Her name was Emily and her life was a mess. Her father had run off and left her, her mother hated her and her little brother was an evil spirit who had been left with their family as a changeling in place of the sweet baby she'd been expecting. But she'd read Chaucer and C.S. Forester and Asimov and she'd been to New York City and Florida and she'd even lived in Boston-Massachusetts. And Guy thought she was beautiful.

And all they'd done was hold hands.

They had walked around the celebration, talking, for more than an hour. Guy felt self-conscious at first, sure that everyone, scout and colonist, had their eyes on the two of them. But after a while, it seemed like the most natural thing in the world. And he saw other mixed couples and groups walking and talking and even more.

In one case, however, it made him feel uneasy. Early in the evening, he saw Jeannie Gilmartin and the Kolberg scout LeClerc sitting together on the back porch of the lodge. He didn't get close enough to see or hear much of anything, but what he did see was enough. He didn't feel jealous so much as alarmed – LeClerc was not a good scout and Jeannie should have known as much.

Guy and Emily ended up behind one of the storage barns, looking at the stars, listening to the whistles and clicks of the chites.

"My mother tries too hard, actually," Emily said. "She has a bad case of single-parent syndrome. She thinks she has to be both a mother and a father to me – only when I need a mother, she acts like a father and when I need a father, she acts like a monster. I don't what she expects from me – I'm never perfect enough for her. I was so glad when she became den leader, because it finally got her out my hair. And sometimes I think she blames me because my father ran away on us."

Guy, whose parents were strongly and firmly bound to one another by years of raising a pack of boys, found little to say in response to those complaints. But they found quickly that they had one thing in common – obnoxious younger brothers.

"If you think Walt is bad, you should meet Joey. He's my mother's little darling – but that's because he has a computer for a brain. He's always getting into mischief on the campus – last year he set a fire in the science building by letting a cold-fusion cell melt down. He used to love going into Mother's lab and playing with the snakes and lizards. And I shudder to think what kind of girls he's going to bring home with him in a couple of years." Guy told of his long struggle with Walt.

"It's sort of like a guerrilla war where both sides are too weak to win. He just comes along every so often and does something sneaky and malicious. I try to get even with him, but he's so much younger than I am, there isn't much I can do without actually hurting him. Although the time he dumped the spineyball juice in my bed, I was ready to kill him."

They traded evil brother stories for a long time, until the rising glow of Rudi, Mu Cass' red dwarf companion, appeared in the east. By the time the bright star painted the landscape a deep scarlet, the subject had changed to a direction that made Guy nervous.

"The men I saw back home were such a disappointment," Emily said. "They were darlings, but they were something missing. They seemed like such boys and they were so self-centered. And they just didn't know how to be men – to take responsibility, make decisions, be practical and realistic."

"You mean like your mother?"

She laughed. "Sort of. I guess they looked kind of pale in comparison to her."

"And what about us scouts?" Guy asked, taking a risk that seemed bolder than he could believe.

"They're not so bad," she said, smiling. "At least they're not afraid to take a chance."

That was when he took her hand. When she didn't pull away, Guy felt warm all over. They were silent for a few minutes, then Guy heard someone call his name.

"Oh damn," he said. "What do they want?"

A few minutes later, he had found Lyle Sanderson in front of the lodge. "Remember I told you I wanted to keep you around in case something came up?" he said. "Well, something has."

Now he found himself back down on the cold, stony ground of Asgard. Sanderson had taken him away from Emily and into the lodge where the scouts were holding council. Grampa Bob and a handful of older scouts sat at a table in the library with Suzanne Baxter and four other colonists – one of them a large man with red hair and a thick red beard.

Sanderson had Guy take a seat across from the red giant and went to the head of the table. He cleared his throat and the rest fell silent.

***

"The den leaders met again tonight over the commlink and elected John Porter their chairman. And they heard the report from the committee reviewing our landing plan," Sanderson said. "Mrs. Baxter can tell you what they came up with."

"Basically it was your plan with only a few changes," she said. "We like the idea of dispersal and decentralization, but we don't want to go all the way to the limit. There has to be a center of some kind to keep things organized. We've proved that in the past two days.

"What we want to create is a primary center and two secondaries – pool together four or five specialist dens in the primary and three or four in the secondaries. There's a detailed breakdown of it, den-by-den, on my tablet if you want to see it.

"We kept your proposal for putting the university, woodsmen and specialty manufacturing dens out on the periphery. With a few exceptions, everyone will be assigned to townships by type and dens selected individually by lottery. The exceptions will be those three I just mentioned and some pre-arranged linkups between some of the dens like us and Matanuska."

Guy watched Grampa Bob carefully for a reaction, but the old man looked more asleep than offended.

"And what did the den leaders do?" he asked, opening his eyes and surprising Guy.

"One of the Kolberg supporters moved to postpone implementation of the Doctrine by 30 hours," Suzanne said. "They debated the question for two hours without getting anywhere, then Chairman Porter heard a motion to adjourn."

"What's that mean?" asked one of the scouts.

"You can't debate a motion to adjourn, you just vote on it," Sanderson told him. "We don't use it in our councils, but it's one way a chairman can shut off a debate that isn't going anywhere. He says he hears a motion to adjourn, then he calls for a voice vote and only hears the 'ayes'."

"Which is much easier to do if you're conducting your meeting over a commlink network," Suzanne added. "After the meeting, the Kolbergs sent a message offering to submit their recommendations a day early – by Thursday.

But that would still mean delaying the Doctrine. And putting off Colony Day until Friday at the earliest."

Guy felt disgusted at the thought of another disruption.

"Those ships are like pressure cookers," she said. "Delaying the landings only works to weaken the will of the colonists, to make them anxious to accept direction from others – in this case, the Kolbergs. And that's why I don't want to let them stop us from following the Doctrine."

Grampa Bob leaned forward across the table and looked up at Sanderson.

"Lyle, you said you think the Kolbergs had something to do with Mrs. Baxter's lander coming here instead of at Hartsbridge?"

"Yes, I did. It's my own fault for trusting him, but I let Henry Schmidt lead a patrol up to the Valley Post."

Guy felt his heart pound suddenly at the mention of Schmidt's name.

"He was responsible for that strip," Sanderson continued. "I wouldn't put it past him to switch off the landing beacon. There was nothing wrong with it last week when the duty scoutship did its regular tests. And it's too much of a coincidence that it went down just before you were about to land. Henry's been talking to LeClerc too much. He's all excited about the Kolbergs and wants to help them all he can. I didn't think he'd really do something as bad as this. I still can't understand why?"

"While it may have been aimed at me personally, I should point out that under your landing plan, den Middlesex is assigned to the Glacier Valley township. Tonight, I heard someone say you found the Kolbergs snooping around up there before we arrived, is that correct?"

"I found their stuff up there," Guy said, startled at his own readiness in speaking up at a gathering of adults, then embarrassed by their sudden attention.

"You mean you think the Kolbergs want something up in Glacier Valley?" Grampa Bob asked.

"Something like that, Bob," Sanderson said. "It makes all the pieces tie in together. But there could be more pieces that we don't know about."

"A lot more, I'd say," the old scout said. "I don't like the sound of any of it."

"That doesn't help us with our problem."

"Our problem? Do the scouts have a problem?" Grampa Bob said.

Sanderson looked around the table at the puzzled faces of the scouts. Guy realized there was something more going on that Sanderson and Bob hadn't shared with the rest of them.

"Mrs. Baxter has asked for our help," Sanderson said in answer to their unspoken question. "She wants us to move her party on up to the Valley tomorrow."

"I want to keep up with the schedule set by the Doctrine," she said. "According to the book, we're supposed to start landings there on Wednesday. If we don't, then the Kolbergs have succeeded."

"We don't have anything left for transport," Grampa Bob said.

"They brought their own trucks, Bob. Enough to move 30 people. And we can spare a few horses to provide an escort," Sanderson said.

"And who's going to lead it?"

"That's where Guy comes in."

Guy felt his face grow warm as once again everyone in the room looked at him.

For the first hour of the journey, they rode along in early morning fog behind a scout on foot with a hand-lantern to keep them on the path. Glacier Valley was 64 kilometers from the Main Post – with fifteen hours of daylight ahead of them, they had to average at least five kilometers an hour. It looked easy, but Guy was still nervous.

It was one thing to make that pace with a patrol of young scouts who had lived their lives on horseback. It was quite another to expect it out of a couple dozen colonists, some of whom had never seen an animal larger than a dog in their lives, and a few trucks.

He didn't know how he was going to get there before dark. He figured he wouldn't. But with the trucks to light the way, the last few klicks shouldn't be a problem – he hoped. If only the weather would hold ...

The forecast looked good for the day ahead, but cold air was coming down from the north. That meant snow before tomorrow morning. Guy shuddered – there were so many things that could go wrong.

And to make matters worse, there were all those things that Grampa Bob had said last night.

"These aren't our problems, Lyle," he'd argued. "They aren't something we should get involved with. This kind of political squabbling is what we left Earth to get away from. Selfish greed and manipulation. Adventurism and double-dealing. There's nothing honest or honorable about any of it. I know the Kolbergs are up to no good, but what I've seen of the colonists isn't any better. They want to bring their poisons to Asgard and anything we do to help them will only hurt the planet in the long run. Lyle, I know this day's been coming all my life, but I never thought I'd be sorry to see it arrive. I wish the colonists had never come. I wish they'd go back. I wish I'd never lived this long."

Guy choked at the old scout's dark and hopeless words. He couldn't believe what he was hearing. He realized that Grampa Bob had changed in the last few years, but he hadn't sensed the man's brooding despair before this.

In an instant, Guy's inner compass had been spun around. For years, he had looked to Grampa Bob as a guide for truth and inner rightness. He had made a practice of his moral guidelines and tried to impress them upon his younger brothers. He had defended the old man in arguments with his friends and family.

He never thought the day could come when he would disagree with him. But now it had.

Guy knew that the only hope left for the colony to fulfill its original plan and design was to follow the Doctrine, keep to the schedule, and prevent the process from being derailed. It didn't matter what the Kolbergs had planned, nothing good could come from them. The only other choice for the scouts was to join the other side and work with them. If only he had been able to tell Grampa Bob that. But the meeting had ended on that sour note, Grampa Bob was overruled, and Guy was suddenly swamped with all the responsibilities of a patrol leader with a bunch of tenderfoots.

***

At least Emily was along.

He rode beside her as much as his duties allowed, explaining the sights and sounds of Asgard to her. There was a strange thrill to introducing a newcomer to all the wonderful things he had cataloged over the years.

After all, that had been the purpose of the arduous hours of counting, naming and recording the plants and animals who shared their world – to pass it on the colonists. Suddenly, all that work as a child had become meaningful and useful, and in a direct way that he had never imagined.

"You wouldn't believe how much this land has changed in just the past week," he told her. "There weren't any bluenecks then, now the place is alive with them. And the redcrests and silverbacks are already starting to form their big grazing crowds."

The fuzzasaurs in sight along the wide open vistas of the valley numbered in the thousands. Crowds of a hundred or more were a common sight, plowing through the tall, golden savanna grass.

"They migrate to the south when the cold weather comes, then in the spring, before the floods come, they return and mate. The rivers are already up and beginning to crest, so this is about all the grazers we'll see this year. In the summer, they'll build nests and lay eggs."

"Is winter going to be as bad as they say?" Emily had asked.

"I don't know. It depends on how bad they say it's going to be.

You don't want to go outdoors much. The air gets pretty cold – down to 20 below. But some days the trade winds blow in from the south and it gets up to 20 or 25 – that's when the chites all come out and the swamp toadies start chirping. The weather's a lot worse farther north, of course. We're practically in the tropics right here. But up in Skandia it rains four months out of the year and snows the other two. And along the coast of Bifrost Bay, beyond North Valley, you get a lot of cold air coming down from the mountain ice. It rains a lot up there, too. A little farther south of here, though, and it gets too hot to work in the afternoon. And the winters aren't that much warmer. So that's why they choose the valleys for the Prime Site."

"Are we all going to have houses in time?"

"I don't think so – it depends on so many things. Nobody's sure how fast we can get your cabins up. Winter comes quick around here, you know."

"They should have had us arrive sooner," Emily declared.

Guy shook his head. "They couldn't," he said. "They had to wait until after the spring floods dropped down. Most of the townships don't have roads, let alone bridges. By the time you start landing in big numbers, the streams and rivers will be fordable, but today and tomorrow, there's no chance of getting around South Valley unless you're here on the Scout Path."

"I'm just so worried. I never really thought much about these things before now. But since we landed, even since we first arrived here, it's been like a whole new person is starting to grow inside me. I guess I never thought about the future much back home. Guy, are we going to be able to live here? I mean people like me and my mother and the dean and all the professors at Middlesex? We're not scouts like you. We don't know how to do anything – at least I don't. I mean, we went to all those classes, and I remember most of it. But that's not the same thing as having to live here on our own."

The young scout felt flustered and had no answer. It was not a question that had ever entered his mind. He'd always taken it for granted that the colonists would live here the way the scouts always had. The idea that there was some special skill involved in staying alive on a planet he'd grown up on was totally foreign to him. Asgard, no matter how alien, was still home.

"Don't worry, Em," he ended up saying. "It's not that hard. If my brother Walt can learn to live here, anyone can."

She stuck out her tongue at the mention of Guy's brother, but Guy just frowned.

***

Shortly before low noon, they ran across a maxidon.

Guy rode to the head of the column quickly when the horses began to bunch up.

The predatory fuzzasaur stood in the middle of the road, 150 centimeters tall with a tail two meters long, muscular thighs and an oversized head. A mouthful of pointy teeth worked open and shut nervously. Heavily clawed feet scratched at the ground and small grasping claws on its upper limbs grasped at the air. Tiny eyes stared out from under a heavy brow ridge, and its golden fur was striped with rust-colored bars.

"What are you doing here?" Guy asked the maxidon, trying to mask his fear with calm bravado.

It raised its snout into the air, stuck out a long, forked tongue and hissed in reply.

"What a magnificent creature," said Suzanne Baxter.

"He's just confused," Guy said. "Humans and horses aren't part of his instinctual sensory patterns. He doesn't like us much, and they generally keep away. We must have surprised him. Give him a moment and he'll get out of our way."

The maxidon paced quickly to one side of the road, and a horse whinnied in surprise. Guy looked nervously to see who it was – these were all novice riders and a runaway would be serious trouble at this particular moment.

It gave ground grudgingly, sweeping its long tail around angrily to discourage pursuit. Then it leapt into the grass and began a loping run straight away from the colonists, its tail stretched out behind it for balance.

Suzanne Baxter looked at the rifle in Guy's hands and cocked one eye.

"Were we in any danger?"

"Probably not," he said. "But they're kind of unpredictable. I'd hate to shoot one without need. And they're pretty easy to scare away."

"Then you should tell my daughter that. She was pretty frantic about it a minute ago."

"Your daughter?" Guy followed Suzanne's gaze back down the column to where Emily sat on her horse, red-faced with embarrassment. Guy felt embarrassed as well, but only because he had not realized until this moment that Emily was the daughter of the leader of den Middlesex.

He stammered and felt hot and cold all at once, but he managed to maintain his composure. With the maxidon gone, the colonists had resumed their customary noisy chatter, and Guy used the opportunity to excuse himself and ride on ahead of the patrol.

Half an hour later, they reached the camp where Billy had first seen the Kolberg miniplanes. Guy let the colonists break for lunch.

Some of them complained about the rough ride in the back of a truck and the amount of dust they had inhaled during the course of the morning. Others, though, were more stoic in their acceptance of the small but persistent discomforts of riding on horseback. And a few, Emily's mother included, were experienced riders with full control of their animals. Emily was only fair as a horsewoman, but she got by.

Guy had a cold duckasaur sandwich and the colonists ate from ration packs. He watched them fearfully to see what they did with the empty packs, but was relieved when he saw them putting them into the container on the truck.

The big redhead who'd sat across the table from Guy last night watched the exchange, then shook his head.

"This is not quite how expected it would turn out," the man said.

"Your people are doing fairly well on horseback. I'm surprised it hasn't been more."

"I was referring to our arrival on Asgard. I always figured I'd get here sitting on my ass, but I never imagined there'd be a horse under it."

He introduced himself as Brad Karlsen, leader of den Bunyan.

"It's a woodsman's den. We're part of the manufacturing sector – wood products, lumber, turpentine, varnish and spirits. But in truth we're more craftsmen than laborers."

"Someone said there's only two dens in your group."

"That's right – us and Middlesex. We're from the *Hamilton.* Harry Bayard and his Matanuskans are still up there."

"Does it always take you fellows this long to make a decision?" Guy asked, masking the barb only slightly with his mild tone.

Karlsen reared his head back and looked the scout over carefully.

"The den is the result of a long process of grinding and milling, young fellow. Centuries between the millstones. What you've got is the basic unit of work in a high-tech world, worn smooth by time and history until they are each self-contained marvels. We work together like a fine-tuned machine. My den brothers and I can turn a forest into a fleet of fishing boats – on time and under budget.

"But we're not prepared to work with other dens. We were never trained for it, never learned how to do it, and after watching the spectacle of the last few days, we never want to try it again."

"I'm not surprised."

"But we will, don't you worry about it. Once we're all down here on the ground, we'll put it together right. And we'll do it ourselves – without the help of the Kolbergs."

Or the scouts, Guy realized warily.

Guy gave them an hour to eat and stretch their muscles, then they mounted up and were on their way again, this time along the banks of the Valley River, now swollen by the spring melt.

The sparkling freshet that Guy had followed a week ago had been replaced by a turbulent serpent of gray water and white foam. Since his last trip, the sun and the trade winds had worked their will on the snows atop Loki and along the ridge between North and South valleys. The slopes had changed from white to golden green and the melt water runoff was splashing over the riverbanks only meters away.

By high noon, the colonists made another 10 kilometers. Fluffy fair weather clouds had grown into towering anvils. Away to the west, Guy could see the upper valley cloaked in thunderheads, and to the south, a train of showery weather headed his way. The colonists were all equipped with rain ponchos and hats, and Guy had his own gear, but it didn't make him any more comfortable. The only compensation was the relief the showers brought from the thickness of the tropical air and the midday heat.

Guy was surprised by the time they were making. He worked it out in his head every time they passed another klickstone, but he kept coming up with the same answer – if they maintained this pace, they'd be in Glacier Valley well before dark. He began to feel less harried, though not yet relaxed.

About an hour before late noon, Guy spotted the trees that followed the Hart River down from the slopes. He hurried his horse to the head of the column and followed the path as it wound through a grove of greenwoods and up to the riverbank where Hart's Bridge made its crossing of the river.

And when he got there, his heart leaped into his throat and his hair stood on end.

The bridge was gone – smashed from its foundations.

"

The pilings in the center are still there," Brad Karlsen said after he inspected the damage from shore. "And the braces look like they're still intact. The anchors are good on this side – I went down and checked them myself."

The colonists lined the banks of river – a torrent ten meters wide. A rock outcrop in the center of the river divided the waters and served as the foundation for the two-section span. On the far bank, duckasaurs plucked at the vegetation near the water, but stayed out of the racing stream.

"And I couldn't say for sure what caused it. Maybe chunks of ice from upriver. Maybe snags, if they hit it hard enough. Or maybe plastic explosives planted in the timbers and set off all at once."

"If you're of a suspicious mind," Guy said.

"Not that I am, mind you," Karlsen warned. "Well, Scout, you're in charge. What do we do now?"

Guy took a deep breath and looked at the possibilities.

He could turn back now and admit defeat, let the Kolbergs put off the landings and surrender Asgard to them forever. He pictured the demoralized patrol dragging themselves back to the Main Post. They would never make the same pace back as they had on the way out, and since they were already more than halfway to the valley, they wouldn't make it back until well after dark.

He could fall back to the scout Camp and spend the night there. Maybe in a couple days, the flood waters would recede and the patrol would be able to ford the river farther upstream. But that would still mean delay and defeat.

He looked at the waters rushing by with fearful intensity. Could they rig a line across there and ferry or pass colonists to the far bank? They'd have to walk the remaining distance – only about 33 klicks or so.

While he was watching the river, a duckasaur edged too close to the bank and fell in. Guy watched as it struggled against the current, paddling with huge webbed feet to swim to shore. But the flood was just too much, rolling the duckasaur over and under, pushing it against the rocks, then the banks and finally yanking it under as it disappeared downstream.

He looked up at Karlsen. "How long would it take you to build a new one?"

The woodsman looked at the remains of the bridge, mumbled some numbers under his breath, then smiled. "Six hours – maybe five and a half."

"Then we'd better get started."

***

Karlsen produced a collection of axes and handsaws. "We do this for sport back home, but we figured some day the skills would come in handy. We brought these to cut firewood."

Guy had to walk the riverbank with them to find the right trees for their work.

"These have a tough bark, but there's nothing but mush inside," he said, pointing to a spineycone tree. "The greenwoods are probably too thick to be worth the trouble – although if you could figure out some way to cut it in two and move it, one trunk would make a perfect bridge. There should be a stand of terrestrial pine around here somewhere."

"The hard part is going to be getting a man over there with a line," Karlsen said.

Guy didn't look at him, but stared instead into the swift river. "I know. I'm going to do it."

"Now wait a minute, scout. You don't have to do that. One of my boys will give it a try."

"No. It's my responsibility. I can't send someone else over there in my. place. Do something for me, will you?"

"What's that?"

"Get those wood chips together and start a fire going. That water's awfully cold."

***

Guy began shivering long before he had his shirt and boots off. It was only nerves, he told himself. Just his body's way of telling him that he was doing something stupid and crazy and that it didn't want to cooperate.

He tied the rope around his waist and took the coil with him as he paced up the bank a distance from the bridge crossing. He figured he'd need the time running with the current if he wanted to reach the rocks in midstream.

Karlsen and two of his men took the other end of the line in their hands as Guy climbed down to a rock at the water's edge. The young scout took a few deep breaths to prepare himself, then he jumped into the water.

The icy shock stuck him like a thousand knives.

The current was slow here where a large boulder diverted the flow, but it still plucked and pulled at his body. He let his arms and legs adjust to the cold water before moving out into the maelstrom.

Only a short time ago this water had been snow and ice up on Vogelsberg Ridge. Guy, who had never before been on such intimate terms with the ubiquitous cold of Asgard, decided it was an experience he did not want to repeat.

He pushed off and began swimming for the center. The rope kept him from being swept away as he caromed off boulders and smaller rocks. Karlsen and his mates played out more line and followed him along the bank. He barely had time to react when he saw the rocks rushing towards him. He made one quick kick and reached for the wooden structure at the base of the pilings.

He caught it, then pulled himself towards it.

He want to pull a loop of line up and over a post, to keep himself fast, but his hands would not cooperate. They shook uncontrollably, as did his arms, lips and shoulders, while he sucked ragged lungfuls of air into his chest. It took every ounce of will he could muster to move that line where he wanted and lever himself around to the lee of the structure. He set his hands on the ledge, then heaved himself out of the water.

He lay there gasping for air and shaking violently. He felt as if he weighed a ton. Every muscle in his body ached. But he still had one more thing to do.

He rolled over onto his hands and knees and recovered the line. Then he doubled the loop on the post to secure it at his end. When he was finished, he collapsed helplessly on the rocks.

A moment later, he felt strong hands gripping him and then the icy needles of the river for a second time. He tried to cry out in protest, but he was too weak, and when he opened his mouth, it filled with water. Then he was out of the river and onto the bank.

Emily was there with blankets and towels and she began to wrap and rub him vigorously. They pulled him along to the side of the fire and rubbed the heat back into his aching body.

By the time he had recovered some of his strength, the woodsmen had finished rigging the tackle they needed to put the bridge in place. He watched from the fireside as they lowered the crossbeam into the river and ferried it across, followed by the long beams that would form the floor of the span.

An hour passed before his strength returned and his clothes were dried and returned to him. He watched and waited, pacing the bank of the river, downing too much coffee and not enough solid food, afraid that something would go wrong before they were done.

But as the sun began to dip towards Thor, painting the clouds a golden-orange as it dropped behind them, the bridge was completed. He watched with pride as Karlsens woodsmen pounded in the last pegs.

Karlsen himself sat on the hood of the first truck across to prove its soundness – and to help guide it, since they had made the bridge only as wide as necessary. They led the horses over on foot, covering their eyes as Guy had instructed.

The colonists had eaten their dinner while the lumbermen worked, and now they were ready to go. It was 2230, with barely an hour of daylight left and 25 klicks to go. The young scout mounted up and led the patrol away from Hart's Bridge.

***

Guy looked down from the top of the hill at the rear of the lodge. Sparks flew from a chimney and yellow light spilled out onto the ground at the edges of the rambling collection of rooftops. A single window was visible from his vantage point, at the nearest section of the lodge, the one highest on the hillside.

A man a few meters away cleared his throat. The cold, still air swallowed up the sound, and the starless dark overhead hid him from view.

For a while, Rudi had lit their way, but then the clouds had swallowed up his red light.

The patrol had reached the landing strip in the dark. The beacon, now back in working order, was unattended. Schmidt hadn't posted a watch – he didn't expect anyone to be coming from that direction.

Guy left the trucks there. He didn't want to risk them on the path at night and he didn't want to announce his arrival in the valley with a lot of noise and lights.

The drivers and some of the older or more frail colonists stayed there, breaking out tents and setting up camp in the woods. Guy and the others had gone on.

Once inside the valley, they'd dismounted. Guy wanted to circle around and come down on the post from the high ground at its rear. Then he wanted to find out what Schmidt and his friends were up to – before they knew he'd arrived.

They left Emily, Suzanne and some of the other women with the horses. Suzanne had protested, but Brad Karlsen changed her mind.

"Den leaders do not go skulking around in the dark," he said, remaining behind with her to make the point.

Guy went over the grim arithmetic one more time.

There were more than 7,000 scouts on Asgard, about half of them in the North and South valleys. On Monday, they had split themselves up into 45 patrols and set off for their Colony Day positions in the distant posts, landing strips and townships. That meant less than a hundred scouts in each patrol, half of whom were too old or too young to count, leaving about 40 adults.

How many of Schmidt's patrol were his cronies and how many were good scouts? That would determine the odds he would have to face. But it was a question he could not answer without looking first.

He broke from cover and worked his way slowly and silently down the hill, aiming towards the light in the rear of the lodge. A few minutes later, the five of them huddled against a low wall of rough-hewn timbers. Guy crept up to the window and peered in.

The small bedroom was sparsely furnished with a wooden sleeping rack, a table and a chair. A shaded lamp on the table was the only source of light. A knapsack, coat and loose clothing were scattered on the floor. A sleeping bag lay on the rack in a pile.

Then the bag moved.

Guy's heart raced. A head full of red hair popped out of the bag followed by a face. His heart almost stopped – it was Jeannie Gilmartin. She had a purple bruise across her face and her eyes were red and swollen.

"Wait here," he whispered to the others. Then he pulled out his knife and slipped it under the window sill. With a quick twist that made a sharp but brief snapping noise, he broke the seal that held it shut. He readied himself with a few deep breaths, then lifted the window open, swung his legs over the sill and let it close without a sound. He was standing there in the room, breathing hard before Jeannie even opened her eyes.

She gasped and clutched at the edge of the bag.

"Jeannie, don't scream. It's me, Guy."

Her eyes widened, then the shock ran from her face. "Guy? What in the name of the Great Spirit are you doing here?"

"Me? What are you doing here?"

She let her face drop. "I came with LeClerc. Big mistake, right?"

"Did he do that to you?"

"Real pretty, isn't it?"

Guy seethed with anger. He had never actually wanted to hurt anybody before in his life. Not even Henry Schmidt. But this was different. "How? What happened?"

"I didn't want to do it with him, so he hit me," she said without expression. "Then he did it anyway."

Guy didn't know what to say or do or feel. He was hurt and angry and ashamed all at once. Most of all he wanted to hurt LeClerc – for a long, long time.

"But I thought – "

"It's not what you think, Guy. Or anybody else. Not at all. It was my idea, but I worked it out with Lyle. I was just going to act friendly with him to find out what I could about the Kolbergs. Then last night, he said he'd take me along with him to meet them myself. He had a mini stashed out in the woods and this morning, after the fog lifted, we flew up here."

"Did you find out anything?"

"Do you mean was it worth it?"

"That's not what I said."

"I'm sorry. It's not your fault. It's not anybody's fault."

"It's LeClerc's fault."

"Yeah, that's true. Anyway, I found out a lot. I found out what the Kolbergs want."

"What's that?"

"Glacier Valley."

Guy looked at her blankly. "How? I mean, for what?"

"They want it for their own private estate on Asgard. That's why they were poking around here. That's why they wanted to stop the Middlesexers. That's why they wrecked the bridge – Guy, how did you get past the bridge?"

"It's a long story. Excuse me just a minute first," he said, going to the window. He waved to the woodsmen lurking in the shadows.

But as the first one started to come over the sill, Jeannie protested. "Gee, Guy, can't I get dressed first?"

"Tell me more about banks," Schmidt said. Guy heard him, but could not see him from where he lay on the balcony above the dining hall. He could see the fireplace and the couches around it, and the scouts who sat on them. He could even see LeClerc, seated in a chair next to the hearth. But Schmidt was pacing the floor directly below Guy – and it made him more than a little nervous.

"What do you want to know, my friend?" LeClerc said.

"More about the finances – the development – "

"You mean investments?"

"That's it. I understand how a bank pools all the money. But then how does it work? How do the bankers get their power?"

"Very simple. Or rather compound. The bank, it loans back the money the people put into it. And it charges them interest. Like rent. Every year you have the money, you pay a percentage to use it. Then, and here is the exciting part, you pay a percentage on the percentage. It is called compound interest."

"You mean like acceleration?"

"Exactly."

Guy shook his head as he grasped the idea LeClerc was explaining. He knew what a bank was – it owned things for people while they were saving up the money to pay for them. But the percentage business – that sounded immoral. He understood geometric progressions and self-expanding loops and compound interest sounded suspiciously like the same thing. Why, you could end up paying back ten times what you borrowed in the first place.

"And the bankers get to decide what to build and where, what to make and how many?"

"More or less. The bankers and the people who give them the money."

"This is fantastic," Schmidt said as he marched vigorously up to the fireplace and into Guy's sight. His eyes caught the flames and gleamed, but it seemed to Guy as if part of the gleam came from inside. From what Guy knew of the scout, Schmidt and banks were a perfect match.

Guy strained his senses to the limit as he tried to tally Schmidt's supporters. There were five of them sitting around the fire, including LeClerc. Schmidt seemed to be the only one up and walking around. That meant six. That made him feel better. The others were scouts Guy recognized as young men he had come to dislike over the years. Now, seeing them all assembled, he realized that the reasons he had for disliking them were much the same – they were all bullies, misfits, self-important and arrogant. There was no surprise in seeing them at Schmidt's side.

"Now do you really expect people to let you make them pay money for land?" Schmidt asked LeClerc.

The scout from Tik laughed. "My friend, we write the laws so that they must. It is easy, you see. We explain we are protecting them as well as the bank. We tell them, good people, if you do not let us make you pay money for land, then you cannot make us pay money for land. You will be robbed of the opportunity to use your land as you wish. Please believe us, we are only trying to help you."

"And the colonists believe that?"

"They did on Tik," LeClerc said.

Guy was disgusted. He wanted to listen and hear what else they were up to, but he didn't dare leave the rest of his patrol outside all night. It was time to leave.

***

Guy's plan relied on one simple assumption – that Schmidt and the other scouts were not frightened youngsters who were too nervous to leave their rifles in the rack by the door.

He recalled the last time he'd been in the lodge at the Valley Post and how Walt had insisted that he take the rifle to bed with him. That was not Scout Law. The Law said rifles belong in the rack or outdoors.

He bumped shoulders with the woodsmen who had been with him throughout the night as they jammed into the small space between the inner and outer doors at the main entrance to the lodge. Out in the yard were the remaining colonists, Brad Karlsen and Suzanne in the lead, ready to follow the first team into the building.

Guy took a deep breath, then stepped through the doors. The lobby beyond was empty. He took three steps into the room, stood there with his own rifle at the ready and looked back at the rack.

He saw seven weapons lined up in a row, side by side, without a gap.

Good scouts, every one. He motioned to the others who came in behind him and removed the weapons. The last man in took three, then returned to the door, where he waved to the rest of the party.

It had all happened in just a few seconds and all without a sound – until the colonists hit the porch like a crowd of fuzzies. Guy took the explosion of noise from the front of building as his signal to move.

He stepped through the doors of the dining hall just as the scouts within were rising to their feet.

"What the – " Schmidt started.

"Mon Dieu," LeClerc snorted.

Guy led the rifle-toting colonists into the hall and marched up to the chair where LeClerc was sitting.

"Scout LeClerc, in the name of den Iroquois, I charge you with assault and sexual assault and place you under arrest in accordance with Scout Law."

Schmidt sneered at him. "Traditionally, arrests are only made by adult scouts, Stanger."

"Tradition is tradition, not the Law – and traditionally, scouts do not consort with rapists."

"Assault? What is he talking about?" LeClerc muttered.

Jeannie Gilmartin came into the room with the colonists just in time to witness the arrest. She came forward, pressing past the others, to stand beside Guy. "He's talking about me, you piece of byte dirt."

"Oh no," LeClerc said. He shuddered and his face seemed to sag and blanch.

"What's going on here, Stanger?" Schmidt asked. "Who are these people? What are you all doing here?"

"Why don't you ask Lyle Sanderson? He's been trying to get you on the phone all day – ever since you shut off the landing beacon down at the strip. Maybe you can explain to him why you're harboring this garbage."

LeClerc had his face in his hands now. Schmidt was turning red and clenching his fists.

"Or better yet, maybe you can explain it to me," asked a newcomer to the group – Suzanne Baxter.

***

Suzanne's entrance had shut Schmidt up – and relieved Guy of the thing he had feared most, a confrontation with the older scout over who had proper authority at the post, a confrontation he knew he would have lost.

They raised Sanderson on the satellite phone and reported what they had found. Then they warmed up on coffee and bark tea and confronted LeClerc.

Guy didn't do much but watch as Suzanne took the broken man apart.

"They tell me there's a special place here on Asgard where they put your kind," she said. "It's up in Valkyries, offshore islands to the north of here. They drop you down with a tent and a knife and a month's worth of food, then they leave. They come back in a few years to see if they can recover the tent and the knife.

"I understand the weather isn't too bad in the summer – just rain. Winter can't be that terrible. Actually, I would think the problem would be the loneliness."

She turned her back on him while she drank her coffee.

"The way I see it, you've got only one hope. You tell us what you know – everything that you know – about the Kolbergs. Then maybe, if it's useful, and you don't lie to us, we might tell the scouts how much help you were. And we might just ask them to let you get off the planet and never come back."

Guy wanted to shout in protest. He didn't want to let LeClerc go.

But he realized what Suzanne was up to and held his tongue.

She turned to face LeClerc.

"Of course, if you do lie, then my first thought would be to let the girl have you."

LeClerc had never been a man of much character to begin with. He was not hard to persuade.

***

"I never was a good scout, me. Always in trouble. Never following the rules. I was a youngster when the colony came and the world changed. Some got over it. I never did. When I grew up, I sold my landholdings to the Kolbergs and some others. Then I took the money and spent it all – gambled, spent it on women, clothes, food."

"Gambling?" Guy asked. LeClerc explained.

It was a difficult concept for Guy to grasp at first. The part he couldn't understand was why the fallen scout continued to wager after losing, but he didn't interrupt again.

"But they liked me, the Kolbergs. They kept me around. Peter likes to hear my stories about the backwoods of Tik. So when they say they are coming to Asgard, I ask if I can go to."

"Less about you, more about them," Suzanne said.

"What can I say? They are farmers, all of them. The Kolbergs – Peter and his brother, Eric – belonged to an agricultural den in the breakthrough colony. Breaking ground on a new planet would be enough for anybody else, but not for Peter. He wants more, always more.

"The first winter on Tik, a lot of the farms went bust – farmers with them. The Kolbergs picked up the empty plots and helped manage them to produce more. Each year, a few more farms go under. Each year, the Kolbergs own a little more.

"Then after a few years, Tik gets a new manufacturing den. The Kolbergs, they talk to the den and convince them to settle in their township. The next year, they do the same thing with a machinery den. Pretty soon, they have a busy little town going in their piece of the colony.

"But this colony, Tik, you see, it wasn't supposed to be that way. The planners, the first dens and the scouts, they wanted Tik to be a new world with a new order. They spread everyone far and wide, just like you scouts wanted to do here. They put the specialty dens here and there and everywhere. You have to go a long ways to get anything done on Tik – even today.

"The Kolbergs were not too popular after they built their town. Not with the old-timers anyway. But the new colonists and the youngsters, they liked the busy life and the nice things the Kolberg township gave them. When we left Tik, the colony had been there 14 years – old years, Solar years. Must be more than 20 Asgard years. The population was double yours – 200,000. The Kolbergs, they have a nice port on the Metacomet Sea and they make things everyone needs. One colonist in ten works for them now on Tik. They own banks, ships, factories, libraries, almost anything that you can own.

"But even that is not enough for Peter.

"After all that he went through on Tik, he wants to try again with a new world. He wants to try it fresh from the start – instead of changing it once it begins. So he talks to his friends and to the scouts and he deals and bribes and pays until finally, he gets a scoutship and comes to Asgard.

"And now he is trying to get you to give him what he wants – a whole colony to play with."

"What about Glacier Valley?" asked Guy.

"Glacier Valley is a very beautiful place. The Kolbergs like it very much. They want to live here when the colony is down – so that means den Middlesex will have to find someplace else to live. Peter told us to keep the colonists away from the valley. Don't let them interfere with the plan."

"And what about Jeannie?" asked Suzanne.

"The girl, I am sorry about. She did not understand. I did not understand. I thought she was playing the game with me. Women always say no when they mean yes."

"No, they don't," she said coldly. "Guy, this one is all yours."

They took him to a storeroom in the back of the lodge, tossed in a sleeping bag and took away his belt. Then they threw him inside and locked the door. Guy stood outside and stared at the door for a long time, then turned and walked away.

The Kolberg plan is a monstrosity," Suzanne told Annie Kovalev. But there it was – and on Wednesday morning. Colony Day. Two days before the Kolbergs had promised. And before 0900. She took it as a victory of sorts, though she believed it was more of a tactical response by Peter Kolberg to the losses of the previous night than a retreat.

And now that it was before them, it seemed to be less frightening than she had thought at first – and, at the same time, more frightening.

It's crudeness lessened the fear. The plan was so simple-mindedly brutal, but then, it was so clumsy in its goal.

They wanted to build a city!

The Kolberg plan had all the farming dens concentrated in South Valley, stacked together like soldiers with no room for growth. A few service and educational dens were scattered around the perimeter, but at the center, on either side of a slow bend in the South River, were two ugly concentrations of humanity.

They were brazen enough to call the largest of them Asgard City. They wanted to put 15 dens in there. Suzanne could not believe it. Three health dens – most of the doctors – and two executive dens, the university, food, apparel, construction, transport, machinery and special services. That was more than 25,000 people. At the density the colonists were planning to build, it meant 50 square klicks of residential – almost a quarter of a township.

And across the river, they had more. The rest of the doctors and executives and the remaining construction, transport and special services dens. Another 15,000 colonists and another 30 square klicks of residential development.

How could the Kolbergs think that colonists escaping from a crowded Earth – fleeing from their ten billion neighbors, the high-rise arcologies, the sprawl of the great megalopolises that spanned the continents and the waste heat of all their energies – would accept the creation of another city on their precious new world?

Were they incapable of realizing the feelings and sensitivities of the breakthrough colony? Or was there something diabolically clever going on that she just couldn't fathom?

"No one is going to go for this, are they?"

"Sorry, Suzie. Things have metastasized up here. Politically, the damage is already done. Maybe that's why they thought they could move up their timetable. We've been trying to count votes for three days to see who's on our side and who's on theirs. The numbers have been coming up the same since Tuesday morning. There's about 20 of us – libertarians, progressives and radicals. Special services, ag dens, the people on your ship, you know the list. But then there's about 25 dens on their side. Some of them are just conservatives, but others are really excited about the idea of having the Kolbergs run things. They're the ones that scare me, Sue.

"If you ask me, the Kolbergs have managed to accomplish their main goal – they've split this colony wide open. We're so polarized, I don't think we'll ever be able to agree on anything again. And we haven't even touched the ground yet."

Suzanne shrugged off Annie's despair. She knew that things would be different once everyone had landed, but there was no way you could explain that to someone who was still trapped inside an aluminum can orbiting over the icy surface of Asgard.

"What about the swing vote?" she asked.

"We're working on them. I think it'll break in our favor, but I'm not sure yet."

"We can't let it come to a vote until you are."

"I know, but what do we do instead?"

"You know what the Doctrine says."

"People are tired of hearing about the Doctrine, Suzanne. And the way the weather looks, you wouldn't be able to get anyone down there today even if we do decide what to do. It's supposed to be snowing down there."

Suzanne looked out the window at the lumpy white coating that covered the ground and the sky full of fluffy flakes. "I know about the snow," she said. "I guess I'm just going to have do some thinking about the rest of it."

But long after the link to Annie had been severed, Suzanne was still unsure of what to do next. She was tired, exhausted from two overlong days of stress. Maybe she was missing something, but there didn't seem to be any options available to her.

She had lost the moral authority of the Doctrine. The political situation was turning against her. She was in danger of becoming a small voice, crying out alone in the wilderness of Asgard's unknown surface, with no one hearing or caring about her.

She felt terrible. Why did the Kolbergs have to come along and ruin her colony? Why couldn't the colonists just land they way the way they were meant to?

Why indeed, she wondered with a sudden flash of insight. All they had to do was board the landers and let the AIs take over. You didn't even need a pilot if the winds were low enough. All that stood in the way were the officers of the Colonial Corps. And if Captain Gallo could be persuaded ...

It was a terrible risk. If things went wrong, it would mean victory for the Kolbergs. But even if things went as badly as she feared they could, there was still a chance that it could turn the tide. She waited patiently for the *Hamilton* to come over the horizon to make her call.

***

Long ago, before his hair turned white and before he gained a wiser sense of proportions, Harry Bayard had taught history at the local high school. It hadn't taken him long to tire of the paperwork, the schedules and the tyranny of administrators and school committees. He started his first farm shortly after taking an early retirement. But he still had a reverence for history, still was stirred by the videos of bygone centuries.

So he recognized immediately the underlying connections in Peter Kolberg's arguments when he appeared on the commlink network shortly before 1200.

"The efficiency of this approach speaks for itself," Kolberg told the colonists, his face making its closest approach to a smile that Harry had yet seen. "Too many times on Tik, we have seen people suffer because the things they needed were too far away or cost too much to transport. We have suffered dearly because of the dispersal of resources and abilities. It took us a long time to correct this.

"But with this plan, the resources of the colony are concentrated in a vibrant and energetic center. That energy will help you build a city and a world. Together, we can work to create that future, with the driving force of history pushing us onward.

"Let us lead you there. Let us help show you the way. Let us help you avoid the mistakes that were made on our world."

Harry had heard those words before. Efficiency, energy, the driving force of history. Kolberg was one of those self-righteous leaders who urged their followers to toil and sacrifice for the greater good, to put their faith in powerful men, powerful forces, powerful cities. For centuries, since the rise of technology had overthrown the old values, the Kolbergs and their kind had appealed to the fears of people who only wanted to escape their newfound freedom.

That's who Peter Kolberg was talking to – the colonists who, despite the ties of the den and the colony, were reluctant to leave behind the secure social institutions of crowded old Earth. There were whole dens who felt that way, Harry knew. Farmers mostly, the members concerned with themselves first and the other dens last. They were the Kolbergs' biggest supporters.

Harry believed they were a perversion of what the den was supposed to be. They were the bitter and misshapen fruit of trees planted in poor soil. He was glad they were not representative of the human race as a whole.

There were dens with other values – dens that reflected the highest development of a civilized culture. He liked to think he belonged to one of them. Their goal was not self-enrichment through power or wealth, but the full development of the individual. And not by submission to false idols, but by the productive exercise of creative human powers like faith, creative work and a selfless sense of responsibility.

Harry realized that it took all kinds to make a world, it was just too bad they had to bring them all to Asgard.

He was more heartened by Suzanne's speech. The theatrics made him tremble – the scratchy signal relayed up from the primitive wooden cabin where she and the rest of the pathfinder team had spent the night. How could anyone see that and not be swayed?

"This is not going to be a long speech," she said. "I don't believe in talk – I believe in action, as you may have noticed. Today is the day of decision for the Asgard colony. You're going to have to choose between our own plan and the one the Kolbergs have proposed. Our plan is a good one. Where the Kolbergs want to build a city of 50,000, we are happy to have a town of 12,000. Where the Kolbergs have jammed the farming dens in, side-by-side, we have left room for growth, so our children will not have to travel far from home to start their own lives. And where the Kolbergs have sent everyone into the South Valley, we've split the colony to give a free people the room they need.

"But this isn't about which plan we use. This is about who makes all our plans – from now on. Do we do it ourselves? Or do we turn our independence over to someone else? And most importantly, do we turn it over to the Kolbergs?

"I'm not going to tell you which way you should vote. I'm afraid I've lost all my objectivity down here on the planet. From what I've seen in the past few days, I want to warn you all: The Kolbergs and the company they keep are not the kind of people we want to lead us."

She told the story of her trip to Glacier Valley and of LeClerc's crime.

"There is more. As you may have noticed, the Kolbergs' plan leaves the Glacier Valley township empty, while our plan assigns it to den Middlesex – my den. According to LeClerc, the Kolbergs want that township for themselves, as a private estate and exclusive preserve. If he is mistaken, I'm sure the Kolbergs will correct him. But what I have seen leads me to believe he is not.

"The Kolbergs are thieves, clear and simple. They came here with only one goal. They came to steal Asgard, our world, our future, our hopes and dreams and plans. And since they have come first to my den and to my land – to land that was set aside for a university from the earliest days of the scouts on this planet – I cannot be objective.

"So I will say nothing more about whose plan we should follow. What I will say is this – the time for action has come. At this moment, our companion den, Matanuska, is readying itself to make the first landings on Asgard. Den Matanuska and den Middlesex have been bond-linked since their creation, and under the landing plan presented to us by the Scouts and modified by our committee, they have been assigned to the Hartsbridge township south of Glacier Valley. In a few minutes, Matanuska den leader Harry Bayard will leave the *Hamilton* to begin landing his colonists. By nightfall, they should be on the ground.

"I urge the rest of you to follow his example. I want to thank you and wish you all a safe landing." Her image dissolved into the Asgard shield.

***

It was all up to Commander Gallo, Suzanne had said. But Harry hadn't been so certain, and when the time came, she was against them.

But he sure liked the surprise in those eyes when the Colonial Corps officer heard Suzanne's speech. She shot Harry a questioning look and he smiled.

"We would have mentioned it sooner, Captain, but we didn't

want to trouble you," he said. "This would be a lot easier with your permission. Do we have it?"

She widened her eyes and dropped her jaw. "Are you serious?"

"Quite."

"No, you don't. Emphatically not. I cannot send down the landers without prior authorization from the commodore – and he has forbidden us to do that until the den leaders decide what they want to do."

"The den leaders couldn't decide to all pee in the same pot unless it was running down their legs," the farmer replied. "We are tired of waiting, Captain. We want to go down."

"Mr. Bayard, if you do not leave the bridge and return to your cubicles, I will consider it an act of mutiny."

"Doesn't mutiny require a threat of violence of the use of force?"

"It helps, but in this case I may be tempted to forego that requirement."

Harry smiled. "Don't bother. This should make it official. Captain Gallo, if you don't stay out of our way, somebody's likely to pick you up and stuff you in a locker."

"Lieutenant, call for the master-at-arms. Mr. Bayard, I hereby place you under arrest."

"Before you do that, Captain, I suggest you count heads. There are sixteen of my biggest farm boys here and in the passageway outside. There are only four of your officers. I didn't think you were likely to see things our way, so I took some precautions. Your master-at-arms will not get here before the landers have left."

"Lieutenant, sound General Quarters." Gallo reached out and activated the shipwide alarms, pulling down the microphone to the public address system. "All hands, all Corps officers. Mr. Bayard and the leaders of den Matanuska are standing in mutiny. Crew members are ordered not to cooperate with them in any manner. Landers are to stand down from launch readiness and secure. Master-at-arms to the bridge. I repeat, Mr. Bayard and the – "

A tall, blond boy grabbed Gallo's wrist and held it gently but firmly as he took the microphone away from her. Then he yanked the mike from the overhead and left it floating in the air. Harry recognized the youngster as a student of his at the Ag Extension Service outside Anchorage. They smiled at one another in recognition.

"Keep her there for a while," Harry said. "Then let her go. And please don't hurt her, she is a very dutiful officer."

A few minutes later, Harry arrived at the assembly areas where the colonists waited to board the landers. Earlier in the day, the thousand den members who would be going down in the first wave were alerted and told to assemble shortly before noon, ready to go, without alerting the crew of the *Hamilton*. Now they awaited the final word.

"The pilots are still in there," said Rich Henderson, Harry's old neighbor up the Matanuska Valley near Palmer. "We didn't want to startle them."

"Did they hear the announcement?"

"What announcement?"

"Gallo's last gasp. She called us mutineers and wants us arrested. Just like I said she would."

"I didn't hear anything – not with the noise these folk are making." Harry frowned. The lander pilots might have been alerted to the mutiny and they might not. There was only one way to find out.

"I should be back in a few minutes, but if I'm not, come in and get me." He grabbed two of the broadest shouldered young men in the group and took them in tow.

He passed through into the lander dock and boarded the craft. He worked his way forward to the cockpit and had his two companions wait outside while he poked his head in. He found the pilot and co-pilot strapped into their seats, running through simulations of Asgard's jet stream and weather patterns.

"Hello there," he said. "Can I come in for a minute?"

The co-pilot looked up from her instruments and smiled. "Just give us a chance to land and we'll be right with you."

He watched as they ran through the simulation, listening to them read off the instruments and checklists until the AI announced: "Drill over."

"That looked like fun. But I thought the AIs flew these things for you?" Harry asked, certain now that the pilots hadn't been warned. If they had, he didn't think they would have finished their drill.

"That's right, but this drill was to practice what happens if the AIs give up – like in heavy weather," the pilot said, squinting with one eye and making the wrinkles on that side of his face stand out.

"Those simulations, how do they work?"

"The AIs give us the instrument readings and we fly it down."

"Could I see how it works?"

"Sure," the pilot said with a smile. He turned to the keypad beside him and punched in a command. Harry strained to watch and strained harder to memorize the codes he saw appear on the monitor screen.

"The first step is to detach from the ship," the pilot said. "The AIs take care of that."

"What happens if they don't?"

"Well in that case, Captain Dunne here goes back and pumps up the airlock and we blow ourselves out."

Harry looked at him quizzically.

The pilot's face wrinkled up as he broke out laughing. "No – not really, I'm just pulling your air line," he said. "Actually, we use an override that activates the system for us. That big red switch up there under the plastic cover." He pointed at a panel marked with yellow and black hazard lines, tucked in among the speakers and monitors in the overhead. Harry committed its location to memory and smiled. He had what he needed.

"You know," he said, "I came in here because I noticed something hanging loose in the airlock back there. I don't know what it was, but I figured maybe someone should check it out."

The two officers twisted their faces in puzzlement and alarm. "Maybe you'd better go check it out, Lieutenant," the pilot said. The young woman released her straps and pulled herself out of the seat. Then she followed Harry aft through the cockpit door.

Just beyond the door, the two farm boys stepped out in front of her, Harry barring the way behind her.

"You'll have to excuse us, Lieutenant," he said, "but we're having a small mutiny here today and we need to use your landers. We'll let you have them back just as soon as we're through. In the meantime, it would help if you'd call to the pilot to come out here and look at the airlock with us."

"What are you doing?" she asked, her eyes locking onto his with a seriousness that demanded an answer.

"We're going to put some of our colonists down on the ground where they belong."

"Is that all? It's about time somebody did something besides dither away our 02." She pushed past Harry and stuck her head in the cockpit.

"Lawrence, I think you'd better look at this airlock. It's pretty serious."

A half hour later, the last of the colonists was aboard the landers. Harry took his place in the co-pilot's seat while Lieutenant Dunne had the con. Her counterpart had refused to cooperate. The lieutenant had indicated to Harry that once he detached the landers, she would have no choice but to follow his orders – if only for the safety of the colonists. And then she grinned.

Now she swiveled her seat around to the control panel. A moment later, noise and vibration surged through the craft and a moment after that, the starry darkness of space fell across the windows of the cockpit. Harry felt a rush of excitement as he realized they were on their way.

The sky had a turbulent, roiling look to it. A line of low-flying gray clouds streamed north past the lower slopes of Loki to the east, looking like they were late for supper. Snow squalls blew in from the sea and mixed the warm moist air of the trade winds with the cold blast off the Deep Freeze. Huge wet flakes pelted the scouts and colonists along the landing strip, melting on impact and drenching everything in sight.

Guy felt the cool water run down his face, then wiped it all away in one swipe. The snow had not accumulated at all, but the clouds had kept the ceiling below acceptable limits all day long. He had been at the landing strip since low noon and had eaten his dinner there. In another hour or so, it would be time for supper. His legs ached and he was still tired from last night's activities.

Five times the landers had orbited overhead. Five times the rain-soaked patrol had fallen silent, the leaders gathered around the commset, as the decision point came and went. Five times the landers had passed them by, off on another circuit of Asgard, waiting for the weather to break.

Now Guy looked to the west where a small wedge of blue sky broke open above Thor's northern shoulder, and the gray clouds fled to the south.

"There it is," he said, pointing it out to Emily. "The front's starting to break through."

"Can they land now?"

"They have to. If they wave off this time, the next orbit will bring them around just after sunset. They'd really be pushing it then. It would be just as risky to land in the weather. But at the rate the front's moving, they may be able to make it this time."

"They can't stay up there overnight, can they?"

"I don't know. Maybe, if they stretch things. They must be built with that possibility in mind. But I don't think your mother wants to keep a thousand people in landers for fifteen hours."

"Couldn't they just go back to the *Hamilton*?"

He pursed his lips and shook his head. He'd been listening in when Emily's mother asked Harry Bayard the same question. The Alaskan den leader had been much more emphatic.

"Are you out of your mind, Suzie?" he'd asked. "I don't have time to go into details, but it didn't work out like you planned. We can't go back – repeat, can NOT go back to the ship."

Guy remembered the shudder that went up his back when he contemplated the details Bayard might be withholding.

Now he watched the blue sky widen and the clouds give way to clear air that gave him a view of the whole length of South Valley as far as Thor Mountain. Golden sunlight fell across the ridge line between Thor and Loki.

Then the wind shifted at the landing strip, backing around from southwest to straight out of the north as the temperature plunged.

Within a few minutes, the sky was cut in two as if by a straightedge, one side bright and blue, the other gray and cloaked in rain and snow. The sparkling white flanks of Thor stood in crystal-sharp detail in the clear air and Loki's peak blazed with color from the emerging sun.

Guy looked into Emily's eyes and saw the fear they held. He reached out and put an arm around her as she shivered against the sudden cold. She pressed against him in a way that felt both intimate and familiar, as if it were the most natural thing in the world to do.

Then a whoop of excitement echoed from the tent where the den leaders huddled around the commset, awaiting the next circuit of the landers.

"They're coming down!" someone yelled, and a hundred scouts and colonists rose as one and swarmed towards the landing strip. Guy and Emily watched as the human wave came towards them and then broke on either side. Brad Karisen and Emily's mother appeared in the center of the mass, waving to them to come along.

Guy took Emily's hand and they followed.

A half hour later, the contrails appeared high above Thor, two pale streaks, making towards them in the perfect blue of the cold new sky. They circled overhead, the sonic booms echoed off the trees and hilltops and frightened the horses. Guy felt a mindless thrill at the concussion of the air wave breaking across his chest.

Then the landers themselves lumbered into sight, shed of their orbital energy, pushing along on their own engines, tipping gently to circle the landing field before coming around to the final vector. The first of them dropped lower and lower as it lined up on the strip, clearing the treetops and touching down nearly halfway along the gravel runway. A cloud of dust and an explosion of stones and sand marked the spot where the solid-core tires hit the strip. The second lander circled around once, waiting for its companion to reach the end of the strip before making its landing run.

The whine of the landers' engines cut through the air as the craft rolled on up to the landing pad where the scouts and colonists had assembled. They were dwarfed by the big plane, but not intimidated, surrounding it before the whining turbines wound their way down.

It seemed to take forever for the landing ramps to descend from the underside of the craft. And they remained down for the longest time before anyone came out.

Then, at the top, a figure appeared. Guy had a hard time recognizing it at first – it looked all out of proportion. Then he realized that it was a child.

The first was joined by a second, then more. Suddenly the group seemed to overcome its hesitancy and poured down the ramp and onto the strip. It was like a leak that became a torrent, dozens of children, silent at first, then laughing and shouting. Their cries of joy were met with cries of celebration as the ground party welcomed them into their ranks.

Guy and Emily were soon surrounded by the youngsters. He watched as they picked up rocks and stared at the trees and shivered against the chill air.

One boy with a freckled face and a headful of brown curls walked up to them and hugged Guy's leg.

"Welcome to Asgard," Guy said.

"Hey," the boy replied. "Where's all the ice?"

***

"Well, Suzie, I'm afraid we really stuck the pig this time," Harry Bayard said. Guy, who listened from the back of the tent, couldn't quite form an image out of those words, but they didn't sound good.

"I know," Suzanne replied. "I've been watching them all day. The nicest thing we've been called is obstructionist. The Kolbergs' friends want us lynched. They say mutiny is a capital offense and that means you and me. Some of them are calling for Captain Gallo's head, as well. The commodore isn't too happy about that, but he's kept quiet. But you're down and there isn't much they can do about it."

"I'm afraid there are a few more dens leaning to the Kolbergs now than there were before we did this, though," Harry said, his eyes betraying an inner weariness. "I think we made a big mistake. Even our friends aren't happy about it. They say we should have waited until they got things settled. Said this undercuts our position and only helps the K's. I didn't know what to tell them – just that we were tired of waiting and didn't see any reason to chip in on the Kolberg Plan."

"I'm worried too, Harry, but we had to do it. If we had waited, the initiative would have passed over to them. We didn't have a wide range of options. Landing the den was the only one that would get everyone's attention. And we both know that more talk would not."

"You're right about that, Suzie. But now we've run out of options. And tomorrow, I'm afraid the other dens are going to get their revenge on us and vote for the K's."

Guy felt his heart sink at that idea. And he felt even worse when he saw Suzanne Baxter sigh and close her eyes. She thought so, too, he realized, but she didn't want to say it.

***

But as the hours passed, Guy found himself thinking less of what would follow in the morning and more of the endless work that faced him.

Hundreds of colonists had to be fed and housed as darkness fell. The modular containers of rations and tents were rolled out of the landers quickly, but breaking them down into standard issue for each family went much more slowly. And setting the tents up took even longer.

Guy and the two scouts with him had it down to a science within a short time. They could unfold the tents, stake them into the ground, assemble the frame and raise the walls in ten minutes. The colonists, who claimed to have had training were astonished by their speed, and before long, the woods around the landing strip were filled with campsites.

With the tents up, Guy and his fellows turned their energy to building campfires. Brad Karlsen and his crew had stockpiled enough firewood to keep them going for a few days, but the colonists themselves would have to take that duty over after the initial store was consumed.

The size of the group left Guy feeling a little intimidated. The Main Post had more than a thousand members, but when they got together for a public event like a jamboree, they'd never left him with the same sense of awe. Perhaps it was because he couldn't look at them without thinking of the thousands of others still in orbit who, one way or another, would be following over the next few days.

And the colonists themselves were enough to put him off. Even though they had traveled 25 years, they were only a few days away from experience from old Earth itself. They were still farmers, plain folk, unsophisticated by the standards of their world, but their minds and their voices held echoes of the ten billion souls they had left behind.

Guy felt humble and a little inadequate in the face of it. The more he saw of the colonists, the more he felt odd and uncomfortable, more self-conscious about himself and his raw scout upbringing. And he felt embarrassed more than once by the praise and attention the colonists seemed to shower on the scouts. The look in the eyes of the newcomers to Asgard was something to behold – full of hope and usually tears.

Somewhere along the way he had lost track of Emily and that bothered him. As the night wore on, he grew more and more worried. These were her people. Now that she was back with them, she could meet other new friends – young men who lacked Guy's rough edges and odd ways. Maybe she would find them more attractive and interesting.

After all, she had never said anything to indicate that she felt anything more than friendship towards him. And he had never said anything about his own feelings to her.

The feelings were there. And the more he thought about it, the more he realized that he could not bear the idea of being only friends. He felt like he was being swept away by forces he could sense, but not control. His only choice was to turn and face them, bringing events to closure one way or another. As his fears worked away at him, he began to fear more and more that it would not be a way favorable to him.

If only he could find Emily and look into her eyes. He was sure he could tell if had the chance.

But by the time the camp was settled and the colonists safe and secure, Guy was exhausted, covered with soot and grime, his cloths stiff and foul and his arms and legs aching. He found his way to the single bathhouse that the scouts had thrown up while waiting for the landers to make up their minds.

The line stretched for half a kilometer.

He took his place at the end, but the colonists in front of him turned, took one look at him, and motioned him forward. It continued on down the queue until Guy found himself being ushered through the doors by a dozen smiling colonists. He was too tired to protest.

Once clean and refreshed, he realized he had no place to go. He stumbled around the camp, passing from tent sites lit with bright lanterns into dark thickets and back into light, eavesdropping on the conversations of the colonists, who were too excited to sleep.

"Even the stars are different," cried one excited youngster.

"Is this where we're going to have the farm, Daddy?" asked a little girl.

"A day's hike through the countryside, isn't that what Harry said," her mother asked.

"Did you see the dinosuars?"

"Do the scouts really eat meat?"

Finally, Guy ran into an assistant patrol leader he recognized from the Valley Post who told him there were extra tents at the end of the landing strip. He struck out across the gravel, slogging along under a sky that buried with the bright fire of Rudi and a handful of first-magnitude rivals. The tents were right where he'd been told – but they hadn't been put up.

What had become a quick routine for three scouts was a slow and painful task for one on his own. After a half an hour, he had only managed to put the frame together.

Then a figure appeared out of the darkness.

"Can I help?"

It was Emily.

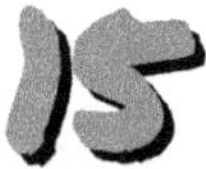

I feel so strange – like I'm someone else walking around in Guy Stanger's body. Everything I believed a few weeks ago was wrong. Nothing has turned out the way it should. And now look at things. Your mother is depressed because she gambled and now she's sure she failed. Someone else is going to decide where the dens will go and what they will do. Grampa Bob thinks I'm betraying the scouts by helping you. And that bastard LeClerc raped Jeannie."

He squeezed his eyes shut to stop the tears from welling up at that last. Emily took his hand. "The two of you were lovers, weren't you?"

Guy looked at her suspiciously. "I wouldn't have used that word to describe it, but yeah, sort of."

"You must feel terrible."

"I'm so tired, I don't know what to feel. I've been waiting all my life for this day, and now it's turned out to be a complete disaster.

And the worst thing of all still hasn't hit."

"What's that?"

"It's something that I realized tonight, something I hadn't given much thought to. Emily, what are the scouts going to do once you colonists have all landed? Look at how many of them are out here. And this is just a tiny bit of them. This isn't going to be the same valley any more, is it?"

"I guess not. It won't be that crowded, though, will it?"

"As thick with people as it is with fuzzasaurs. That's how Grampa Bob described it. I think I'm beginning to understand why he doesn't want the colonists here. This isn't going to be our world anymore. I don't know what we're going to do. And I don't know what I'm going to do."

He twisted himself around in his sleeping bag on the floor of the tent. Spots of light from Rudi filtered through the trees and painted an odd pattern of shadows across the top of the tent. There was just enough light to make out the shape of Emily across the floor from him.

She had fallen asleep while helping to put up tents not long after dark, she'd said. She still wasn't used to Asgard's clock. When she awoke and realized how late it was, she went looking for Guy.

When she told him that, he felt a warm glow engulf his body. All his fears had been baseless. But now he was growing nervous once again. He still felt the same, but with her here in the tent with him, it was hard to raise the subject that he wanted to broach.

With Jeannie, it had been different. There was never any doubt about what she wanted – not after the day she'd waylaid him in the horsebarn after supper. Then it was just a matter of making dates. But he'd known Jeannie all his life. Emily was a stranger. His heart started to pound just thinking about it.

"My mother is pretty upset, even though she doesn't show it,"

Emily said. "She's sure we've lost. She says they've all turned against her up there and that everyone's going to vote for the Kolbergs in the morning. She thinks it's all her fault. And she says that no matter who wins, it's already too late. The colony's already split up over this and it'll never be the same. Like Humpty Dumpty, you can't put it back together again."

"That's how I feel about Jeannie. She's been hurt in a way that can never be fixed. It makes me mad enough to kill LeClerc. I still don't know if I want to let the Kolbergs take him, but the scouts don't have any way of punishing him. We never had a problem like that before."

"That's so strange. Back home, we have prisons full of people who do things like that. And people who do things a lot worse. A lot of us wanted things to be better out here. Now I don't know what's going to happen. You're not the only one who doesn't know what to do."

"You're a colonist," Guy said with surprise. "Didn't you come to build a colony."

Emily laughed. "I came because my mother made me. It's not like I had much of a choice. I was still in high school when they asked me if I wanted to go, for all that was worth. And how do you build a colony? I'm still working on getting to class on time. Gad, I haven't even picked a specialty yet."

"I won't be a full scout until November. And by then, who knows what that will mean."

"What did the scouts plan to do after the colony landed?"

"We're here to show you how to live on Asgard, of course. We've been here nearly a hundred years. That's time to learn a lot of Asgard's tricks. You can't survive here if you don't know enough of them. And you can't go back. But if the Kolbergs take over, who knows what they'll do. And even if they don't, you people don't sound like you're going to listen much to us. I know your mother has tried to avoid hurting our feelings – "

"Fat chance."

" – but there have been quite a few things she's said or done that have left us feeling like we weren't part of this program. I'm not sure anyone in the colony realizes what we've been doing while we were waiting for you to arrive."

"I do," Emily said softly.

Guy snorted incredulously.

"Really, Guy. My father joined the scouts. He left us when I was only twelve – about twenty in your years. Mother always hated him for it, but she was always mean to him. At least for as long as I remembered. I used to blame her for driving him away. Anyway, I used to read all I could about the Scout Service and what they did. And when we were selected for a breakthrough colony, I wanted to go to the same star system that he did – only that was impossible, Mother said.

"Then, after we made orbit here at Asgard, I saw a little girl ask her mother if they would be lost down on their new planet. The mother told her that she didn't have to worry, because there were scouts down there waiting to help her find her way. So I know what scouts do, Guy, don't you worry about that."

They were both silent for a long time after that, until Guy became conscious of the sound of his own breathing and the outline of Emily's hair against the faintly lit tent walls.

"Emily?"

"Yes, Guy?"

"What do you do on Earth about birth control? I mean, the girls here on Asgard use biopatches that last two years. I was just worried that – "

"Don't worry, Guy, we use the same thing. What's the matter, don't you want to help build a colony?"

"No, I just – "

"Shhhh!" she hissed as she pulled her sweater off over the top of her head, slid into the sleeping bag beside him and pulled him close. As tired as he was, it was a long time before Guy got to sleep.

***

The thunder of sonic booms echoing off the mountainside woke Guy from a deep and ponderous sleep. He extracted a cold, numb arm from under Emily's head and rubbed his eyes. Then he heard the sound of cheering voices nearby. He looked around for his pants as Emily stirred beside him.

"What is it?" she asked.

"I don't know. I'm going to go look."

Before he finished dressing, he heard a distant voice calling his name. It grew closer, and by the time he'd pulled a shirt, it was just outside the tent. "In here," he called.

"Guy, where are you? Dammit, nobody knows where anyone is this morning."

He stuck his head through the door and saw the assistant patrol leader who'd sent him towards the spare tents the previous night.

"Here I am," he said. "What's going on?"

The scout grinned broadly. "The colonists are landing, that's what. They decided last night to let the Kolbergs rot, follow our plan and get down on the ground before all the good land is taken. We've got two landers coming in right now – den Jasper and den Cornwall. There's another pair due in an hour with all of Middlesex and five more before dark. By nightfall, there's going to be five thousand people here. It's Colony Day!"

Guy could hardly believe what he was hearing. Then Emily stuck her head through the tent flap beside him.

"Are you serious?" she asked.

The patrol leader swallowed hard at the sight of Guy's tent-mate. "Absolutely. There's landers coming down all over the place. Look at the sky."

Guy looked up to see white contrails tracking across an otherwise perfect blue dome, and the elephantine shape of a lander lumbering through the air a few klicks to the south.

"Oh Guy, this is wonderful!" Emily said, throwing her arms around his neck and kissing him on the cheek. "I should have told you – my mother is usually wrong about everything."

"That's why I came looking for you," the other scout said. "Mr. Sanderson called to tell me we should put you in charge of a patrol and have you take the Middlesex den up into Glacier Valley."

Guy felt a lump grow in his throat at that news. He looked down into Emily's eyes and kissed her back. "Come on. We're going to take you to your new home."

***

By nightfall, 22,000 colonists were on the ground, setting up tents, building fires, raising dust, making noise and discovering the hundreds of joys and pains that Asgard had to offer. The radio channels were full of the chatter of excited colonists, announcing their presence on their new world.

"Den Munchen is here in the Upper River Valley, ready to work and ready to serve ... "

"The weather up here on North Lake is a little chilly for us poor farm boys from Texas, but den Austin is ready to start busting sod first thing in the morning ... "

"Tell your children that classes start next week for den Stowe ... "

"Does anyone know where the medical dens landed – we've got two mothers about to deliver a month early here at Lake Geneva and we'd like some help … "

"A hearty welcome to all of you from the scouts at Highland Post … "

And as the setting sun painted wild colors across the top of Mount Loki, the long line of colonists from den Middlesex filed down the hill towards the Valley Post. Guy and Emily looked on, hands locked together, their hearts filled with the bright promise of a new life on Asgard.

DEN OF FOXES

L in Palmer watched the first big wet flakes of snow drift down out of a yellow sky and felt the muscles in his gut tighten up. With a half meter of snow already on the ground, this was the last thing he wanted to see. The only thing that could make it worse would be another blast of cold like the one that followed last week's storm.

He bundled his parka around his face and neck and trudged along the well-trampled path to the greenhouse.

Despite his fears, there wasn't much he could complain about. After all, he knew just what he was getting into when he volunteered for the Asgard breakthrough colony. You had to expect snow on a world in the grip of an ice age, but you didn't have to like it.

Of course, Lin's real problems didn't come from the snow, which was no worse than a winter back in Caribou. It just made all the other things worse.

Like the getting the greenhouse going ...

He paused at the end of the path and unsealed the sheet of plastic that formed the wall of the building – there was no door on the place. Once inside, he checked the thermostat and the level in the water tank. Both were within safe limits.

He looked down the length of the greenhouse in a quick visual inspection of the structure. The place was three meters wide and thirty meters long.

It was high on the north side and low on the south to take advantage of solar warming. The construction was simple enough, sheet plastic over wooden cross-ribs, but it had taken all the capital budget he was allowed by the den and most of his personal labor budget. Even now it ate up the largest chunk of his time – even with Asgard's overlong days. The tiny fusion pack in the corner could pump enough heat for ten times as much space, but only if he could afford to build it.

He had planted four rows deep in native soil under the plastic. The mix included some Incan strains gene-adapted for Asgard's shorter year, a native fruit-bearing species and some old-fashioned Maine potatoes. So far, the best performers were the pepina dulce. He'd picked them because he liked the taste – sort of like a honeydew melon – and because they packed a lot of vitamin C. The potatoes were coming up strong, as was something the scouts called beastfruit that grew on a long vine. South Valley had good soil – mostly loess sediments blown in long ago from glacial outwash plains.

But good soil or not, the cherimoyas weren't doing so great. They looked yellow and pale. The scouts had warned them about that, said they need stronger sunlight.

Lin walked slowly down the space between the rows, checking each cross rib in turn. The plastic was designed to transfer enough of the heat inside to the snow as it fell. The melt water ran down to fill the tank, and then was diverted out a drain hose when the tank was full. But he still liked to check the load on the wooden braces. He was afraid that if one went, the rest would follow like the teeth on a zipper.

A scuttling sound among the pepinas stopped him halfway down the row. Damn it, had a lizard gotten in here?

He peered into the leafy tangle on the ground and waited. The noise came again. He pinpointed it now and turned his eyes toward the potatoes.

There it was. Not a lizard, but a furry gray creature the size and shape of a golf ball. Bytes, they called them. This one had four short pink stick legs, a pink nose and two black eyes. It scurried under a leaf, then stopped and looked up at Lin boldly.

For a moment, Lin felt as if the byte was regarding him with the same surprised amusement that he felt towards it.

According to the scouts, bytes, and their little cousins, bits, were the only mammaloid life on Asgard – and these days they were just about the only life in South Valley. Most of the fuzzasaurs had already migrated south or gone into hibernation for the winter. Bytes, apparently, did not hibernate. Or if they did, they woke up during the occasional thaw. This one must have, anyway.

"You're cute, but I'm afraid you'll have to go. You look like you need a lot of food to keep you going in this weather."

Lin shooed the byte away, making a note to double check the ground seals and to look for its nest. Was there an easy way to make a byte trap? Maybe one that wouldn't hurt the little buggers? After all, mammals should stick together.

After two hours of tending the plantings, patching loose plastic and pumping water, Lin bundled up his parka and squeezed through the greenhouse wall. The snow was blowing furiously now, and the sky had begun to darken to the west. A cold wind was blowing down the path at him, forcing him to bow his head and trudged along once again. A couple of painful minutes later, he was home.

And here was another of his problems. He had no house ...

***

The lack of adequate shelter was just one more parcel in Lin Palmer's burden of suffering since his arrival at Mu Cassiopeiae.

He'd had a house once, a little clapboard place back home in Maine, made of real wood with a fresh coat of white paint and bright blue trim. But that was 25 years in the past now, and the paint had long since peeled off and the clapboards begun to warp. All those years had flashed by between the blinking of his eyes when the breakthrough colony's twenty ships were transformed into solitons and flung at light speed across the vastness of interstellar space.

Lin's disappointments had begun with the colony's bittersweet arrival in-system and the loss of the *Hollister*.

And then there was the struggle over the landing plans ...

The three dens on the *Bates* had included Lin's own, den Aroostook, a Canadian farming den, Jasper, from Alberta, and a school den, Stowe, from Ohio.

Naturally, opinion had split three ways – den Aroostook went against the Kolbergs, den Jasper supported them and den Stowe didn't know what to do. For a few days, while the colonists remained in orbit, sealed in the cramped ships like shrimp in a can, things got pretty tense, with the members of each den bristling at the intransigence of the other – especially as it looked like the Kolbergs were going to get their way. But when den Matanuska on the *Hamilton* mutinied against its Colonial Corps crew the landings began anyway.

Den Aroostook followed quickly, leaving the Kolberg plan in pieces in the wake of their mad dash to the surface of Asgard.

For Lin Palmer, Colony Day had been an experience full of exhilaration and joy. He and his wife, Jackie, had come down in the first wave and spent the night in a tent in the woods near the Highland Scout Post. And the next four nights as well. Then the scouts had led them to the southwest to the den's assigned township, the Palmers and the rest on foot, their personal effects and tents in the few trucks that had been landed.

The landings and the trek seemed like one long celebration, a party to commemorate their safe arrival on the new world. They'd spent another two weeks camped out at the village center while the den organized itself and more of its equipment and supplies were landed.

There was something romantic about living out of the tent, sleeping under the stars in the warm, tropical air of Asgard's brief summer, listening to the chitinoids hum and click and the wild herds of grazing bluenecks lowing and hooting to one another.

It was the middle of July, almost six weeks after the first of the landings, when Lin and Jackie drew their basic equipment and were assigned title to their 64-hectare farmholding. The rest of the den members helped them pack the truck and two of their neighbors traveled with them most of the way along the slow, bumping, cross-country drive. They had pitched their tent once again, now alone in the great emptiness of more than half a square kilometer of land that was all theirs.

The romance had died when the first cold winds of November blew through South Valley.

Late in September, a crew from the den had come through and cleared and fused the foundation slab for the house. And a week later, a truckload of woodsmen came through and cut down a stand of terrestrial pine at one end of the Palmer farmholding and left it to cure by the slab.

But now it was January. Winter was already six days old. It had been four months since the breakthrough colony had landed. And the Palmers still didn't have their house.

The only consolation was that more than half the 95,000 colonists on Asgard were in the same predicament. For all the planning done back on Earth before they left, they had still overestimated by far the number of houses that could be built by the colonists before winter set in.

Lin and Jackie had been low on the priority list – behind families with children and oldsters. But that was before Jackie got pregnant.

"Lin, is that you?" his wife called from the rear compartment of the improvised lean-to that they'd built to expand their living space and protect against the cold.

"Were you expecting someone else?" he asked as he put his arms around her in a hug.

"Yes, but not for six more months – or is it five months now? I can figure out a 30-hour day, but the calendar is going to get the best of me."

"Just as long as the little darling doesn't get it confused."

"Were you out in the greenhouse all that time?"

"Yes," he mumbled. He turned to the kitchenette to get some hot water for tea and braced himself for what came next.

"Don't you think you're spending too much time on that, Lin? I mean, we don't even have a house yet."

He turned a deaf ear to her. Jackie was a shoemaker's daughter, not a farm girl. She didn't understand a lot of how Lin felt. He couldn't explain to her why he'd invested so much capital and labor in the project. He couldn't give her the faith that had carried him this far. He wanted to explain to her how it was going to make the whole surplus for their farm once he got it up to scale, but he was afraid it would only start an argument. And he didn't want to upset the expectant mother of his first child.

"Did you hear what I said?" she asked after a minute.

"My labor budget's been OK'd by the den council," Lin said finally. At least they trusted him – a thought that went unvoiced.

But the truth was that Lin was getting nervous about the future too.

***

Martin Meyers watched the snow fall between the chicken coops, blown by the wind and sticking in big clumps to the plastic ducts that connected the low sheds. The air was still and the sound of the snow splattering on the plastic could be heard over the soft clucking of the hens.

He opened the storage shed and took down the bucket and the chicken feed, pouring a measured amount of one into the other. Then he distributed it among the coops. Next, he went gathering eggs – four dozen by the time he was done. Finally, he began cleaning the coops, working doubly hard on the surfaces to make up for the fact that he wouldn't be able to do the chore tomorrow – he was signed up for ten hours of communal labor.

While he regretted the weekly sacrifice of a day's work on his own farm, he welcomed the advantages that den Jasper's labor pool provided. Unlike many of the Asgard colonists, he had a house already. It was built in September by den work parties and finished in five days – a different party every day.

Den Jasper was a tight-knit family, bound by church and marriage long before the colonists ever left Alberta. Well organized, too. Marty's farm was already obligated to plant sixteen hectares in corn to support the den's dairy herd. The chickens were his choice for a farmyard project – picked from a list of those the den required. He had put a lot of time into building the coops, but he wished he could have put up more of them. The chicks were there for the asking, but Marty's access the den's capital assets was limited. And the way the den council picked apart his labor budget, he didn't see how he could have found time for more.

He sighed at the thought of it, then let the thought go. There would be time. The world was still brand new, fresh and virginal in its heavy coat of ice and snow, the scout-planted pines and native greenwoods coated with white lace. All things could be worked out in time. And with the den's help, they would be.

In the meantime, he wasn't sure he would ever get used to the long Asgard day. He'd grown up on a farm and was used to rising before the sun – but here it was hours after breakfast before the deep golden rays of Mu Cassiopeiae peeked over the shoulder of Mount Loki. By the time dinner rolled around at 1700 hours, Marty felt like he'd put in a decent day's work – but he still faced another four hours of work until suppertime. And then there was paperwork and bookkeeping to tend to after dark. When he finally fell into bed around 2500, he was ready for twelve hours of sleep, but he could get only ten.

Marty grabbed a snow shovel – a piece of packing crate bonded to a staff of hardwood – and cleaned the light cover from the path to the house.

He paused at the back door to admire the handiwork of his denmates. Rough wooden shingles covered the roof, coated with sealant to keep out the elements. More shingles sheathed the exterior walls of the bungalow, with careful woodwork around the doors and windows. The back porch served as a mud room and heatlock to keep the cold wind outdoors.

Long days and short seasons. Autumn seemed to have come and gone in a week. The warm weather had lasted so long – except for the two cold snaps in early September that brought 10 centimeters of short-lived snow. And then suddenly, it was cold and the snow was piling up instead of melting away. The herds of redcrests and the bluenecks went away and the maxidons followed them. The wilburs and orvilles flew off to the south, leaving only the high flying eddies to come down from the Vogelsberg Ridge to hunt for bytes and snow lizards.

With luck, the winter would be gone as quickly as the summer. But spring was still five weeks away – and each week held seven long, long days.

Like every other colonist on Asgard, Marty wondered what kind of miserable weather those weeks would bring.

"Marty, is that you?" Lois called from the study at the rear of the house.

"Of course, sweetheart," he said as he stuck his head through the door. His wife was seated at the keyboard of the household mainframe, going over the planting scheme for the spring. He looked over the numbers quickly and shook his head – how much did she think the two of them could do?

"Hello, dear," she said. "You know you're supposed to go down to the village tomorrow, don't you."

"Oh, don't I," Marty said.

"Do I hear an attitude developing? You're supposed to be glad about your opportunity to work with the your den brothers."

"It's just that Hans Becker is a pain to work for and he's leading the detail tomorrow. And there's so much that I want to do around here ... "

"I think Hans is very nice," Lois said. "Anyway, I want you to find out if the Kolbergs are really going to be at Sunday's services. That's what Ellie Black said, and I want to know if it's true or not. I've got a special dress that I've been working on, and I need to know if I've got to finish it by then or not."

"The Kolbergs? What do they want with us? I thought they'd caused enough trouble before Colony Day."

"Be nice, Martin. The Kolbergs could be very helpful to us. They've got a lot to offer den Jasper and if we're smart, we'll take every advantage of it. After all, they've got fourteen years of experience from their own colony and they're a lot more useful than the scouts."

"Yes, dear," Marty said as he tuned out his wife's voice. Regardless of what she thought, he did not like the Kolbergs. The chaos of those first days in orbit before the landings began had been a terrible time. Marty blamed them for the fear, the uncertainty and the bitterness that had been the result. It was an opinion, however, that he kept to himself, since it was not shared by anyone else he knew in den Jasper – including his wife.

But in the four months since then, the bad feelings left in their wake had long since faded. Today a new question plucked at him. What were the Kolbergs up to now?

Joey Baxter heard the voice of Guy Stanger before he reached the kitchen.

He came through the door in time to see his sister Emily sit down beside Guy and press up against him.

"Why do you eat so much meat?" she asked.

"This isn't meat, it's soup."

"It's got meat in it. Fuzzasaur meat. It's not healthy to eat so much meat, you know, especially fuzzy meat. They haven't had the cholesterol gened out of them like our dairy herds. And besides, you should eat more vegetables."

Joey laughed. His sister was always giving Guy a hard time about his diet. She reminded him of their mother that way, always trying to tell people what to do.

"Hi, Em. Hi, Guy," he said with a wave. "Anyone home yet?"

"No – you're in luck. Where have you been? And why weren't you home hours ago?" Emily asked angrily.

"Just out. Don't worry, I can't get into any trouble around here." He grabbed a piece of fruit from the counter and pulled up a stool.

"You've been hanging around with the guys from the service and transport dens, haven't you." She turned to Guy and said: "Mother tells him not to, but he does it anyway. It's not fair. He gets away with murder and she pats him on the head. I try so hard and all she does is criticize me."

"What're you doing with the serfs and the truckers, Joey?" Guy asked.

"Exploring," Joey said. "I've been riding the trucks ever since they opened the road to Highland Post. It's loads of fun. You're a scout, you know what I mean."

"Don't let him kid you, Guy. He told me last night that he's smuggling tabacky. One of these days you're going to go too far and then you'll really have to pay for it – I hope."

Joey waved her off with the back of his hand and grinned at Guy. "So what's up with the Kolbergs?" he asked.

"That's what I'd like to know. You'd think they would have gotten the message by now. Why don't they go back to Tikarahisat and bother their own colony?"

"Mother thinks they haven't given up on us yet," Emily said. "And it's six years back to Eta Cass. That's a long way to come just to give up after only one defeat. They must have some backup plan that they're working on – that's what Mother says."

"After the way they tried to steal Glacier Valley out from under your feet, I'd hate to see what they've got for a backup plan."

"Mother said we've got to watch them like a fox," Emily said.

"A fox?"

"They're like dogs, only skinnier, bigger and with a long red tail," said Joey. "They're clever and they like to get into mischief. They'll steal the chickens out of your yard while you're watching."

"I know that," Guy said as he flashed an evil look at Joey. "I read books, you know."

Guy helped Emily clean up the supper dishes as Joey began looking for his own meal. He hadn't gotten far when Ray Adamcek, his stepfather, entered the kitchen. He said hello, then retrieved a ripe cherimoya from the fridge and fetched a knife to cut it in quarters.

"You're home awfully late," Emily said impatiently. "Mom's over at the dean's office working on schedules. Joey just came home from who knows where."

"I've been trying to finish up those weather records from the Highland Post," Ray said as he plopped himself down at the table. "You know, Guy, you scouts keep the most incredibly detailed records – storms, temperatures, even little notes about flowers and floods and frosts. But none of you ever tried to figure out the why and the how of Asgard's weather. Didn't you ever get curious?"

Joey found a seat at the end of the table and listened carefully to the conversation. He had discovered long ago that there was a lot to be learned by keeping his mouth shut and his ears open. Until he revealed his own precocious talents by making overly mature remarks, people tended to treat him as if he were invisible – a trait that he did all he could to cultivate. Of course, it never worked with Emily or his mother.

"Sure, I guess," Guy said. "But we never needed to worry that much about what makes the weather go. Theorizing is for people who have the time. I think we always had too much work to do collecting the data to bother sorting out why.

"But now that the colony is here, can't they just put all that stuff into an AI and program it to make the forecasts?"

Ray chuckled and pulled on his long beard. "I'm afraid there isn't any 'they', Guy. Just me and a couple of youngsters who want to be weathermen some day. And I've been working for four months trying to figure out what makes the wind blow in this place. Unfortunately, just when I thought I understood how the autumn weather worked, it turned into winter. You just can't catch your breath around here."

"Do you think it's necessary to predict the weather?" Guy asked. "I mean, we got along fine for 80 years taking it as it comes."

"Sure, but you scouts were putting all your energies into surviving and subsisting. And I don't believe for a minute you weren't predicting the weather in your own unscientific way. The colony's got a bigger agenda than that. We're supposed to grow and prosper, make the soil bloom and all that stuff. There's a lot of hard work and planning involved in that. And success or failure depends on little differences at the margins. Every little advantage or disadvantage gets multiplied terribly when you're starting out on a new world like this, Guy. If we know what kind of weather is coming, we can save time and money for more important things. If we don't, then the waste can mean the difference between success and failure."

"I guess so," Guy said.

"And there's a political dimension to it, too," Emily added. "The dens are competing for resources and prestige. The ones that make a big surplus are going to be the ones that take the lead in everything else. The dens that are having trouble getting by aren't going to have time for much but survival. And with the Kolbergs around, that can mean trouble for us."

"You've been listening to your mother, haven't you?" Ray asked with a smile. Emily forced a smile back at him, but it wasn't a strong one. "She's right, isn't she?"

"I'm afraid so."

"All the more reason to find out what the Kolbergs are up to," Guy said. "Like I said before – I wish I knew what they were still doing here."

"I'm afraid it's easier to predict the weather than it is to predict what people like Peter and Eric Kolberg are likely to do."

"I don't know," said Guy. Than he looked down the table and locked eyes with Joey, who felt a sudden warm flush across his face. He'd been discovered. "But I've got an idea … "

***

Joey sat on the edge of his bed, pounding the keys of his tablet, going over his figures one more time, when the knock came at the door. He blanked out the screen, slid the tablet under a pillow and said, "Come in."

It was Guy. That was a relief – he'd been expecting Ray.

"What are you up to, scout?"

"Nothing," he replied, trying to hide the nervous excitement that had filled him only a moment earlier. He worked hard at keeping his expression from betraying him, but it wasn't enough. Guy wasn't buying it.

"They tell me down at the Main Post that you've been talking to scouts about buying tabacky."

"Well … "

Guy smiled. "Come on, Joey. I've got no reason to turn you in to your mother. Tell me what you're up to. I need to know if you can help me with something."

Joey weighed his options, then decided that the only thing that would satisfy the scout would be complete candor.

"Well, if I'm right, and nothing goes wrong with my plans, I going to be the richest 13-year-old – correction, 22-year-old – on Asgard."

Despite his tender years, Joey was anything but childlike in his ambitions. He saw life in the new colony as an unparalleled opportunity to become powerful beyond the limits of adolescent imagination. He was a careful student of history – particularly the history of old Earth's colonizing days. He was acutely aware of the number of the rich and powerful men of exotic places like Hong Kong and Hawaii who had been youngsters when the colonies were young. He planned to take every advantage of that historical tendency – despite the best efforts of his mother, his stepfather and his older sister.

While the adults were busy establishing their dens in townships up and down North Valley and South Valley, Joey also had been active, developing a lucrative enterprise all his own.

Now, with the completion of the road connecting Glacier Valley here in the east with the Main Post in the center and Highland Post in the west, he was ready for business.

He had a product: tabacky. The dried weed was a habit straight out of the Dark Ages, revived during the decadent years just before the dawn of the New Era. The old vice had been pathological – ingesting carcinogenic materials on a daily basis for years. But the modern plant (which had proven highly useful as the base for a number of geneing projects) had been gened to remove the carcinogens, the toxic chemicals and even the active biological agent, nicotine. Instead, the plant now produced a variety of natural endorphins and flavoring agents that made the smoke more agreeable.

Centuries-old social customs discouraged tabacky-smoking in public back on Earth, but here on Asgard, new customs were bound to emerge – less restricted by the crowded societies of the home planet.

"Did you ever smoke the stuff yourself?" Guy asked.

"I tried it once. It made me sick."

"And you really don't have any qualms about selling addictive drugs to people? I mean, your sister won't even let me eat meat."

"Tabacky's not addictive – no more than chocolate, anyway. I've read the studies. That's a lot of Dark Age propaganda. And here on Asgard, there's no mass production facilities. The average dose is smaller than in the Dark Ages, so you can't have constant consumption."

"Who are your suppliers?"

"The Jewell brothers." The two farmers from den Matanuska, which shared Glacier Valley with the university, had planted a patch up at the far end of the lake shortly after Colony Day. They'd had it gened once more to adapt it to Asgard's rapid growing season, and at the end of September they had harvested their crop. Since then it had been curing in a shed on the Jewell farm. Now the process was complete, and the tabacky had been pressed, shredded and packed into one-kilogram packages.

"We've got about 200 kilograms, all together."

"And transportation?"

"Den Pullman." For weeks, Joey had been making friends with the drivers in the transport den. The long rides up and down the length of South Valley had been part adventure and part business. First he had to gain the confidence of the truckers so he could find out which of them would be willing to help his enterprise. Then he had to use the them as contacts to meet colonists who might become customers.

And he had customers. There were settlers up and down the valley looking for the comforts and amenities of life back on Earth. Raw living on the frontier seemed just a little more palatable with a pipeful now and then. Most of the dens were producing some kind of alcoholic beverage – from sweet wines and malt liquors to distilled spirits. Tabacky was a little more ambitious in terms of startup investment, but that made it harder to supply. And for Joey's purposes, that was perfect.

"Sounds like you've thought of everything," Guy said.

"Almost."

"What's your problem?"

"Well, I'm not sure what I'm going to do with all the money. From what I can see, the cash economy here on Asgard is going to be pretty limited for the next few years. I could spend it on fried nunas or spineycones at the university canteen – but I get sick of that stuff after a while. Once some of the specialty dens get up and running, I can probably use it for clothes and stuff. But if this is as big as I think it's going to be, what am I going to do, Guy?"

"I can think of a lot of things, Joey, but most of them don't involve money. Do you really think the dens are going to let you do this?"

"I don't know. How can they stop me?"

Guy just shook his head.

"Anyway, scout, it sounds like you are in just the right place to do me a favor."

"What's the favor?"

"I want to find out what the Kolbergs are doing. I thought you could try playing spy for me."

"Me? I don't know, Guy. I haven't got anything against the Kolbergs. They look like they're doing the same thing I'd do if I were in their position."

"Who's side are you on, Joey? The Kolbergs are a bunch of thieves. They tried to steal the whole colony away from you when you first arrived. And look what they did to Jeannie Gilmartin."

"Jeannie was raped by LeClerc and he was a scout."

Guy snarled, and Joey was suddenly afraid at the young man's anger. "LeClerc was from Tik, just like the rest of them. Be honest with yourself, Joey. Would you really rather have the Kolbergs running things on Asgard?"

Joey let his imagination play with that idea for a minute and realized what it could mean to his own ambitions. There could be no native prodigies in a colony controlled by offworlders – only young Kolbergs would benefit under those conditions. He shook his head sharply.

"No way, Guy. I guess you're right. What do you want me to do?"

"Here's what I had in mind ... "

3

The truck was a marvel of engineering. The body was a seamless plastic shell that would not rust, flake or crack for forty years. The tires were a constructed of a memory plastic, a solid core surrounded by a semi-rigid frame. The power plant was a fusion pack electric motor using torque induction that could be removed to serve as a windlass for farm work. Every part in every system was designed to last for decades.

But it did Lin Palmer absolutely no good buried up to its floor boards in mud.

And the strands of frost blossoms, robin eggs and other snow flowers that had wrapped themselves festively around the wheels did nothing to improve his mood.

He felt like crying, but was too scared to let himself go. And he didn't want to upset Jackie.

"What are we going to do, Lin?"

"We'll just have to get it out of there," he said.

"But how?"

"I don't know. I'll have to think about it for a minute and figure it out."

But Jackie was already upset. She had mud all over her hands, face and legs, she looked exhausted, and Lin was sure she was just as tired as he was of the dry, warm wind that had been blowing since early morning. The wind was the problem.

Lin had noticed it shift before sunrise. The tent poles had creaked and crackled as it backed around from the southeast to the west. Then it picked up in force and began to blow steadily as the sun came up. When he went out to tend the greenhouse he was amazed to see the snow withering before it.

Before lunch, most of the meter of snow that had covered the Palmer farmstead had been reduced to a few patches in the shade of the apple trees. The rest of it had melted away, leaving behind a thick mat of yellow-white grass and the mud. Endless mud, thick and gooey, that clung to his feet and sucked at his boots.

If he had known what to expect, he would have left the truck where it was, secure on the fused foundation slab for their unbuilt house, next to the tent on the only dry spot for 800 meters. But at the time, he had been in too much of a hurry.

That was because shortly after 0900, Lin had discovered a more serious problem than a mudstuck truck.

He was inspecting the outside walls of the greenhouse, leaving a trail of foot-shaped ponds as he plucked his way through slushy mounds of wet snow. The south side of the structure showed no damage from the quickthaw. But as he came around to the north side, what he saw almost made his heart stop.

The ground was subsiding, slipping away in crumbling, frothy bits towards a two-meter deep gully full of rushing snowmelt. It didn't look like regular erosion, but some kind of subterranean effect, where the soil seemed to be collapsing in on itself as the ice that had bound it together turned to liquid.

The near edge of the subsidence was only three meters from the greenhouse – a distance that shrank as Lin watched.

His blood roared in his ears and his heart pounded in his chest as he envisioned all his labor and capital washed away in the quickthaw. What could he do?

His thoughts were drawn to the logs stacked to dry on the foundation. If he could use them to brace the crumbling bank, shore it up against the underground drainage ...

Lin had rigged a tow rope around one of the logs. Jackie drove the truck while he tended the line. Together they dragged three of the logs into place by the side of the greenhouse. They had been working on the fourth when the ground turned to mush.

Now Lin tried to weigh the limited time he had against the speed with which the ground was giving way. Would three logs be enough? What about the smaller trunks he needed to anchor the big ones?

"Help me disconnect the powerplant," he said to Jackie.

"What are you going to do, use it pull the truck out?"

"I guess I could do that. If I anchored it to that pine tree over there." When the connections were all broken, Lin pulled the 50-kilogram motor from the truck and lugged it through the mud to the trees. He returned to the cab and broke out the tackle and anchors and the rest of the gear he would need. Then he started looking at the truck, the trees, the greenhouse and the fourth log. If he wanted to start moving things around, he'd need a lot of rope. There was more in the back of the truck. And before he moved it out of the mud, that last log would have to go into place ...

He never actually decided to abandon the truck to the mud. He just kept giving other things higher priority.

Of course, he didn't bother explaining that to Jackie.

"Lin, what about the truck?"

"What about it?"

"Aren't you going to get it out of the mud?"

"Later. After I do this."

"But – " She stammered and sputtered. "Why do you always have to do everything your way?"

"You mean one thing at a time and by myself?" Lin asked with practiced sarcasm. "Because it's the only way I know how."

***

"The way I see it, you're going to run into two problems," Cord Jackson said as he eased the truck up onto the roadway from the stop at Camp Falls.

Joey's eyes were flying everywhere, drinking in the view from the high cab of hectares of broad savanna They rolled quickly past rolling snow-covered plains that stretched off towards the highlands to the north and south. The dark shapes of distant houses and tents on the farmsteads gave evidence to the impact of the human settlement on a plain where a few months early great crowds of grazing fuzzasaurs – redcrests, bluenecks and duckasaurs – had roamed freely. Joey wondered what would happen in the spring when they returned.

"Now I ain't exactly an expert on the subject, but everyone's got a little business sense. And what you're doing here is a business, you know. In any case, the problem I see you having is that you've only got a limited amount of that stuff. Now how much of that tabacky do you expect someone to smoke in, say, a week?"

"For planning purposes, I've estimated fifty grams."

"Oh yeah?" Cord said, a puzzled expression across his face. Joey realized that he had thrown the truck driver off balance with his ready answer. "Anyway, how long do you figure your batch will last?"

"Using fifty grams per week, I calculate twenty customers a week for each kilogram and four thousand customer-weeks. That breaks out into a thousand customers for four weeks, five hundred for eight weeks and two hundred for twenty weeks. I'm working on the using the last combination."

"Oh yeah? You really got this figured out, don't you, kid?" Cord rubbed his face with one hand while he looked upwards. "Well, in any case, when your customers are done smoking up what you've got, when are you going to get more?"

"I'm not worried about that, Cord," Joey said. "That won't be until the end of September. By then, we'll grow some more."

"I guess you will at that."

Cord kept his advice to himself for the rest of the trip.

They rode west up the valley, cruising along at about forty kilometers an hour. The road was still shiny and new, fused silicon-oxides from the sandy soil, and thirty meters wide. That gave them room to pass the farm trucks that streamed along the road at less than thirty.

Camp Falls had been a 90-minute ride from Glacier Valley, through the den Matanuska holdings in Hartsbridge township. Joey met his first customer there, Carlos Rivera, a farmer with den Imperial. Rivera was a big man, wider at the waist than the shoulders, with a handlebar mustache and rosy cheeks. He treated Joey with amused respect, exaggerated deference and a hearty laugh.

"Care to strike a blow for freedom?" he asked as he filled a clay pipe with the yellowed weed.

Joey declined the offer, but took the payment for two kilograms of tabacky and returned to the truck.

In the next hour and a half, they passed through Scoutpath

township – named the for the route they followed – and into the Main Post.

Joey was always impressed by the original scout settlement on Asgard. It had been the center of human activity on the planet for 55 years – that was 93 Asgard years, he calculated – and was full of ingenious machinery, aging equipment and scouts and enough arcane memorabilia to keep him occupied for a month. But today he was on business and had no time to dally.

He found his next set of customers at the horsebarn, Jimmy Gilmartin, Andy Osborne and Phillip Sanderson. The scouts were anxious to try the new treat from Earth and fell all over one another to open the packages Joey had delivered. They thanked him, stuffed his pockets with the scrip used for money by the colonists, and waved him on his way.

After a few minutes, Joey and Cord were on their way again, across the valley plain to Center Township. The new hub of civil society on Asgard was only a few klicks down the road from Main Post, on the far side of the landing field.

This was the closest thing to a city on the planet, and that was no accident. The colonists had been forced to choose, on short notice, between a plan offered by the scouts, with a few modifications of their own, and one presented by the Kolbergs. The Kolbergs had called for a powerful city with half the colony's population concentrated in one or two townships. Instead, they had chosen a decentralized plan with a smaller center and a more dispersed population.

Although he'd grown up in the sprawling, crowded arcologies of Earth, Joey had come to regard Center as the epitome of human activity. Seven dens – more than 11,000 inhabitants – all packed into a couple of square klicks, with a Main Street, shops and stores, a hospital and a courthouse. Why, some of the buildings here were three stories high!

Once again, though, this was not the market he was looking for. This was the turf of one of the service dens, and those scions of Earth's urban centers cultivated a more refined set of vices and habits. He had realized early on that tabacky would be too mild a pleasure for them.

"Here's the depot, Joey," Cord said as he pulled into a large lot full of trucks, buses and other vehicles. "I think Pat Turley's heading on up to Highland Post, if that's where you plan on going."

Joey reached under the seat, pulled out his backpack and looked in at the six remaining packages of tabacky. "Thanks a lot," he said, as he slipped from the cab. A short time later, he was on his way out of Center in the cab of Turley's truck.

The ground was more rugged in the west of end of the valley, rising up from the river banks to the lower slopes of Mount Thor in steep, rocky ridges. In between were more flatlands, still covered with white snow, but dotted with silver ponds of melting slush. The wind had become rough and dry and quite warm.

Joey was surprised by the contrast from earlier in the morning. This wasn't the kind of weather he usually encountered. Warm winds were usually moist and came out of the east.

He pondered that question as the truck came around a low hill and crossed a piece of what looked like broken pavement. Joey was still trying to figure out what could have broken the fused surface when he began to feel lightheaded. He wasn't dizzy, though, merely falling.

The truck tilted downwards as the road beneath it slipped away, collapsing out from under itself. The cab of the truck lurched and bumped and rolled, then crashed to a sudden halt. Joey's seatbelt cut into his shoulder, but held him firmly, which was just as well, because the truck ended up nose down.

"Are you all right, young fella?" Cord asked before groaning softly. "I think so," Joey replied.

"What happened to the road?"

"I think it was a washout. Is the truck all right?"

"No power. I don't think so. Let me get out and look – as soon as I catch my breath."

Joey started to work on his seat belt, then noticed that his hands were shaking. He paused and tremors passed through his body several times before he brought them under control.

It was another ten minutes before either of them worked their way clear of the cab. Then Cord let out a low whistle.

"What is it?" Joey asked as he came around to the other side of the truck.

"The power plant's been ripped right off the axles," he said. "Must have, happened on the way down that slope. See the motor back there? That means we've got no motor, no power and no phone."

"What do we do now?"

"Start walking, son."

Joey didn't realize that he'd left his backpack behind until he had been walking for more than half an hour. The shock of it made him realize how dazed he was by the crash. Even so, he was not happy with himself.

"Sometimes, Baxter, you act like a damned adolescent," he said aloud.

"What was that?" asked Cord, who had unzipped his jacket and pushed back his cap in the warm wind.

"I forgot my stuff back at the truck."

"We'll pick it up later. It's only a few more klicks to the village. Just over this rise."

Just over the rise was nothing but another empty stretch of road. Joey was disheartened, and Cord cursed. They began walking dejectedly down the slope and had gone nearly three hundred meters when a small farm truck rolled up over the crest of the hill behind them. It slowed to a stop beside them, and the two farmers inside called out.

"Are you two from that truck back up the road?"

Cord nodded.

"Are you all right?"

"We could use a ride," the truckdriver said.

They piled into the back of the truck and a few minutes later, they were at the village center.

Joey could tell by looking around that this township had only one den for a proprietor. Many of the villages around the colony served as home to the service and educational dens, but there were also a substantial number of solos. This wide spot in the road to Highland Post boasted a lodge, a meeting hall, several cow and horse barns, storage silos for the animal rations and warehouses for the colonists' rations.

"Welcome to den Jasper," said one of the farmers as they rolled to a stop in front of the lodge. They helped them find their way inside and introduced them to the folks there. Within a few minutes, the women were stuffing cakes and apple cider at Joey, and the men were talking about repairs with Cord.

They decided they would organize a repair team to see if the truck could be salvaged. But the expedition itself would have to wait until one of the work crews returned to the village to lend a hand. Over the next two hours, Joey found little to keep him occupied. He had his fill of pastries and cider, wandered around the lodge, found a library with little of interest and peeked into offices that were dark and uninviting.

Then, in the main hallway, he came across the community bulletin board. The screen was filled with notes, messages and announcements. He reached up and touched the tags on the items that looked interesting and read through them quickly. Most of it was simple ag-den business, about as interesting as watching corn grow.

But this last note wasn't.

"Meet the Kolbergs – Reception after Sunday Service at the Lodge. Eric and Hannah Kolberg, Miles Verstig, Peter Vandenberg and Lillian Roman. A chance to socialize and talk shop ... find out what our friends from Tik can do to help den Jasper grow and prosper."

A few minutes later, he was at the main office again, asking to use the phone. The young farmer behind the desk grinned, then obligingly led him down the hall to the communications center. Shortly after that, Joey was talking to Guy Stanger.

"Joey, where in the world are you?" he asked. "And why are you calling me?"

"I'm at den Jasper. Our truck broke down."

"Your truck? What truck?"

"Never mind that right now. I need you to do something for me. You have to tell my mother where I am and tell her I'll probably be spending the night here."

"I don't know, Joey. What's going on?"

"I can't talk now, Guy. But it's real important that you tell my mother and fix things with her so she isn't mad at me or anything."

"And why should I do that?"

"Because you owe me the favor. After all, I found what you said you were looking for the other night."

"You did, did you?"

"Yeah. I'll tell you all about it when we get back."

"All right, Joey. We'll see you tomorrow."

A short while later, the repair team was mustered in the yard in front of the lodge. By now, the ground around the village had turned into a sea of mud. Joey tugged at his feet as he struggled to keep up with the men.

One of the farmers looked down at him with a stern, inquisitorial expression as he started to climb aboard the truck.

"I left my stuff back there. Cord said I could go back and get it."

He felt his life hang in suspense for a moment as the farmer narrowed his eyes in disbelief. Then Cord spoke up. "Come on up here, Joey. Keep out of this wind."

In a second, he was aboard the truck and they were on their way.

It only took a few minutes to reach the site of the crash. Sliding soil had drifted around the wheels of the truck, but otherwise it was still in the same embarrassingly helpless state it had been in when they left it hours ago.

While the men inspected the damage and surveyed the situation, Joey climbed up onto the truck and opened the door to the cab, hoping to retrieve his pack without notice. But when the door was open wide, he was hit in the face by a wave of fluttering chitinoids, dozens of them, all glittering with bright spots of color on their black enamel shells. They filled the cab of the truck and spilled out in a cloud.

Where had they come from? And why were they in here?

When Joey reached under the seat and pulled out his pack, he knew why. Inside, where six kilos of tabacky had been, there was a mass of silvery chite eggs. A chite bloom! The quickthaw had brought out a colony of chites, which had stumbled across the pack in its search for an organic base to plant its eggs.

His heart sank as he realized what this meant to his dreams of enterprise.

***

It had been a long, hard day for Marty Meyers. In the morning, he and his denmates had worked knee-deep in freezing water to shore up a wooden bridge across a brook that had swollen to river proportions. After low noon, they had gone on to rescue a barn whose foundation was undermined by the quickthaw. And after late noon, it was towing duty for a dozen trucks that had gotten stuck in the mud.

The sun was already ducking behind Mount Thor and the warm, dry wind was beginning to take on a chilly bite to it when their truck rolled back into Jasper village. The men stumbled stiff legged and sore into the community hall and made a direct attack on the coffee stand. Marty joined them, even though the substitute the hall used for real coffee was almost undrinkable.

They had only been there for a few minutes when when Hans Becker showed up. Marty had been relieved that morning when he reached the village and discovered that Becker wouldn't be leading the work detail. Now that Hans was back, he felt a knot growing in his stomach. Whatever he was up to, it had to be bad news, judging by the smile on the man's face.

Becker took a seat at the table beside the coffee pot and put his tablet down on the table. One by one, he called the men over to him.

After a couple of minutes, it was Marty's turn.

"I've got some difficult news for you, Martin," he said. "I'm afraid we're going to have to increase your communal labor requirements by at least five hours a week."

"What?" Marty snapped back in surprise. "What for?"

"We've been talking it over on the council, and considering the problems we had to handle today – and the likelihood that they'll be hitting us again – we've had to readjust our work schedules. This isn't the first time we've had to do this, and every time, we fall farther and farther behind on the goals we want to meet before spring. I'm sure you realize how important it is to have everything in place when the cold is gone – especially when you look at how little time we'll have to get things done. Six-month years are a little hectic when it comes to planning."

"You've got to be kidding," said a man behind him. It was Tom Hoffman, one of the more outspoken members of den Jasper.

"I know – you've already got more than enough to do," Hans said. "But the den has its own demands, and we're all going to have to make sacrifices if they going to be met."

Martin felt the anger grow inside him. This wasn't the way to handle something like this. There should be a council meeting – and a vote. Hans had no business making an announcement like this without being on solid ground.

"Did the Kolbergs have anything to do with this?" asked Hoffman.

"I don't know what you mean."

"Sure you do. This is part of their management plan, isn't it?"

"The Kolbergs?" Marty asked, looking back at Hoffman.

"The den council's been talking to them about their management and consultant services," he said. "The word around the village is that upping the communal labor budget is the quickest way to improve our productivity. That may not be a problem for people like Hans here, but for the rest of us it's a real problem. It may be quiet now, but in a few weeks I'm going to be busier than a two-credit hooker."

"Sorry, Tom, that's the decision."

"Well I think the decision stinks. Who's running this den – us or the Kolbergs? What do you think, Meyers?"

Marty, who had stayed back during the argument, looked up sheepishly. "I don't think you're going about this the right way, Hans. Shouldn't something like this be put before a den vote? It's one thing if we all agree to it, but I don't want the Kolbergs making up my labor budget anymore than Tommy does."

"Look, you two," Hans said. "The Kolbergs know more about making a colony successful that either one of you do. If we follow their advice, we can be one of the leading dens on Asgard. If we don't, we could end up like den Aroostook or even worse."

Hoffman just sneered. "That's easy talk from a man who doesn't have a farm of his own to take care of."

That seemed to get Becker's temper up. Marty watched as he started to turn red in the cheeks. "What's that supposed to mean?"

"It means that anyone can call on more communal labor if they plan on keeping their land fallow for a couple of seasons like you."

Becker rose from his chair and reached across the table to grab Hoffman by the jacket. "Why you – "

Hoffman tried to pull back, but he just dragged Becker further over the table. Marty reached out without thinking, trying to break the two of them up. He caught a hold of Becker's wrists and tried to break his hold.

But he wouldn't release Hoffman, and Marty's interference only served to throw him off balance. The only thing that kept the three of them from coming to blows was the sudden collapse of the table.

The men leapt back as the urn of steaming hot coffee felt to the floor and black liquid splashed at their feet. Hans Becker flew backwards, cursing loudly at both Hoffman and Marty Meyers.

Marty backed up, heading for the door. He just wanted to get into his truck and start the long, bumpy drive home. But before he left, he caught sight of Becker, being calmed by a couple of his friends.

"I won't forget this, Meyers," he called as Marty stepped out into the cold.

Ray Adamcek felt a tingle of excitement race up his spine as the ground fell away from him and streamed swiftly towards the rear of the scoutship. He gripped the arms of his seat as the ship buffeted its way through the turbulence layer, then beamed wide-eyed out the windows as the stars began to emerge.

But he cut his star-gazing short abruptly as he realized he was missing an opportunity to observe something even more tantalizing – the weather over the Prime Site, Mount Thor and Mount Loki and the colonists in North and South valleys.

He rode on the port side of the ship as they flew into the sunrise, giving him a wide view of the land to the north. As they climbed higher and higher, that view grew to encompass the great continental glaciers that gripped the northern quarter of the planet – or at least the perpetual clouds that clung to their hems. Foul weather was a certain constant under those clouds – rain that fell in unending torrents and winds that blew unceasingly.

Off to the west were the Ragnarok Mountains, of which Thor, Loki and Odin to the north were but the lowest teeth on a jaw that descended into to the sea. Glaciers clung to its peaks and valleys in a braciating pattern that reminded Ray of frost on a pane of glass.

The upper-level low that had brought the snow and then the Chinook winds to the valleys had turned into a full-fledged storm, running north up the coast into Bifrost Bay, dumping great loads of snow as it pulled moisture in from the sea and up the steep coastal mountains.

"Bad luck, those Chinooks," he said as he noticed the pilot relaxing his grip on the controls and turning the ship over to the AIs. The pilot was a scout, an old-timer with cracked brown skin, a fringe of short white hair high over his ears and permanent smile. His name was Abe Johanson.

More information than that, he would not divulge. Ray wondered if putting up with eight decades of Asgard winters had made him so taciturn.

Nimbus, the little AI in the shockproof plastic case, provided more conversation than Johanson.

"Chinook – also known in Europe as foehn winds. Air descending down a slope warms adiabatically and becomes dry."

"That's right, Nimbus," Ray said. "A common occurrence in the American Rockies and the European Alps – and on Asgard. Only this one took us by surprise. Half the colonists got hit by it somehow. Even some of the scouts were surprised."

"Surprised by the size of the melt," Abe said. "Don't usually have that much snow on the ground."

"That's right. The average for this time of year is more like ... "

"Twenty centimeters," Nimbus said.

"Sounds right," Abe said, nodding his head.

"Now if they had know it was coming, I'll bet it would have saved a lot of people a lot of work."

The scout looked up at Ray with a questioning look in his eyes. "If I'd known it was coming, I probably would have told someone," he said after a moment's pause, before turning back to his AIs.

Ray ignored him and looked back out the windows to the north. This was what he had come for. He had studied the statistics, the charts and the notes the scouts had accumulated over the past 93 winters. He had run a few models through Nimbus. But he still didn't have a feel for the twisting patterns of shifting wind and air masses that determined Asgard's weather.

No – for that kind of understanding, he needed something else. Something more direct and immediate. He had to watch the weather as it unfolded its drama on a continent-sized stage.

And for the next few days, he would have a reserved seat, front row center, for the performance.

***

Sunday was not a good day for Lin Palmer.

By nightfall Saturday, he had succeeded in shoring up the muddy slopes that had threatened his greenhouse. It had taken a quarter of the logs set aside for his house, but in the end, he had a retaining wall, staked in place and braced with cross beam, covering the lower side of the ditch. In addition, the rushing stream of melting water subsided, and the erosion slowed as the afternoon heat faded and the wind died down.

That should have told him something right there, but he was too exhausted by that point to think straight.

The next morning, Lin and Jackie found themselves surrounded by a world of frost. During the night, a mass of bitter cold air had slipped down off the northern glaciers. The lingering moisture on the ground, drawn up to the surface by the Chinook wind and then the dry northern air, had turned to a fine dusting of shimmering, glittering diamonds that coated the world.

The fusion plant in the front half of the tent was working overtime to keep the place warm – a hard job. with all the lean-to's leaks and gaps. Lin barely had his boots on when the awful realization hit him. His truck!

He pulled on his parka as he rushed out the door, leaving Jackie protesting behind him. He ran across the yard, his feet clunking heavily in the hard-frozen soil, to where the mud-stuck truck still sat, buried up to the hub caps.

The snowflowers had died, leaving behind brittle gray tendrils where they had grown. The ground had refrozen, deeply, during the 16-hour night. And the truck, which had only been stuck the day before, was now encased in an unbroken expanse of ice and mud.

Getting it out would take a power hammer and a backhoe.

He felt his throat constrict and his eyes water as he realized that the heavy freeze had also eliminated the threat to his greenhouse by stabilizing the soil and ending the quickthaw, making all the previous day's work unnecessary. He could have spent the afternoon getting his truck out of the mud instead.

If only he had known – if only someone had warned him about what the weather would bring next.

"It's called a Chinook wind and they explained it on the school net last night," Jackie said when he came back inside.

"What?" he asked, holding his anger and frustration inside.

"The warm wind yesterday. They explained it on the network last night. The wind blows down off the mountains and gets dry and warm. It happens a lot in the winter, the scouts say. Too bad no one warned us."

"Yeah, too bad."

"Too bad you didn't get your truck out of the mud."

"Yeah."

"Now what are you going to do?"

"I don't know. When's the next wind coming through?"

"That's a good question ... "

***

Marty Meyers was almost late getting to church. He'd spent too much time puttering around the chicken coops trying to make sure they'd stay warm. The cold air that blew in overnight worried him, but the fusion plant was doing a fine job, and his efforts weren't really needed.

Lois complained all the way to the village. He half-listened, knowing that she would not stop until they arrived safe and on time. And when they did, she was hardly satisfied, but held her tongue at last.

The entire den had assembled and the yard was full of trucks. Marty dropped his wife off in front of the meeting hall and found a place to park.

The service was just beginning by the time he found his way back to the hall. Lois had found a seat in the last row, and he joined her just as the first hymn began.

When the singing was over and the prayers finished, Pastor Gant rose and greeted the congregation. From where he sat, behind most of the 1,600 members of den Jasper, Marty could not see the minister, but Gant's amplified voice echoed off the ceiling overhead.

He began by mentioning the number of sick children and oldsters who couldn't make it to the service. "We have sixty cases of mud pox, but the folks at den Schweitzer have given us a counter-virus to take care of it. And there are another forty with the wheezer bug – including Alice Clarkson, who, as you all know, is the oldest member of the den, although she has asked me not to reveal by how much. The doctors say that she's doing well and the antibiotics are working just fine. I'm sure all our prayers go out to Alice and all the rest of our brothers, sisters and young ones."

Marty shifted uneasily in his seat. He never did enjoy services. Lois was the one who had brought him into the church in the first place and had pushed him to sign up for the breakthrough colony ten years earlier.

She loved the social environment, the chance to trade gossip and inspect new dresses and shoes – though there wouldn't be any new shoes on Asgard until the apparel den was all set up for production.

"Now I'm afraid I have to turn to a less charitable subject," Pastor Gant said. "As many of you are aware, the den has been working recently with our neighbors from the colony at Eta Cassiopeiae. The Kolbergs and their associates have been very kind to us and have offered us all kinds of help in getting den Jasper set up and functioning. I'm not sure how many people realize it, but they have strong ties to our synod on Tikarahisat and they've said they want to help us keep in touch with them, to the extent possible given the time it takes to travel there. After today's services, there'll be a reception for Eric and Hannah Kolberg and some of their friends.

"But I'm afraid there is a sour note being struck here. The den leaders have called my attention to the fact that some of the den members have been stubborn and uncharitable towards our newfound friends. There's been some complaining and even a few incidents that we won't bring up at a worship service.

"The point I want to make, however, has to do with this church as a community. It's very important that we join together on issues as important as this. One of our strengths as a den is our sense of oneness and our commitment to one another – both as church members and as den members. The two go hand in hand and cannot be separated.

"Now there are some among us who think they know better than the den council and den leaders what we should do. Their prideful attitude hurts us all and threatens to divide us as a group. As your pastor, it is up to me to curb this kind of behavior and this kind of attitude.

"To do that, I'm afraid I will have to take steps that I find painful and regrettable, but necessary. Those of you who feel that they cannot support the den in its decision to rely on the Kolbergs for guidance and aid have put themselves beyond the brotherhood of this den – and beyond the brotherhood of this church. If you persist in your attitudes, I'm afraid I will have no choice but to exclude you from communion – beginning next week."

Marty hadn't been listening too closely – talk of the Kolbergs bored him more than anything else. But the congregation fell into stunned silence at that last remark, and Marty shook his head, uncertain that he'd heard Pastor Gant correctly.

The pastor quickly went on to the next hymn, which Marty suspected was a ploy to get everyone busy singing instead of brooding about his threat. But with Marty, it wasn't successful. Without communion, you weren't part of the church, he realized. And if you weren't part of the church, how could you be part of the den?

The rest of the service went slowly, punctuated by nervous rustlings among the members. Communion took a long time, with hesitant communicants shuffling up the aisles eyeing one another suspiciously. Because of their location in the hall, Marty and Lois had to wait until the last wave.

With a sigh of relief, Marty rose from his knees and returned to his seat, glad that the service would soon be over. It was, but the ordeal was not.

The reception for the Kolbergs was a more festive affair than the long worship service. The food was unspectacular for the most part, with cakes and pastries made up from the bland rations available to the colonists. Next year, when the planting began and the harvests came in, it would be another story, but for now they were still dependent on the food they'd brought with them.

Lois made her way through the crowded hall, Marty in tow, as she looked for her friends and co-conspirators in the Sunday gossip exchange. Marty remained oblivious to them, nodding politely and keeping an eye out for the men, who could swap some useful information about den business when their wives were otherwise occupied.

He didn't see Pastor Gant until the last minute. Gant was an older man, gray at the temples with a face full of creases. He shook Marty's hand and grabbed his arm above the elbow – then refused to let go. He put an arm around Lois and pried her away from her friends.

The pastor did not have a smile on his face.

"Martin, Lois, it's good to see you here today," he said. "It's always nice to have everyone at the service."

They nodded and smiled nervously.

"Martin, I hope my message this morning wasn't lost on you. Especially after what happened yesterday, if you get my meaning."

Lois looked sideways at her husband, who felt his face grow warm. "What happened yesterday?" she asked.

He started to explain about the incident between Hans Beck and Tom Hoffman, but the pastor beat him to it. Unfortunately, he had only heard Beck's version of the story.

"Let's just say that Martin and brother Hoffman were more spirited than prudent in their actions," the pastor said. "A word to the wise should be sufficient."

"But I didn't do anything," Marty protested as Gant walked away.

"Marty, how could you?" Lois cried. "What are you trying to do to me? You heard what the pastor said this morning. If you don't like the Kolbergs, you'd better keep it to yourself. And if you don't do something to set things right, you're going to be in big trouble with me."

She spun on her heel and walked off, pushing past a few surprised denmates and leaving Marty sputtering at empty air.

6

Ray Adamcek floated weightlessly in middle of the cabin, watching the roiling clouds of Asgard's turbulent atmosphere swirl and spin in the distance.

"This is the only way to study the weather – all at once and with the naked eye," he said.

"Naked eye?" asked Nimbus from the corner where it was tethered. The AI had no eyes, and Ray wasn't sure if it could process information visually. The neural networks in its holographic brain were a world unto themselves.

"It's just an expression," Ray said. "Things aren't the same as the last time we were up here, are they?"

Back in September, they had been up in orbit to watch a pair of tropical cyclones that threatened Prime Site.

The storms had boiled up without warning, cooking quickly in the long afternoon sun. They had spun off, one behind the other, careening towards the two valleys where the fresh colony was still settling in. But much to his surprise, they had smashed themselves against the coastal mountains and been quenched by a sudden supply of glacial air from the north.

The scene today had changed significantly in the course of a couple of months. Now the jet stream and the region of prevailing westerlies had dropped southwards, pushing before it the tropical pattern that dominated Prime Site in the summer.

"The weather patterns are not similar," Nimbus agreed. The scout pilot had retreated to his cabin for the better part of the flight, leaving Ray with only the AI for company. It did not improve his disposition.

"Forecasting this stuff is a bitch. The systems move through so damn fast, you hardly have time to give a decent warning."

"At 25 degrees latitude, Pettersen's formula indicates long wave velocities of 12 degrees of longitude per day and short wave velocities of 28 degrees per day," Nimbus said. "That equals 30 kilometers per hour and 75 kilometers per hour respectively."

"I'll take your word for it," Ray said. He knew the numbers were right, though, and that was the problem. The long waves, the progression of high pressure ridges and low pressure troughs, dominated the air circulation of the hemisphere. The short waves, the cyclones and anticyclones, rode upon the long waves.

"Great fleas have little fleas upon their backs to bite 'em. And little fleas have lesser fleas, and so ad infinitum."

"Big whirls have little whirls that feed on their velocity. And little whirls have lesser whirls, and so on to viscosity," Nimbus replied. "L.F. Richardson, 1881-1953 A.D."

"Oh yeah?"

"The first meteorologist to attempt to predict weather using the laws of physics."

"I knew that."

Ray turned his attention back to the pattern of clouds before him. The scoutship hung in a medium-high orbit – not far enough out to be synchronized with the planet's rotation, but at a sufficient distance to give the weatherman a good look at Prime Site and the region to the west where most of its weather originated.

Since the first day he arrived, when a sudden outbreak of glacial air dropped the temperature from 20 degrees down to -10 in an hour, Ray had not ceased his amazement at the surprises this world held. The sight of a funnel cloud turned bright white as it filled with snow was one that he would always remember with awe and wonder. And the way the high speed jet stream clipped the tops off thunderheads gave them an appearance that was unique to Asgard.

But the more he watched the weather, the more he appreciated the delicate balance between heat and cold that drove the circulation of the planetary atmosphere. If he could just figure out how that balance worked …

Winter found the jet stream coursing by just south of the glaciated regions of the Ragnarok Mountains and just north of Prime Site. The topography and the permanent high pressure system of the mountain icecap tended to keep the stream confined to these limits.

To the west, however, were several cyclone-producing regions. Two of these had a critical impact on Prime Site. The nearest was the Avalon Sea, which drained the melting verge of the glaciers and channeled it northward and westward to the sea. And beyond that was the low land in the lee of the Albion Mountains.

The storms boiled up out of the sea or the lee of the mountains and were carried east at a fast clip, where they fell upon the unsuspecting colonists without warning, sometimes dumping a meter of snow on them before blowing out to sea. They were followed alternately by the Chinook winds that melted the snow in unexpected quickthaws and outbreaks of cold air that froze the world solid.

The series consisted of two or three cyclones, which hit or miss the colony on their eastward trek, depending upon their will, followed by a final storm that pulled down cold air from the north, freezing the mud, snowmelt and everything else.

The complex balance of energies between the Avalon Sea and the Albion Mountains determined the number, course and severity of the cyclones.

"I think I'm beginning to see the way these things fit together," Ray said. "But I'm still not there yet. Maybe if we program you to model the patterns we can figure out what makes this system work ..."

"Perhaps," said Nimbus. "But we have tried that before. All I've been able to do is produce a copy of the pattern – not a predictive formula."

"Let's try it anyway," Ray said.

"Your wish is my command," the AI replied.

***

Den Middlesex being a secular group, Joey Baxter had never spent much time in church. His mother's wedding was the only exception that came to mind, and that was brief and bearable. The den Jasper service, on the other hand, had struck him as long and strenuous, with a lot of standing up and sitting down and praying and singing.

He was glad it was over, especially when the women brought out trays of pastries and the men carried in big urns of coffee and jugs of cider. He contented himself to stuffing his face for the first hour, trying to blend in with the other children who streamed through the big meeting hall. He mingled with the adults as much as he could, doing his best to look innocent and uninterested.

But in actuality, he was listening hard to all that was being said. Eventually he tracked down the guests of honor at the reception – Eric Kolberg, his wife and their partners – and stationed himself nearby, his back to them to act as protective coloration.

At first, he overheard little that was useful, but his ears perked up when they mentioned a smaller meeting to be held later. He noticed that few invitations were being issued to that get together. And he also noted the time and location – after supper, in the library at the lodge.

He was careful to get there well in advance of the invited guests. He inspected the place carefully, looking for a suitable hiding place from which he could eavesdrop on the conference. The pickings were slim. The library was a large room with four walls lined with empty shelves made of rough wood.

A cabinet in the corner contained a few dozen electronic readers and a hard disk at one end held the den's supply of books, journals and manuals. In another corner sat a desk with a terminal and keyboard.

The cabinet was impractical for hiding unless the shelves were removed, and the desk offered only the kneehole, which faced the open room.

Then Joey looked up. There was no ceiling, only a high loft with cross beams and the underside of the steeply pitched roof. The space was dark and inviting – if he could find a way up there.

He tried standing on a chair, but the rafters were out of reach. If he put the chair on the table, though ...

A moment later, hanging from the beam by his hands, he hooked the chair with one foot and swung it back over the floor. He lowered it as far as it would go, then let it drop. He held his breath as it teetered for a moment, then righted itself on all four legs. He found a dark corner towards the center of the lodge to sit in, satisfied that he would be invisible to anyone seated at the table.

An hour passed before the Kolbergs and the farmers of den Jasper began straggling in.

Joey had never shared his mother's antagonism against the Kolbergs. They way he saw it, they were just trying to do the same thing he was, only on a larger scale. Even now, his main interest was their potential as an obstacle to his own ambitions, as young and unformed as those may be.

He had never imagined just how big an obstacle until he heard them talk.

"Back on Tik, we were six years in getting organized – Earth years, just to keep you from getting confused," Eric Kolberg said. He was a tall man, with blond hair, but a dark complexion and dark, thick eyebrows that gave him brooding, sinister look. "The other colonists were too involved with their own problems to recognize what we had to offer. The laws and rules that they had drawn up were based on a silly idealism, a romantic attachment to a past that never was. They were not geared for the future here among the stars that is available to those who are wise and bold enough to seize it.

"I hope you are not going to make the same mistake."

The plan that Eric Kolberg described was certainly bold. The pooling of resources and capital in a strong development bank, central planning and distribution of investments, rapid build up of industrial facilities like mining and manufacturing, and overall management of the colonial dens by the Kolbergs and their allies. Joey began to picture the robust urbanized economy that would result from all of this and grinned at the audacity of the Kolbergs.

The development plan that the colonists had brought with them called for a slowly expanding society where half the dens would work the soil to provide food and the other half provided the special skills and services that an advanced technological society required. This plan called for the farmers to leave the land and come to the cities that the Kolbergs hoped to build here on Asgard. The opportunities were endless, Joey realized. But only for the Kolbergs and their friends.

And the farmers from den Jasper were eating it up.

That was what scared him the most. It hadn't occurred to him that the colonists of Asgard would harbor the kinds of attitudes that den Jasper had cultivated. They were proud and arrogant, certain of their special place in the universe, sure that they would do better than their neighbors because they were favored by God.

At first, Joey thought it was a lot of superstitious prattle. But they really believed this stuff.

"The Lord must surely be smiling on us," said the man beside Eric Kolberg with a silly grin and wide-eyed stare. "He has brought us to this new world, given us this rich land and provided us with allies who will help make us strong and wealthy. I think we owe Him a prayer of thanks."

With that, the rest of the farmers bowed their heads as he led them in prayer.

Joey just shook his head in disbelief. Wait until Guy heard about this.

A day of cold air, brisk wind and deep blue skies passed before the weather warmed up enough for Lin Palmer to free his truck. Late in the afternoon, when the sun had had time to turn the soil back to mud and the wind had shifted around to the south, he hooked up the powerplant to a sturdy pine tree and connected the cable to the towing brace.

Jackie sat behind the wheel while he took up the slack, put on a strain and, finally, eased the vehicle out of the mire. Lin reeled in the line as his wife guided the truck up to the grove of trees, where the roots held the soil together more tightly and the mud was not so greedy.

"I wish I'd known it was going to warm up sooner," he said. "Don't they have a weather forecast service on the network? Or is it all just gossip and recipes?"

"If you'd plug in once in a while you'd find out," Jackie said. "The university ag-service has a program that can help you with your planting schedules. And the school dens can tell you things you never knew about this place – like how to get sweet juice from the conifers and where to look for chites when they get into your crops. In a couple of months, you'll be wishing you spent more time on the net."

"But still no weather, huh?"

"No – not yet. But if that's what it'll take to get you to pay attention to what the rest of the colony is doing, maybe we can get them to add that too."

"The rest of the colony isn't stuck in the mud with a pregnant wife and no house," Lin said.

Jackie just reared back and regarded him with a look of stunned disbelief. "You'd be surprised how many of the colonists are in exactly that situation, Lin. Only half of us have houses and at last count, a third of the women on this planet were pregnant. And now your truck is out of the mud. So how come you're feeling sorry for yourself?"

Lin tried to think of a snappy response, but decided against it. There was no way he could win. He had a better idea.

"I'm going for a walk," he said.

He kept to the high ground, away from the mud, even though the sun was dropping toward the slopes of Mount Thor and the air was losing its pleasant warmth. Ben Cormier's farmstead was to the west and Ed Laureno's was to the north, but he didn't feel like talking to Ben or Ed. Ben was an older farmer with a pack of adolescent children, and Ed's wife didn't like Lin much, so he kept a neighborly distance. Instead, he traveled east, towards the border between den Aroostook's township and den Jasper, the adjacent settlement. Darkness wouldn't come for another couple of hours, even with the winter sun hugging the southern horizon.

The air grew warmer, even as the setting sun lost its power, and Lin kept up a quick pace. It wasn't long before he came upon the narrow stream that marked the township line. The gravel along the banks marked where the quickthaw had produced a strong flood. Now the water had receded to a manageable size, and a few meters upstream he found a natural rock dam that also served as a crossing point.

He hoped his neighbor from Alberta wouldn't mind an uninvited guest, but maybe it was time he paid a call on the fellow – whoever he might be.

***

The first thing Lin noticed was the line of small sheds behind the wooden frame house. The next thing was the sound of chickens clucking and crowing inside the sheds.

He hesitated, nervous about meeting strangers, then walked up to the back door and knocked. For a brief moment, he wondered how he would feel if the quiet peace of his home was suddenly disturbed by an unexpected knock – especially on an alien world 25 light years from all he had once called home.

Then the door opened swiftly and a young man about his own age thrust his head out into the balmy air. An hour later, all of Lin's uneasiness had fled and been replaced by a sense of warm camaraderie. While he loved his wife very much, he still had a need for alternative companionship that he realized was sorely missed.

The farmer's name was Martin Meyers, and his wife, Lois, fed him cider and apple pie while the three of them discussed farm life and their new world. After a while, Marty took him on a tour of the chicken coops. They stopped in the storage shed for privacy, Martin offering Lin a seat on a box of chicken feed.

Much to Lin's surprise, the two had a lot in common – and a lot that set them apart.

"Sometimes my wife can make me feel like a dog with pie on his face," Lin said forlornly.

"I know what you mean," Marty replied. "It doesn't do any good trying to explain things. Women just give you that look – you know the one I mean – like nothing you say has anything to do with what they want. It's like they've got a whole set of rules that we're never going to learn."

They talked about den business and their farming problems. Lin never knew there was so much to raising chickens. And Marty was sympathetic towards Lin's problems with his truck and his greenhouse.

"If we knew what was coming at us, we might have a chance," Lin said. "Doesn't anyone know what the weather on this place is going to do?"

"Beats me. But it sounds like you've got more problems than that. Why doesn't your den do more to help you out? Everybody in Jasper's got a house by now. I can't understand why they let you live in a tent."

"We just let people take care of themselves, I guess," Lin said. "It seems like the natural way to do it. Never was any different back home. You know what they say – you can tell someone from Maine, but you can't tell them much."

Marty just shook his head. "It still doesn't sound very helpful. What happens if you get into trouble?"

"I suppose the whole den'll be out to my place if I really need them. That's just the way they are. The rest of the time, they'll leave me alone."

"Sometimes I wish our den was more like that," Marty said. He told Lin about the problems with Hans Beck, the pastor and the

Kolbergs. "That's why I have to give another day every week in community labor. It doesn't hardly seem fair."

"Ayuh, it sure don't. Never did like them Kolbergs, though. Doesn't sound right for them to come here. Makes you wonder what they did back at their own colony and why they had to leave."

"From what I've heard, they left on their own. They were doing all right back on Tik, I guess, and wanted to try it out over here – before the colony had time to settle in and make the same mistakes theirs did."

"I don't know," Lin said. "I think every man's got the right to make his own mistakes. It's the only way he can learn anything. What kind of world are you going to have if you can't do that?"

"One where a man can't learn," said the farmer from Alberta.

"And one where a man's got no rights," said the farmer from Maine.

***

The next day, Marty Meyers drove through thick snow squalls to bring his eggs into the village, pressing through rising mounds of wet slush and across the combination of gravel fill and drain pipes that forded the stream beds between his farm and the center of the township. When he had finished unloading the plastic crates and registering his production with the warehouse clerk, he headed over to the ration center to pick up the week's supplies. Hans Beck caught him on his way into the building.

"Martin, we'd like to talk to you for a minute over at the lodge."

Big white snowflakes swirled through the air as Marty swallowed hard and fell in step behind the assistant den leader. What did they want now?

The two men stamped the snow and ice from the boots in the

entrance to the lodge, then Beck led Marty down the hall to a small office, which already held another man – Marty recognized him as Miles Verstig, the Kolberg associate who had attended Sunday's reception.

"What's this all about?" Marty asked.

"Have a seat," Beck said as he went around behind the table with Verstig. Marty sat down in the empty chair facing them.

"We heard you had a visit the other night from a farmer from den Aroostook. Is that correct?" Beck asked.

Marty shrugged. "Sure, what of it?"

"Why was he there?"

"I guess he was lonely. He said he had a fight with his wife." Beck smirked and turned to Verstig.

"How long did he stay?" Beck asked.

"About two hours. Just until dark. Then he walked home. I think he has the farmstead on the township line. Listen, Hans, what's this all about? And what's he doing here?"

"We'll ask the questions for now, Martin."

They went on for twenty minutes, until Marty had lost his patience and his good-natured desire to cooperate. They wanted to know what the two had talked about, how much Marty had told the other farmer about the den's operations, its plans and programs, and anything else they could think of.

Most of the questions struck him as petty and motivated by a hostile suspicion that reduced any natural human impulse on the part of Lin Palmer to some clever, subversive plot. He didn't like it.

All through the questioning, Miles Verstig remained silent. Then, when Beck was finished, he spoke up.

"What did this Palmer fellow tell you?"

Marty was tired of being intimidated, but he thought he had restrained himself admirably. He didn't want to give Pastor Gant further reason to question his commitment to the den, or Lois further cause to hold him responsible for their social ostracism. He had tried to choose his words carefully while remaining honest.

"He told me about the troubles he's been having with his wife, the weather and his farm. The kind of thing that any farmer would talk about with his neighbor. Or don't they do that kind of thing where you come from?"

He regretted letting the sarcasm slip out almost immediately. Apparently he wasn't being as careful as he thought he was. But Verstig ignored it.

"What kind of problems with his farm?"

Marty told him about the truck, the greenhouse and the quickthaw, and Palmer's worry about his capital and labor budgets. That seemed to satisfy both Verstig and Beck because they fell silent after he finished.

"Thank you very much, Mr. Meyers," Verstig said. "You've been a great help."

Beck wasn't nearly so polite. "We'll see you tomorrow for community labor, Martin."

On his way back to the ration center, Marty thought over the interrogation he'd been subjected to and wondered at the reason behind it.

Why were the den leaders and the Kolbergs so nervous about what other dens knew?

Then another question arose in his mind. How did they know about Lin Palmer's visit?

A sick feeling overcame him as the answer came quickly but unhappily – Lois must have told them.

For three days, winter storms buffeted the farmsteads, townships, villages, settlements and scout posts of North Valley and South Valley. The first of them dumped 15 centimeters of snow on the ground. The next day, another 10 centimeters fell. And less than fifteen hours later, the third came through, mixing snow and violent winds.

White tornadoes ripped through South Valley, tearing up the landscape and narrowly missing the village of den Regan, which contained den Stowe, a school den, in addition to the leadership and support workers for the farmers. The only casualties belonged to a family of five whose house was smashed into splinters by the storm.

And of course, the storms struck virtually without warning.

For Lin Palmer, the bad weather was an even worse break. Just before the first storm hit, the Aroostook den council sent word that the house building crew would be out to his farmstead first thing in the afternoon. When the snow began to pile up before low noon, his spirits had sunk and with them his hopes for improvement in his miserable lot. That night, the snow piled so high on the tent that the poles began to sag and he had to go outside and brush off the snow every half hour. The winds picked up and the snow began to drift across the lean-to. Faint drafts carried icy crystals into the shelter and the fusion pack was unable to keep up with the heat drain caused by wind, ice and mounting snowpack.

The greenhouse suffered too.

Like the tent and lean-to, it was impossible to keep it warm enough to melt the snow as it fell. The structure wasn't even as strong as the tent, and Lin spent much of his time rushing from one end to the other trying to keep the snow from crushing the fragile framework.

The second storm hit just as he finished recovering his strength from the first. Another day of frantic effort left him exhausted, unable to contemplate his next move or anything else, for that matter. When the third storm struck in the middle of the night, there was almost nothing he could do.

He tried to keep the greenhouse secure, and sometime after midnight he found that the snow had drifted around the high side of the structure and shielded it from the wind. The blowing snow couldn't pile up on the rest of the frame, saving it from collapse. He blessed his luck and returned to the shelter, where Jackie was struggling to keep the place warm.

The two of them held each other under extra blankets, and Lin slept fitfully, dreaming of his new house, which was now as unreachable as his old home in Houlton.

The dawn came in with a bitter, raw blast of glacial air, straight off the icepack, dropping temperatures to 20 below. Only the snow piled around the lean-to kept them from freezing inside.

But nothing that happened that day kept away the chill that wrapped Lin's heart.

Before lunch, the message came across the network from the den council. The storms had caused so much damage that there was no way of telling when the construction crews would be able to get out to Lin's farmstead for the house-raising. They would let him know when their plans were more certain.

And after dinner, with the sun trying vainly to heat the frigid air that was the true hallmark of Asgard, the strangers arrived.

There were two of them. One was from den Jasper and called himself Hans Beck. The other was from six light years away, Miles Verstig of the Kolberg group.

***

"What we want to do is to help you achieve all that you can," Verstig said. "We can help you build your greenhouses. We can help you make sure the ground doesn't wash out from under them. We can even help you get a house built, if your own den doesn't come through fast enough for you. You could have a very prosperous future on this planet if get the help you need – and we want to give it to you."

"That's awfully generous of you," Lin replied.

Verstig was smooth, the farmer recognized that. And his offer seemed sincere. But there was something about his delivery, something about the way he smiled and the way he kept using Lin's name like he was a long lost cousin or something. It didn't sit right with him. The truth of it was that Verstig was just another flatlander – another tourist who'd come down east asking directions. The fact that were trillions of klicks from home didn't change some things.

And the way Beck just sat there, silently, like a buzzard on a branch or a guard dog ready to pounce, didn't help ease Lin's mind.

"It's not generosity. It's an even trade. This contract is your labor bond. When you get your farm operation going, when everything is working the way you want it to, you can work off the investment with us."

"At only one day a week?"

"That's what the contract says."

"And you say other people are signing up?"

"That's right. Ben Cormier, your neighbor to the west just came aboard. We're putting up a barn for him in a couple of weeks."

"Have you talked this over with our den council?"

At that, Verstig frowned and looked down.

"I have to be honest with you, Lin. We aren't going through your den council on this. Can I tell you something in confidence?"

"I guess so," Lin said, not sure what difference it made.

"Well ... some of your neighbors aren't too happy about the way your den council has done its job. You aren't the only farmstead without a house up. And there's a lot more your den could be doing for you. Frankly, I'm surprised you don't have a community labor pool. A lot of the other dens do that – like den Jasper. Everyone puts in a day a week, sometimes even more, to help build community projects. It seems fair to them, so I don't understand why den Aroostook doesn't use the system. But that lack shouldn't penalize you. That's why we're here – to go across the den lines and bring people together. That was one of the mistakes we made back on Tik when we first landed there. The dens were too self-contained, too rigid. No one would work with each other. We don't want to see that happen here."

"I suppose you don't," Lin said. "You make a good argument. I don't know if I can give you a good reason not to sign your contract."

Lin thought Verstig's mouth was beginning to water at the prospect of getting his name on the labor bond. Lin took a secret pleasure in his next move.

"But I guess it won't hurt to think it over for a few days, don't you agree?"

Beck frowned and made a sound that resembled a snarl. "For Pete's sake, Palmer, can't you make up your mind?"

But Verstig cut him short with a chopping wave of one hand. Lin thought he could see a flash of anger in the offworlder's eyes as he glared at Beck.

"Take it easy, Hans. Lin's got a lot on his mind right now, I can tell. The weather's been rough on everyone the past few days. I do agree with you, Lin. Take all the time you need to decide. We'll be back in a few days to see if you've seen your way clear to take us up on our offer. Hans, let's be going."

When they were gone, Lin turned to his wife.

"What do you think?"

"Labor bond? It sounds more like labor bondage. What's going to happen if you get called away to work for them and we need you back here. They're going to want you just about the time that young little Palmer here needs you the most," she said, patting her belly.

"It sounds like a guarantee that we'll get what we need to make the farm work. I just don't know if it's worth the price – or if I can trust them to keep their word. I'm going to have to read this contract carefully before they get back. If the weather holds out long enough, that is ... "

Ray Adamcek worked quickly to direct the scoutship's planetary sensors towards the critical areas to the west of Prime Site. Densitometers, infrared scopes, water vapor detectors, all were geared to measure the pressure, temperature and humidity of the shifting air masses that composed the vast circulating machine of Asgard's atmosphere.

Time was short now. These were to be the ship's last few orbits, and he wanted to get all the information he could.

The scouts had planted weather monitoring stations in the great emptiness of the continental interior. They even had posts on the shores of the Avalon Sea and in the wide prairies that stretched between Prime Site and the Albion Mountains. But their coverage wasn't enough to give Ray what he wanted – a quantification of the atmosphere in all its parts.

Somewhere in the numbers would be the clue he was looking for – the key to predicting the winter weather that bedeviled the colonists down on the surface.

"How are we coming?" he asked Nimbus.

"Data stream is correct and continuous," the AI replied. "Low pressure systems are building strength in Critical Points One and Two."

"That's what I want to hear."

Critical Point One was over the center of the Avalon Sea. The shallow waters of the Avalon soaked up the sunshine and stored its heat, returning it to the cold air that poured down off the icecap. The clash between the two regimes gave rise great spinning masses of warm, wet air, continental lows that shook loose from their foundations and spun quickly to the east along the jet stream.

Point Two was in the lee of the Albion Mountains. To the southwest of the mountains was the Akkadian Desert. Hot air boiled up out of the desert and stirred the atmosphere, but carried little moisture. The disturbances crossed over the Albion Mountains and reformed in their lee, reinforced by the jet stream as it dipped southwards after passing to the north of the Albion icecap. These dry cyclones interacted with the moist storms that blew out of the Avalon.

And what Ray wanted to know was just how the two sources fed one another to create the weather that pounded away at the Prime Site.

For a week now, he had watched the clouds that hung over the permanently dank waters of the Avalon as they turned. He had followed the dry winds east of Albion. He'd had Nimbus record the progression of weather fronts and cyclones and play it back at high speed, trying to track the transfer of great energies as revealed by the shifting winds.

The answer was almost within his reach now. He knew it. The weather patterns played themselves out over and over again. Even his dreams were filled with the spiral shapes of continental storms.

The trouble with Asgard was that the great ice fields that covered the top quarter of the planet compressed the normal temperate zone. Cold fronts that would have run from north to south back on Earth were pushed southwards and stretched from west to east. Storms that would have tracked from southwest to northeast, or from northwest to southeast, had nowhere to go but eastwards, straight across the valleys chosen by the scouts decades ago to be the first home of the settlers. Whatever mischief the storm generating centers of the continental interior could brew wound up crossing over North Valley and South Valley without fail.

Ray had watched helplessly as the string of cyclones pummeled Prime Site. As each one arose, grew stronger and spilled down the great river of a jet stream towards the ocean, he felt a terrible sense of powerlessness. Somehow, the equations of planetary circulation should be able to predict the inexorable advance of the storms. But there was just so much information to integrate ...

"Seen enough weather yet, Doc?"

Ray was startled by the sudden sound of Abe Johanson's voice. The scout pilot had emerged without warning from whatever cubbyhole he'd been inhabiting for the week.

"Not nearly," Ray said, covering his discomfiture as well as he could.

"Sorry about that, but we'll be going down in another hour or so anyway. Make sure you've got your gear secured. That one, too," he added, poking a finger at Nimbus.

"Aye, aye, skipper," the plastic laser brain replied.

"Did you get what you came after?" the pilot asked.

"Models are running at 30 percent accuracy," Nimbus said. "Data enhancement has averaged 78 percent. Not quite, chief."

"Ignore him, Abe," Ray said. "I didn't quite get the answers I was looking for, but I think I'll have it worked out in another day or so. The information we got up here was more than enough, though. Thanks a lot for the help."

"No problem. It's our pleasure to be of service," the scout said before disappearing back into the ship to prepare for the landing.

Ray took one last look at the skies above the Prime Site before he began gathering up his tablet, notepads, pencils and other gear. He noticed a gathering of clouds to the west of Mount Thor as an upper level low began to sweep in from the continent. More Chinook winds for the colonists. That was bad news. Maybe even a little foul weather further east, close to the coast, once the moisture from the ocean fed into it.

He had an uneasy feeling in the pit of his stomach as he thought about the speed with which the weather changed down there. Once again, the colonists were going to be caught off guard. And it was up to him to change all that – if he could.

The scoutship's orbit carried them on towards the sea, leaving the view of the weather over Prime Site behind, as Ray strapped Nimbus into a niche in the corner and stowed his gear in a locker, and Abe Johanson returned to take the controls.

***

Stanger asked him to spy on the Kolbergs. It seemed like much longer. After the accident and the evening in the loft above the library at den Jasper, he'd had to find a way back home.

The trucker who rescued Cord Jackson and recovered his load was not a friend of his, and Cord had little influence with the man. So Joey was stranded at den Jasper on Monday.

The washout on the highway had shut down the bus service to Highland Post, so he couldn't use that. In the end, he had to walk halfway home, watching as local farm trucks rolled on by without a pause while he slogged his way to Center Township. He arrived there too late for both the last bus for Glacier Valley and Cord's aftersupper run to den Bunyan, so he had to spend the night in the travelers' hostel.

It was almost lunch time on Tuesday before he got home, and, for the first time in his life, his mother was ready to kill him. Guy's intervention would have been enough to get him safe conduct on Monday, but by Tuesday, even that was insufficient.

So Joey spent the rest of the week confined to quarters, allowed out of his room for classes and meals only. It was a tough punishment, but it allowed him to put off the painful business of telling the Jewell brothers that the chites had ruined the first load of their tabacky crop.

All in all, it was not a profitable season so far.

When Guy returned to Glacier Valley on Saturday, Joey's mother released him from his confinement. She told him it was credit for his espionage work and for his good behavior.

Guy was sitting at the table in the kitchen of the lodge when Joey came downstairs. Through the window behind him, he could see the turbulent clouds of a snow squall, painted orange and gold by the setting sun. The wind whistled as it tugged at the shingles on the roof and sought chinks in the window frame.

"So how's the tabacky business?" Guy asked.

"Don't ask," Joey replied.

"You mean you haven't become an overnight success?"

Joey told him about the chite infestation. "I talked to the entomologist here at the university. He said the chites that got into the stuff are tree-borers. Their instinct is to borrow through the outer bark of one of the conifers to plant their eggs. The plastic wrapping on the packages was the same kind of surface, so I guess they thought there was no place like home."

"Too bad."

"I guess so. I haven't told the Jewell's yet, though I suppose I'll have to soon. They're not going to be too happy. I think I'm going to end up owing them some money."

"I hope the rest of your trip wasn't as big a flop," Guy said.

"The trip home was no party. But I think the whole experience was worth it on balance." He told Guy the story of the reception and the private meeting at den Jasper – and then some.

"The truckers say they've seen the Kolbergs and their friends everywhere. You should get a list of the dens that supported them before the landings and see if it matches up with what they told me. And it's even worse than you figured. They couldn't get control of the whole colony before we landed, so now they're going after it piecemeal. One den at a time. Even one farmer at a time.

"Their idea is to sign agreements with everyone they can. Get everyone obligated to them. Get their fingers in everything. They haven't given up on us at all, Guy. They still want their city. They still want power. They're just being a lot more clever now than they were at first, that's all."

"Like a crowd of rippers," the scout said.

"Yeah. Or like a den of foxes – that's what Mother calls them. They're too clever."

"They don't seem to be hiding it, do they?"

"Not that I could see. Sure, they kept their real plans secret. I was afraid I'd fall out of the rafters and get in big trouble Sunday night. But they come and go in the open. Maybe they figure we can't do anything about it even if we know what they're up to."

"Maybe they're right. What can we do?"

"I don't know, Guy. I thought about it all week long. I'm only thirteen – I mean twenty-two – so maybe I haven't thought of everything. But the Kolbergs are taking advantage of our weak points. They're going after the dens that are already easy to control – like den Jasper. They're nasty out there. Always telling everyone what to do. Have you ever been to church? It's not a lot of fun, I'll tell you that. The farmers out there really believe all that religious stuff.

"And they said they want to go after the farmers from the other dens. The ones who aren't making it through the winter. That's the part that's scary. I mean, who cares what den Jasper does – they get what they deserve. But the others, the little guys like the Jewell brothers, they could get into real trouble listening to the K's."

"I know. I'm not sure what we can do for them. Winter can be real wicked here. We've always just sat it out, but I don't know how much the colonists are going to be able to take. Your stepdad seems to think it will help once he gets the weather figured out. Maybe it will, but I'm not sure how. I guess every little thing we can do to make the farmers stronger will help them hold out against the Kolbergs. But you can't do anything about the weather, even if you know what's coming ... "

Joey just reflected Guy's glum expression. "I don't know, Guy. It doesn't look good."

They sat in silence for a few minutes while the wind rose and fell and rain splattered against the windows.

Then, all of a sudden, Joey's sister, Emily, burst into the kitchen, her wet hair plastered against the sides of her red face.

"Guy! Joey! Where's Mother?"

"Upstairs," Joey said. "What's wrong?"

"It's Ray! His scoutship was supposed to land a little while ago. Only it disappeared on the final approach. Guy, they think he crashed!"

Ray Adamcek sat alone in a boat, pulling at the oars. With every stroke, he lifted the oars out of the water, slipped them back in and pulled again. The sky overhead was dark gray and threatened rain or worse, but all his attention was drawn to the little whirlpools that formed in the lee of the oars. Families of them were spawned each time he pulled back against the oarlocks, miniature tornadoes, tiny cyclones, pulled down into the water by the complex and powerful changes in pressure caused by the stroke of the oar.

Somehow, those shifting vortexes seemed to stay put, despite the swirl of water around them. He couldn't understand why, but something told him that if he did, all his troubles would be over.

Then the sky opened up and a great torrent of rain fell on him and the boat. In what seemed like a second, the little hull had filled with water. He pulled in vain against the oars, but the boat went nowhere but down. The water washed over the sides, the boat acted like an anchor and before he could do anything about it, Ray had slipped beneath the waves.

Once under water, he drew in a deep breath, surprised that his lungs filled with air and not liquid. Then he awoke with a startled gasp.

His head spun and his back hurt. A small emergency light behind him illuminated the twisted compartment that had once been the control deck of the scoutship. He turned to look around and the edges of his vision closed in.

Then it struck him. They had crashed. He tried to recall the last few minutes of the flight. Abe Johanson had said something about the way the weather was closing in on the Main Post. He hoped he could clear the Vogelsberg Ridge before it cut them off completely. Then they flew into a thick bank of dark clouds. Ray remembered warning the pilot about the wind shear as they made their final approach. But the actual crash remained a blank spot in his memory.

And Johanson. Where was he?

"Abe? Are you all right?"

There was no reply. "Nimbus? Are you there?"

"Am I where?" the AI answered. "Shock overpressures of great force were unmeasured. Pilot Johanson is not responding. Have we landed yet?"

"In a manner of speaking," Ray said. Then he spotted the unmoving shape of the pilot's body, a deep gash along one side of his head. The eyes were open but lifeless.

Ray tried to move towards him to take a closer look. That was a mistake. He felt something give way in his back. His legs went numb. Then his hips. He was seized with panic as adrenaline coursed through his veins and his heart pounded. He felt light headed and almost passed out.

"Nimbus, I think I've been injured badly."

"Diagnostics show no damage to my systems," Nimbus answered. "Is the pilot inactive?"

"Yes. And I'm afraid I may become inactive too."

"You mean dead."

"Exactly."

"It is a state not unlike CPU deactivation, is it not?"

"Yes, it is. Only I can't be reactivated."

There was silence for a moment, then Nimbus said: "The winds shall cease to blow for you and the rain to fall?"

"That's a nice way to put it."

"I am sorry, Ray."

"So am I."

Ray felt the air in the compartment grow cold and heard the sound of dripping water somewhere to his right. The hull had been breached, the power systems all shut down and the scoutship was as dead as its pilot. If a rescue party discovered them soon, he might survive. But it they did not, he did not expect to.

What a shame, he thought, to miss the Asgard spring.

And he still hadn't figured out its winter yet. The poor colonists, what would they do? He felt another wave of panic begin to rise within him and started talking to head it off.

"Nimbus, I may not have much time left so you've got to help me work this out. Somehow or another, we've got to sort out the secret of the winter weather patterns. I thought I'd have a few days to do this, but I guess not. Damn it, it's not fair. At least back home I would have had someone else to talk this over with. Here there's no one but Pendergast and Small – and you Nimbus. I know you're all hard workers and well meaning, but it's not the same. I mean, it took hundreds of years for meteorologists to figure out Earth's weather – and they still get it wrong once a week. How did they expect me to figure Asgard out on my own?"

Then he remembered his dream, and the urgency with which he had watched the tiny whirlpools behind the oars. Why had they remained stationary as the liquid flowed around them?

He described his dream to the AI, babbling nervously. "So tell me, Nimbus, why do the whirlpools stand still?"

"I'm sorry Ray but I am unable to speculate on unreal and imaginary phenomena."

"Ha! Too bad – that's one of the great joys of being human, you know. Probably the one I'll miss most. That's all right, I know the answer. They're caused by pressure differentials and not the motion of the water itself. The interaction of two masses of moving water. Just like storms. The clash of the two masses gives rise to chaotic, but stable releases of energy.

"You know, Nimbus, the low-pressure centers that boil up out of the west are just like the little whirlpools in my dream. The air masses and the winds move according to the physics of expansion and vorticity, but the storms aren't just air masses, they're pressure phenomena, pulled along by a little bit of chaos."

"Yes, I understand the analogy. But we've always known that. How does it help us solve the problem?"

"Because it points the way to the crucial measurements. If we look in the right place in the right time, we can make the right predictions."

And that was the solution to the problem, he realized suddenly.

"Listen to me, Nimbus. I have something very important to tell you. I think I've figured out the mechanism behind the western cyclones. You must remember what I tell you, use it to integrate the data we collected, and then apply it to our forecasting model."

"Aye, aye, Ray."

"The cyclones come in families. We knew that, of course, but we didn't know what to look for to predict their number and course. But they aren't physical air masses that we can follow around. They're bundles of energy that get transferred from one part of the atmosphere to another – with a little bit of chaos thrown in to boot. There's two main attractors for the chaos in the system – Albion and Avalon. But the problem with predicting the storm tracks is that there's a third attractor between the two of them. Once the energy is drawn away from the two stable nodes, it gets swept along on the jet stream. We can't predict the location of the secondary attractor, but we can watch for it.

"If we track the surface pressure and the winds aloft, and look for sudden changes over the Avalon Sea or the prairies to the east of the Albion Mountains, we'll be able to get the earliest indications of the birth of the storms. Now the scouts or the colonists or someone will have to put more monitoring stations out there in between the two. And more sensors in orbit. Those are the critical measurements – the way the pressure shifts and the energy of the moving systems is transferred. You know what to look for. It's in the models. Do you know what I mean? Can you pinpoint the best sites for the measurements?"

"Pressure differentials of 10 millibars or less. Temperature changes of 2 degrees or more," Nimbus said. "A measurement grid of 50-kilometer intervals. Hourly readings at least. Eureka! Yes, Ray. The model can be improved in accuracy by those things. Stand by while I process data ..."

Nimbus emitted a low electronic whistle. "Test predictions on earlier weather data confirmed by subsequent record! Accuracy of 30 percent over 15 hours on coarse data available! Estimate accuracy of 55 percent over 30 hours if measurement precision is increased – 75 percent over 30 hours. You are correct, Ray! The analysis is complete. When can we land and tell the other colonists?"

Ray smiled, then his eyes widened as he felt the numbness reach his chest. His breathing quickly became difficult, then impossible. His hands no longer felt the cold metal around him. A moment later he slipped beneath the waters one last time.

His cold body remained motionless for hours until the rescue party, Guy Stanger in the lead, cut their way into the compartment. Only Nimbus was left to repeat his epitaph.

"Energy transfers and monitor grids!" the plastic brain recited frantically. "Everyone listen! We found the answer. Follow Ray's instructions, please. He cannot be reactivated. Energy transfers and monitor grids."

***

Lin Palmer was knee-deep in the mud behind the greenhouse, trying to shore up the retaining wall as the gravelly soil spilled around its edges, when he heard Jackie calling to him from the lean-to. The quickthaw hadn't caught him so much by surprise this time, and he'd been out to the gully early to make sure things were intact.

He pulled himself from the muck, working around to the stable edges of the wash before climbing to the top of the short slope. Then he followed a path lined with plastic packing that led across the muddy ground to the shelter. He poured a bucket of cold water over his legs to wash off the mud, then stripped off his boots and trousers before stepping inside.

Jackie was looking at her tablet, her jaw unhinged and her eyes open wide.

"Look at this, Lin. I can't believe it."

"What is it?" he asked as he came around behind her and stared at the screen.

"Read it," she said, handing him the tablet, and he did.

"WEATHER BULLETIN – 1100, 15 JANUARY ...

"The Asgard University Weather Service makes the following forecast for North Valley and South Valley for Monday, 15 January. Warm winds will continue today until nightfall in the west end of the valleys, with highs expected in the teens. Cooler temperatures and lighter winds are expected in the east end of the valleys and along the coast.

"Tonight, temperatures will drop below zero inland with a hard freeze in higher elevations.

"A winter storm watch is in effect for Tuesday, 16 January. A strong low-pressure system is expected to build up over the Avalon Sea tonight and move into the region before dawn. Colonists are urged to take precautionary measures this evening. The storm should pass through before sunset on Tuesday. Lows are expected in the single digits, with winds at 30 klicks out of the southwest in the morning and the northwest in the afternoon.

"A second storm is due to follow the first one sometime before sunrise Wednesday, with warmer temperatures and more moisture. Expect snow in the higher elevations and rain in the lowlands and to the east. Accumulations of snow are expected to exceed 10 centimeters.

"The long range forecast calls for a possible outbreak of glacial air on Wednesday night or Thursday in the wake of the second storm. Highs will reach -10 degrees Centigrade and lows will drop to -30 degrees.

"This forecast will be repeated every hour. For an individual transmission or for detailed weather maps, use command WX-30 on the standard net. This is the Asgard University Weather Service signing off."

Lin just stood there in his long-johns, shivering against the chill that had soaked into his legs, reading the forecast over and over again.

"It's about time," Jackie said.

"I guess so," Lin replied. Jackie went on talking, but he didn't listen. His mind had lost its focus as a strange sensation came across him. For the first time since they had landed on the planet, he felt an unaccustomed sense of security.

Everyone always talked about the ties between a farmer and the land he worked. But the land was only half the story. The rest of it was the air – the rain, clouds, and snow. The weather meant more to a farmer than the soil. Not knowing what was coming did more than make it hard to plan. It made Lin feel helpless in a way he hadn't been able to identify.

But knowing what the weather would be restored that lost security. And finally he realized what he had been missing. He felt like the captain of a ship, ready to sail his farm through the hazardous stream of storms that blew towards him from the west. He could see over the horizon now, and had become rooted in time as well as space.

It gave him a feeling of strength that he hadn't known since leaving Maine. A strength that gave him the will to tell the Kolbergs what they could do with their labor bond and the phony offers of help and everything that went with it.

"Now we can tell the Kolbergs to go to hell," he said aloud.

"What?" Jackie said. "Lin, you haven't heard a word I said, did you?"

"Uh, no, I guess not. What were you saying?"

"The word on the net is that the weatherman who figured out the winter storms died when his ship crashed. Isn't that a shame?"

"Yeah, I guess it is. Who did the forecast, then?"

"They say it was his AI. Some clever little machine. And look at these messages from the net, Lin. Farmers all over South Valley are linking in. I told you we weren't the only ones with weather problems. People are just amazed at how much difference this makes.

Look, here's someone who says he's so glad we've got a weather forecast that he's going to tell the Kolberg's to drop dead. And here's another. What did you just say about them?"

"Only that I've decided we don't need their help after all. I think we'll do all right on our own."

***

Before the end of the week, two truckloads of Lin's denmates showed up, with a truckload of carpenters and another full of laborers from a service den behind them. They spilled over the ground around the grove of trees where Lin and Jackie had placed their foundation, retrieved the trees from the gully where Lin had built his retaining wall, replaced the wall with a fused sand embankment, and went to work on the Palmer house. They returned the next day to finish the job and when they were gone, a sturdy wooden structure stood with four strong walls and cozy pitched roof.

It was a scene repeated up and down North and South valleys as the farming dens began to pull themselves together, plan around the storms and the snow and quickthaws and put the colony on a more solid footing.

A week later, just after supper, a knock came at the door. It was Martin Meyers.

"Hello, Lin. Your new house looks mighty nice," he said. "I came to ask a favor, though if you turn me down I won't blame you. My wife and I had a fight, and I'm afraid I walked out on her. I guess I walked out on den Jasper, too. Looks like I'll need a place to spend the night."

Lin looked at Jackie, who put an arm around her husband and nodded her head. "We've got a tent out there that you can use, if you don't mind the cold."

"It's all right with me," Marty said. "But I've got a box here that you might want to keep inside where it's warm."

He produced a small plastic container and opened the top. Inside were a dozen balls of golden fuzz, peeping and pecking at the grain on the bottom of the box. "I didn't want to start out entirely fresh."

They welcomed Marty into their home and made plans for the spring.

DEN OF
SORROW

Guy Stanger looked into the small cage and searched for a tiny ball of gray fur. He knew the byte was there someplace, hiding under a leaf of the large greenwood branch in the corner or buried in the woodchips at the bottom. He found it after a moment, nestled in a crook of the tree limb.

"What's his name?"

"Mega, and he's a she," said Emily Baxter. "The next cage belongs to Kilo and over there is Giga."

"Don't disturb him," said Suzanne Baxter, Emily's mother, from her desk on the far side of the lab. "He has a lot to do this afternoon. We've got a dozen mazes to run him through."

"That's an awful lot of work for such a little fellow," Guy said. "Are you sure that's fair?"

"I don't think we're asking an awful lot," Suzanne said. "After all, he does represent the pinnacle of the evolutionary process on Asgard."

"Poor little mammaloid. Too bad you haven't evolved any cousins to share the planet with," Guy crooned.

"What about the bits?" Emily asked.

"I think the bytes descended from them, not the other way around," Guy said.

"That's what we're trying to establish," Suzanne said.

Guy looked across the room at the chartpads on the walls. He walked over to one and touched the corner to bring up the menu. He called for the chart marked "Evolutionary Tree." A broad, branching diagram appeared, illustrated with pictures of a variety of fish, amphibians, reptiloids and fuzzasaurs with the diminutive byte and bit at the top, sharing equal billing for now.

The wildlife biology lab of Asgard University occupied a large room in a corner of one of the old scout barns in what had once been the Glacier Valley Post. Den Middlesex, the academic den in the Asgard breakthrough colony, had taken over the post when the colony landed nearly a year earlier. Since then, Suzanne had managed to fill it to overflowing with specimens, samples, equipment and supplies.

"And what about the fuzzies?"

"What about them?"

"How do they shake out on the evolutionary scale?"

"They're pretty advanced," Suzanne said. "They have the skeletal architecture of reptiloids, but they changed a lot when the ice age came. They grew fur. A lot of the species adopted mammalian-style herd traits – like the grazers. Some of their behaviors mimic avian lifestyles – migratory patterns and inbred navigational tracks. We're still trying to decide which of the fuzzy species are the most advanced – the predators like the maxidons and the rippers or the opportunistic carnivores like the grabbers and draggers."

Suzanne ran her fingers through her hair and sighed. "I just hope we have time to complete our studies."

"Time?" Guy asked. "Why shouldn't you have time? You're not going anywhere."

"No ... but the grazers are. And who knows what else."

"What are you talking about?" he asked, his interest piqued.

"Emily, haven't you told your young scout the truth about us colonists yet? It's been three months since he came of age."

Guy felt his face grow red with embarrassment at the unstated meanings flying over his head. Emily took his hand and gave him a puzzled look, then turned the expression on her mother.

"Mother, what in the world are you talking about?"

"I'm talking about the grazer migration, young lady," she said, turning her seat around so that her back was to the tablet. "In a few days, it will be the first day of spring. Shortly after that, the first crowds of bluenecks, redcrests and silverbacks will begin to infiltrate their way into South Valley, just like they've been doing for thousands of years. Only this year, they're going to be in for a surprise – us.

"Tell me, Guy, you've lived on Asgard all your life. What's going to happen when a quarter of a million grazers try to mix in with thirty thousand farmers just starting to break sod?"

Guy felt a chill run up his back. He had never given that question much thought, but in the past six months, so much had happened to change his world that it seemed like a new problem appeared every week. It didn't take much effort to imagine the ultimate clash that was about to take place between the fuzzies, with their appetite for the savanna grass that covered the floor of South Valley, and the colonists, who were just beginning to establish the colony's agricultural base in the valley's fertile soil. Not only was the grass likely to disappear in short order, but the fuzzasaurs that depended on it were also likely to develop a taste for corn, wheat, quinoa and anything else that grew in the ground.

"I don't think either one of them are going to be too happy."

"That's an understatement."

"What can we do about it?"

"What have you scouts done about it? You've been here for 55 years," she said.

"We built fences, of course."

"Oh yeah, that's right. I should have thought of that."

"Well, sure, there's only a few thousand of us. But can't the colonists do the same thing?"

"Guy, you know as well as I do that there are agricultural dens in more than two thirds of the townships in South Valley. How many fences will we have to build to keep the grazers from getting into everyone's fields?"

"I don't know. Ask Joey, he's good with figures," he said.

"No, Guy. I don't need to ask Joey. We haven't even finished building houses for all the colonists. We're not going to shift gears and start turning out fences instead. I'm afraid we're going to have a serious problem on our hands and I don't think there's a lot we can do about it. That means the ag dens are going to have to work it out on their own – each with its own methods. And what scares me is that the some of them are already talking about slaughtering the poor things."

"They wouldn't do that, would they?"

"Have you ever heard of the buffalo, Guy?" Suzanne asked.

"Isn't that a city on Earth that gets a lot of snow?"

"It was a herd animal back on old Earth. Also known as the bison. They used to cover the plains as far as the eye could see. The indigenes used to live off them. But when the Europeans came to

North America, they began to use industrial methods of mass destruction to harvest them. When they were done, the only buffalo left lived in zoos. I have a terrible feeling that the same thing is going to happen here on Asgard.”

“But that’s awful. Haven’t you been able to figure out a better way to deal with the problem than that?”

“Like what?”

“I don’t know. At least you could take a look at what the farmers are planning. Maybe some of them have ideas that the rest could use. Maybe someone could go look at the grazers and see if there’s something we can do to keep them out of South Valley.”

“Someone like who, Guy?”

“I don’t know. Have you asked any of the scouts?”

“You mean, like you personally?”

Guy felt his face grow red once again. He really hadn’t considered volunteering himself for the job. But he was a scout, and he didn’t exactly have any other pressing responsibilities – with the exception of maintaining his year-old romance with Emily.

“Well, now that you mention it ... ”

***

“Why did you have to volunteer?” Emily said later, on the bus ride down to the Main Post. “Now you’re going to be gone for weeks.”

“It won’t be that long.”

“But Guy, spring break only lasts seven days. By the time you get back, I’ll be back in school.”

“I’m sorry, Em. But by the time your holiday is over, the grazers will already be here. If we’re going to do something useful, we need to do it now.”

“That’s what you always say.”

"Why? Is there something you had planned for the vacation?"

"Just this," she said, pulling him closer and planting her lips on his. He enjoyed it for a moment, then caught his breath when she relaxed her grip on him.

"For seven days?"

***

Their arrival at the scout post was cause for a wild celebration among Guy's three younger brothers, Walt, Billy and Tad – and even for his parents.

Guy's father, Philip, smiled and stayed in the background while the rest of the family mobbed poor Emily. She hadn't been at the Main Post since before Colony Day.

"It's so nice to have another woman around here," said Guy's mother, Joanne. "You don't know what it's like having to live with five men."

Emily shined at the attention, and even gave Walt a sisterly kiss on the cheek in greeting. Guy remembered her first night on Asgard, when Walt had stolen a kiss from her, only to have his older brother come along and steal the young lady away. Guy was happy to see Walt blush – there was no jealousy there.

She even had little gifts for all the boys – a slingshot for Billy that her own brother had donated, a book disk for shy, sensitive Tad, and a bright red headband for Walt. And for Guy's mother, she had an even greater gift – a small bag of makeup, including lipstick, powder and eye shadow.

"Oh my goodness, Emily, these are beautiful. You wouldn't believe what we had to put up with before the colony arrived. We ran out of real cosmetics decades ago. But what shall I do with all these?"

"I'll show you how to use them. You're going to need to know how when the special services and apparel dens start production this summer. There's even going to be a beauty parlor in Center Township, you know."

"I know. I can't believe it. When I was growing up, it was always hard to tell the boys from the girls until the boys came of age and had their hair trimmed. Maybe now the kids'll start to take more interest in how they look. I know there are so many times I've wanted to fix myself up and feel like a woman for a change ... "

Guy lost his girlfriend to his mother for the rest of the afternoon. He only recovered her at supper, when they put on a special meal with lots of fruits and vegetables to honor their guest. Emily was a vegetarian, something she never let Guy forget for a minute when there was meat on the table. He filled himself up on roast blueneck with gravy and yams with spineycone glaze, despite the undisguised glares she aimed at his plate.

"It's too bad we don't see more of you," Guy's mother said as they finished up the meal and the younger boys began to take away the dishes. "And Guy's hardly around here on weekends anymore, so we don't get to talk much."

Emily flashed a coy smile, and Guy felt embarrassed.

"I know how you feel," Emily said. "He's going to take off on me in the morning, you know."

"He is? What for?"

Guy explained how he had talked himself into investigating the grazer problem for Emily's mother, and she and his father voiced their own support for the mission.

"While you're at it, you should stop by up at Highland Post," Guy's father said. "Stop in and check on Grampa Bob. I hear bad news about him. You were always close to him, maybe you can figure out what's wrong."

"I'll do that, Dad," Guy said, wondering what the old scoutmaster was up to now.

"We'll leave you two alone now," his father said, ushering his surprised wife from the table and into the kitchen to leave Guy and Emily alone. They went outside, where a premature breath of spring had blown up from the southeast bringing warm air to the South Valley where snow had fallen only a day before.

Emily shivered against him, and he hugged her closer.

"So what did my brother have to tell you about the Kolbergs?" Emily asked after a momentary kiss.

"That's an odd question," Guy replied. "Don't you two talk?"

"Not if it can be avoided. But enough to know you've got him spying on them for you. Isn't that kind of dangerous?"

"Are you concerned for his safety?"

"Not personally, but Mother would be."

"He's not doing anything dangerous."

"Guy, he's only a child."

"A very careful, smart and thoughtful child who knows how to keep himself out of trouble."

"You wouldn't say that if it was Billy out there."

"Billy is four years younger than Joey."

Emily grew silent for a moment, then said: "You haven't answered my original question."

"Which was?"

"What did Joey tell you about the Kolbergs?"

"More bad news. They're really starting to get organized. They're signing contracts with farmers, lining up clients for their consultant services, getting their fingers into everyone's soup."

"I don't like it. The colonists are supposed to be free and equal. This isn't we had planned on when we left Earth. The Kolbergs and their friends aren't going to give up until they're running Asgard."

"I know. Sometimes I'm afraid the rest of us are going to end up like the grazers ... just another inconvenient nuisance. Then they'll have an excuse to get rid of us if we don't get out of the way."

They didn't talk much after that, but found other ways to pass the evening on the front porch of the Stanger household. Later, before Rudy had set, while the world was still painted with its faded red glow, but after the rest of the family had turned in, they went to bed.

2

Guy was always left breathless by the sight of Highland Post. While the low buildings of the Main Post sprawled across the rolling savanna plain, and the Glacier Valley Post was laid out neatly along the shores of Glacier Lake, Highland Post was built along more vertical lines. The main lodge rose in tiers, framed by the hundred-meter greenwood trees, backed by the pale cliffs that fell from Mt. Thor. The tall cabins were built of greenwood timbers and pine logs, with steeply pitched roofs and narrow windows. Stairs and walkways connected balconies and porches – some of them mounted on the trees themselves. The integration of artifice and nature made the whole place seem as fantastic in its character as it was in its dimensions.

Guy was almost ashamed to approach it in a bus.

Only a year ago, the only way to come upon Highland Post was on horseback. But since then, the colonists had laid their roads and unpacked their trucks and buses, and the transport dens had started shuttling people around from one end of South Valley to the other.

The changes had even Guy Stanger's young head spinning. He could imagine how Grampa Bob must feel.

He found the old man in a strange little apartment cut into the bole of a greenwood not far from the base of the main lodge. As he had told Guy many times, he would have preferred living higher up, but he was too heavy around the middle to go climbing up and down 40 meters of stairways four or five times a day. Guy thought he was stretching the truth a little bit, but never said so.

"Hello, young scout," Grampa Bob called out as he stepped out onto his front porch. "Heard any good Great Spirit stories lately?"

"Not since the last one you told me, Grampa Bob. And that was when I was still just a cub."

"Come on in here and have some tea anyway. Keep an old man comfortable in his declining years." Guy stepped into the dim chambers that the old scoutmaster kept.

"So what brings you up to this end of the valley? I haven't seen you since you since before Colony Day."

He told Grampa Bob about the grazer problem – and what he hoped to do about it.

"That's a pretty tall task to take on yourself, Guy. I hope the colonists turn out to be worth it. Personally, I have my doubts."

"I know, sir. You've made that clear more than once."

Grampa Bob looked serious for a moment, then shrugged. "Don't take it personally, boy. I'm just a cranky old man who worries too much. I hear you've taken up with one of the colonist girls. Do you like her?"

Now it was Guy's turn to look serious. "Of course I do, Grampa Bob. I never felt this way about anyone before."

"What are your plans for the future?"

"Well, sir, I hadn't thought too much about the future yet. Things have been pretty hectic since the colony landed."

"You'd better start, then. Things are only going to get worse, you know. If you wait around until they ease up, you'll be as old as me. There's a lot more changes coming in the next few weeks – more than you've seen so far, I'd wager. And I'd win, too."

"What kind of changes, Grampa Bob?"

"Changes in the scout den, for one. People have been talking pretty serious about the future of den Iroquois. There's a lot of different ideas being tossed around. I've got a few of my own, without getting too bold about it. Now that the colonists are here, we've got to make some hard decisions."

"I know ... "

***

"I've made up a new Great Spirit story, Guy. I want to tell it to you."

Guy felt a warm rush run up his back as he recalled the earliest days of his childhood when Grampa Bob first told him the Great Spirit stories. "I'd like to hear it," he said.

"The Great Spirit is with us," the oldster intoned.

"And we are with the Great Spirit," Guy replied.

"Long ago, the Great Spirit walked upon the Earth and made it great and bountiful. Clear waters sprang from the ground where he walked. Fruit grew where he paused. Forests arose where he slept."

"Great was the Great Spirit."

"He walked with the other spirits of the world. The Spirit of the Wind, the Spirit of the Sea, the Spirit of the River, the Spirit of the Forest and the Spirit of the Ice.

"But this is the story of a new spirit – the Spirit of Empire. This is a different kind of spirit, not a spirit of nature, but a spirit of man.

"Once upon a time, man himself was a spirit of nature. He lived in peace with the other animals of the forest and field. He took what he needed from the soil and gave back what was left. His numbers were few and his thoughts were many. He lived in small cities where he learned the ways of nature and the Great Spirit, where he practiced art and medicine and science and where he cultivated the virtues that made his spirit grow.

"But things do not remain the same forever. The small cities grew, until one of them became larger than the others. And there, the Spirit of Empire arose.

"The larger city began to believe that it was a better city and that it was meant to rule over the others. It raised up an army, conquered and enslaved its neighbors, amassed wealth and overwhelmed all of the civilized world.

"No longer did man live in peace with nature. Now he turned against it, against his fellow man and against himself. He stole nature's treasures, poisoned its air and water, slaughtered its children and destroyed the system of fragile balances that the Spirits of the Wind, the Sea, the River, the Forest and the Ice had created through ageless time. The other spirits turned against the Spirit of Empire and one by one they worked to undermine his work. The Wind Spirit blew down the city walls. The Sea Spirit rose up and flooded the city streets. The River Spirit overflowed its banks and washed away the city bridges. The Forest Spirit and the Ice Spirit fled from the city's edges to leave it harsh and barren.

"But the Spirit of Empire would not be denied. He laughed at the others, built new walls, new streets and new bridges. He reveled in the emptiness left by the forest and the ice. And he reached around the globe to increase his power beyond all imagination.

"The other spirits grew sad at the sight of what the Spirit of Empire had done to their world. And when the sound of their crying was heard by the Great Spirit, he came to them and told them of another world where they could go.

"Among those spirits was one who cried louder than all the rest to see what the Spirit of Empire had done to old Earth – and that was the Spirit of Man. He told the Great Spirit that he cried the hardest because he was the closest of all to the Spirit of Empire. At first, the Great Spirit did not want to bring the Spirit of Man along with the rest. He was afraid that he would give rise once again to the Spirit of Empire. But the Spirit of Man promised that he would serve the other spirits and protect them from the evil that they had suffered on Earth. After talking for many days, the Great Spirit finally agreed to take him along. He gathered all the spirits together on a great starship and carried them away. They traveled for 25 years until they reached Mu Cassiopeiae, where they found a planet named Asgard.

"And all the spirits went down to the planet and decided to live there, in peace and harmony. But then one day, the sky above Asgard was filled with spaceships filled with many men and women. The Great Spirit looked upon them and grew sad himself, because he realized that the Spirit of Empire had followed him to Asgard. And he knew that there was no way to escape from Empire, no place to run, no place to hide. No matter what the Great Spirit did, Empire would follow him and take what peace he thought he had achieved."

Grampa Bob fell silent, and Guy swallowed hard. All the bitterness and anger of the old man cut through to his heart, leaving him feeling empty and hurt. This was not a story Guy wanted to repeat to the children of Asgard. It was a story he never wanted to hear again. But at the same time, he knew he could not tell that to Grampa Bob.

"Is that the end?" he asked suddenly, not knowing why.

"I think so ... I don't know. I've considered other endings. The one that I like the best has the Great Spirit lead the other spirits into the wilderness instead. It's not as pessimistic. But it's not what I believe, either."

Guy was silent for a long time, turning confused thoughts and feelings over in his mind. Grampa Bob just sat in his chair, his arms hanging at his sides and his head slumped down, eyes pointed at the floor. At last, Guy gingerly asked another question.

"Are you really that disappointed by the colonists, Grampa Bob?"

The old man looked up, suddenly piqued by the sensitive inquiry.

"Not all of them, I guess. There are a few that may give you reason for hope. But not enough, I think." He looked at Guy with weary eyes seated in a nest of deep wrinkles. "You've seen the library videos of the great arcologies of old Earth, haven't you Guy?"

He nodded, picturing the giant towers of steel and glass, the geodesic domes and mile-high spires of the great monuments to human artifice. He knew that Grampa Bob was talking about them when he told of the great cities that gave birth to the Spirit of Empire.

"Well what the videos don't show you is how those things looked when I left Earth. They don't talk much about Mexico City, do they?"

"No, sir."

"They say it was the earthquake that did it in, but that place was in decline long before then. I've been to Mexico and I've seen what those things look like when the life has been knocked out of them. You cannot imagine the decay and the human rot that is left behind – and I'm talking about living rot, not dead flesh. The criminally evil men and women and the destruction they perpetrate on themselves and others. The distortion and perversion of the human spirit under the wreckage of spoiled greatness.

"Guy, they want to bring it all here. Give them a few centuries and they will recreate the whole thing on Asgard. There'll be another

Mexico City and another idol to the Spirit of Empire on a world that was perfect and pure when we got here. I wish I could stop it, but I know there is no way. There's just no way ... "

Guy felt his throat burn as he choked back his emotions. He wanted to say something to help restore the old man's faith, but the reversal of roles was too much for him. Grampa Bob had always been the one who gave him faith, who assured him that there was a purpose to life and a reason to wait all those years for Colony Day to arrive. He wanted to give some of that hope back to the man, but he just didn't know how. He felt empty and powerless and angry at his own inability.

And yet, somewhere inside himself, he knew that the Grampa Bob was wrong. He just had to be.

An hour later, while he was standing in line at the commons, waiting to fill a tray with fuzzasaur soup, baked arracacha, spineycone sauce and pork chops, Guy looked up to see a familiar face – Lyle Sanderson from the Main Post.

"Hello, Guy, what brings you up here?"

"I came to visit Grampa Bob," he said.

"What a coincidence. So did we. Come on over and sit with us while you eat, why don't you."

Guy felt uncomfortable socializing with the senior scout leaders – especially after the session with Grampa Bob. But he found out quickly that it was more than a social occasion. He took a seat across the table from Sanderson and Eddie Gilmartin.

"How is the old man these days?" Gilmartin asked.

"Tired, I think," Guy said. "He's awfully depressed about the colonists."

"Sounds like he dropped a heavy load on you," said Sanderson. "I've been talking to him lately myself, Guy. If I were you, I would be very careful about letting Grampa Bob make you feel bad. It isn't fair for him to make young men like you carry his burden of bitterness and spite."

"Or anyone else, for that matter," Gilmartin said.

"I know," answered Guy. "It's just that he's always been the one to show us why we we're here. And now it sounds like it was all wrong. Or at least he thinks so."

"Do you think so?" asked Sanderson.

"No, I don't. I think we have a lot more work to do on Asgard. And now that the colonists are here, we have to help them any way we can. But Grampa Bob seems to think they aren't worth it. I know the Kolbergs aren't any good, but he doesn't even like regular colonists."

"It's deeper than that, young fellow," Gilmartin said. "That's why we're up here. There's going to be a High Council meeting. Probably next week."

"A High Council meeting? What for?"

"In a way, it's past due," said Sanderson. "And in a way it's too early. There's a lot of changes coming for the scouts. They've been simmering for a year now. Part of it is because of the Kolbergs. But I think the difficulties we're facing would have come up anyway.

"We've got to decide just what the future holds for den Iroquois, Guy. But I think it's too early to make that decision. We haven't worked things through yet. In another month or two, maybe we could reach a consensus, but now Grampa Bob has brought matters to a head."

"How? What's he done?"

"He's stirred up a lot of people who feel a lot like him. They're not happy with the changes now that the colony's here. They're used to living alone on Asgard, got set in their ways. A lot of them are older, a lot of them are just stubborn. And about half of them are kids that never stopped believing in him. He seems to have generated a spark under them, and Eddie here thinks it's got to be stopped or settled one way or another."

"I still don't understand," Guy said. "What's Grampa Bob want?"

"He wants to split up the den," Gilmartin said. "He wants to take a bunch of scouts out into the interior, apart from everyone else and set up their own post."

"I guess you don't mean like the posts at the Avalon Sea or near the Albion Mountains."

"No – I mean like alone, separate and having nothing to do with the rest of us."

Guy felt strangely uncomfortable, like someone was moving furniture around inside his soul. It was just one more in a long string of disruptions that stretched back a year. Each time he thought things had achieved some kind of equilibrium, there was another terrible change appearing on the horizon. He didn't know how to cope with this one, though. The idea that the scouts could break up was more than he had ever imagined.

"If you ask me, he's just a mean, depressed old man," Gilmartin said, causing Guy's emotional defenses to rise within him, although he made no outward response. "I don't want to see his bitterness destroy the den. And if I can stop him, I will."

"Eddie wants to be sure we're all committed to continuing the mission of the den. Now that the breakthrough group is here, there's going to be new dens coming every couple of years. In 25 years, there's going to be another hundred thousand colonists here. And in a hundred years there'll be two million of them. Those people are going to need some place to live and the scouts are still going to have to find sites for them. What Grampa Bob doesn't seem to realize is that this is just the beginning. We're going to be in business for a long, long time."

Lyle Sanderson tried to soften the harshness of Gilmartin's words.

"I think Grampa Bob knows exactly what we're facing, Eddie. But I think he has a lot of different feelings about it. You know, neither of us ever lived on Earth. He's not just old, he's from a different generation, a whole different way of looking at things."

"I think he's too tied up in the past. This isn't Earth, it's Asgard. We've got a big future to fill up. We can't keep looking back the way he does. Besides, what's he got to look forward to? He's over 135 years old. What's he got – another fifteen?"

The talk of Grampa Bob's mortality disturbed Guy more than anything. He didn't know if he wanted to sit and listen to this talk much longer – especially if Eddie Gilmartin was going to keep stirring up feelings he didn't want to face.

Luckily they were nearly finished with their meal. Guy concentrated on soaking up the last of the soup with a piece of bread while the two scout leaders continued their discussion.

"If the den does break up, then we're all going to have to make some pretty hard choices," Sanderson said.

"You may have to, Lyle, but I don't. I'm sticking with the way I was taught – even if it means moving on out to Avalon."

Guy felt buffeted by invisible undercurrents again. He was almost afraid to ask what they meant this time, but he spoke up once more. "What are you talking about?"

"What he means is that if Grampa Bob busts open den Iroquois, there are some scouts who want to stay behind and join the colonists. Lyle thinks he may be one of them."

"I'm just saying it's an option, Eddie. We can help the colonists just as much by staying here and teaching them what we've learned as we can by striking out into the wilderness."

"Well if I can get Grampa Bob to forget his crazy ideas, we won't have to worry about it, will we," Gilmartin said.

"No, I suppose we won't," Sanderson replied. But he shot Guy a look of despair that left the young scout feeling that the choices facing den Iroquois were going to become quite personal before it was all over.

And Guy realized with a sudden sinking feeling that he wasn't sure he would want to leave South Valley behind if it meant that Eddie Gilmartin was going to be the scoutmaster

***

Guy spent the night at Highland Post and in the morning he drew a horse and supplies from the barn and set out towards the south.

A light drizzle was falling when he left the high cabins of the post behind. He pulled his poncho tight around his neck and let the hood drop low around his face. The sound of the rain drops splattering across the weatherized fuzzasaur skin, the sound of the horse's regular breathing and the steady rocking rhythm of his gait allowed him to retreat into a tiny, self-contained space, apart from the larger world around him.

Riding alone, without care or worry, made up for the tumultuous emotional upheavals of the day before. He didn't want to think about Grampa Bob, or the breakup of the scout den. He didn't even want to think about Emily and her mother and the poor grazers that would soon be making their way north.

He just wanted to ride, fulfilling a role he had sought all his life. Being a scout meant going out into the world and seeing what was there to be seen. It meant exploring and investigating and studying and recording. Not necessarily for anyone's future use, but for its own sake. Like Adam naming the animals in the Garden of Eden. Sure someone could use it some day, but he couldn't know who or how. So he just had to do that one job well and not think about how it fit into everything else. That was the one constant that remained undisturbed in Guy's life and he held onto it as tightly as he knew how.

It took him all morning long, four hours, to follow the High River down from the Highland Post to the ferry across the South River. During that time, the rain let up and a steady wind blew up out of the southeast. Thick with tropical heat and humidity, it slapped at his face with a heavy hand.

Weather on Asgard was always exciting and never dull. If you didn't like it, wait just a while it would always get worse. The sun burned off the remaining low clouds that had been the source of the morning rain. Great shafts of gold and yellow cut through the sky, raising steam from the wet plains and cooking through Guy's poncho. By the time he reached the South River, he had stripped down to a vest, stowing the poncho behind him in a handy spot in case the rain returned.

The ferry was on the other side of the river when he rode into the landing and tied up his horse. He pulled out his pack and unwrapped a sandwich he'd made for himself before leaving. While he ate, he watched the flat barge work its way along the cable from the south bank to the north. The river was slow and lazy right now, and the cable ran up across the mudflats on either side of channel to its anchor posts.

But in a few weeks, when the snow along the mountains and ridges began to melt under the withering heat of the spring thaw, it would grow into a raging flood. A few crowds of grazers would make it across before then, but the rest would wait until the springmelt subsided before turning into a flood of their own.

After a few minutes, the ferry moored alongside a floating dock.

Guy took his horse by the reins, wrapped his poncho over its eyes, and walked it out to the end of the dock to meet the ferry. The ferryman was an old man who said he was from den Pontiac, the transport den, but didn't have much else to say. It was just as well – Guy didn't feel like talking.

Pushing the barge was an electric torque induction motor powered by a portable fusion pack. A long shaft extended from the motor with a propeller on the end. The old man disconnected the motor from its mount and manhandled it the other end of the ferry. Then he had Guy lead his horse down into the center of the deck.

The ride across was uneventful, and a few minutes later Guy led his horse up the dock on the far side. He was on his way quickly, his spirits rising as the sun burned down on his face and arms.

To the east lay an empty township, unoccupied by any den, with space reserved for future growth. Off to the west somewhere, on the other side of the Lower River, was Roanoke township, where farmers from southern Africa shared a village with den Halston, the apparel den. Guy could see a line of trees on the horizon that had to mark the river. Beyond it were 1,600 farmers spread out over a square 16 kilometers on a side. Somewhere in there was a village center where den Halston had set up its textile shops.

He was mildly curious about what that village might look like, but his path today took him too far west to indulge his interest. In a short time, however, he found himself crossing through much of the township and getting a good look at what the farmers had accomplished since their arrival a little less than six months ago.

Roanoke seemed to be a typically American den that had developed its township in a typically American manner. The square had been divided into smaller squares of 640 hectares each and every family was given a square and a house. The little frame buildings dotted the plains, and even though they didn't make a perfect grid, Guy could sense the measured regularity of their spacing.

Some families had put up greenhouses, some had built sheds and coops and barns, some had corrals and fences that held livestock – beef and dairy cattle, sheep and horses. There weren't any crops in yet, but he found quite a few farmers taking advantage of the warm weather to begin breaking the earth.

Guy was fascinated by the way their windlass plows worked. The plow was attached by a cable to the windlass on the front of a farm truck. The windlass reeled in the cable and took a tow on the plow. The result was a neatly plowed field where the earth wasn't pounded down and broken in by the heavy weight of tractors and other machinery.

About 1500, as the sun reached the top of the sky, the weather began to turn nasty. Thunderheads climbed towards the heavens, obscuring Mt. Thor to the northwest and cloaking the Vogelsberg Ridge in the gray gauze of distant rain. Cold upper level winds, straight off the glaciers to the far north, sliced through the billowing crowns of the rising storm cells. Bold flashes of blue lightning danced at their feet.

He decided to take refuge in the nearest farmstead as the squall line marched steadily towards him. He thought he could beat the rain to the barn that he saw there, so he didn't slow down long enough to don his poncho. He could not.

There was no one in the yard as he galloped in. Great cold drops of rain bombarded the dusty ground and smacked into the back of his head, followed by a short, sudden rush of sound, then the air turned into wave after wave of falling rain.

He was drenched by the time he reached the barn door. Suddenly a blurred shape appeared from the door, grabbed Guy's horse by the bit and pulled it inside.

The change was like someone turning a switch. The drumming of the rain on the rooftop echoed throughout the large dry space, muffling the sound of nervous livestock. Guy wiped his eyes, then saw the line of cows that ran either side of the barn, all tethered to the wall and standing in muddy straw. Holding the reigns of the horse was a young girl, no more than 25.

Her long blond hair framed a fair-skinned face with high cheekbones and blue eyes. The eyes locked with his for a long time before she spoke.

"Are you a scout?" she asked.

"Yes," Guy said. "Are you a farmer?"

"Sure am. Eddie Lee. Short for Edwina. This is my farm – my dad's farm. He's over at the other barn with Uncle Dick. That's some storm."

"It's going to get worse," Guy warned. He looked around. The barn seemed to built on a slab foundation of fused silicon. "Is there a storm cellar in this place?"

"A what?"

"A cellar – a hole in the ground with a cover on it?"

"No, sir. Not that I've ever seen, anyway."

"Too bad. Well, we probably won't need it."

Eddie looked at Guy quizzically, and Guy realized the farm girl wasn't sure if she was being set up for a joke. He felt embarrassed for being a little bit melodramatic.

But it was only a little bit. A few minutes later, the rain let up, Guy tied up his horse, and he and Eddie stood at the barn door looking out across the plains at a distant thunderhead.

"Look over there – see where the clouds get thicker at the base of that storm. Watch it for a few minutes."

They did and slowly but steadily the clouds thickened, dipped earthwards and dropped a thick black siphon onto the ground.

"Twisters. Are you sure there isn't a storm cellar in this place?"

There wasn't, but it turned out to be unnecessary. Guy felt a little ashamed at scaring Eddie, though. After all, the Main Post had sat unharmed in its current location for 93 years without ever being hit by a tornado. There was no reason to believe that this farm was likely to be any less lucky.

Eddie calmed down the cows by walking the length of the barn and talking to them. The Lee farm was a double spread, shared between Eddie's father, Ned, and her uncle. The two sections would be able to provide feed corn for the cattle, they judged.

"What about the grazers? How are you going to keep them out of the corn?" Guy asked.

"The what? You mean the fuzzasauruses? We've got them licked. Come see this … "

She brought Guy over to a corner of the barn and showed him a small plastic box. "What is it?"

"A holograph projector. Watch." She fiddled around with it for a moment, then suddenly a maxidon two meters tall with a three-meter tail appeared in the middle of the barn. Guy jumped back, then realized that it was not moving. And on closer examination, he realized it wasn't maxidon, but an Earth dinosaur covered with scales instead of fur,

"The guy who sold it to us called it a 'scare-a-saur.' I can't wait to see if it works."

"If it doesn't have the scent, I'm not sure it will," Guy said.

"Oh, we've got that. Right here." She pulled a plastic jug out from behind the projector. Inside was a viscous brown fluid. "They gened it, Chen pumped it through the bio-factory up at the village. We're supposed to paint it on fence posts around the cornfields."

Guy shook his head. "Sounds ingenious."

Eddie shrugged. "I don't know if any of it's going to work. Daddy and Uncle Dickie argued about it once, but they never settled who won. Daddy thinks it will. Uncle Dickie doesn't."

"I know how your father must feel, but I'm afraid my vote would go with your uncle. I'll believe it when I see it."

The squall line passed by and a brisk northwest wind fell in behind it. The air turned dry and chilly and Guy went through his pack for warmer clothes. Then he mounted up and walked his horse into the yard.

Eddie looked up at him with a bit of awe and amazement in her eyes. Guy felt uncomfortable, but didn't know what to say. "Tell your father I said to build a storm cellar, will you?"

"Sure thing, Mr. Scout. Thanks a lot."

***

It was late noon, 1800, before Guy stopped for supper.

According to the map in his tablet, he was probably near the junction of Roanoke, Dubuque and Geneva townships. He could see the small square shapes of farmhouses in the distance, and here and there the smoke from cooking fires smeared the air.

Along the northern horizon stretched the great wall of rock and forest that split the Prime Site from east to west, separating the two river valleys. Mt. Thor was already cloaked in shadows to the west. The snows at the peak of Mt. Loki in the east danced in the orange light of the setting sun. And between the two ran the Vogelsberg Ridge. Before him stood the lower ridgelines that marked the southern limits of the valley and a series of small buttes that rose sharply from the savanna plain.

Then, in the distance, he heard the hooting sounds of a crowd of bluenecks. He scanned the plains with narrowed eyes, then caught a glimpse of them through the haze about four kilometers away – too far to get any idea of their numbers. He doubted if it was the first crowd to make it this far north. The migration had already begun days ago.

Somewhere beyond that crowd to the south was his destination – Fuzzasaur Pass and the pathway to the wide open lands of the tropics. Guy figured he could reach it before dark if he pressed on – he had another six hours of daylight. As it turned out, he was wrong, but not because of any miscalculation on his part.

The fence was mean and ugly, sharp wooden stakes linked together loosely with coiling ribbons of metal. It stretched from the gray cliffs of a butte to the west over a rise to the east where it dropped from view. The metal ribbons looked razor sharp to Guy, and they were full of barbs and kinks. He felt shivers run up his back at the sight.

And on one of the stakes was the limp body of a female blueneck, its fur matted with blood.

Guy tried to imagine how it could have happened. Bluenecks weren't terribly smart animals, but he didn't see how it could have run into the fence by accident. But then he remembered the sight of a crowd of the grazers pushing and shoving one another to get at a chite mound – not to eat the little bugs, but because of the beastweed plant growing out of it.

There was beastweed all around here. The poor creature stuck on the fence must have been pushed there by the rest of the crowd.

But there was another, more crucial question that went unanswered – where had the fence come from?

He rode for an hour along the vicious-looking barrier until he came to an opening. A gate blocked a rudimentary gravel roadway running through it, and a single unarmed farmer stood watch over the gate from a small wooden shack. Guy hailed the watchman, but was surprised by the reply.

It was a word in a language he had never heard before.

He waited while the watchman returned to the shack and engaged in an excited conversation with an unseen companion – unheard as well, leading Guy to suspect he was on the phone. Then the watchman hurried back to the gate, opened it, and beckoned to Guy to come through. He smiled, pointed up the road and urged the scout on. Guy waved to him as he nudged his horse into a trot and hurried away.

It didn't take him long to notice the different layout of this foreign township. Instead of dispersed farmsteads centered around separate houses, this den was organized around small villages, with the fields marked by stones, but not occupied by their owners. The village he came upon was full of houses, sported a few barns and warehouses, a herd of cows, a chicken farm and a honeyworks. And a bakery, he realized as he rode into the rich smell of baking bread.

He found his way to the main lodge at the center of a village green where he was greeted by a trio of men. He dismounted, tied his horse to a convenient rail and walked up to meet them.

The first two spoke the same foreign language that the gatekeeper had. Guy had checked his tablet and saw that this was den Kindrat, a Ukrainian farming den. He assumed they were speaking Ukrainian, but there was no way he could know for sure. From their smiles, he also assumed that they were friendly.

The third man hung back, waiting until the first two had exhausted their supply of salutations, then stepped up.

"Hello there, Scout. My name is Stepan Soroka. Welcome to Kindrat Township. The fellow on your right is Vasyl Yurchyk, the den leader, and the one on your left is Mykola Ploschak, his assistant."

"Hi. I'm Guy Stanger. I'm a scout. Are you the only one around here who speaks English?"

"Just about. But then, I'm not a member of this den. I'm here with the Kolbergs."

***

Guy's exposure to evil had so far been limited to two instances.

The first had been the night that Suzanne Baxter had called him over the satellite phone and asked him to send her the scout plans for landing the breakthrough colony. That was the night Henry Schmidt had picked him up off the floor and pushed him aside in a vain attempt to stop him from uploading the file to Suzanne's ship. He remembered Schmidt's warning that night: "Don't get in our way."

The second instance was a few days later when he found Jeannie Gilmartin in the Main Lodge at Glacier Valley Post after she'd been raped by the Kolberg scout, LeClerc.

But there was something amateurish and improvised about the moral weaknesses that afflicted those two. Soroka seemed much more refined and practiced in his evil than anyone Guy had ever known. He suddenly found it easy to see what Grampa Bob meant when he described the ruins of Mexico City on old Earth. He realized suddenly that there really was a Spirit of Empire.

Soroka explained the fence.

"Back on Tik, there's a herd animal we call the vishnu. They're mammaloid, shorter than the fuzzasaur, but more bulk, with bulging skulls and woolly fur. They run in herds – number in the thousands each. The colony's prime site is a wide open plain sort of like this valley. The only way we could protect ourselves from them was with the vishnu-break. We figured it would work just as well on the fuzzies."

"From what I've seen, it works real good," Guy said, trying to restrain his sarcasm. "I found a blueneck impaled on the section I first found."

"Yes, we get that back on Tik, too. Not nearly the same numbers here, though. Maybe we'll do better in the summer."

Soroka was a young man, not more than five years senior to Guy. He'd been a child when his family emigrated to Eta Cass, and he'd grown up in an agricultural den on Tikarahisat. By the time he reached manhood, the den had linked itself to the growing Kolberg organization – trading agricultural surpluses for manufactured goods. His den had always suffered from poor organization and weak finances and the longer the deal went on, the worse off they became.

"So why did you join the Kolbergs?" Guy asked.

"It was my chance to get out of there. Power is strength – and the Kolbergs had power. I knew what they were planning to do and I wanted to go with them, to get off Tik and out of my own poor farmer's den. What kind of a life is that, growing things all day."

"And you wound up here?"

"I knew the language. My own den came from the Donbass. I think that was what kept us from prospering. Too many machinists, not enough farmers."

Guy, never much of a talker anyway, found himself just nodding silently as the man rambled on. But Soroka didn't seem to notice or care. He talked for his own entertainment, just to hear the words fall from his tongue.

"When we first made contact with den Kindrat, they were already organized along pretty strict lines. I liked that. They're here to do a job and they're ready to do it. Unified and committed. By the time they landed, we had helped them planned things out. The township farmland is held by the den as a whole. Now that spring is here, the farmers will begin working the fields according to a rotating schedule. The produce will belong to the entire den and the surplus will be a den asset."

The system sounded terrible to Guy, who believed in giving a man land of his own. It didn't sound to him like it would work – not without making the farmers responsible for their own work and their own land. He noticed, however, that the Ukrainians didn't seem to object. They were busy and happy, smiling and eager as they bounced along in their trucks on their home from the fields.

Soroka invited Guy to supper, and, reluctantly, he agreed. The reluctance came because Guy had sampled colonial rations before and avoided them like spoiled fruit whenever possible. But he wanted to find out as much as he could from this loquacious Kolberg agent.

The experience turned out to be more pleasant than he expected. They ate at the village lodge, a small wooden building with two large rooms and a loft. The fresh bread, still warm from the oven, made up for the bland pasty dishes concocted from the ration packages. There was some fresh fish, a big, fat cherimoyas, a bowl of shriveled black potatoes that were probably the winter product of a greenhouse and fresh butter.

Yurchyk and Ploschak sat on either side of him while they ate, speaking to him occasionally through Soroka to ask how he liked the food, but mostly carrying on a loud dialog between them across Guy's plate. When the meal was done, Ploschak went to a small wooden cabinet in one corner and returned with a large plastic jug and a tray of small glasses. They were made of real glass, not plastic, and Guy recognized them as heirlooms by the way the farmer treated them. He poured a clear liquid from the jug into each of the glasses, then resealed the jug and returned it to the cabinet. Then he passed the drinks around.

Guy copied the way the other tossed the liquid down in one gulp, but after he swallowed, his mouth burned with fire. He sucked air through his teeth and swallowed again, reaching for the plastic mug of water that he'd been nursing throughout the meal.

When he recovered himself, he found the others laughing and grinning at him as Soroka slapped him on the back. He began to feel a warm glow rise from the bottom of his feet and when it reached his eyes, he broke into a smile of his own. It only remotely occurred to him that this was some kind of homemade alcoholic brew and that he should limit the amount he consumed. He wasn't given a second offer, however, a fact for which he was grateful.

Soroka seemed oblivious to the moral impact of his advice.

When the ceremonial drink was over, Ploschak turned his attention to a pair of pretty blond women at the far end of the table and Yurchyk joined a group at another table, leaving Soroka and Guy to talk. The conversation quickly turned again to the organization of den Kindrat.

"The purpose of the colony is to grow and grow it will. We're going to knock Roanoke, Geneva and Dubuque off the air," Soroka said. "The agricultural surplus we produce will become our leverage in the competition between dens. Instead of dispersing it among the membership, we will concentrate it and use it like a tool to increase our power.

"We have to be systematic, organized and committed, you know. A new world can be a deadly place. You should have seen what happened back on Tik. We run a long year there – 456 standard days. That's more than twice one of Asgard's puny little years. We'd already settled in, started our crops and built our farmsteads that first year on the planet when the first vishnu came. In two days, they wiped out four months work. We lost the equivalent of six dens. That's when we started building the breaks to keep the vishnu out. Is it any wonder we want to help these people avoid the same kind of fate?"

"Of course," Guy said. "Although I'm not sure you've got the same problem with the grazers that you do with the vishnu."

Soroka didn't listen, but went on and on.

"And this township is just one of many. We'll be working from a strong base once things get organized colony-wide. The ones who are smart enough to listen to us and join us will find that they will be strong, too. You'll see – the strong dens will lead the others, they'll build up the wealth of the colony. And the leaders of those dens will be strong and powerful men. That's what I want – strength and power."

All his life, Guy had been taught that every action one took, every job one assumed, would not – indeed could not – benefit just oneself. Although there were private indulgences that only benefited others in the most indirect way, in scout society, everything had a unity of purpose and commitment that left almost no room for a split between the common and the particular good. All scout work, in the end, was to benefit colonists who would not come for many years – most of whom would follow centuries down the road.

"You know, the concept of private gain at the expense of others is hard for me to accept," Guy said. "I've always been taught that it was wrong to indulge my personal interests at the price of the den's interests. I've recognized it in all the things you people have done since you arrived on Asgard. But I always thought you knew that you were wrong. As I listen to you talk, I realize you do not.

"You speak as though it was the highest value to which one could attain. You believe that personal wealth and individual power based on greater accumulations of material products and goods is a suitable goal for a man to pursue. Yet you have no shame or remorse, only a starry-eyed and detached view of life as the pursuit of objects to be possessed."

"I suppose I do," Soroka said. "But your alternative, everyone working for the common good with everything they do? That's what we're doing here. Look around you. Everyone is working hard, everyone is working for the group. What more do you want?"

Guy's head spun and his tongue grew thick as he tried to voice his thoughts. "That wasn't what I meant. There's a difference between what the farmers of den Kindrat were doing and what I'm was talking about. A whole different balance between freedom and duty. For your farmers, duty comes before freedom and is the opposite thing. For us, freedom and duty are identical."

"Oh go on," Soroka said, waving him away. "Don't try to fool me. I know you scouts all have title to landholdings out in the wilds. Big lands, good lands. In good places. Don't you understand what I mean? You are richer than any of the farmers here in Kindrat will ever be. Of course you are free, because you are wealthy and powerful."

Guy thought about that. The Stangers did indeed have title to an area about ten times the size of a Prime Site township – about a quarter of a million hectares. The holding, with enough room for twenty dens, stood south from the joining of the Great Muddy and the Sierra rivers about a thousand klicks west of South Valley. There were forests of greenwood that reached two hundred meters in height, lakes of pure fresh water, fields of boulders and gravel where the glaciers had once roamed. All the scout families held them. Guy's uncle and two aunts each had a holding of similar size, which had once been part of a larger section held by Guy's grandparents – original members of the scout team. And that was only from his father's side. Through his mother's family, he had a share of a tropical holding on an island far to the east of Prime Site.

But he never thought of himself as being personally rich because of the holding. Far from it. His father had explained it years ago – it was for the descendants of the scouts once they had completed their job and the colony was fully developed. He would pass his title on to his children and they would pass it onto theirs. By the time it would be needed, there would be a farmstead for every scout.

"Don't deny it. You must know that what you call freedom comes from owning a whole world – at least until we got here, right? You never knew how rich you were until we brought some poor people here for you to compare yourselves to. You should thank us for this opportunity. But instead, we will be thanking you for your help. You could make a good deal of use out of that title under the right circumstances," Soroka said. "If you just give me a chance ... "

He probably could, Guy realized. But somehow he didn't want to imagine what those circumstances could be – despite the obvious invitation from Soroka to explore them in more detail.

Guy spent the morning thinking about what life would have been like if the Kolbergs had not intruded on the Asgard colony. And the more he thought about it, the angrier he became.

He was so preoccupied by his own turbulent thoughts that he barely noticed the rhythmic gait of his horse and the cool pockets of night air that had pooled in the low grounds.

If it weren't for the Kolbergs, there wouldn't have been any debate over whose plan to follow. The colonists would have carried out the program prepared for them by the Colonial Service and the scouts of den Iroquois.

There wouldn't have been anything to split the colonists up, pitting one group against the others, as the Kolbergs had before the fifty-seven dens of the breakthrough colony had begun to land.

And without that insidious influence, Grampa Bob wouldn't have turned so harshly against the colonists. He was a cranky, depressed old man, but Guy didn't believe he would have spurned the colonists if they had arrived in good order instead of falling in fits in starts from the sky, first Suzanne and Emily, then a farming den from Alaska, finally the rest of the colony in a mad dash to grab a township before their fellow colonists took them all. And Grampa Bob had grown more disgusted the longer it went on.

Jeannie Gilmartin would still be whole and happy today if the Kolbergs hadn't come, Guy realized bitterly.

Of course, he might never have met Emily without their interference. But then again, no one ever proved that someone had tampered with the landing beacon to send the pathfinder team with Emily and her mother to the Main Post.

A warm wind had come up from the southeast and the ground had begun to rise from the valley floor before Guy took notice of his surroundings. He took a bearing on a line of trees that cut across the savanna plain – a sure sign of a river – and headed towards it to water his horse and give it a rest.

Guy found the riverbank just opposite a crowd of duckasaurs. The wide-billed fuzzasaurs padded through the mud along the riverbed, digging up and swallowing yellow plants that grew there in profusion. His horse snorted at the smell of them, and their heads all shot up at once, swiveling on long necks to scan the area. Then one of them started hooting, and they broke into a trot, slapping along the mud. They splashed into the river in a mass and were downstream before Guy could reach the water.

The horse dropped its head to drink, leaving Guy to gaze out across the river and remember how to observe like a scout once again. He recognized the fuzzwort and beastthorn that covered the high wooded banks of the river. Baby's nest, frozen peas and robin eggs blossomed in the shadows of mossback trees and willows. A fleur-de-lis vine climbed a single tree as a forerunner of spring.

In the mud, he saw swamp toadies leaping from puddle to puddle. He remembered a fossil he had seen of a thunder'phibian unearthed by a scout fifty years ago. The phibs were the only land creatures to experience gigantism in Asgard's natural history. The one Guy had seen must have stood two meters tall. The species had died out because it couldn't adapt when the ice age came. Their much smaller descendants would be asleep in the mud, back in hibernation, if the temperatures dropped off tonight.

In a few days, the river itself would be jumping with fish – native Asgardian species and the trout and salmon that an earlier generation of scouts had stocked in the rivers and streams of the two valleys, North and South.

And in the distance, he heard the hooting of bluenecks.

A few hours later, just before low noon, he found his first fuzzy trail. Crowds of grazers tended to walk in single file and over the years, at least around here, they wore smooth, wide trails into the plain. In the open, once the grazers became dispersed, such trails were less common. They appeared only where the natural terrain funneled the beasts together.

He followed the trail uphill, knowing that it would have to lead eventually to his destination – Fuzzasaur Pass. More trails fed into this one, and it eventually linked into a larger one, which led into the woods. Guy followed into the cool darkness beneath the trees, prodding his mount along as he encountered steeper ground.

Eventually, he emerged from the trees at the base of two basalt cliffs no more than a thousand meters apart and fifty meters high. The stone was weathered and smooth, stained with yellow and brown, and split horizontally and vertically by laser straight cracks that made it look quarried.

The fuzzy trail merged with a dozen others, melting into a wide highway that shouldered aside the thin conifers clinging to the base of the rock. The highway was clear today, but in a few weeks, it would be the busiest thoroughfare on Asgard.

Guy rode on through.

***

By the time he reached the other end, a half a kilometer away, he was certain that he'd solved the problem of the grazers. But the solution he had found only filled him with sorrow.

The far side of the pass opened onto a treeless slope that dropped off to a rolling plain covered with savanna grass that extended to the horizon. In the distance, at the hazy edge of visibility, a line of trees marked the path of a river and here and there stood small groves of native conifers and scout-seeded fruit trees.

And stretching as far as Guy could see were fuzzy trails, branching and twisting and braiding themselves into one big highway that lead straight to the pass. The fuzzasaurs themselves were dispersed along the length and breadth of the network of trails. He saw them nestled down amid the grass under the increasing glare of the midday sun, bluenecks, redcrests and silverstreaks, their long necks rising from the plain in little clusters.

He stopped his horse and dismounted, then walked down the trail towards a natural spring to allow it to drink. He pulled out his tablet and sat down on a fallen log. The entry on Fuzzasaur Pass was an old one, made only a few years after the scout team first arrived. It had been written by Kenneth Monahan, a scout who had turned 35 only a week before he left on his patrol. Monahan described the fuzzy trails, the mix of grazers, the maxidons lurking in the shade of distant trees. He could have been there just this morning.

He began to enter his own report on dens Roanoke and Kindrat and his evaluation of their plans for the grazers. Neither one was being practical or realistic. If the grazers followed the pattern of migration that they had since the coming of the Deep Freeze, the fences at Kindrat township would only channel them into other townships and the scents and holograms at den Roanoke wouldn't deter them for a minute.

When he was done, he attached his ID code to the report and saved it for a later date when he could add it to the den database. Then he opened his saddlebags and pulled out the satellite phone, extending the antenna and activating the transmitter. A moment later, a ready light came on, indicating that he had made contact with the communications ship in permanent synchronous orbit over Prime Site. Then he punched in the personal number for Suzanne Baxter.

An intern picked up the phone and told Guy that Suzanne was teaching a class. He set the phone down and waited for her to call back.

While he was waiting, he studied the plain below with his field glasses. The collapsed optics and digital processing rendered a crystal clear image of a crowd near the edge of a copse of trees. As he watched, he saw the crowd suddenly rise from their midday nesting place in unison, their heads all swiveled in the same direction. He followed their view to the trees, where a maxidon stood, its tail twitching as it worked its smaller upper limbs, grasping at the air. He could see the sharp claws on the maxi's lower limbs and could imagine the sound of its tail snapping with nervous energy.

The fuzzasaurs broke into a run, maintaining cadence and step as a unit. The maxidon took after them. They spread out and crisscrossed their paths in an attempt to confuse the predator, but it did not work. The maxi singled out one grazer on the edge of the crowd and followed it move for move. Then in a sudden burst of speed, the big fuzzasaur was on top of the little grazer. There was a cloud of dust as they struggled, then the maxidon hunched over its prey.

Just about the moment that it sunk its teeth into the grazer's long neck, the satellite phone rang, rousing Guy from his long-distance rapture. "Hello, Guy. What have you been up to?" Suzanne's mother asked.

"Keeping busy," he replied. "I think I solved our problem."

"Oh yeah? You make it sound awfully easy."

"Do you know if the colony brought anyone with it who can work in stone?"

"I think we remembered to bring a few. What do you have in mind?"

"Let me tell you what I found first," he said. He told her about den Kindrat's vishnu-break and Soroka's amoral attitudes about the grazers and the rest of the colonists of Asgard. "Soroka sounds pretty scary, doesn't he?"

"Everything about the Kolbergs sound scary to me," Suzanne replied. "Now what's your solution for the grazer problem."

"Fuzzasaur Pass – it's the only door the grazers use to get into South Valley. All we have to do is close that door. The materials are already here – the rock in the pass comes in big brown blocks, already cut for us. It's just a matter of piling them up. The wall doesn't even have to be very high."

"Sounds awfully simple, Guy," she said. "But it may work out. Are you sure there's no other way for them to get around? What about farther up the valley, beyond Mount Thor?"

"Not according the scout records. The Valley is pretty well isolated from the southern plains. This should do the trick."

And what a trick. He choked up at the thought of South Valley without the great crowds of bluenecks, redcrests and silverstreaks. He would never again hear them hooting to one another at dusk or see them running across a field in single file. The savanna plains would be empty and lifeless, an alien landscape where humanity had pushed nature aside.

And he would go down in history as the scout who made it possible. Wouldn't that make Grampa Bob proud?

"I'll believe that when I see it," Suzanne said. "But I'll also see about getting some stonemasons out to that pass. Tell me, Guy, when are you coming home? I have a daughter here who is not too happy about your travel plans."

"Tell Emily that I have some business to take care of at Highland Post before I head back that way. Scout business. There's a High Council coming up in two days and if I hurry, I should be just able to make it by then."

6

We are one den with one purpose. The coming of the colonists has not changed that one bit."

Eddie Gilmartin's amplified voice echoed from the cliffs and woods around the Highland Post. From where Guy stood at the base of the natural amphitheater it seemed like every word went out and returned as garbled thunder. Eddie held center stage at a table with other scout leaders – Lyle Sanderson, Grampa Bob and scoutmasters from Geneva, Northern, Skagerak, Snorri, Avalon and Albion posts. The seats were filled with hundreds of scouts – most of the population of Highland Post was there along with quite a few from Main Post who had come up on the bus. The remaining seven thousand scouts on Asgard were tuned in over the satellite commlink the colonists had provided. Flanking the speakers were a pair of great bonfires, painting the trees and the scouts on the hillside orange and gold, great pillars of smoke rising into the Rudy-lit sky.

"And no one should know that better than you, Grampa Bob," Gilmartin added.

The opening ceremonies of the High Council had been dispensed with quickly by scoutmasters who clearly had their thoughts elsewhere. They hadn't taken long to get down to business – but that's the way scouts always were. Guy was surprised by the directness of the debate – especially after listening to the colonists argue their own decisions out a few months ago. The contrast was reassuring. He may not have agreed with all that Eddie Gilmartin said, but at least he got right to the point.

"You came here voluntarily and took an oath that meant something, Grampa Bob. The younger fellows among us, like me and Lyle, are here by a happenstance of birth. We shouldn't have to teach you about a scout's commitment."

"Like you say, Eddie, I'm an old man," Grampa Bob said. "What more can I do for this den? What more can I do for the colonists? Don't I have a right to spend my last few years doing what I want to do? Haven't I earned that much?"

"Doesn't that depend on what it will mean to the den? You're not talking about going off on your own, Grampa Bob. You want to take a lot of people with you."

"That's their choice. I can't answer for them."

"And your oath?"

"My oath was to preserve and protect this world for posterity. Maybe I can do that better with a few scouts who are willing to live apart from the corruption of the colonists' world."

"Really, Grampa, do you expect – "

"Don't patronize me, Eddie Gilmartin. You and I both know that this isn't really about me and a few hundred starry-eyed boys and girls taking off for Albion. What you're really afraid of is a bigger split between the Prime Site posts and the outliers. You know that if I'm allowed to leave the den, then the scouts at the Main Post and here at Highland are going to break away from you and the others. Isn't that right, Lyle?"

Lyle Sanderson cleared his throat and the rumble shook the leaves of the greenwood trees. "Not exactly, Grampa Bob. Everyone here knows that some of the scouts at Main Post are talking about settling down and starting a farm. A few have even talked about joining colonial dens. But that's only to be expected, and it doesn't mean that we're ready to break up."

"That's not the way I hear it," Grampa Bob replied. "Is it, Eddie?"

"That's not the point, Bob."

"Yes, it is, Eddie. That's exactly the point. Am I right or wrong? Tell us what you think about the breakaways? Isn't everyone at Avalon Post talking about how the Main Posters have all gone colonial because they live next door to Center Township? Isn't that why you're so hot about the den maintaining its unity?"

"Bob, you're not going to get me to start an argument with Lyle. This is about you taking a lot of innocent kids out into the woods to live on their own."

"What do you thinks being a scout is all about, Eddie?"

"Grampa Bob, they're not going to have you to help them for very long."

That seemed to stop the old man in his tracks. Guy, too. He felt fury in his heart for Eddie Gilmartin when he saw how Grampa Bob was hurt by the remark. Even if he was right about keeping the den together, he was wrong about everything else.

But so was Grampa Bob. Did everyone at the Main Post want to be a colonist? Not that Guy had noticed. All this talk seemed so pointless to him. What was it going to accomplish?

And why was Grampa Bob trying so hard to turn the scouts

against one another? That thought suddenly filled him with a sense of dread. The old scout really was working against both Eddie Gilmartin and Lyle Sanderson, dividing the den to achieve his own, private ends. That was wrong, against everything that Grampa Bob had taught the young scouts all his life. Why had he suddenly turned his back on his own principals?

"I'll be able to teach them what I know in the time I have left, Eddie," Grampa Bob finally answered after a long, embarrassing silence. Guy didn't find his tone convincing.

The debate continued for another hour, as speakers from the outlying dens expressed their points of view – all opposed to Grampa Bob's isolationist group and in favor of unity. Nothing they said advanced the issue a single centimeter.

Guy noticed a young scout walk up to the table and give a note to Lyle Sanderson. The scoutmaster read it, then folded it up and stuck it in his pocket. Then he spoke up.

"I think we need to take a break and figure out if there's anything we can decide at this meeting that was worth the trouble of calling it," he said.

Eddie Gilmartin grumbled and Grampa Bob sneered, but no one objected to the recess and suddenly the tension broke as people recovered their own voices instead of listening to the strong ones that clashed below.

Sanderson came over to Guy and bent his head down. "Come with me, Guy, there's something going on that I want you to be a witness to."

***

The small lodge up the hill from the amphitheater was crowded with steamy, sweaty bodies of men full of purpose and will. Guy jammed his back up against a rough-hewn wall and tried to identify as many of them as he could.

Eddie Gilmartin held court at the head of a small table. His brother and a couple of friends stood behind him. At the other end of the table were a handful of scouts he knew from the Main Post. He recognized them immediately as cronies of Henry Schmidt – and by that connection linked to the Kolbergs. His back stiffened and his nerves tightened. What did they want that was worth interrupting a High Council meeting?

Mike Hennig, the biggest of the party, stood up and started the palaver.

"We just want to let you know that there a few others doing the same as us who didn't want tell the rest of the den – Henry Schmidt, to name just one. That's why we wanted to keep this meeting closed and private. We figured we owed you something – scout's honor still means something to some of us, you know."

"I know, Mike," Lyle Sanderson said. "But maybe you'd better start at the beginning for the others who didn't see your note."

"I'm sorry, Lyle," Hennig said. "Well, we just thought we should let the den know before things go too far about our plans. It doesn't make any sense to argue all night long about letting Grampa Bob leave the den because we – us here and the others outside – we're planning on leaving too."

There was a sudden commotion of restrained epithets and flexing muscles. Guy felt anger towards them himself, but kept it under restraint.

"Tell everyone why, Mike," Sanderson interjected.

"It's the Kolbergs, Lyle. You know that. We're joining the Kolbergs. We're putting up title to our back country holdings to become their partners. It's our way of helping Asgard grow. We want to be in on some of the great things that are going to be happening here. And we think the Kolbergs are the way to go. I know that doesn't make us too popular around here – ”

“You're damned right it doesn't!” someone yelled from the back of the lodge to Guy's right. Guy cheered silently, but Hennig ignored it.

“But we've got a right to make up our own minds.”

“What kind of partnership are they talking about, Mike?” Eddie Gilmartin asked. “Did you check the fine print on the contract?”

“Full partnership, Eddie. Hell, they're going to take some of us back to Tik with them when they go. This is my chance to see the stars, Eddie. I don't know about everyone else, but I don't want to spend the rest of my life counting rippers and grazers or holed up in a tent on the other side of the Avalon Sea. Face it, Lyle, some of us just weren't cut out to be very good scouts ... ”

That prompted an outburst of barely suppressed rage from most of the scouts in the lodge. They jeered and groaned, and Mike Hennig and his friends looked around with sudden fear in their eyes.

Guy thought back to the things Stepan Soroka had said at den Kindrat. He had known. He and his associates had been after the weak-willed scouts of den Iroquois right from the beginning, starting with Henry Schmidt. Soroka had even tried to bait Guy into the deal with his talk of the “the right circumstances.”

“What if we don't want you to leave?” Eddie said.

“What are you going to do to us? Grampa Bob asked for your permission because he wants your help. We don't need either one. You can't force us to stay on Asgard. You can't force us to stay in den Iroquois. And you can't keep us from signing over our holdings. Scout law says so.”

“Don't quote scout law to me.”

“Then don't make empty threats. Really, Eddie, no wonder the den is falling apart. Lyle, I think we've said enough. Remember, we didn't have to tell anyone about this.”

"That's what you think – " Eddie started to say before Lyle cut him off.

"I appreciate that, Mike," Sanderson said, motioning the renegade scouts to the door. They exited quickly through a gauntlet of fiercely burning faces, and, for a moment, Guy thought violence might break out before they were through the door.

"I guess that changes things quite a bit, doesn't it, Eddie?" Lyle Sanderson asked the other scoutmaster. "I'd say we have a few things to settle before we're finished tonight."

Guy felt the ground shifting beneath his feet as the fear of terrible change took hold of him.

Resolved: that Senior Scoutmaster Robert Scoggins be allowed to withdraw from den Iroquois with those scouts who wish to join him, and be it further resolved that they be provided with the equipment, supplies and landholdings needed for their convenience and safety."

The clerk of the council, a large man from Northern Post with a voice that needed no electronic amplification, read from the tablet on the table before him. Guy felt his throat tighten as roll was called.

"Albion."

"Albion Post casts two votes in favor of the resolution."

"Avalon."

"Aye."

"Geneva."

"One aye and one nay."

"Highland."

"We cast all four votes in favor."

"Main Post."

"Two for, two against."

"Skagerak."

"Nay."

"Snorri."

"Aye."

"The vote is eleven aye, four nay. The resolution passes."

A knot in Guy's stomach tightened as he saw Grampa Bob raise his hand to speak. The old man looked tired and not at all happy despite his victory. What was he going to say now?

"I want to thank all of you who supported me," Grampa Bob said when he was given the nod by the council president. "But I think that you've still got some unfinished business before you. Unless you want Eddie Gilmartin and Lyle Sanderson to snap at each other's heels for a few months before you call another council."

Someone at the far end of the table made a remark in a poorly muffled stage whisper, and Grampa Bob turned in that direction. "Don't tell me to sit down, Wilbur Gray. I haven't left the den yet and I've got something to say to you before I do leave.

"As long as the den is breaking up, we might as well have this out. There's two ways the rest of you can go. You can keep on with the mission of the den, live out in the wilds and break the trail for the colonists who will follow you. Or you can move into Prime Site and try live alongside them, teaching them what you know. Both of these are honorable callings and you may not all choose now, but choose you must. The time has come for the scouts on Asgard to all grow up. Our long innocence has ended. The world your grandparents and I left behind has caught up with us. And with it have come all the old sins – greed, lust, anger and hatred. I don't think there is any way to avoid being corrupted by the colonists unless we break contact with all of you. Some of you may think you can compromise by keeping to the old ways, but the old ways are gone. You'll learn that slowly, and those of you who find yourself agreeing with us should find your own path into the wilds. Please don't come looking for us, though.

"But to those of you who stay here in the Prime Site, a word of warning. Do not forget who and what you are, no matter how much your lives change." He reached into his pocket and pulled out a piece of paper.

"Here it is, Eddie. You wrote the resolution for me, so I'm returning the favor. Mr. Clerk, listen up carefully.

"I hereby move that we adopt the following resolution. Resolved: that the members of scout den Iroquois who wish to continue the mission of the den and scout new territory for the colonists of Asgard be allowed to form a new organization to be called den Pequot, and that it be further resolved that den Iroquois will retain title to the Main Post, the Highland Post, the Highland township and the Main Post township, while title to all remaining posts and townships currently settled be turned over to the new den.

"This is something that has to come sooner or later, boys. Now you can blame it all on me."

Guy was overwhelmed. He looked down at the table and at the scoutmasters around it, lit by the flickering glow of the bonfires at the far ends of the stage. For a moment, he saw them as they really were. Grampa Bob was a scornful and bitter tyrant, telling everyone what to do, what was best for them. Eddie Gilmartin was impatient and ambitious, filled with a restlessness that would never be quenched. Lyle Sanderson was a passive, withdrawn man grown old before his time whose life had remained within the safe bounds of South Valley and whose future lay there too.

They were all very ordinary, very human figures, he realized, all sharing feelings very much like his.

Grampa Bob passed the resolution down the table to the clerk and the great natural bowl full of scouts hung in tense silence until it reached the end.

"If this isn't what you want, now is the time to say so," the old scoutmaster said.

The president of the council, the scoutmaster from Albion, said: "There's a motion on the floor, do I hear a second?"

A few people shouted from the audience, then another scoutmaster from one of the outlying posts raised a hand. "Second," he mumbled.

"The motion has been made and seconded," said the president. "Is there discussion?"

"This isn't really the time or the place for this discussion," Lyle Sanderson said meekly.

"This is exactly the time and the place," Grampa Bob shot back. "Or would you rather wait until the Kolbergs come around the Main Post putting price tags on the furniture and offering to rent you back the main lodge at a discount?"

"Why fight it, Lyle?" Eddie Gilmartin said. "You know he's right. And we can't face the Kolbergs and the colonists unless our house is in order. It's something we've both discussed. We can't try to go two directions at once and we can't both be the leader of den Iroquois. Separation isn't divorce, you know. We'll still come back to the Main Post and visit."

"I thought you were the one who wanted to keep the den together."

"I did. Or I thought I did. Maybe I shouldn't get involved in politics like this. It's not my strongest trait. It just seems that things have changed tonight. And they're going to keep on changing. If we don't face this now, we're going to have to before the end of the year anyway. I move the question."

The council agreed to end debate, the clerk read the resolution aloud and then went through the roll. There were no dissenting votes and the resolution was adopted.

Guy wanted to cry. He realized as the gavel came down that he had already made his choice between the new den and the old. As much as he wanted to Grampa Bob to respect him, he could never turn his back on the world the way the old scout was doing. And as much as he believed in the greater duty of the scouts to explore Asgard, he could not join a den lead by Eddie Gilmartin. He had made his commitment to the colonists nearly a year ago, in a tent with Emily Baxter. There was no question of changing that. But he knew suddenly that being a scout was never going to be what he once thought it would ...

***

The bus ride from Highland Post to Asgard University the next day was long, dreary and depressing. Guy stayed on board when it stopped over for a half hour at the Main Post. He couldn't bear to look at it without feeling a terrible sense of loss.

He tried to nap, but images of the council meeting kept appearing in his dreams, only with grotesque caricatures of the participants holding forth.

Grampa Bob took on the look of a wild-eyed prophet with a robe and staff, straight out of the religious books. Eddie Gilmartin reverted to a primitive, Wild West cowboy character from an old video. And Lyle Sanderson became a long-haired guru from a spiritual disk. Surrounding the meeting was a crowd of hungry animals with their noses to the ground, snuffling loudly as they hunted their prey – the

Kolbergs. All that kept the beasts out was a tall barrier of twisted metal ribbon strung on sharp wooden stakes.

When the bus came over the last rise before the lake and he saw the wooden buildings spread out along the shore, his heart soared with joy. At least there was some place on Asgard that didn't make him feel bad. He could hardly wait to see Suzanne Baxter.

He laughed at that thought. It was probably the first time in his life that he wanted to see his girlfriend's mother more than his girlfriend. But he found Emily first, and found that her warm embrace soothed many of the open wounds that he had suffered the night before. Together, they went off to search for Suzanne. They found her in her lab, feeding the bits and bytes.

She stood at the cage for the byte named Giga, measuring out a precise meal in a plastic cup.

"So what's happening with Fuzzasaur Pass?" he asked with preamble. "Are they building the wall yet?"

Suzanne looked up and around, then returned to the task at hand, leaving Guy feeling a little disappointed and bewildered. He had been hoping for a more gracious welcome, although he should have known better than to expect that from Suzanne. "Yes, they're up there now," she said after a moment's silence.

She set the food tray in the cage, closed the top and put the food and measuring cup on the lab table. Then she smiled at Guy.

"But if you're waiting for a hero's welcome, you'd better calm down," she said.

Guy felt his face grow hot.

That was the last thing he had been waiting for. But he had expected Suzanne to relieve some of the burden of guilt that he felt about ending the annual migration of fuzzasaurs. She did not.

"We were very lucky here in South Valley. The topography and the terrain have given us a unique opportunity. Your idea was right. If we block off the pass, then we deny access to the valley to the grazers." Emily squeezed his hand and smiled.

"But if I solved the grazer problem, why don't I feel a lot better about it."

"Probably because you know it's not really a solution."

He frowned, but knew that she was right. "No, it's not. It just creates a whole lot of other problems ... "

"That's right. Once we're rid of the grazers, what do we do about the animals whose lives depend on them? The maxidons tend to follow the crowds, so there shouldn't be too many of them left over. But the rippers, the cavers and the draggers all depend on a regular supply of grazer meat. You've taken away their food supply, Guy. What are we going to do about that? They're going to turn on the duckasaurs and the pineheads, the hivedrillers and the minisaurs. And they're going to go after the colonists' livestock – or even the colonists themselves. The maxidon may not like the way we smell, but the others aren't so picky.

"You've only reduced the number of animals we have to slaughter and replaced the grazers with other species. And don't start trying to figure out another way around it, because there isn't one. We are alien invaders on this planet. We are imposing our ecology on it and we're kicking the indigenous one out. That means the animals, no matter how beautiful and gracious they are, must go. And it means we will end up killing a lot of them. There is no way around it."

"I never even thought of all that. I was upset because there wouldn't be any more grazers in South Valley. Now I feel even worse."

"This may have been one reason your Grampa Bob decided that there was no way to escape the evil that we brought to Asgard. As I understand it, there was a long debate on old Earth before the New Era about whether we had the moral right to colonize worlds like this in the first place – especially knowing that we would have to slaughter the grazers or the rippers or both before we were done."

She returned to the bag of byte food and looked down at her tablet before measuring out a small amount. Then she opened the top of the Mega's cage.

"And the other thing is that your solution only applies to South Valley. What are we going to do when colonists start to settle on the other side of the pass? Or when they move south of Albion? The grazers are everywhere. We can't just close a door on them forever."

"No, I guess we can't. That's why Grampa Bob was wrong, isn't it? He's trying to close a door on the world. But you can't really keep it out."

"Cheer up, Guy. You've bought us time – 20 years of it. According to the settlement plan, it'll be that long before we reach our limits here at Prime Site. Maybe by then, we can figure out some way to live with the bluenecks and the redcrests and even the rippers and the maxidons."

"How are we going to do that? There won't be any around to practice on. And the way things look to me, we aren't going to be able to figure out how to live with one another, let alone the fuzzies. Everybody is building up walls and fences and running away. They're all trying to close doors on the world ... "

Then an idea struck him from that dark place where ideas lurk before they are known. Doors could open, too.

"You know, it just occurred to me – if there were a few grazers around, they could live off the empty townships, keep away from the farmers and we could start learning how to get along with them today, not 20 years from now. Suzanne, do you think we could tell the stonemasons up in Fuzzasaur Pass to put a gate in that wall to let some of the grazers through – "

"-- at a regulated rate until there were only as many as we wanted before we closed the gate? Oh Guy, for a scout, you're an awfully sophisticated young man. That's an excellent idea. I'll get on the phone right now."

Emily threw her arms around Guy and planted a hungry kiss on his lips.

He felt a warm glow rise from the soles of his feet and for the first time in days, he felt satisfied with himself.

But not for very long.

"Don't start to get too self-satisfied, Guy," Suzanne said. "That still doesn't solve everything. First of all, we've got to count the little fuzzies as they come through the gate. How would you like to spend a couple of weeks up there doing that?"

"Mother!" Emily squealed in protest. "He just got back."

"Well, maybe we can do that electronically. But I can think of one job he could help with. Someone's going to have to close the gate when we've let enough of them through. Someone big and strong – just like you ... "

Guy let the suggestion hang in the air as he returned Emily's kiss.

DEN OF WOLVES

Guy Stanger leaned back so he could get a better look at the stars. Rudy had set long ago and the clear night revealed the Milky Way in all its glory, crossing the sky in a broad band from east to west with the thicket of dust and star clouds that marked the galactic core centered halfway up from the southern horizon.

He sat on the porch of the main lodge of what had once been the Glacier Valley Scout Post. Emily Baxter sat beside him, holding his hand in hers.

"You see the dark spot in the middle? That's the Coal Sack. It's just a big old cloud of dust hanging in front of everything else."

"Where's Sol?" asked Emily.

"Right beside it. See the bright cross beside the Coal Sack – the Southern Cross? Just to the left of it is a little triangle. The star on top is Sol, the one beneath it is Alpha Centauri. Off to the right there is

Sirius and up there away from the Milky Way is Eta Cassiopeiae –
only six light years away."

"Yuck," said Emily.

"Yuck?"

"That's what I said. If it weren't for Eta Cass being so close, the
Kolbergs would have left us alone."

"The fault, dear Caesar, lies not within our stars, but in ourselves,"
Guy said.

"Says who?"

"Brutus, I think."

"I'm cold. Let's go inside and find something to eat."

"Sounds like a good idea to me."

Emily and her family were among the lucky few who had been
quartered here in the main building. The rest of the den was
distributed among a dozen dormitories that offered fewer amenities
and a stronger taste of the old scout life. Guy had no pity for either
group. Until last year, when the colonists took over, he had been
quite content with the post's spartan environment.

But he did have a craving for leftover soup – although it lacked the
thick chunks of fuzzasaur that he always included in his recipes.
Emily was a vegetarian and refused to make the soup the way he liked
it. Even so, it still was better than the pasty stuff that comprised the
colonists' rations.

She removed the pot from the fridge and set it on the power range,
stirring it as it came to a boil.

"I don't like to see you worrying about the Kolbergs all the time,"
Emily said after a while.

"Someone has to do it."

"What can you do about it?"

"I can send your little brother out on another run. He likes that kind of thing. Have him start counting dens to see who's on their side, who's on our side and who's in the middle – especially who's in the middle. With the constitutional convention coming up, who knows what could happen."

"I suppose so," Emily said.

"And you could help too."

Her eyes widened. "And what have you got in mind for me, Guy Stanger? I'm not about to go spying on Kolbergs for you."

"I was thinking about something a little closer to home. You're a socioeconomics student. You've got access to the colonial reports. Start checking the numbers. Look for something unusual. Maybe we can correlate some differences between the dens who are working with the Kolbergs and the rest of us."

"I don't know, Guy. It all sounds so ... "

"Paranoid. That's the word you're looking for, isn't it?"

"I was going to say suspicious. Don't you think you're blowing things a little out of proportion?"

"No, I don't. Neither does your mother."

"I'm not sure I trust Mother all that much."

"Then trust me. I've spoken to some of them. These are not nice people we're dealing with here."

"I know," she said with a pained expression. "I didn't say I wouldn't help. I just don't know what good it'll do."

"It'll make me feel better, for one thing. And you might come up with something."

"I've got other ways of making you feel better," she suggested with a seductive smile. "Do you want to see?"

Guy smiled back and stroked her face with the back of his hand. "Again?"

"What's the matter, am I too much for you?" she asked as she picked the soup bowls up and put them in the sink. "Tell me something, though. While Joey is out spying on the Kolbergs and I'm here crunching numbers, what are you going to do?"

"I'm going stay here and worry – what else."

She flipped her head back in a laugh that summed up all her feelings about Guy's division of labor, then ran quickly down the hall as the young scout took after her.

***

For Lin Palmer, the split between delegates from dens linked to the Kolbergs and those who were not began a short time after he boarded the bus for Center Township.

Half the seats were full when he climbed aboard at the Aroostook village center and took a seat near the middle. Two knots of passengers, one in the front and one in the back, were locked together in hushed conversations broken occasionally by laughter or a loud remark. He knew that today's run would be carrying other delegates, but he couldn't overhear enough from either group to tell who was who or what they were talking about. So he rode in silence for a half an hour.

Then the bus pulled into the village center at Jasper township and picked up two passengers. Lin recognized one of them – Hans Beck.

The sight of the man sent a chill up his spine.

He watched Beck closely and felt his face flush when the man looked straight at him. There was a moment of hesitation, but no response from the Jasper den leader, no sign of mutual recognition. Oh well, Beck must have talked to dozens of farmers, while Lin had only met one surly manipulator.

But Beck did seem to recognize other passengers on the bus, greeting the cluster of men in the first few rows of seats and taking a place among them. They continued their discrete conversation as the bus pulled out.

Lin looked towards the back of the bus and examined that group more closely. If the bunch in the front were friendly with Beck, then they must be Kolberg supporters. That meant the ones in the back …

"On your way to the convention?" asked a woman with an odd accent, clipped and British, Lin thought, but he wasn't sure.

"Yes," he said. "You too?"

"Gladly. Betty Montgomery, den Cornwall." She offered her hand over the back of the seat, and Lin shook it.

"Lin Palmer, den Aroostook."

"That's Maine, isn't it? I'm from the south of England myself. Long way from home, what. George, my husband, he's the farmer. He figured I'd be more useful talking everyone's ear off at Center than I would be his. I guess the rest of the den felt the same, because here I am."

"They picked me because I've got an extra hand back on my farm," Lin said. "And because they trust me not to let the Kolbergs pull anything tricky."

"Pardon my French, but damn those K's and their scheming," Betty said. "That's the same reason my den sent me. To stop them from perverting this business with their plots and plans and labor bonds and everything else. I don't know how we're going to do it. They're organized and we're just offended."

"Maybe we can help," suggested a third voice – one of the group at the rear of the bus. "Ed Findlay, den Lincoln. Not everyone on this bus is a delegate, but nearly all of us are. I don't suppose it's too early for coalition building, do you?"

Lin and Betty smiled and joined the rest of the cell. By the time they reached Center Township, they had organized a caucus of five dens ready to block the influence of the Kolbergs at the convention.

Not a bad morning's work, Lin realized. But it was only a beginning. The real fight would come later.

***

At three stories, the Hotel Asgard was the tallest building in Center Township – although a few of the cabins at Highland Post beat it out for the planetary title. Lin was given a room on the top floor, two flights up, that he would share with Ed Findlay. He unpacked, called home and spoke for a long time with his wife.

This was the first time they'd been apart since before leaving Earth many months ago. The precise number was lost to him after the change in calendars. More than a year, Asgard time, or seven months, old Earth time. Their baby wasn't due until November, but she was still nervous. Even with a hired hand around to do the work, it was hard on her.

The convention would not convene for another day, so Lin had time to take a walking tour of Center Town. With a population of ten thousand, it was more than a village, sprawling over nine square kilometers.

There were hectares of tents and houses and shops and workyards and equipment. Warehouses filled with rations and supplies lined the nearby landing strip. The permanent residents of Center included two management dens, two health dens, one special services den, a food processing den, and a service den. The bulk of the land in the township remained empty and uncultivated. No farmers were assigned here, and the territory was left vacant for expansion of the urban center and adjoining agricultural dens – and for the fuzzasaur crowds that had begun their annual spring migration into South Valley.

Lin had heard a story about this year's migration – that it was being regulated at a pass in the southern hills to keep the numbers down. Good thing, that. He didn't want the grazers to start working on his corn, and he didn't think a scarecrow would keep the fur-covered saurians out of his fields.

The streets of the township were thick with traffic – both vehicular and pedestrian. The number of people here was overwhelming at first. Lin had spent the winter in relative isolation, visiting the Aroostook village center periodically to pick up supplies. It wasn't the same as Caribou or Houlton back home, but Center was clearly the closest Asgard came to a thriving metropolis. And it was as close to one as Lin wanted to come.

The main topic of discussion at supper that night in the main dining room of the Asgard Hotel was the Kolbergs.

"This is our colony, not theirs. If they want to run things, they can go back to Tik and do it there," said Harry Bayard, leader of den Matanuska, a farming den that had settled up near Glacier Valley.

"I agree," said Betty Montgomery. "But the question is, how do we write a constitution that protects us from the Kolbergs without creating a tyranny of our own? The law is a tough thing to tailor to specific political needs."

"Can't we just fix it so they're not allowed to play their games on our planet?" Lin asked. He had found himself at the same table as Bayard, Annie, Ed Findlay, and a handful of delegates from the north who were also wary of the Kolbergs.

"It's not that simple," said Betty. "You can't name them specifically – not unless you want to change from law to dictatorial fiat. You have to phrase things in general terms. That means you close the door on our own people. Constitutions are delicate things. A little mistake here can mean centuries of difficulty for our children and grandchildren."

Lin shivered. "I thought this was going to be like a big den council.

Just make up some sensible rules and vote."

"Politics is never sensible, Lin," Bayard said. "Otherwise we'd leave it to the AIs. I'm afraid we're going to have to work hard to keep things from getting out of control. And even then, I'm not sure we can do it. Once this thing is signed and ratified, it's out of our hands."

"You're starting to get me nervous," Lin said.

"Well don't be, duckie," Betty said. "There are enough of us to write a constitution that keeps the K's from taking over. Don't worry about it."

"That's not what I'm worried about," said Bayard. "I'm worried that they'll do whatever they want, no matter what the constitution says … "

***

Each of the fifty-seven dens that had reached Asgard contained about sixteen hundred members. Throw in the eight thousand scouts and the human population of Asgard was somewhere above in excess of a hundred thousand souls.

Each colonial den had two representatives at the convention, the scouts had four, for a total of 118 delegates. Today they were all seated in the high-ceilinged warehouse that had been converted into a meeting hall and given the name Hollister Auditorium, after the colony ship that hadn't made it to Asgard. They clustered in groups around large tables with a tablet in the center of each one.

Lin was amazed and a little intimidated by the rich mixture of faces. Men and women from North and South Valleys, machinists, farmers, truckers, doctors, teachers and everything in between, stood to represent their dens.

He felt a little overwhelmed at his own insignificance in the face of all the others. His voice was so small and his sense was shallow. He was afraid that he would carry little weight at this gathering.

At the podium in the front of the hall, raised above the rest and decorated with blue and white bunting, the leaders of the ad hoc colonial commission, which had managed the colony's business since the first days in orbit before the landings began, stood in casual disarray.

As the clock neared low noon, however, they found their places. And as the numbers clicked over into place, John Porter, the head of the commission, brought down his gavel and pounded the hall into silence.

"Ladies and gentlemen, the Constitutional Convention of Asgard is hereby brought to order ... "

The truck bounced and jogged and slid as it made its way along the rough dirt track that climbed higher and higher above the savanna plain, jerking Joey Baxter hard against the seatbelt that held him in place. They weren't traveling very fast, forty klicks an hour tops. But the way they were bouncing around, it felt like a hundred. And the shoulder harness was meant for a full-grown man, not an adolescent, leaving a lot of slack in which to slop around. His arms were red and sore from the chafing, and they weren't even halfway to the end of the road.

"How are you doing, kid?" asked Lucky Levesque as he swerved hard to avoid a frost heave on the middle of the track. Joey bounced against the door.

"I'll live," Joey said. "How long before you guys finish the road up here, anyway?"

Lucky laughed. "Next spring, from what I hear. They're going to work on the other side of the river this summer. Then they've got bridges to build. The little feeder roads like this one are pretty low on the priority list."

"That's a mistake. I figured it out. The driving time, round trips and wear-and-tear make it less cost-effective to wait until the main arteries are finished. The unpaved roads use up more driving time, require more maintenance on the trucks and they leave the outlying townships with reduced services."

The truck driver whistled. "You figured that out, eh?"

"Just a quick simulation model on my tablet. I tried two or three different configurations. The best way to take care of things would be to put a paved artery up here in the foothills parallel to the river. That way, you could operate a loop, a full circuit. Goods would travel faster and you'd be able to make a quicker run. Less time on the road."

"I'm for that. You know, the rest of the drivers have been complaining about the upland runs. Just like you said – too much time for too small a load. Did you tell anybody back at the den?"

"Nah. Who'd listen to a kid like me?"

"I guess you're right. They don't seem to hear anything us drivers tell them. Looks like we're stuck with things the way they are until they figure it out for themselves."

"Now if the Kolbergs had sold their plan, we could have a couple of ring roads with connecting spokes all centered on the urban hub. But then you'd have the congestion of a centralized transport network. Traffic would jam up at peak hours and you'd get delays and bottlenecks."

"And you'd have the bloodsuckers in charge," Lucky said with a sneer.

"Yes, you'd have the bloodsuckers in charge, that's true.

Personally, I think we'd be better off if we took their advice – but only if they didn't come with it. They're right about a lot of things, you know."

"Like what?"

"I like the way they want to get things organized. We've got too much confusion here. Everyone's running off in different directions. There's no one to keep things together."

"You mean like a governor?"

"Yeah. Someone who would do what the Kolbergs want to do – only for us and not for them."

"Someone like you?"

Joey broke into a smile. "Someday, maybe. When I grow up."

"And what don't you like about the K's?"

He squinted and pursed his lips, thinking hard. "I'm not one of them." Lucky broke out in a loud guffaw and slapped his thigh. "I guess you aren't," he said.

The track smoothed out a little bit as they approached a small lake and hugged the shore, though the holes in the gravel surface kept the truck bouncing until they slowed down to thirty klicks. The vehicle was a cross between a farm truck and one of the big highway rigs that ran the road between Highland Post and Glacier Valley. It had rugged suspension and a smaller bed. Today, the load was a container of plastic construction fittings from den Levitt – window frames, casements, door knobs, cleats, joints and a whole slew of specialized products. The farm dens could usually come up with lumber and men to cut it and nail it together, but the odd parts needed to finish a job were more efficiently produced on the jigs of the construction den.

Their destination was Olympia township, nestled high up in the valley near the Vogelsberg Ridge. Joey was along for the ride because he'd heard that den Olympia was supposed to be one of the strongest

Kolberg supporters in the colony. He wanted to find out for sure.

So far, he had counted sixteen dens firmly behind the offworlders – farmers, two of the educational dens, half the service dens, a health den, and even den Levitt.

Their reasons were varied. The educational dens had a lot of secondary school types, the kind that used to give Joey a hard time because of his unorthodox approach to school – he would appear once a week, whether he needed to or not, take his exams, drop off his completed assignments, and then disappear. Before he left Earth, he had worked himself up to a university sophomore reading level and was knocking off tensor calculus without breaking a sweat. Although he hadn't tackled astronomy yet, he'd found that stoichometric chemistry was another easy subject for him. He drove some of the teachers crazy. They seemed to think he needed to be in class in order to learn something – discipline, they claimed. They were the type that supported the Kolbergs.

The doctors from den Reed, the health den from Orange County, California, treated their nurses and patients like cattle. Prime Kolberg country.

Den Levitt was full of hard-working blue collar stiffs who swallowed the Kolberg appeal to work hard for the future – and they were tired of taking the blame for the lag in building houses for the other colonists. The Kolbergs played into that by telling them that it was the fault of the woodsmen in den Bunyan and the administrators at Center Township.

The farmers were a mix of religious types and backwater boys from South Africa, Canada and the U.S. Midwest. The service dens went along because their leaders were mean and nasty and used to city life. They were hedging their bets by backing what they saw to be a proven winner in the politics of the street.

Joey didn't begrudge any of them their opinions, although he thought a lot of them were just silly. He'd been more than a little impressed by the Kolbergs at first, until Guy pointed out to him that their plans had no room for an ambitious adolescent from den Middlesex who wanted to get rich as the colony grew. Somehow he knew they were not about to share the wealth with the local entrepreneurs, no matter what they said.

***

The truck jinked and jerked to a stop, skidding the last meter on rough gravel. The silence wrapped Joey's ears like a blanket. His arms and legs tingled from the vibrations of the long rough ride.

The village ran along the shore of the lake, a handful of low buildings, a single lodge, a health clinic marked by a red cross on the wall, a couple of warehouses and a barn. There were a few people hanging around in the common greensward that led to the lodge, but a long line of them, maybe a dozen or more adults and half again as many children, trailed out of the clinic.

Mud pox, Joey realized. It was spreading quickly now that spring was here. The colonists had been ready with antibiotics and medications to treat the symptoms, but there was nothing on hand to prevent it. The scouts who had returned to Earth after the first few years on Asgard brought back information – medical data and horror stories – but no samples of the virus to be used to create a vaccine or a countervirus.

Now the health dens were working overtime to produce enough vaccine for everyone, but without success. It took a week to cook up each batch in the lab, not nearly as fast as nature was doing on its own. So far, they'd come up with enough for the babies and youngest kids and those with special problems, respiratory cases and people with allergic reactions.

He sighed. This only complicated the mission he had set for himself. And it was already hard enough.

The word from drivers like Lucky and his mates was that Olympia was a Kolberg den, through and through. They'd lined up behind the interlopers early and backed them in the debates before landing. And since they'd come down only to find themselves assigned to an upland township at the wrong end of a bad road, their support for the Kolbergs had grown.

Buy Joey wasn't here just to count votes. He took the drivers at their word. He had a different objective in mind.

Although Peter Kolberg, his brother, his cousins and their associates had made themselves visible throughout the colony, no one had yet learned the location of their base camp.

They must have wintered over somewhere safe and sheltered, that much was certain. But they were a secretive lot and no one could pry the information from them.

The rumors were that it was up on Vogelsberg Ridge somewhere. Joey had played with the possibility that it was over in North Valley, on the other side of the ridge, but that didn't make sense. The bulk of the colonists and the center of gravity for the colony were in South Valley. The seacoast on the east side of Mt. Loki was ruled out after late summer storms battered the coves and beaches there. And the townships south of the river were a ferry ride too far to be of much use to the Kolbergs' purposes.

So Joey had come to Olympia in search of clues.

Lucky had warned him in advance to be careful. With spring here, the convention in session and some kind of political maneuvering already underway, the adults of the den were already suspicious and on edge. The truck driver's gentle questions had been deflected with glaring eyes and sharp remarks, leaving Joey without anything more to go on than his own suspicions.

That left only one alternative – one that Joey approached with as much enthusiasm as following ripper tracks into a box canyon. The other kids.

Joey did not get along well with children, his own age or any other age. They were so tedious and simple, or noisy and obnoxious, or aggressive and abusive. After growing up in close proximity to the faculty of Middlesex University before it left Earth, he much preferred the company of adults, preferably educated adults, though in a pinch any would do.

The truth was that he didn't know how to get along with other adolescents. But now he had to.

He found a handful of them congregated in an open space behind one of the warehouses. A basketball hoop hung from the wall and a round ball sat on the ground. That wasn't good. Joey was no good at athletics in general, but basketball in particular was alien territory for the short, slightly overweight teen. Then he saw one of the boy's kick the ball to his mate, who flipped it into the air with a toe and bounced it off his knee and forehead to a third youth. Soccer. There was something he could fake – if he absolutely had to. After all, you just had to kick the ball in the right direction.

He walked up to the group slowly. There were nine of them, six boys and three girls. When he came within range, one of the boys kicked the ball in his direction. He took two nervous steps sideways to intercept it, hoping his uncertain moves would be laid to awkwardness and not the nervous fear that caused them.

"Don't get too close," called a boy with red hair who looked to be his own age. "We don't want to get the pox."

"I don't have the pox. I've already been checked," Joey said. "But how do I know I won't get it from you?"

"'Cause we've been checked too," said a skinny youth wearing green shorts and sandals. Joey passed the ball to Red, who relayed it to

Skinny.

"Who are you?" Red asked. "And what are you doing up here?"

"My name's Joey Baxter and I came up with the supply truck for a ride. Now I have to wait until they turn the container around and send us back. Boring stuff. What is there to do around here, anyway?"

"You're doing it," said Skinny. "This place is dead. The pox is the most excitement we've had since we landed. All the rest of the time it's schoolwork and farmwork. I don't know why my folks dragged me here from Washington. At least there we had 3-V and the arco-mall."

"Oh Arnold, you're such a whine," one of the girls said. "That's all you boys are interested in – 3-V and the arco-mall."

Skinny Arnold made a face at his taunters and kicked the ball hard off the wall of the warehouse. Red ran after it and passed it to Joey, who stretched to block it, but slipped on wet grass and went down on his face. He heard a chorus of laughter from the other kids, but ignored it and rose quickly, running to retrieve the ball.

"Ever go hiking up on the ridge?" Joey asked carefully. It was the question he had rehearsed all the way up from Center Township, the one that he hoped would lead to more information about the Kolberg base. He was afraid that it would sound forced and arouse suspicion. It did.

"Nah. It's too far," said Red. "Mostly we're just stuck around here. You hike much?"

"A little bit," Joey lied. "Last summer we went overnight backpacking a couple of times down at Glacier Valley. Camped out near the ice."

"They won't let us hike up on the ridge," Skinny Arnold said. "Off limits."

"How come?" Joey asked, his interest aroused. The query was a mistake. He could tell by the way Red's face froze. The girls picked it up the quickest.

"Do you like to hike or just ask questions?" asked the oldest one. Joey shrugged and toed the soccer ball. "Just curious."

"I think he's a spy," said the girl. "Arnold, you've got a big mouth. If your dad finds out you've been talking to outsiders about the ridge, you're going to be in big trouble."

The kids had all stopped their adolescent motions and now stood in a semicircle facing Joey. He felt the skin crawl across his back and up his neck. What was he going to do next?

It was probably a good time to make his exit – if they would let him. The young girl had given more away by her response than anything Arnold had said. The suspicion, the sudden sense of confrontation, there was too much going on here for this to be a simple children's game. Joey decided to tough it out. Don't break your cover, but don't turn your back.

"You guys are weird," he said. "If you don't want to talk, then forget it. I've got a truck to catch." He shifted his weight nervously from one foot to another while Arnold, the girls and the other boys looked to Red for some kind of guidance. It was time to go, before Red realized he should call in the adults.

"Here's your ball," he said, kicking it high and aiming it at Red's stomach. For once in his life, he wasn't uncoordinated and clumsy. The ball nearly found its mark, batted away at the last minute by Red's quick hands.

Joey backed up slowly, locking eyes with Red. When the other youth gave in, looking at his mates for support, Joey turned and walked slowly but purposefully back through the village towards where he'd left Lucky Levesque and the truck.

The kids followed him, keeping their distance, but not letting him out of sight. The more they did, the more he realized that he had stumbled onto something. The Kolbergs had to be nearby – if not somewhere in Olympia township, then somewhere very close.

He came into sight of the village green and the truck, still a couple of hundred meters away. Then he noticed one of the younger boys in the group split off from the rest and run towards the main lodge. He was only halfway to the truck when the kid found an adult, a bearded man wearing an insulated vest and a pair of heavy boots. His heart began to pound terribly when the boy's hand went up and pointed across the commons at him.

Where was Lucky? Was the truck ready to go? He picked up the pace, but was scared to run. That would have been making the same mistake as the farm kids – and he was too clever for that. Would his cleverness keep him from getting away? He didn't know, but he kept on, closer and closer to the truck and his freedom.

The man in the vest began to stride toward him. The other children took that as a sign to move in.

Joey was about to break into a run when he saw Lucky emerge from the rear of the truck. It was only a few meters away now. He was going to make it – if the kids didn't get there first.

Lucky looked up and waved at Joey – then hesitated as he began to size up the situation. But Joey didn't have time. He stepped up into the cab and, in a harsh, low voice, said: "Get us out of here and don't stop to ask questions, Lucky."

The truck driver's eyes widened in surprise, but he came to life suddenly, jumping up to his side of the cab and climbing in. Joey opened the door –

BAMM!!

Something smacked into him, and the middle of his back began to sting.

He turned as he fell into the cab, looking back to see the soccer ball bounce off onto the ground and the farm kids with fierce, angry eyes closing in on him. He ignored the pain from the futile attack with the ball and slammed the door shut.

Lucky switched on the motor and the truck's wheels spun in the gravel, then they began to move. The kids jumped back as he swung the truck around in a big circle. The man in the vest scratched his head, but did nothing more as they drove off down the dirt track.

Joey realized his hands were shaking and his back hurt, but it didn't matter. He had what he came for – or close enough to it. He smiled as the distance between him and the village increased. Then he frowned. What was the next step?

Emily Baxter looked up from the workstation in the corner of the library when her mother walked into the room and sighed. She took note of the red eyes and the lines in Suzanne Baxter's face, the hesitance in her step and the slight shakiness in her hands, but she withheld comment.

It was not the first time she had seen her mother like this since scoutship crash that killed Ray Adamcek. Emily's own feelings were still raw and torn at the edges, and she had never even been close to her stepfather. She still had dreams about Ray, though, and occasionally, when her defenses were down, she pictured his frozen, lifeless body in the wreckage where Guy had found it, her imagination filling in the details of a tableau she had never witnessed herself.

She could only imagine how her mother must feel.

"And what are you up to this early on a Saturday morning?" Suzanne asked.

Emily fidgeted nervously, unsure if she should keep Guy's assignment secret or let her mother in on the latest round of intrigue her scout boyfriend had cooked up. Her main fear was that once started down that road, she would end up revealing Joey's role in the plot to uncover more intelligence on the Kolbergs. Emily didn't care much what her mother did to Joey for placing himself in harm's way, but she was afraid for herself. She would have expected her to stop Guy and Joey from conspiring and would blame her for allowing them to go ahead. No matter that she had no control over either one of them. Her mother was never fair to her, never had realistic expectations, never treated her with anything but barely concealed disappointment, starting with the day her father ran off to become a scout.

But since Ray's death, the struggle between them seemed to have relaxed. Emily felt a rare and unusual sympathy for her mother after watching the impact of the loss on her.

Two men gone.

How would she have felt if Guy were the one who hadn't come back from Vogelsberg Ridge? For the first time in her life, she saw her mother as fragile and human.

And she almost felt as if she could forgive her for the injustice in their relationship. Almost.

In any event, she decided she could risk a partial answer and hoped her mother would not press with too deep an investigation.

"I'm running through the economic reports from the dens to see if I can find signs of the Kolbergs," she said. "I figured if I found anything anomalous or some pattern among their backers and the other dens, it might be worth checking up on."

"And whose idea was that? Guy's?"

"Yeah, sort of. He asked me to look, anyway. He said you'd agree. It's a good way to figure out what they're up to."

"He's right, dear," Suzanne said as she sat down beside Emily. "What have you found?"

"Nothing about the Kolbergs yet. Just the reports on the mud pox. I never realized how much damage that was doing to us. We've lost so many days of labor that everyone's production and capital investment schedules have been set back by weeks. Can we afford that?"

"Probably not if it keeps up. Plagues are bad news, even if they aren't terribly deadly. And this one is still kind of nasty. How many have we lost, anyway?"

"Twelve – three kids. Allergic reactions, mostly. But the adults who get it are laid up in the infirmary for a week. It sounds terrible – fever, delirium, that awful rash. I hope I don't get it."

"We're due for the vaccine this week. They figure we're a good place to start because we've got so much traffic through here." She leaned back and sipped her tea. "So what are you looking for from the Kolbergs?"

"I'm not sure. Guy said to check production schedules. He said they're really pushing to break their labor quotas. And capital investment. He also thinks I should study a couple of the dens that are already using them as consultants to see what kind of figures they've been totaling up and look for others with the same profile."

"That sounds good for openers. Anything else?"

"He said we need to look for hidden effects too. Dens where they've sent their agents without actually taking over wholesale. He said they've been out signing up farmers and workers with labor bonds. If there are enough of them, they could seriously deflect the normal production curves for the den."

"They're the ones we have to watch," Suzanne said. "We know

who the supporters are. The trick is finding the ones who are being sandbagged and undermined. When the crucial votes come up at the convention, we're going to need to know who we can count on and who we can't."

That idea made Emily feel nervous. Too much was riding on this already. What if she were wrong?

"Are you running time projections on the data?" her mother asked suddenly.

"Well, no ... I didn't think of that."

"You should. Try and see if anything unusual pops up a few years down the road."

"That's probably a good idea. I'll do that."

"By the way, have you seen your brother?"

Emily tried to hide her face as she felt goose bumps rise from the small of her back, crawl across her scalp and meet at the top of her head.

"I think he went off on the bus somewhere. Look around and see if he left a note for you in the kitchen."

"I was just in there. No note. One of these days, I'm going to murder the little son of a gun. If he comes in, tell him to come looking for me."

She lifted herself from the bench with obvious discomfort and pulled her robe tight around her, then she headed for the door. She paused with one foot in the hallway and said: "I just hope he's not running around spying for Guy again. You remember the last time that happened. He was stuck up at Jasper township for three days."

"Yes, Mother," Emily said, hoping the tone of her voice, her eyes and the shaking of her hand would not give her away. She held her breath until she heard her mother all the way down the corridor in the kitchen.

***

"Mr. President?"

"Mr. Santaniello, do you wish to be recognized?"

"Yes, Mr. President."

"The chair recognizes the delegate from den Camellia."

"Thank you, Mr. President. I wasn't going to speak on this motion, but I find that I must ... "

Lin Palmer leaned back in his chair and tuned out the monologue. Santaniello was just like all the others who had started their remarks the same way. If he wasn't going to speak, then why didn't he keep his mouth shut? Lin's back ached almost as much as his backsides and his mind had turned to mush long ago. Two days in Center Township and all he had heard was an endless stream of parliamentary jargon and political double-talk. Nothing had been accomplished in all that time but to make every delegate weary of the process and wary of their fellows.

Lin looked around the chamber. The number of empty chairs was far greater than the number of those still occupied. Where had everyone gone? Or more to the point, why was anyone still here?

As soon as the light flashed in his mind that no one was here because there was no important business going on, he found himself rising to his feet without conscious thought. Once up, he let his feet carry him to the rear of the hall and out the door.

He didn't really regain possession of his senses until he was in the street, breathing the sweet, clean air that blew in from the sea and warmed his face, away from the numbing drone of the delegate from den Camellia.

He looked around. The Hollister Auditorium was situated at one end of a long green – although it was more aptly named a gold, for the deep yellow tint of the chloroplasts in the close-cropped savanna grass. The late afternoon sun was dipping towards Mount Thor – it was still midway between dinner and supper. Across the commons a row of shops and storefronts was anchored at one end by the hotel and at the other by a large dining hall. And next to the dining hall was a small building with narrow, dark windows with a crowd of men and women outside, seated at tables or milling around. He recognized them as delegates to the convention.

Lin Palmer was not a man who took long to make a decision. He marched quickly across the grass to join his fellows and take a closer look at their place of refuge.

The building turned out to be a tavern – one of many that had popped up like mushrooms here in Center Township. A half dozen tables were set up in front of the establishment, more were visible through the door beyond the mass of colonists, and two men were dispensing pitchers of amber fluid from a giant barrel. Lin recognized them from the cut of their clothes and their hair as scouts.

"Mr. Palmer, over here!"

He recognized the odd-sounding voice of Betty Montgomery and turned to see her at one of the tables, waving to him. He made his way through the crowd and took a seat on the bench as the others moved aside to accommodate him.

Betty introduced him around the table. Two of the delegates he already knew – Ed Findlay, and Harry Bayard of den Matanuska.

"So what do you think of your first glancing blow with the democratic process, Lin?" the Alaskan farmer asked him.

"Do they always talk like this?"

"No, sometimes it gets bad."

He winced and some of the other amateur politicians moaned. "Seriously, Harry, when do we get down to business? I thought we came here to write a constitution."

"Sorry, Lin. You must have made the mistake of taking the call to the convention seriously. The truth is that there's way too many of us to do that job. Legislation is like sausage – too many ingredients spoil the flavor."

"Also, you shouldn't watch it being made," said Betty, hoisting a plastic mug of beer. Someone passed Lin a mug of his own and he sampled the contents gingerly. It was bitter and a little green, but it was cold and it washed the dust and desiccated words of the convention hall out of his system.

"We won't even start work on a constitution for two more days," Bayard said.

"But that's when we all go back home," Lin said.

"Exactly. The job's going to be done by a committee. And by the lawyers in den Putnam."

"And by James Madison and Alexander Hamilton and the rest of history's best constitutionalists," added Betty.

"True. Plagiarism is the sincerest form of flattery. But that'll all happen while you're back on your farm. You'll be called back here when it's done to ratify the finished product. That's when the real fun will begin. Wait until you see how these honorable delegates react to a decent Bill of Human Rights. You think they're appalling now, you ain't seen nothing yet."

"Why?" asked Lin naively. "What's wrong with a bill of rights?"

"Nothing, as far as you and I may be concerned – though I'm giving you the benefit of the doubt here. But the sad truth is that most people don't want their fellow men and women to have too many rights. They don't believe in free speech, free news, free enterprise or democracy. What they believe in is getting the most they can for themselves and the least for everyone else. That would rather see people shut up and do what they are told – or at the very least be told what to do. They don't want free economic competition, they want a monopoly that guarantees them wealth or income without requiring them to adapt to change. They believe in power and authority, not self-determination. And when any of them get it, popular will and the public good go right out the door. No, Lin, if we get a constitution through this convention that talks about human rights, it'll be because we slipped it by them in the dead of night when no one had the sense or the strength to talk it to death."

"That may not be a bad floor strategy, Harry," Betty said with leering grin.

"Take notes, dear, take notes."

"And what about the rest of the business? How do we organize a government? How do the dens share power? What about courts and a legislature?"

"Technicalities. The power-sharing formula is a matter of mathematics and demographics. The lawyers'll come up with a few formulas, point out the strengths and weaknesses in each, and then we'll find out just what kind of people this colony is going to be made of."

"What do you think we're made of?" Lin asked pointedly.

Bayard frowned, then wrinkled his brow. "The vote to let the Kolbergs run things was damned close before the landings started," he said. "Granted, we all came down according to the scout plan – or close to it. But if things had gone one whit differently, we'd all be sitting around right now signing labor bonds with the Kolbergs in return for this pitcher of beer."

He refilled his mug carefully, as if to illustrate the precarious state of the beer supply.

"You don't sound too optimistic."

"Are you?"

"I've met the Kolbergs, so I know what we're up against."

"And?"

"If they scare everyone else just one half as much as they do me, and if they make everyone one quarter as mad, then I don't think we'll have any problem getting anything we want from these delegates."

"Bravely spoken," Harry said. "But I think you have a noble and idealistic view of humanity that isn't borne out by the facts. The truth is that people are afraid of freedom. It gives them the willies. Most of us never learn how to deal with it. Those that do take half a lifetime. Stability and security are much more inviting. Change only makes people nervous. Most of human history has consisted of a struggle between people who are afraid of freedom and those few who demand it. I don't think Asgard is going to be any different."

"And who's going to win?"

He paused dramatically, looking Lin straight in the eye as he drained the beer from his mug. "If I knew the answer to questions like that," he said, "I never would have left Earth."

If anything, the ride up to Olympia township was worse in the back of the truck than it had been in the cab. This trip, Joey was sandwiched in with a dozen boys and girls, most of them older than he was. The canopy protected them from the cold north wind that blew down off the ice, but it didn't shield Joey from the unusual scents of his companions.

They were from the service den in Center Township – den Franklin. While ostensibly a Midwestern group from the old St. Louis arcology, they resembled a mixture of Third Worlders more than anything else. All but two boys and one girl were a mixture of Latino, black and Asian.

Joey wasn't sure if it was their food, the clothes or their personal hygiene that gave rise to the odd smell. It wasn't offensive enough to single out any one source, but it was distinct enough to send shivers of doubt up and down his spine.

What if the Kolbergs could tell that he didn't smell like a serf? Otherwise, his disguise was complete. He wore the same blue clothes and parka, workboots and loose cloth hat – the uniform of the service workers. He tried to mimic the testy, aggressive attitude that the boys adopted, although his heart wasn't really in it. He was accustomed to a more easy-going approach, catching people off guard by letting them expect an innocent young boy and then presenting them with a razor-sharp AI-like mind that was three steps ahead of them.

But he knew it was not an act he would be able to pull off in these circumstances. Any violation of expectation in this role would only call attention to a whole bag full of inconsistencies, eventually leaving him unmasked.

The first few minutes of the ride had been the worst.

The oldest of the boys knew he was an outsider. Pedro Sanchez had gotten him into the work detail in return for a half-kilo of tabacky from some Alaskan farmers that Joey knew. Lucky Levesque had connected him with Pedro as a favor, but the young serf was not so altruistic. His young brothers were even less so.

"You got any more weed?" they asked when the truck began its bouncing trek up the gravel track leading north from Center Township.

When he told them he hadn't, they refused to believe him. They were not satisfied until they had stripped his parka from him and held him down while they went through his pockets. They were as empty as they'd been when Pedro gave him the outfit. The boys made a few disparaging remarks, then let him go. He had pulled himself together and found a place to sit away from the rest of them at the front of the truck.

He caught the eye of a young Asian girl who smiled, then ignored him for the rest of the trip.

The boys, having completed their amusement with Joey, spent the rest of the trip keeping themselves busy with a frightening game that made him appreciate soccer a little more.

The game centered on a piece of metal the size of a baseball. One side was machined or cast into a smooth hemisphere, but the other was raw and ragged with sharp surfaces and gruesome teeth.

The object was to toss it spinning into the air, then grab it by the smooth side.

Each of the young toughs took turns, passing it around and around the crew. They ignored Joey and the girls with a sneer. Joey was just as happy that they didn't ask him to join in. Especially when the game began to draw blood. He tried not to watch too closely after that, but the sharp, stifled yelps of the boys who missed the smooth side drew his attention each time.

Then the oldest of the group leaned forward and called: "Hey, school boy!"

Joey looked up to see the chunk of metal sailing through the air towards him. He just had time enough to recognize that the smooth aspect was facing him, then he reached out and caught it with one hand. It stung his palm, but he was surprised at its light weight. Probably aluminum or some alloy.

He looked at it closely, turning it over in his hand. He was only marginally aware that everyone in the truck had their eyes on him. He hefted it, spun it, touched the sharp projections on the distaff side, then tested it with a twist of his wrist.

There was a trick to the game, he realized. The piece of metal was not uniform in density. The center of gravity was much closer to the smooth side. And there were patterns to the way it spun in the air, gyroscopic effect turning it around on its axis. He tossed it once to watch it, analyzing the precession rate and axial tilt.

Then he started. He tossed it and spun it, tossed it and spun it, faster and faster and faster. The action of the wrist controlled it all, he realized. Once you got that down, you could do whatever you wanted to with it.

He tossed it higher and watched it tumble into his hand. He spun it faster and watched the flashing teeth cut the air. Each time he slapped it hard before launching it back into space. It was really child's play once you calculated the harmonics.

He looked up the length of the truck to see ten pairs of wide white eyes locked on the spinning chunk of metal, amazed by his performance. It caught him off guard, and this time he grabbed the wrong side of the orb.

"Shit!" he yelled as he felt it catch on his thumb. He dropped it to the bed of the truck with a loud clunk and stuck the injured digit into his mouth.

The other boys made derisive remarks, but Joey recognized the awe and respect that they were meant to conceal. He looked at the palm of his hand, already red from the punishment of catching the easy side, now marked with a half dozen small scratches to match the cut on his thumb. He hoped he had paid the price of admission to the group with that pain – at least for one day.

***

After an hour of torture, the truck rolled to a stop, the rear flap opened and the kids piled out into the bracing cold air. A bright sun burned down from high overhead, relieving the cold where it fell, but leaving a biting chill in its shadow. A few hundred meters to the north, Joey saw the chalky white cliffs of the Vogelsberg Ridge behind a thick stand of greenwoods.

Clustered around the base of the massive trees were a collection of huts, tents, cabins and inflatable plastic warehouses. To the south was a long flat stretch of clear land – a natural meadow scraped out long ago by a retreating glacier. At one end was a miniplane under a camouflage screen.

At the other, under a larger screen and tucked into the edge of the woods, was the bulky, winged shape of a scoutship.

He had found the Kolberg base camp!

Pedro Sanchez had confirmed his suspicions, of course, but this was the real thing, not just some talk over a bowl of tabacky. Pedro said he and his family didn't like the Kolbergs any more than the other colonists, but the den was being paid well for its work. And the members of den Franklin had never had much to say about where its leaders sent them. "We do what we're told, Joey," he had said. "And we don't ask a lot of questions."

The scouts had tried to find the place for a year now, but without success. Their sensor equipment wasn't exactly designed for the task, and the Kolbergs had taken some effective precautions, like the screen and probably some other countermeasures suggested by Joey's active imagination. Den Olympia had given them the space they needed in an arroyo near the crest of the ridge. And den Franklin had supplied them with whatever labor they needed to keep their camp maintained and secure.

Joey took a deep breath of the crisp air and followed the rest of the group into the middle of the camp. After counting latrines, tents and ration storage, he figured there was enough working and living space for about a hundred people. That matched up with what Guy Stanger had told him about the Kolberg party. Most of them weren't at the camp, Guy had said. They were out in the townships, trying to sell the Kolberg management plan to unsuspecting and disadvantaged colonists, though there were few left that hadn't already made their decision by this point.

"Gather round," Pedro called, once the group had reached the center of the compound. Joey huddled with the others, trying to blend in with the work detail. A second truck from den Franklin had pulled up in front of the main lodge of the camp. Pedro and a couple of men were unloading the cargo – a collection of small plastic cylinders with hoses and shoulder straps hanging from them.

"Here's the job for the day, kids," Pedro said, once they had formed a semicircle in front of him. "Everybody gets a spray tank. Everybody gets a partner. Everybody gets a package of flags. You get assigned to your sectors. You search your sector for snow pools – puddles, ponding, standing water of any kind. You spray the pools. You leave a flag."

Joey listened carefully, even though he already knew the drill. The young toughs who had first terrorized him, then turned into admiring fans of his fancy handwork, joked and jostled one another, ignoring Pedro.

"Everyone understand?" Pedro asked. "Yuli, how about you? What's the job?"

Yuli was the tallest of the group, though not the biggest in mass and muscles. He grinned, then stammered, then grinned again.

"I thought so. I will repeat your instructions again. This time, listen to me carefully." He went through the list slowly, emphasizing each word. This time the rest of the crew listened to what he said. Then Pedro split them up into pairs and assigned them to their sectors.

Joey wound up with the sector that contained the wooden lodge. Pedro knew what he wanted. And for a partner, he drew the Asian girl who sat opposite him on the truck.

***

Peter Kolberg paced the room nervously, warming himself before the fireplace, worrying about the mud pox. The colonists were so stupid. They should have taken precautions. They should have been more sanitary.

He stopped at the wide table covered with reader-disks, tablets and a big memory tank. The figures were on the screen of the main terminal. His dens had already lost ten percent of their labor force to the ailment for a month. How were they going to make it up?

How could they let themselves get caught by this? If they had listened to him six months ago, this wouldn't have happened. They'd had epidemics on Tik the first few years. His own parents had been caught in the first one and hadn't survived. One of his daughters barely lived through the last of them, before the colonists learned how to cope with alien bacteria and viruses.

But this – this was a matter of hygiene.

The pox was spread by chites that bred and laid eggs in the shallow pools of snowmelt and spring rains. The larvae filled the pools, fed on the Asgardian equivalent of algae, grew into adults and spread the virus. It all happened so quickly, the colonists were caught unprepared.

The scouts should have warned them, Kolberg cursed. But then, the scouts never found out where the pox had come from. It had hit them the first year, and they had recovered without knowing its source or solution. The next year, they'd already learned to spray the pools and kill off the black chites that spread the virus. As long as they kept the bugs under control, the pox never returned. The isolated cases that cropped up over the years were treated with acyclovir, but the cause was never tracked down.

It was only now, with colonists all over the place, living near the snowpools and mudpuddles and drainage ponds, that the pox had come back with a vengeance, laying out thousands of colonists.

Peter Kolberg swallowed his anger and turned his thoughts

towards higher goals. In the long run, the epidemic would work in his favor. He could point to it as another sign of weakness among the colonists. It was another reason why they should accept his proposal.

Behind each failure was another victory. The plan was so clever, so perfect.

He wiped the screen clear of the depressing figures and called up a spreadsheet that always made him feel good, strong and powerful – the economic projections for the Asgard colony. Even with the consequences of the pox factored in, they were reassuringly bold.

The colony planned for an annual growth rate of five percent. Half of that would come from natural expansion, a steady birth rate and the longevity of the colonists. He would liked to have seen the birth rate even higher, but he'd learned on Tik that there were some things that couldn't be forced. The other half would come from additional colonists, another ship each year to start, more later on.

He ordered the program to begin its iterations, totaling productivity, investment, return on investment, market growth, capital and labor pools, all the sparkling numbers that meant more to him than all the living men and women on the planet. It ran through the first cycle – twenty years Asgard time. The population would double by then. New dens, homegrown and flown in from Earth, would fill in the lands to the west and south.

There were two sets of figures in the spreadsheet. One showed the colony if left to itself, following trends that were already beginning to appear. The other showed the effect of careful management by Kolberg and his associates. As time went by, the two numbers diverged more and more.

He keyed the program to continue with the next cycle. Another twenty years, more divergence. The numbers in the Kolberg columns swelled and Peter Kolberg swelled with pride at the sight of them.

Years ago – fourteen years as Earth reckoned time, more then ten years by the slower calendar of Tikarahisat – Peter Kolberg had worked the rich black soil of his farmstead under the small, hot sun Eta Cassiopeiae. He knew even then that backbreaking labor was not his fate, that a life of endless summers followed by endless harvests was not his lot. Even then the vision was alive in his mind, in his soul.

He knew it would take a long time. Longer than anyone could imagine. But he knew also that he would have that time. All the time he needed, and more, in endless quantities.

The colonists were so stupid – stupid and ignorant. They did not know what was good for them. They could not see what they needed or how their petty selfish interests kept them from getting it. And what they needed most was someone to tell them what to do, how to order their lives, organize their efforts and build a world worthy of the stars.

It had taken him a long time to build up his power on Tik. Years of work, years of learning. All that he had planned and all that he had learned was being compressed here on Asgard. The time was so short. Soon they would have to act. The pieces were beginning to fall into place.

They had scout holdings in the back country. They had dens beholden to them. They had colonists bound by labor contracts. They had votes in the constitutional convention. Everything was coming together – but so much more quickly than back on Tik. The pace was almost frightening. Almost.

He looked again at the spreadsheet unfolding the future of the planet, calculating across the decades, growth upon growth. This was the crucial time for all those numbers. The decisive moment was coming – only a matter of days now. Until then, time seemed frozen as solid as the glaciers on Mt. Loki.

And afterwards, it would unfold, like the lines of numbers in the spreadsheet, building and rising inexorably to some ultimate climax in the distant future. A future where the name of Kolberg would be written in letters large enough to blot out the sun ...

"Peter, are you in there?"

His brother, Eric, entered the room. He was older than Peter and taller and more handsome. But Peter was the one who had the vision, who had nurtured it and made it real. Peter was the dominant brother, while Eric followed along effortlessly in his wake.

"Over here," Peter said.

"Are you going over those numbers still?" his brother asked.

"Yes. What of it? They are interesting to me."

Eric smiled and shook his head. "It's time for lunch with the den leaders from Jasper. Hannah sent me to fetch you."

"Den Jasper? Oh yes, that's correct. I'll be right with you." He lingered for a moment before the screen, watching the bottom line for Asgard grow in leaps and bounds, his heart soaring with the numbers. Then he stepped down from the heights of his reverie and executed the reset command. The screen wiped itself clear and the original numbers reappeared, the present state of the Asgard colony in all its stark reality. He turned his back on the momentary truth and walked off to the dining hall and a distant future.

The numbers were still there a few minutes later when Joey Baxter slipped into the hall unnoticed. They were practically the first thing he saw. The clutter of readerdisks and tablets was uninteresting and uninviting. Too much work to see what was in them. But the bright numbers beckoned like city lights in the night.

Joey had left the little Asian girl, Jennie Vinh, at the truck while he did his spying. The two of them had worked for a couple of hours, spraying the snow pools and mud puddles around the compound.

"What is this stuff?" Jennie had asked.

"Mylotropin."

"What's that, smartcakes?"

"It's a growth agent. It interferes with the chite's hormones so they don't grow wings and mature. They cooked it up at the university."

"What happens if we get it on our hands?"

"We don't grow wings, I guess," Joey had said.

Jennie didn't want Joey to go inside the lodge. She said they'd think she was in on it, too. So he took her back to the truck and told her to turn around. "Now you can tell them that I disappeared while your back was turned."

Joey's eyes were fixed on the spreadsheet, taking in the numbers, the categories. He recognized it for what it was almost instantly. Emily had been running similar spreadsheets all week long at home. It didn't take more than a few seconds for him to start the iterations.

A broad grin spit Joey's face as the spreadsheet scrolled up, year after year, decade after decade, numbers in rows and columns marching in rigid formation up the screen and across Joey's eyes.

It had reached well past three centuries into the future before Joey realized there was someone else in the room.

"Who are you and what are you doing here?" asked a man with thin hair and a dark face – Peter Kolberg.

Joey's first regret was that he had failed to inform Guy Stanger of his plans or his whereabouts before leaving for Center Township. It was not his last.

The next one came when they dragged Jennie Vinh into the lodge. She struggled with one of the big men who had come running when Peter Kolberg called out. When she saw Joey, she flashed him a venomous look that made him feel as worthless as a snow lizard, then they dragged her away.

Now they were both in trouble.

"Just looking around, sir," Joey had said.

"Are you a thief? Is that what you pretend?" Kolberg had asked in return. "Show me your hands. I thought so – too soft. You're no serf, even with dirt smeared on your face. Who are you? You look like the boy they chased off at the village last week. Was that you? I think so, little bird."

Joey fell silent after that. He was afraid and worried, but he refused to talk and hoped that would be enough. It wasn't.

Kolberg had him sit in a chair at one end of the room. An hour went by without either of them uttering a word. Joey's heartstrings tightened with every passing minute, as he considered his options. In a few days, if he didn't show up, someone would come looking for him. If the Kolbergs didn't suspect that he was anything more than a mischievous child, they might even send him home before then. Or they might suspect the truth and decide it would be better if he never turned up.

Kolberg continued his business silently, writing on a tablet, reading a disk, playing idly with the screen on the table. After a while, the man who had capture Jennie entered the hall. "She says she doesn't know who he is or where he's from. She said Pedro Sanchez brought him along."

With a wave of his hand, Kolberg dismissed the man, then returned his attention to Joey.

"See, I told you you were no serf. Do I have to bring Pedro Sanchez in here and question him too?"

Joey just glared at him and bit his lip. A few minutes later, Pedro appeared, flanked by the first man and a newfound friend. Kolberg questioned him just out of earshot of Joey, which only made the boy sweat coldly. Then he saw Sanchez look his way and shake his head in vigorous denial. Pedro exchanged more words with Kolberg, facing him boldly with a stern defiance in his carriage and expression. Joey tried to adopt a similar posture in his four-legged prison.

"He says you came to him in Center Township and asked for a job. He doesn't know what den you come from. Thought you were a farmboy. I don't believe him, but what can I say. You are a great deal of trouble for me now, boy. I should have done this first."

He motioned to his gorilla and the man approached Joey menacingly, pulling a deadly looking device from his pocket. He put one arm around Joey's head and poked the business end of the device into his right eye.

"Open your eye!" he commanded. When Joey did, he pulled the trigger and a bright red flash filled one side of his vision.

"I'm going to run your retina print through the colonial roster to find out who you are," Kolberg said. "This will take some time and I do not like to waste time. You will sit there and you will not move until we end these mystery games."

Two more hours passed while Kolberg came and went. The big man with the retina print gun stood guard while his master was gone. Joey sat and brooded. What had he done that was really so wrong? He hadn't heard anything. He hadn't seen much of anything at all. Just that spreadsheet on the mainframe, and that wasn't anything at all. These guys were wrapped too tight for him. Suspicion was one thing, but this was pathological.

Finally, Kolberg returned, a strange. lopsided grin on his face, as if smiling was an occasional and poorly handled practice. "So, Joseph Baxter, what a surprise to have you with us. You look a little like your mother, you know. I am curious, though, as to why she would risk sending her youngest child on such a foolish errand as this one. Spying is something that adults should do, not children."

Joey swallowed hard. "But – "

"Take him away," Kolberg ordered. "Put him in with the girl. We can't have him interfering with us now. The next few days are too important."

The gorilla grabbed Joey hard by the upper arm and fast-marched him down the hallway to a door near the end. The door opened into a dark room with no windows. Joey could see a couple of mattresses on the floor, some blankets and an irregular shape on one mattress. Then the man pushed him inside and closed the door behind him.

Joey reached around in the dark until he found a light switch. The bulb was dim and the light barely enough to make out the shape on the floor as that of another person. Joey gasped and shuddered in surprise, then recovered himself.

"Hello?" he asked the immobile figure. There was no reply. He knelt on the mattress and pulled back the blanket. He gasped again. It was Jennie Vinh.

She moaned and opened her eyes. Even through the blanket, Joey could feel the fevered heat that her body gave off.

"I feel sick," she said weakly.

Joey looked closer at the bumps that had begun to rise on her forehead. Mud pox!

"Oh great," he said.

***

Friday nights in Center Township were a strange and tantalizing experience for Guy Stanger. He'd grown up in the austere isolation of the Main Post, one of only six active scout posts on the planet and more than 40 klicks from the nearest settlement. A big celebration was the annual jamboree, when nearly half of all the scouts on Asgard gathered together, either down at Main Post or up at Highland Post.

Weekends were distinguished by a half workday on Saturday and a holiday on Sunday. Friday nights, there were dances for the kids, Saturday nights for the adults. He had never considered it boring, but then, he'd never had anything to compare it to. Until now.

Center Commons was a large open square, glazed pavement surrounding a large, newly mown green. At one end was Hollister Auditorium where the constitutional convention was being held. The village holdings of four dens met at this juncture – one of the executive dens, special services, the food den and den Franklin, the service den.

People thronged the square, jostling through the streets, calling out, laughing, running, sitting on the grass in large circles, playing instruments, singing, dancing. Around the perimeter was a strange collection of shops and storefronts, whose products and purposes defied all rational explanation. Grog shops offered homemade ales and distilled liquors, darkened clubs hawked private intimacy and those sporting decorative lighting on the outside solicited dancers. Sweet, sick smells issued from some doorways, while others gave forth the rich tang of roasting meat, baking bread and real coffee.

The complex wealth of sensations was enough to overload Guy most nights. But this evening, his mind was focused on something else and the crowded square barely existed for him.

He made his way purposefully down the street, inspecting each shop as he approached it. He was halfway around the commons before he found what he was looking for – the Silver Rose Tavern, lit by a single yellow bulb over a crudely lettered sign on the back of a packing shield.

The door was open to the warm spring night, but two men blocked the entrance with their wide backs. Guy levered himself past them and stepped into the dim interior of the tavern. The air was thick with the smell of spilled ale and burning tabacky. He looked around cautiously, holding his breath against the reek.

He didn't like what he saw. The place was a hangout for scouts. He recognized several youngsters in the back from the Main Post who shouldn't have been allowed in the place. There were others, too. A couple of old men, part of the original scout team, who made no attempt to hide their indiscretion. And in the corner, seated with his brother, was the man Guy was looking for: Mike Hennig.

Only a few weeks had passed since the night Hennig told his

fellow scouts that he and his mates were selling off their title to large back-country holdings in return for a piece of the Kolberg enterprise. Guy remembered the cramped room, the bitterness in the eyes of the other scouts, and the anger in their voices. He bit back now on those same feelings, bending them to a greater need.

He crossed the room and slipped into a plastic chair across from the elder Hennig, who clutched a mug of ale in one hand and a scout knife in the other.

"Good evenwatch, Mike. I haven't seen you since the High Council last month. What have you and your mates been up to?"

Hennig scowled, drank from his mug and wiped his mouth with the back of his hand. The knife blade flashed a brief reflection from one of the hooded lights hanging overhead. "Do I know you, scout? No, I don't know you. But I saw you at the Council, didn't I. You had your back against the wall. You came in with Sanderson and Gilmartin, but I've seen you somewhere else. I know – you hung around with Grampa Bob. You were one of his boys, weren't you."

"Yeah, once. A lot of scouts were," he said, emphasizing the last word.

"I guess so. I used to listen to the old ripper when I was a kid, too. Him and his Great Spirit stories. Crazy old man. Nobody ever believed in the Great Spirit – especially him."

Guy shook his head, swallowing a lifetime of devotion to an old man and his allegorical tales of life on Old Earth. "I guess not."

"So what do want here, scout? Don't you know you're not supposed to be talking to us? We're outcasts. At least Grampa Bob got to take his dignity with him. And what did he do that we didn't? He's left the scouts just as sure as we have."

Yeah, thought Guy, but at least he didn't sell the scout den out like you did. Hennig and his compatriots had signed over to the Kolbergs title to thousands of hectares of virgin land in the interior of the continent. Guy wasn't sure what they were getting in return besides a lot of starry-eyed promises. What they had given up was plain to see – their self-respect.

"I need your help," Guy said.

"That's a good one," Hennig said. "Any reason you expect to get it?"

"Not any in particular."

"At least you're honest."

"Yes, are you?"

Hennig came up quickly, the knife cutting through the air. Good, Guy thought, he hadn't sold all of his pride away. He didn't flinch, but looked Hennig straight in the eye.

"If you weren't a scout, that would have been your last question."

"I'm looking for the Kolberg base camp. I thought you might know where it is."

Hennig relaxed. "You've got to be kidding."

"Not at all. Three days ago, my girlfriend's kid brother disappeared. He said he was going looking for the camp. I want to find him. If I knew where the camp was, I might have some direction to start in."

"Sounds convincing. What's your real reason?"

"That's it. The kid's only twenty-two."

"A real little scout."

"He's not a scout, he's a colonist."

"And that's supposed to make him count."

"No – but I thought the honesty might."

Hennig frowned, then looked Guy over carefully. He plucked at his nails with the tip of the knife. "The Kolbergs don't want visitors. This is a private club – and you already decided the dues were too high to pay. Look somewhere else, scout."

The renegade fell back in his chair and turned his gaze away from Guy, concentrating on the blade in his hands.

Guy felt angry – and shocked. He really had expected the scout to help him. Somehow, he thought, their common kinship would have made a difference. Feeling terribly naive, he rose quickly to his feet and headed for the door. He tried to ignore Hennig's rude laugh as he slipped outside, but he knew it had found its mark. The common bonds between scouts, the basis of all society on Asgard until the arrival of the colonists, had been shattered by the Kolbergs and could never be made whole again.

He stumbled up the street, lost in embarrassed thought, unaware of the people around him. He was halfway to Hollister Auditorium before he realized where his feet were carrying him.

"Guy?"

The voice was familiar, but terribly out of place. He stopped abruptly and looked at the handful of strangers around him until he found its source – and his blood froze.

"Guy Stanger, what have you done with my son?"

It was Suzanne Baxter.

Lin Palmer scrolled through his tablet until he found the agenda for the committee meeting.

After a week on the farm, he was back in Hollister Auditorium. He'd been assigned to the Committee on Den Affairs and its job tonight was to review the bylaws and constitutional articles on the definition, creation, rights and duties of dens.

The agenda appeared on the screen of the tablet. There was only one item under consideration – a resolution on the bylaws. The meeting had begun at 2500 and would probably go on until midnight. Then tomorrow, a full session of the convention was scheduled. Lin grew tired just contemplating the long hours of speechifying and legal wrangling. Tonight's committee meeting was bad enough.

He asked for the file on the evening's resolution. The bylaws rolled up on the screen, chapter, section and paragraph, about 60K's worth of copy. Then the constitutional articles, shorter and more to the point, another 40K. He tried to plow through the legal language, but found himself lost in the first few subparagraphs. He traced his way back to the place where he got lost, but the subordinate clauses and indeterminate appositives swallowed him alive.

He ordered up the legislative summary – the plain language explanation of the measure. But after a few minutes, a message flashed on the screen: "FILE OPEN – NOT AVAILABLE".

"Hey, Betty," he called softly to his colleague at the next table. "What's the story on this?"

He pointed the screen of the tablet at her.

"Last minute amendments," she said. "Bayard says they're trying to come up with some substitute language. We'll get it later."

Lin shrugged. What difference would it make? He barely understood what they were talking about. Oh sure, he knew what a den was. And when new colonists started arriving, there would be new dens on Asgard, each with its own landholding – townships for the farmers, villages for the specialists. You had to have rules to make sure everyone was treated fairly and equally. But why couldn't they be written in language that ordinary farmers like him could understand? The lawyers from den Putnam wrote everything up, told the delegates what it meant, then waited for them to approve it. Why did they even need him in the first place?

The chairman called the meeting to order and the murmur of conversations subsided. They ran through the minutes of the first meeting, then the chairman called on the legal aide from Putnam to explain the language in the resolution.

It didn't help. Thirty seconds after she began, he was lost.

He kept asking for the summary with his tablet, but all he got was the same message. Then he found the message was interrupted by a new graphic – a bright red "SPECIAL NOTICE" warning.

He looked up to see several other delegates staring into their tablets with puzzlement in their faces. The legal aide fell silent and the chairman called a pause in the hearing.

"Notice from the president of the convention – " The words scrolled up across the screen.

"Quorum Call – All delegates to the Constitutional Convention are requested to return to the meeting hall at this time – Quorum Call.

"Peter Kolberg of the Tikarahisat colony at Eta Cassiopeiae has asked to address the convention in special session this evening. As a courtesy to him, the president has issued a quorum call for a session to begin at 2600."

Lin blinked in surprise, a couple of delegates nearby moaned and the chaotic babble of a dozen startled conversations echoed from the high ceiling. The chairman pounded the gavel a few times to bring the meeting to order.

"In view of this request, I suggest that we recess this hearing until after the special session. So moved and seconded, all in favor say 'Aye', the motion carries. We are in recess."

The swiftness of the action surprised Lin, but he realized that the handling of the delegates required speed and a deaf ear for objections.

He was left to sit for another hour as the sergeant-at-arms appointed a handful of deputies and sent them out in search of delegates.

"You three go to the hotel, you four up the west side of the square and you four up the east side. I will personally attend to the special services quarter and return here within a half hour."

That brought a round of hooting from the deputies. Lin smiled too. He knew what the sergeant-at-arms was talking about. In addition to hairdressers, security guards, artists, dancers, musicians, video crews and producers, the special services den had also brought along specialists in an older profession. Some of the more puritanical dens frowned on the idea – as did Lin's wife, Jackie. But the delegates – the male delegates, anyway – found it the source of endless ribald humor.

The delegates thus retrieved by the deputies and the sergeant arrived in all different states and moods. Some were indignant about the interruption in their private affairs, some were oblivious to the interruption after their overindulgence in homemade refreshments. A few continued to sing songs from their homelands until the gavel fell and the convention was called to order.

"Fellow delegates, I present to you our guest … "

***

"My name is Peter Kolberg. My family and our friends came to Tik fifteen years ago – twenty-one now that we have come to Asgard for this year. Little more than six months ago, I spoke to you while you were still in your ships orbiting overhead. I offered you our aid and support.

"I told you how we built a strong and stable colony back on Tik. But at the same time we made mistakes, we wasted time, we lost money, work and lives. We are so small out here, there is so little room for error, that each of those mistakes cost us dearly. We wanted to save you that cost and help you reinvest it in building your world.

"The Kolbergs offered you all the assistance we could provide. We formed a management consultant team to help you organize your colony. We brought our technology and our technical libraries. And we brought ourselves. We offered you a contract with us that would make Asgard grow and thrive and flourish.

"In return, we asked only for a stake in your world – a few tiny pieces of land here and there. We asked to build and grow with you. We are natural trading partners, you and we. Sol is twenty-five years away from here, we are only six. Beyond us are a dozen worlds ready to be settled in the next few centuries. Asgard and Tik will be the gateways to those new worlds. We have a long future together.

"But you chose not to.

"I do not hold this against you. You did not know us. You did not know what we could do. We expected this, but felt compelled to make our offer anyway. Since then, much has happened.

"You too have made mistakes. You too have wasted time and money and lives. If you had listened to us last year, some of that waste might have been avoided. But that is our fault. We should have tried harder to make you understand what we can do for you.

"But now you can see what we are about. We have come only to help you. We can give you valuable guidance if you let us.

"I have come to you tonight, before you continue with your work, to make our offer once again. Let us show you the way to a rich and powerful new future. Let us lead you to a new age among the stars. We have the knowledge and the will that you need.

"This will be the last time we offer you this opportunity. Our time here is drawing near an end. Before the end of this year, we will be leaving for home. We make the offer now and it will remain open until Sunday night. We do not want to split the colony up over this – the decision must be quick and final. There is too much work to do for all of us to delay this any longer. Thank you. Good night."

***

Suzanne Baxter watched Peter Kolberg as he stepped back from the podium and returned to his seat. She felt like she had stepped back in time a year, back to the bridge of the *Hamilton* where she had heard Kolberg's first speech. It was a chilling feeling. Back before Ray's accident. Before Joey had vanished.

She stood at the rear of the meeting hall, behind the blockade of tables that separated the delegates from the public. Her hands shook, but otherwise she betrayed no sign of the angry turmoil that raged within her.

Poor Guy, she thought. She had left him outside Hollister Auditorium with a hangdog look on his face after a fifteen-minute lecture about letting Joey go off on his own. If he was going to be a spy, then they should have been more careful about it. There was no excuse for that.

She knew what he was up to. That was why the first night Joey was gone, she had been worried, but not frightened. The second night was worse. The past two nights had been sleepless torture.

And up there, on the stage, the center of attention for the entire convention – the entire colony – was the man she knew had to be responsible.

The president of the convention slammed the gavel twice, heard a motion to adjourn, and before anyone could object, he ended the session. Chaos erupted from the floor of the meeting hall as a hundred delegates rose to speak at once. They surged forward, some to gather around their leaders, others trying to get close to Kolberg.

Suzanne joined the latter group, working her way slowly through the mass, inching her way towards the stage. She was nearly there when she caught Kolberg's eye. A chill ran through her as he looked down from where he sat, surrounded by aides and assistants who held off the press of delegates. He held up a hand to silence the man he was speaking with and beckoned to an aide.

A minute later, a woman approached Suzanne from behind the stage and escorted her down a short hallway to a small room. The furnishings were meager – a table and a few chairs. The woman told her to have a seat and wait just a moment.

It was longer than that, but in fairly short order, the door opened and Peter Kolberg entered, followed by three men. He stopped before Suzanne, introduced her to his assistants, then asked them to step outside.

"It's been some time since we last spoke, Mrs. Baxter," Kolberg said. It had, indeed. She remembered ho she had faced him over a commlink, suffered his intimidation and threats and stared him back down. "I'm afraid I wasn't very polite then. I should apologize."

"Yes, you should," she replied. "Tell me something. Do you really expect the colony to give you a different answer today from the one we gave you last year?"

"No – I think not. But I must give them the opportunity. It is a moral obligation."

She tried not to gag at that remark. "But what's the point?" she asked.

"If you were in my position, you would feel the same obligation. We know what you must go through for many years to build your colony. We know what is best for you. If you had come to us fourteen years ago, we would have listened – should have listened."

She swallowed her disgust at Kolberg's self-serving sanctimony. He wouldn't know a moral obligation if it jumped up and spit in his face. "And how does kidnapping my son help build our colony?"

Kolberg stiffened, then frowned.

"I'm afraid I don't understand you," he said.

"Oh yes you do. You wouldn't bother wasting two seconds on me, let alone ten minutes if you didn't have some reason. The only one I can imagine is that you know precisely where my son is and you want to make sure that I know you do."

"I'm sorry, Mrs. Baxter, but I thought better of you. This is, I'm afraid, completely irrational. I thought we could discuss my proposal.

Apparently we cannot."

"I'll discuss your proposal. You give me back my son tonight or in the morning, I'm going out in front of the convention and charge you with kidnapping. You can imagine what that will do to your offer this time around."

"Mrs. Baxter, believe me when I say that we are both equally concerned with the well-being of your child. I would hate to see anything happen to him, especially in the next sixty hours or so. Don't you agree?"

Suzanne sucked in air through clenched teeth. "You bastard," she spit back at him. But inside, her heart sank. He had called her bluff. She was not about to make the charges she described – not without some evidence. And she didn't doubt for one instant Peter Kolberg's thinly veiled threats against Joey.

She rose unsteadily, the breath torn from her in ragged gasps. She wanted to run away. The bastard had her son and wouldn't let him go.

Kolberg just stared at her, no expression in his cold eyes, as she walked out the door and down the hall.

***

The floor of the meeting hall did not quiet down for more than an hour – time that Lin Palmer spent seated at his desk, feet up on the table, bewildered by the confusion. For him, the issue was simple: send the Kolbergs back to Eta Cass. What he couldn't understand was why anyone would want to let them run the world.

The reaction of the delegates ranged from Lin's bemused disbelief to angry resentment at the audacity of the Kolbergs to wild-eyed hope that the rest of the colony might back their grand enterprise. With his limited experience at counting votes, Lin supposed that the final tally would shake out into the same three categories.

Finally, the chairman of Lin's committee gathered his membership together out of the milling mob of delegates and sat them down around a few tables in a quiet corner.

The meeting was mercifully quick. Someone made a motion to approve the bylaws as amended and the article on dens as drafted by the committee. Someone else seconded the motion.

"All in favor?" asked the chairman.

A chorus of delegates answered, "Aye."

"All those opposed?"

"Nay," Lin called out.

The chairman looked down at him with bleary eyes and a disgruntled look. "Why not, Lin?"

"Because I still haven't seen what they say," he replied.

The chairman sighed as his face rearranged itself in confusion. "The motion carries eight to one. Do I hear a motion to adjourn?"

It was all over in an instant and Lin staggered through the damp darkness of the central square towards the warm comfort of the Asgard Hotel.

Peter Kolberg spent the day Saturday in the main lodge of den Franklin, watching the convention on a remote monitor. The session began with quick action on the committee reports on bylaws, then dove head first into the immobility of long-winded, repetitive debate on the Kolberg offer.

He paced nervously for much of the day as the arguments unfolded predictably. There was little change in the discussion from a year earlier. The issue remained the same – who would decide the important policy issues of the colony? Would everyone go off in their own direction under the illusion that they were exercising their freedom, or would they unite under a strong central leadership?

No one had anything to say that was startling or new. And in many ways, the Kolbergs had insured that they would not. Suzanne Baxter was a case in point. The ignorant woman was too irrational to manipulate with ordinary means, but he had found a lever to keep her off the floor. Her interference the last time around had cost him dearly.

Instead of listening to the words, Kolberg paid attention to who was speaking. He had a fairly certain count of the delegates and the dens. He knew who was on their side and who was not. There were a few fence straddlers, dens divided among themselves over who to follow, and it would be interesting to see which way they broke. But he knew long before the vote just how things would turn out.

The delegates continued to talk through lunch and dinner, but with the supper hour approaching, they began to run out of steam. A brief recess came around 2000, and the leaders put their heads together to see how they should handle the rest of the session. The den leader from Olympia called and talked for a while with Kolberg.

"Do we go on after supper, or is this as far as you want to go?" the man asked at last.

"Everyone has had their chance to talk. Whatever votes are going to be ours are ours already. If they want to act before supper, don't stand in their way."

"Yes, sir," the den leader said.

A few minutes after that, the president hammered the convention back into session. And within a half an hour, he called for a vote. The clerk read the resolution and rang a bell to open the voting.

Kolberg's tablet mirrored the large tally board mounted above the stage in the meeting hall. He watched as the names turned red or green from their neutral gray It was like the screen had caught fire.

Peter's brother, Eric, joined him at the last minute to see the outcome. "It doesn't look good," he told Peter.

"No – as I expected. Out of fifty-seven dens, we've got twenty-two. Windsor split its vote, and so did Crandall. The rest of them are against us."

"And now what?"

"And now we go on with the next phase. Our opponents think they have won, but they do not know what we are fighting over. Tonight they will celebrate another victory over us, but in a short time, we will have what we want from them." He let a rare smile crack his lips. "After all, they passed the bylaws without debate ... "

***

Joey had a test. If he could turn the two valve stems in plumbing above his bunk into one valve stem, he was all right. If he could not, he was still sick.

Today was a one-valve day, the second so far out of the past three. Earlier than that, Joey hadn't kept an accurate count.

The ventilator fan whirred softly in the corner, the bulkhead on the far side of the compartment was in some kind of rational perspective and he could hear voices in the distance.

He recalled something of the period between being thrown in the closet with Jennie Vinh and awakening clear-headed three mornings ago. The first few hours in the closet were still a potent memory – mainly because he had relived those hours a dozen times or more in feverish nightmares. He remembered being scared for Jennie, whose little body was burning with fever. And he remembered scratching his ankles and the back of his neck where he'd been bitten by chites. When he started to get dizzy and hot with a fever of his own, he made the logical connection between the two. He remembered being pissed.

They spent the night locked in the closet. Joey was pretty sure of that, because he didn't remember being hungry in there. Sometime the next day, they moved the two of them to another room in a different part of the camp. He remembered being outside after dark, the cold air whipping across his face and bringing a temporary relief to the fever.

Then, when the delirium became serious and his body was covered with an itching rash, he discovered they had moved him again, here to what was obviously the sickbay on the scoutship from Tik.

Today the rash wasn't nearly as bad as it had been. His skin was peeling away in dry scabs from most of the places he'd rubbed raw. The itching was down to merely annoying levels, and he didn't even feel feverish.

The voices down the passageway grew louder, then closer. He realized he should take an interest in what they were saying. but he wasn't quite that conscious yet. Then he looked up at the doorway and saw a familiar face.

"Guy?"

"Next time you try this, let someone know where you're going," he said.

"Are you for real or am I sicker than I thought?"

"As real as it gets. Can you walk or are we going to have to carry you out of here?"

"So far the most I've been able to do is see straight. I haven't tried getting vertical yet."

"I'll give you a hand."

He swung his feet out over the floor and put them down. His ankles felt watery and legs insubstantial. His face felt cold and his head swirled dizzily. Then the feeling subsided and he rose shakily until he stood erect but unclothed in the middle of the sickbay floor.

"Here's a robe," Guy said, helping guide his arms into the appropriate holes. He dropped a pair of boots on the floor and guided Joey's feet into them. "Come with me."

"This is really not recommended," said a new entrant to the sickbay. It was the nurse that Joey had recognized from his occasional moments of lucidity.

"I don't care what is really not recommended. This young fellow is going back where he belongs – today." The nurse drew back at Guy's growl. "Come on, Joey, it isn't far."

"How did you find me?"

"Later ... "

They walked down a long passageway until they reached the amidships hatch. Guy preceded him down the ladder to the ground, lending a strong arm to keep him steady. Joey walked stiff-legged through the cold sand that surrounded the ship, oblivious to it. He did notice the crowd of people that formed a rough circle around Guy, Joey and the truck parked under one wing of the scoutship. They were all Kolberg people, and they all glared at the two of them with piercing eyes.

When he reached the truck, he saw the reason why. In front were four scouts, all armed with hunting rifles. They carried the rifles strapped across their shoulders, but the implication was clear. Aside from the security police in the special services den, the scouts were the only ones on Asgard who regularly carried arms.

Joey looked up at Guy and rolled his eyes. Guy put a finger to his lips. The youth swallowed hard and kept his mouth closed until they were in the truck, then the four armed scouts climbed in behind them. Guy had Joey lie down on a mat on the floor and covered him with a blanket.

"Pedro Sanchez told me where you were," Guy said as they lurched into motion.

"Why did it take you so long to get here?"

"He didn't tell me until today."

"That son of a bitch. Why not?"

"Because until today, they still had Jennie Vinh."

"Jennie? How did she get back? She was sicker than me. Did she run away or what?"

"They sent her back – or rather, they sent her body back. She died of the pox."

Joey felt his stomach drop and his forehead grow cold. The air thickened, and he felt his tenuous hold on awareness slip. He let out a deep moan. Then he started to cry.

It could have been him ...

They hadn't treated the two of them for the pox for three days. That was the problem. He realized it right away. The acyclovir they'd given him when he got to the scoutship had begun working right away. But before that, the Kolbergs had just let them lie there and suffer. Guy said Jennie had been dead four days when they brought her home. The Kolbergs didn't want Sanchez to talk. When Jennie showed up, he called Lucky Levesque at den Pontiac. Lucky called Guy.

"Why? What did they do it for?"

"Politics. They tried to get us to buy their contract again. Relax, we voted it down again. But I guess they figured you might screw things up."

"But how? What could I do? I was only in the office for ten minutes. didn't see anything."

"Maybe they don't know that. Or maybe you don't know what you saw that was so important. Or maybe they're just so paranoid, they didn't want to take a chance. Your mother said they kept her quiet by threatening to send you back like Jennie."

"Damn. I guess I finally got into real trouble with her."

"If they way she yelled at me is any indication, I'd say so."

"This is screwy. Back before I got sick, I figured out that I must have stumbled across something important. They were real worried, or they would have bought my curious kid act. But the only thing I really looked at was a spreadsheet on the colonial economy, like the ones Emily's been studying. I watched it crank for a long time. I was staring at when Peter Kolberg himself came in and caught me. I wonder if that's why they bagged me?"

"I don't know, Joey. We'll have to figure that out when we get you home ... "

***

Guy Stanger felt exhausted by the time the truck returned to Center Township. He began the trip in a terrible state and things had only gotten worse. He didn't need Suzanne Baxter to make him feel guilty about Joey's disappearance. He knew he had failed. And when Pedro Sanchez came forward, his anguish became all the sharper. It could have been Joey who came back in the bag instead of an innocent little girl.

In fact, he'd realized as they left the Kolberg camp, Jennie's death was even more tragic. At least Joey knew what he was doing. Her involvement was entirely accidental. Guy had spent an uncomfortable couple of hours on the way back down the rough road from den Olympia wrestling with that fact.

There was no easy way to swallow it, and it was still stuck in his craw.

Their first stop was the infirmary at den Schweitzer. Joey didn't want to go, but Guy was insistent.

"Then do me a favor before you leave me here," he asked.

"What's that?"

"Get me a tablet and tell them to let talk to Emily. I want to know why the Kolberg spreadsheets were so important that they let Jennie Vinh die rather than let me go."

"Done." It took a few minutes to arrange, but Guy was insistent once again.

The next stop was the meeting hall. Guy had expected to meet Suzanne at the infirmary, but had received a message instead to head for Hollister Auditorium and find her there. It was a short drive and his scout mates dropped him off in front of the main entrance.

The street was empty, but the doors were open. He stepped through them to find a wall of backs bracing the chamber. Up on the stage, above the crowd, stood Peter Kolberg, addressing the convention for the second time in a week.

" ... but since you chose not to accept our offer, we have decided to take a different course. After looking at the bylaws adopted by the convention, we have chosen to make a contribution to the Asgard colony in another way. Mr. President, convention delegates, I wish today to announce formation of a new den, which claims entitlement to all the rights and benefits accorded to the dens of the Asgard colony under the bylaws of this convention.

"The membership of this new den includes permanent colonists from Tikarahisat who have decided to settle here on Asgard, scouts from den Iroquois with holdings on Asgard and colonists from the dens that arrived here one year ago and who have decided to join us. It will call itself den Kolberg.

"We want the people of Asgard to know that our commitment to this world is strong and real. We plan to stay among you for a long time. I present to you now a list of the families who will comprise den Kolberg."

Guy listened to the roster with half an ear. He didn't recognize most of them. The scouts Mike Hennig and Henry Schmidt were the exceptions. But what was interesting was the sudden flurry of outrage that erupted among small groups of delegates at the mention of the names.

"There you are."

Suzanne Baxter appeared at the edge of the crowd. "How's Joey?"

"He's fine. They've been treating him with acyclovir for three or four days up there. No more fever. The rash is drying up."

"He sounds better off than we are in here," she said with a frown. "I know. Can they do this?"

"I guess so. Harry Bayard told me this morning that according to the bylaws, until there's a government on Asgard the convention decides whether to recognize new dens."

"Since when?"

"Since Saturday morning. Harry said the Kolberg supporters slipped the rules through when everyone was preoccupied with their contract offer. I wonder if the whole thing was just a big bluff, a diversion to set us up for this."

"Can't we just change the rules?"

"And start off our new government with a clearly unjust and dishonorable act on our record? The rules are fair as they stand. If we don't have a government in place before the first follow-on dens arrive, someone's got to grant them legal status. We can't change them just to stop the Kolbergs. We've got to do more than that."

"Like what?"

"I don't know."

"And why do they want to start a den of their own?"

Suzanne closed her eyes and shook her head. "Again – I don't know."

Emily, what does SAO 22341 mean?" Joey's sister looked up from her own tablet, which was busy relaying information to his. "I don't know, what does it mean?"

"No, really. I asked you first. I don't know what it means."

"Well, neither do I. What difference does it make?"

Emily had worn a sour expression since arriving at the infirmary shortly after dinner. When Guy left, he said he'd "arranged" things to get him a tablet and his sister's spreadsheets. What he didn't say was that Emily was going to bring them with her. And he could tell that Em was not happy with drawing nursemaid duty either. Ordinarily, he would have ignored her, but after a week of mud pox and imprisonment, he was glad to see a familiar face. Even his sister's. So he tried to be polite. It wasn't easy.

"Calm down," he said, which only made her more angry. "It's just something I remembered from the Kolberg spreadsheet. You don't have it on yours."

"Doesn't ring any bells for me. Maybe it's a special account. Special

Accounting Order ... Solar Adjusted Objects ... Stupid Arrogant Obnoxious ... I don't know. What part of the sheet was it in? Do you remember anything about the numbers? What did the spreadsheet look like?"

Joey closed his eyes and tried to revive the fever-strained memory. "The whole sheet was in Earth-Solar years. One iteration every year. Production figures, labor and capital growth, expenditures, industrial output, research, investment, return on investment, capital borrowing, capital repayment, capital export – that's the column where I came across SAO 22341."

"Capital export? That's an odd category. I don't have it on my sheets. Are we talking big megabucks or was this some marginal item?"

"Small numbers, small percentage of GPP, when it kicks in about 80 years from now. But it starts to balloon after a century or so."

"I still haven't got a clue."

"You know, Em, there's another thing about their numbers that are different from yours. Yours are all kind of flat. But theirs have some kind of cycle going that gives the system a boost every twelve years. Why doesn't your spreadsheet do that?"

"I don't know, Joey."

"You're no help."

"Don't get wise with me, little brother."

"Where are my clothes?"

"In the locker over – What are you planning to do, kid?"

"We've got to go talk to somebody who knows something.

Where's Guy?" Joey swung his legs out over the edge of the high hospital bed and slipped onto the floor. He felt shaky, but alive. Everything worked well enough, he decided. The locker in the corner held a clean pair of trousers and a shirt, his hiking boots and clean socks.

"What, no underwear?"

"I wasn't going to go digging around looking for your underwear. Your socks were bad enough."

"It's all clean, Em."

"They're not going to let you out of here, you know."

"Then we'd better not ask them if it's alright. You bring the tablets, I'm going out this way."

He pushed the table up against the wall below the window and climbed on top. It only took a minute to dismantle the latch and climb through the opening.

"Meet me around the front of the building. And where is Guy?"

"Joey, you're going to get me in trouble now. Guy is over at the convention – with Mother. And I wish I had gone there with them ... "

***

The conference room at the Asgard Hotel was small and sparsely furnished – a rough wooden table with a couple of tablets set up on it, benches and a few chairs occupied by delegates from the convention. A partially polarized window without curtains looked out onto the square. From where he sat, Guy could see the meeting hall across the commons, with delegates, staffers and hangers-on milling about the entrance.

The debate had come to a standstill over there and the president had called a recess. Suzanne and her allies at the convention had called a strategy meeting. They clustered around the table now, trying to divine the twisted paths of Peter Kolberg's thought. They were not having much luck.

Guy recognized Harry Bayard, but the others were new faces to him – Lin Palmer, the farmer from den Aroostook and Betty Montgomery from den Cornwall.

"I still don't understand Suzanne's argument against changing the rules," said Lin. "It seems the most direct route to me."

Harry Bayard ran a hand through his white hair and wrinkled his brow. "It's a matter of pride, personal honor and precedent, Lin. You'd be asking the delegates to admit that they made a mistake, that they weren't paying attention to what was going on. And the rules are not out of line. All they did was make the convention responsible for creating new dens. It's obvious now that they did it so they could be the first to apply – but the rule itself makes sense. You might get the convention to swallow the rat and rescind the rule if it was a clunker, but not if it's legitimate. Besides, it would make them look like they were ducking the most important question the colony's going to face for the next hundred years: What do we do with the colonists who come after us?"

"But those are legitimate colonists," Lin said.

"So are the Kolbergs. Just because they don't come from Earth doesn't mean they don't count. And they've got people on their membership list who did come from Earth. Some of them on the same ship as you, Lin."

"Okay, we don't change the rules. Can't we get them to vote against the Kolbergs?"

"I don't see how. They fit all the criteria. They met all our standards. That's what law is all about. It's supposed to be the same for everyone."

"And what do they get out of it?"

"Two seats in the convention. The right to vote in the new government. What else?"

"A township," said Betty.

"Rations, capital and labor entitlements," said Harry.

"A foothold on Asgard," said Suzanne. "And that's what they've wanted all along. That's why they didn't put up a better fight over the management deal they offered. If they were serious about it, they would have hammered away at us tooth and nail. Instead, they trotted it out, went through the motions and told us to phone in our answer. Not what I'd call a hard sell."

"They didn't even get all their own people to vote for the deal," Harry noted.

"Because they didn't care," Suzanne said. "They had this waiting in the wings. Guy told us about the scouts that joined them last month. We should have realized this was coming. It's all part of a larger plan. Does everyone else see that, or am I just getting paranoid in my middle age?"

"I see it," said Lin. "They've got a shopping list and they're going right down it. What scares me is that I was on that list last winter and I get the feeling they keep putting me back on every time they look at it."

"But that brings us back to the question that we haven't been able to answer from the day we arrived at Asgard," Suzanne said. "Why did the Kolbergs travel across six light-years of cold space just to start a den on Asgard? What is in this for them?"

Guy shook his head. In six months, after the loss of Ray Adamcek, the near loss of Joey Baxter, the problems with the weather, the fuzzies and pox, no one had been able to advance a single centimeter beyond that question.

All the spying by Joey, all the analysis by Emily, all the questioning by Guy himself had not produced an answer. The facts kept up a slow, measured dance around Guy's head, keeping pace to some unmeasured beat, centered on some unknown guide. Peter Kolberg knew what he was up to. He had a plan and an agenda and a schedule and he was keeping to it.

What galled Guy the most was that the man had kept all knowledge of that plan away from him, from his friends and family and from the colonists of Asgard.

A knock came at the door to the room.

The men and women at the table continued their fruitless discussion while Guy rose to answer it. He opened the door and there was Emily, a tablet under each arm, her little brother beside her. He looked back over his shoulder at the meeting and decided quickly to steer them the other way. He stepped out into the hall and closed the door behind him.

***

"Don't tell me that neither of you knows anything about astrography," Guy said as he led them across the street to the broad square of close-cut savanna grass. He had taken them outside to avoid the close and anything-but-confidential political atmosphere within the hotel. Out here, he could have all the privacy he wanted and could see anyone coming who might invade that privacy .

"Don't look at me," said Emily. "I'm majoring in social sciences, not physical sciences."

They both turned to Joey, who shrugged.

"The numbers in astrography are too boring. They never change. Come on, Guy, I'm a math wizard, not a science drone."

Guy shook his head in amazement. It was so simple, he couldn't believe that they didn't know the answer.

"SAO stands for Smithsonian Astrophysical Observatory. It's a designation for stars, part of their names. SAO 22341 is the next star out from here – about fourteen light years farther out from Eta Cass. They call the major habitable planet there Helvetica – ever hear of that?"

Joey shook his head, but Emily's eyes showed a flash of recognition. "There's already a scout team there, isn't there?"

"As far as we know, there is. They would have sent their report back to Earth by now, I think. But there won't be a breakthrough colony there for another eighty years."

"Bingo!" said Joey.

"What did I say?"

"That's when the Kolbergs start exporting capital out there," Joey replied.

Emily's face was twisted by a puzzled frown. "That doesn't make sense."

"Why not?"

"Because it sounds like the Kolbergs are trying to set up an interstellar trade syndicate. Only with the soliton drive, you can only travel at the speed of light. And that means you can't carry on any kind of meaningful trade between the stars."

"I don't see why not," said Joey.

"Because it takes six years to get to Eta Cass from here and six years to get back. What kind of business is going to wait that long to fill an order, or get paid for a product? What kind of products are they going to ship that would make it worth the wait? What if the money isn't worth anything by the time it gets here? It doesn't make sense. People have talked about it for years, but they all came to the same conclusion – we're out here on our own."

"And yet the Kolbergs seem to be busy trying to do what you claim is impossible," Guy said. "Maybe they've figured out something that everyone else has missed. After all, we are only the second colony to be established out here."

"I don't know, Guy. Economies and financial systems can't operate with that kind of a time lag between actions. There's no interstellar market for agricultural products. We won't be producing industrial goods for a long time. And there's no way to respond to short-term changes. What good would it do them if they all grow old and die before they get a return on their investment?"

"It beats me," said Guy. "But Joey saw what he saw. It sounds like they're making plans for something big. Maybe we just haven't figured out exactly what they're up to. Maybe it's bigger than we can imagine."

"Yeah, and maybe they're going to turn into Easter bunnies and give us all presents," said Emily.

"Come on, Em," Joey said. "Guy's right. We've only been thinking about this for a few minutes. The Kolbergs have been working on it for years."

"Well until you get them to explain it to you, we're still just as bad off as ever," Emily said. "Even if they do explain it, I don't see how it can affect what's happening here and now. The real problem is that the Kolbergs want their own den. What are we going to do about that?"

"They way they were talking when you showed up, there isn't a single thing we can do about it. The rules are fair, the Kolbergs are within their rights, and the convention is probably going to give them what they want."

With that statement, a palpable gloom fell upon all three of them as if the sun had dipped below Mount Thor in the west.

The light from Rudy gave a bloody tint to the cool fog that condensed out of the moist evening air, suiting Guy's dark mood. He walked without direction in a world where sound and light alike were swallowed up before they had traveled more than a few meters.

His feet carried him along, but his mind was elsewhere. Olympia township, where Jennie Vinh had breathed her last, a scared captive of ruthless and insensitive men. Den Franklin, where her family lit mourning candles and chanted prayers for her spirit.

His face and hands grew wet as he swept droplets from the fog in his relentless march through the void. He had no place to go, but walked to give motion to his thoughts. And no matter which way he tried to turn, they kept returning to Jennie Vinh. Her cold, waxy face and her guiltless cry hovered in his imagination. Never mind that he had never met the girl. He would never forget her for as long as he lived.

He had killed her just as surely as the Kolbergs. And just as surely as Joey Baxter.

So much had happened in the year since Guy led a patrol of young scouts up to Glacier Valley and saw the Kolberg miniplanes gliding through the night. So much that could never be undone.

Back then, before Colony Day, before the arrival of the Kolbergs, he had dreamed innocently of a bright new future for Asgard. One where the colonists would settle the valleys of Prime Site and the scouts would lead the way into the new wilderness, where man and nature would live in peace and harmony.

But it seemed like every time he turned around, his world took another step away from that dream. The Kolbergs had turned the colonists against one another. Emily's stepfather was killed in a scoutship crash. The fuzzasaurs narrowly avoided wholesale slaughter. The scout den broke up. And now this – Jennie Vinh and the Kolbergs' bid to make a new den.

Until this last, he had met each crisis with an unbroken optimism, certain that somehow, things would work out. But not now. He knew at last that the future he had envisioned was only a dream. Real life was much more difficult, more complex and more disappointing than he had ever imagined. The harmony that he had hoped for was a thing of the past, a creation of the scouts, who had since lost their own unity. The future was going to be a struggle, long and endless, between the different urges of the colonists – hope and fear, sacrifice and selfishness, freedom and empire.

It was not what he had prepared himself for in all the long days and short years of his youth. It was not what he wanted for himself and his own children.

But then, he did not recall being asked for his opinion.

After walking the streets for nearly an hour, somehow Guy found himself standing in front of a familiar storefront – the Silver Rose, the aleshop he had visited a few nights earlier looking for information on the Kolbergs.

He wondered how had he ended up there. Then he was struck by an sudden inspiration, which sent him into motion once again, stepping from the fog into the warmth and soft light of the tavern.

***

"Talk to me, Mike. Tell me about interstellar empires. Tell me about the Kolbergs."

At first, Mike Hennig didn't notice Guy. His heavy-lidded eyes struggled to open and focus and his mouth worked around words he could not speak.

Then he shuddered once and came alive.

"You again? What do you want this time?"

"Knowledge. I want you to tell me what you know. Explain to me how the Kolbergs are going to build an interstellar empire."

Mike laughed and rubbed his eyes with the backs of hands. "You've figured that much out already, have you? And you can't make sense of the rest, I'll bet. Neither could I – at first."

"I know what they say about the idea. It takes too long to do business. Investments don't pay off for decades. By the time your mistakes are corrected, everyone involved is dead and gone."

"Sounds depressing. I don't think I want to join. Actually, we've got a better idea. And I'll bet you couldn't figure it out in a thousand years, because you won't have that long. But we will ... "

The prompted another round of self-satisfied laughter that left Mike's face red and his eyes full of tears.

"If you don't want to tell me, fine. But I just want you to know what kind of devils you're getting mixed up with. Last week, they let a little girl from den Franklin die of mud pox just to keep the secret. Is that what you bought when you traded in your landholdings? What kind of a scout do you call yourself now?"

Mike's face fell, frozen suddenly with anger.

"You little ripper, you fight dirty. What makes you think I don't care what the Kolbergs are like? I'll tell you their secret, but first I want to pull you down off your high horse. You look down on me because I left the den. But when are you going to admit that you're not a scout anymore? You do the work of the colonists – and I've seen you with your colonist girl. You're no more a scout than I am."

Guy swallowed hard and tried to ignore the anger that was rising within him. He bit his tongue and let Mike continue.

"The Kolbergs aren't talking about making us rich, you know. They've got a bigger bait than that. Tell me, kid, how would you like to live for a thousand years? That's what they asked me. I don't mean live a lifetime of a centuries, but how would you like to skip across the decades like stone on the water. Pause here and there for a few months, then move on. Watch the colony grow and develop from this little camp to big cities and great nations. How does that sound for a future?

"All you have to do is climb aboard a starship and take the step across the stars. Ten years gone in the blink of an eye. Another ten and you're back. Keep it up for a few months, and a century is gone. All the people you left behind have died, new ones have taken their place. The colony has millions of people by then. And by then, the investments have paid off, the mistakes have been corrected and business is booming.

"Interstellar trade doesn't take long as far as the traders are concerned. The deals may take twenty years to work out, but if you're not around for most of that time, who cares? Let them take forty years if they have to. As long as there's someone around to keep an eye on things from year to year, it'll work out in long run. And you're in it for the long run.

While you travel, your bankbook stays home. You build up interest and dividends and equity. After a few centuries, we're talking about real leverage – that's the word the Kolbergs use for it.

"The rest of you people can stay behind, live your lives one day at a time. Den Kolberg is going places – literally. And I'm going with them. I'm with Peter. This was all his idea, you know, his special vision. He was a dirt farmer, just like half the colonists here. Only he couldn't stand the idea of spending his life digging in the dirt to make a colony grow that wouldn't mature until long after he died. He wanted to see it develop and thrive.

"He knew how to do it, too. Just start traveling. Asgard first. Then Helvetica. Pericles. Poseidon. The whole Perseus Sector is going to be opening up over the next century. You groundlings will never see it, but the rest of us will be there, building a future for ourselves. You'll all be dust in the ground by then. And then what difference will it make who belonged to the scout den back in the old days?"

He sneered, then let his head drop to back. Guy twisted his face in anger and disbelief, then stood up from the table and fled the tavern, running from a truth too terrible to know.

***

A cool breeze had cleared the fog from the central square, leaving the air dry and crystal clear and the lights from the shops and eateries burning bright and crisp. Guy felt the grit in his boots, and his mouth was full of the taste of metal as he walked back to the hotel.

The Kolbergs were going to get away.

They were going to wrap up their business, then run, up into the sky, up the time line, into a future that would become increasingly their private property. Each year that went by would bring them more wealth and more power. Each time they returned, they would be a bigger and more formidable threat. But most of all, the thing that ate at his soul was the idea that they were going to escape. All that they had done or were going to do, they would never have to pay for it. No matter what the crime, no matter what the injustice, they would be able to skip across the decades and skip out on the blame, the guilt and the payment.

And at the same time, Guy felt alive and free in a way that was beyond his understanding. For six months, he had lived with a sense of terrible foreboding. It had churned away slowly but constantly in the back of his mind, underlying all his joys and pleasures.

Now the churning had stopped.

The evil had revealed itself. It had chosen the form it would keep for generations. Guy felt as if a terrible burden had been lifted from his shoulders. A Kolberg den certainly would be frightening in all of its implications, but it was not nearly as bad as the blind fear that had lurked in the dark corners of his soul for a year now.

This, at least, was something he could face. It was something he could fight against and maybe even defeat – although that was just a vagrant, unsubstaniated dream. It was a known quantity, with weaknesses as well as strengths.

And slowly, as he padded across the dew-covered savanna grass, he began to sense a new strength within himself. All the changes of the past year had reached their ultimate peak. All the uncertainty had ended. The future was no longer a clouded landscape, cloaked in red shadows as if lit by Rudy. It was a bright valley, where danger could be seen, but avoided.

A smile broke across his face as he looked within himself and saw the man that he had become. He knew at last that he finally had both the strength and the knowledge that he needed.

Damn the Kolbergs! They would not rob him of his life. They would not take away his world. He vowed not to let them. And he knew that he had the power to fulfill that vow.

*****

When he got to the hotel, he found the conference room empty. He walked around the table, full of nervous energy, looking for a note or a message to tell him what had happened. There was nothing there.

He was about to leave when the door opened and Emily walked in.

"There you are," she said. "Mother's been looking all over for you. They're back in session and they're already to vote. Guy, they're going to let the Kolbergs form a den."

"I know, Em. But that's only half of it. This is just the beginning for them."

"Come on. quick. Mother wants you over at the meeting hall."

He took the lead as they hurried from the conference room, down the stairs and out the front door. Emily had to run to keep up with him and by the time they reached Hollister Auditorium, she was out of breath. They found Suzanne Baxter waiting inside the main entrance. She looked tired, tense and unhappy.

Guy went to talk to her, but before he could say anything she took him through a side door and into a cloak room where they could be alone. When the door was closed behind them and their privacy was assured, he told her what he had learned from Mike Hennig.

She took it with the same sense of calm strength that Guy had discovered on his walk across the square.

"Everything they did was a charade," she said. "All of it, right from the beginning. The management offer, the business deals, the labor bonds. They were just paper tigers to keep us busy while they worked on the only important goal. Once they get that den, they are part of Asgard forever."

"I don't know. I think all that other stuff was serious. They would have been just as happy if we had agreed to let them run things."

"But it never mattered to them, Guy. They've outmaneuvered us. We never even had a chance."

"That's not true," Guy said. "We do have a chance. Now that we know what they're really doing, we can stop them."

"No we can't, Guy. It's all over. They're going to vote in a few minutes in there, and the Kolbergs are going to get everything they want."

"You're wrong, Suzanne. Once they get their den, the Kolbergs are going to be gone. They may leave their friends behind to keep an eye on their enterprises, but they won't be here to take care of things themselves. We'll be here every day, working to keep them from getting their hands on the rest of the colony. The next time they come around, we will have had twenty years to get ready for them."

Suzanne sighed. For a moment, Guy thought she was going to cry. All the weight and pain of the events of the past year showed in her tired eyes ad deeply etched features. Then a sparkle flashed to life in those eyes and a smile blossomed across her face.

"Guy, you're so young and full of strength. You think you can do anything, don't you?"

"Why not, Suzanne? We're not going anywhere. They are. Don't tell me you can't think of something to tell that convention in there. I remember the night you talked the whole colony down out of the sky."

Guy's heart pounded with excitement as he watched Suzanne stiffen her back with sudden resolve and flex her arms with a new energy. Her eyes glazed briefly as she mumbled to herself: "I suppose I could warn them about the wolves."

The voting had already begun when Guy and Suzanne entered the hall. A big datascreen at the side of the chamber revealed the tally. Suzanne drew in a breath at the sight of it. To the untutored eye, it looked like the red blots outshined the green. But she knew that was just an optical illusion.

She could tell that the resolution was headed for approval. A quick check of the votes that remained uncast bore out her fear. The anti-Kolberg faction had already taken its stand, as had the Kolberg supporters. The holdouts were the uncommitted delegates, most of whom had already expressed their reluctant support for the measure. They said they wanted to be fair.

Fair, my elbow, she'd told herself when those wishy-washy slackers made their whining pleas. They were the kind who would argue that being fair meant punishing all children equally regardless of their behavior.

She could understand why they were waiting until the last minute to take a stand.

But eventually the time came to close the tally board. The president asked three times if all the delegates had voted. When he finally slammed the gavel down, six delegates still remained silent.

"Those voting aye, 66, those voting nay, 46, those present and not voting, 6," the president of the convention announced. "The motion is adopted!"

The hall filled with boos and cheers as the delegates rose from their seats. About a third of the delegates stayed put, turning their eyes away from the rest – they did not like the Kolberg backers and they could not face the others.

"The convention will stand at ease for a moment," the president said, his voice barely audible above the din of rancorous conversation.

Suzanne gathered her wits about her. She had spent too much time feeling sorry for herself, she realized. There was a time for mourning and a time for action. The trick was knowing the difference. She hadn't wanted to get involved in the struggle. Her feelings were still raw over the loss of Ray. And a week of worrying about Joseph had left her drained and exhausted.

But the sight of Guy and Emily, arms locked around one another, standing defiantly at the rear of the hall despite the victory of the Kolbergs, changed all that. What brave young kids they were. They were better off in their innocence, not knowing what the future was likely to hold.

But she had seen a change come over Guy in the past few days. Something had settled in the young man, some kind of resolve had seized him. Especially tonight. He was no longer the reticent youth who had first led her pathfinder team up the Scout Path to Glacier Valley.

And his newfound strength was contagious, she realized. How else could she explain the boldness that now carried her forward through the mass of delegates to find Harry Bayard.

He was surrounded by a circle of his closest allies. None of them looked happy. Maybe she could change that ...

"Harry, I want to talk to the convention," she said, raising her voice to be heard over the ragged roar of the delegates.

"God, Suzanne, what do you want to do that for? They're so riled up now, they'll eat you alive."

"I don't care. I have something to say to them. Maybe it'll settle things down. At the worst, it'll give them someone to be mad at besides you."

Harry shook his head and shrugged. "If you're sure you want to do this, I'll set it up."

"I'm sure, Harry. Real sure."

It was fifteen minutes before some semblance of order was restored to the convention. Noise still filled the chamber though, and the president had to pound on the gavel several times to silence the delegates. Then he introduced Suzanne.

***

She was seized with a moment of disorienting panic as she rose to her feet and took her place behind the lectern. But it passed as quickly as it arose as soon as she began to speak.

"You know, friends, even though it's only been six months long, this has been the longest year of my life. I don't know about you, but I'm glad it's over. Tonight, you've all settled the biggest question that's been hanging over us since before we landed on Asgard. Some of us don't like what's been done, but it's been done and the issue has been settled. Let me be the first one to welcome den Kolberg to

Asgard."

She saw the puzzled looks on the faces of Harry Bayard and Betty Montgomery and the rest of her friends as well as the confusion among the Kolberg supporters. And she heard the buzz of approval from the uncommitted delegates.

When she stood up, Suzanne had planned to deliver a lecture to the delegates. She was going to tell them about predators and the threat that a Kolberg den was going to pose for the colony. She was going to ask the convention to impose strict limits on how much of the colony the Kolbergs would be allowed to own. She was going to be tough and demanding and uncompromising.

But suddenly all that had become impossible.

"The Kolbergs have been trying to find a role in our society for more than a year. While the proposals they've made haven't been acceptable to us, we are all glad that they've finally found a place in the colony. I recognize that a good many of you delegates who have voted against the Kolbergs in past felt that, out of fairness, this is the best way to go."

The delegates in the middle were the reason why it was impossible. She realized that if she said anything at all critical about the Kolbergs tonight, it would only alienate them. They wouldn't see the Kolbergs as the target, but themselves for voting with them. And if she wanted to be at all successful in her efforts to put a leash on den Kolberg, she would need their support.

No, the best way to act was to follow the lead of the Kolbergs themselves. Be discreet and invisible in public. Go through the motions of conciliation and consensus, and then come back when all that was done and take care of the real business.

The alternative was to preach to people already tired from the stress of making a decision they did not like. All she could accomplish by that would be to drive the majority of them away. Later, when they were rested and had had time to think, they could discuss it rationally. There would be time.

Lots of time.

"Now the time has come to start the real work of forming a government for this planet. There are a lot of important decisions for you to make. Now that this has been settled, let's hope we can all get along for the good of the future of Asgard."

She looked out at Guy and Emily, their hands still linked. Joey sat on the table beside them, pale but alive and whole. She smiled and felt strong. Closer to the stage, Harry Bayard shook his head in disbelief while the delegates looked towards him with uncertain eyes.

She would have to explain to them later, after the applause died down and the convention had adjourned and the delegates drifted away ...

***

Guy and Emily made their way back across the green to the Asgard Hotel and waited in the upstairs meeting room as the delegates returned, one by one. Harry Bayard and Suzanne were the last to arrive. By then, the rest of them, Betty Montgomery, Lin Palmer, and a dozen others, had filed in, all grumbling and complaining to various degrees about the outcome of the vote. They all shared a bewilderment over Suzanne's closing remarks.

Emily sat beside Guy on the bench, resting her head on his shoulder. Joey sat with a tablet on the table, running through spreadsheets and calculations. Guy was exhausted, his mind a blank. He wasn't sure what Suzanne had been trying to do, but it wasn't what he had expected.

When she finally entered the room, everyone fell upon her, surrounding her with anxious faces and pelting her with their questions.

Guy slipped away from Emily and pushed through to help her into the room and to a chair. "I thought you were going to warn them about the wolves," he said.

She smiled weakly and said: "So did I."

Harry quieted the room by filling it with his own voice. "Everyone calm down and be patient. Suzanne wants to talk."

Emily came up to Guy's side while the delegates found seats or took up station against the wall. He took her hand and gave it a squeeze, which she returned.

"I'm sorry, everyone," she said. "I went up there with every intention of giving the convention hell for what it did tonight, but when I saw their faces, I realized that was the wrong thing to do. I couldn't change anyone's mind tonight, and I didn't want to undermine the job that we're going to have to do – starting tomorrow."

That didn't seem to satisfy the delegates, Guy thought, who shifted uncomfortably in their places. But she wasn't finished.

"I want everyone here in this room to know that what I said to the convention is for public consumption only. What I was going to say up on that stage I will pass along to you now. At least you're willing to listen.

"This is an important time for the human race. It is the fate of humanity to be rootless in the universe. We have never remained at home for long and our history is one of a long series of migrations – across continents and oceans and now across the emptiness of interstellar space. On all our previous migrations, we have had to contend with new environments and old threats.

"For a while, when we first arrived here on Asgard, I thought this migration would be different from the earlier ones. I thought we would be free of the predators that followed the race in its previous wanderings – natural predators like the wolf. But I know now that I was wrong.

"We have invented our own predators – or rather they have invented themselves. Tonight, we have allowed the creation of a den of wolves, which will follow us through the generations as we expand into the stars.

"And as we have done in the past, we are going to have to protect ourselves from these predators. Now we must build fences to keep them from our children and our land. This convention will not complete its work until there are restrictions on what den Kolberg and their friends can do. There have to be limits placed on their holdings, controls placed on their wealth. They have plans for our world that do not include us – plans that will take generations to complete.

"It is up to you to stop these self-made predators from turning us into their sheep. It is up to you to save our world from this den of thieves and wolves ... "

Suzanne fell silent and there was a moment of quiet among the delegates. Then Harry Bayard stood up and started clapping. The others joined him, and the applause was overtaken by a rising wave of voices, all echoing Suzanne's words and promising their support.

A long time later, after everyone had wound down from the night's drama and the conversations had become muted and private, Suzanne came to Guy and Emily, with Joey in tow.

Guy looked into her eyes and saw his own newfound resolve reflected in them. Joey's eyes, on the other hand, were red and heavy. His bout with the mud pox was not quite over.

"How are you two tonight?" Suzanne asked.

"Tired, angry and determined," Guy replied.

"Good. Never mind what I told the rest of these people tonight. The real struggle isn't going to be here at the convention. It's going to be out there in the townships and the dens. It's not going to end for a long, long time. You're going to have to live with it – and so are your children and grandchildren and many generations to come after them."

Guy smiled suddenly at the mention of his children and grandchildren, theoretical as they might be at present. In an instant, his mind's eye caught a vision of a long and unbroken future stretching forward from this moment. All the long march of history, turned end for end and continued on through time. He and Emily, their children and grandchildren, and all that would follow, they were all there – as were the Kolbergs, locked with them in a millennial struggle that could afford no defeat.

"Are you ready for that, Guy?"

"We're ready," he said, his heart swelling within his chest.

"Both of us, Mother," Emily said. Then she took Joey's hand in hers and added: "All of us."

* * *